Say Your Goodbyes

BOOKS BY LINDA LADD

CLAIRE MORGAN HOMICIDE THRILLERS

Head to Head

Dark Places

Die Smiling

Enter Evil

Remember Murder

Mostly Murder

Bad Bones

CLAIRE MORGAN INVESTIGATIONS SERIES

Devil Dead

Gone Black

WILL NOVAK THRILLERS

Bad Road to Nowhere

Say Your Goodbyes

Say Your Goodbyes

Linda Ladd

KENSINGTON PUBLISHING CORP.

www.kensingtonbooks.com

First electronic edition: June 2017

ISBN-13: 978-1-60183-858-2
ISBN-10: 1-60183-858-1

First trade paperback edition: June 2017

ISBN-13: 978-1-60183-859-9
ISBN-10: 1-60183-859-X

Chapter One

"No, no! Please! Help me!"

Will Novak opened his eyes and stared into utter darkness. He had been drinking earlier that evening before he passed out. He wasn't drunk anymore, maybe hungover some, but he could think straight. He knew who had been calling for help. The same dream had come to him every night. It was Mariah Murray's voice, his beautiful sister-in-law who called to him from the dark corners of his troubled mind. She had died on his doorstep, not a fortnight ago. He had promised to protect her. But he had failed, and now she haunted him, just like his dead wife and his dead children haunted him. All those voices that he loved so much and missed so desperately called out to him, distant and tinny, like static on an old Motorola radio. But he couldn't help any of them. They were gone forever. Sarah and Kelly and Katie had perished when the south tower came down on 9/11. He had watched it happen, unable to help them in that terrible moment, and unable to help them now. He couldn't help Mariah, either. She was dead. Everybody he loved was dead. Those voices calling to him were why he drank himself to oblivion, hoping to stifle the pain and forget his guilt and regret. But it never worked.

Eyes bleary and bloodshot, he sat up and looked around. He was out in the middle of the Caribbean Sea. His sailboat, his prized forty-foot custom-built Jeanneau Sun Odyssey 379, rocked beneath him. The waves were gentle, but the wind was picking up and buffeting the masts and riggings. A gale was probably developing somewhere far away. Maybe it would hit him eventually, but so what? He laid his head on the back of the seat and stared up at the stars above him.

Novak squeezed his eyes shut and felt his heart begin to constrict in upon itself. He dropped his head into his hands. Deep inside his mind, he remembered the day his family died, trapped up so high in the south tower. He had been working the streets of Manhattan in his NYPD cruiser. He'd seen the first plane hit and tried to get to them but couldn't make it through the snarled traffic. He had gotten out of his car and watched the tower, with his family inside, as it began to buckle. He had heard the grinding and snapping of steel beams and breaking glass, the people screaming all around him. And then it had come down, far ahead of him, in clouds of gray dust and fluttering papers and black smoke, with a roar of finality and death.

Will Novak forced that image away. Time to shake it off. Come to terms once again. Pull himself together. But his skin felt clammy in the cool night air, and his hands trembled. The darkness closed in around him, thick and impenetrable, but softly, as if the breeze that touched his face was made of smooth black velvet. It was very quiet, floating out there in the dark ocean. He felt utterly alone, anchored where he was at the edge of a coral reef. He figured he was somewhere off the east coast of the Yucatan Peninsula. The boat's running lights were off. All the lights were off. Around him was nothing but a silent, watery, swaying world.

Novak stretched back out on the padded bench under the dark blue awning. Behind his boat, a billion stars spread out in a spangled canopy, vast and glittering, but also cold and distant and unfathomable. He stared up at the heavens, always awestruck by the clear, impossibly vivid spectacle of the universe when so far out at sea. In the west, a falling star streaked for several seconds and burned itself out. Sometimes Novak felt like that meteorite, like he was burning out. Sometimes he just wanted to burn out, end his mental suffering, end the memories of a life that had been so good, so perfect, but was now dead and gone forever . . .

Novak cursed his maudlin thoughts and stood up. He leaned down and pulled a cold beer out of the ice. He'd been sailing due south, away from his home deep inside the bayous of Louisiana. Wanting solitude. Wanting to mourn for all he'd lost. He thrust one hand into the cooler and brought up ice to rub over his sunburned face. Then he just froze, with the ice still held against his skin. A woman had just screamed. He'd heard her clearly—far away from the boat, but resonating in the silence around him. Frowning, he put down the beer and peered out over the water. Then she cried out again. A long, hysterical scream.

Novak held on to the gunwale and steadied himself. Those screams were not figments of his imagination. No way. Another scream came. Novak strained his eyes, searching the inky black night. He still saw nothing, just endless, restless water. He rubbed his eyes and scanned every direction. He wished he hadn't drunk so much. He felt a little sick. A full moon was climbing up the sky, easing through the myriad of bright stars and out from a thick cloud bank. Moments later, a glittering trail of white moonlight stretched across the sea. That pale lunar gleam was all he could see. The sky and ocean melded into black nothingness on the horizon. Then he caught sight of a light. Maybe a hundred yards off his port bow. Just a momentary flash. A boat's spotlight, maybe.

Novak grabbed a rifle out of the rack beside the helm, the Colt AR 7.62 NATO. He'd had the gun for years. It felt good when he wrapped his fingers around it. He brought the high-powered scope up to his eye, blinked away some of his grogginess, and adjusted the knob. The dull green night vision screen reacted and slowly pulled the distant lights in close. A large motor yacht was out there. It wasn't running, just floating in the darkness. Predominantly white. One stripe down the side. Sleek, modern, expensive. A honey of a boat, all right, and big, probably sixty, seventy feet, at least. Dim lights glowed softly along the main deck, probably from the state-rooms and lounge, illuminating the waterline and the silhouette of the vessel. It looked as if it was anchored, maybe, the captain taking advantage of the coral reef. No screams now. Just quiet.

Novak moved his crosshairs slowly up the length of the boat, up to the bow, where he spotted another light shining in a large plate-glass window. He twisted an adjustment and picked up a couple of dark figures moving around in the bow. One was small; looked like a woman or child. Probably a woman. She was hightailing it back toward the stern, moving at a full run. He could pick up shouting now. This time it sounded like male voices. Loud. Angry. Sounded like they were speaking in Spanish. Novak was fluent in Spanish, but he was still too far away to hear what they were yelling. Then Novak saw a man chasing the woman. He was small, too, didn't look much taller than she did, but he had a gun in his hand and he was almost on her. She screamed shrilly when he grabbed her from the back. She was in big trouble.

Another guy darted out of nowhere, taller, bigger, and thrust the struggling woman behind him, trying to shield her from the little guy. They were all arguing and shouting at each other. Then the little guy raised his arm and fired the handgun at the tall man. Shot him right in the face. Point-blank. That's when the woman went crazy, screaming her head off, her shrieks echoing out over the water to Novak. After that, she put up one hell of a fight with the killer, kicking and scratching and trying to wrestle his gun away. While Novak watched, she twisted loose and made another mad dash down the gangway toward the stern.

Novak shifted his scope down to the waterline and picked up a small Zodiac inflatable boat bobbing at starboard stern. All he could see was the end of it, the rest hidden behind the boat. That's where she was heading, all right, but she only made it a couple of yards. The little guy grabbed the back of her shirt, swung her bodily around to face him, and then slammed his pistol butt hard against her forehead. She went down like a felled tree. Her assailant went down after her.

To Novak, cowards like that guy on that boat were the scum of the earth. Misogynists and bullies and abusers irked the hell out of him. He did not like men who shot unarmed victims in the face for trying to shield a woman, either. Both things he had just witnessed were big triggers for Novak. To him, that kind of behavior labeled them as black hats destined to be put down, and without a doubt. He liked to take them down hard and make it as final as he could. End them. So he calmly and methodically lined up the crosshairs on the little man who was having fun bludgeoning the scared lady. The bully had already jerked the woman back up to her feet. He hit her again, with his fist this time, so hard in the right temple that she went back hard, slammed up against the port rail, and went backwards over the side. The guy followed her movements, leaning against the gunwale above where she was floundering in the choppy swells. When he started taking potshots down at her, Novak shifted his finger to the trigger. Enough's enough, tough guy.

Slowly building anger was coursing through Novak's bloodstream and had been since the first time that guy had hit the woman. Maybe her attacker was a hijacker and was forcibly commandeering the luxury yacht, most likely to sell it on the marine black market. Bulletin alerts from the Coast Guard had been coming in daily about modern-day pirate bands operating in the Gulf and off the Mexican coast. They targeted small and undefended pleasure vessels. He had been on the lookout for them himself. Almost wished they would attack so he could put them down. He was heavily armed and knew how to use weapons. He was going to use one now.

He sat down, held his rifle nice and steady, the barrel propped atop the canopy rigging, gauged the rocking of his hull and the force of the breeze, and set his aim. Slowly, carefully, no hurry, he sighted on the killer and squeezed the trigger. The bullet burst out into the darkness, followed seconds later by a deafening retort that echoed thunderously out across the water. If the killer had not chosen that exact moment to move left, he would have died where he stood, a bullet in his head. But he had moved, bending forward to take another shot down at the girl in the water. The slug might have nicked him; Novak wasn't sure. The guy had disappeared behind the rail and stayed down. So Novak waited for him to stand up again, his finger on the trigger, ready to fire—his version of whack-a-mole.

Novak expected the guy to return fire, be it haphazardly out into the blackness around him, shooting aimlessly at an unspecified target in an unspecified area. No way could he see Novak. No way could he know who was firing at him, or why. Patiently, left eye shut, right eye fastened on the scope, Novak waited for him to pop up again. But nothing happened. Maybe the guy was smarter than Novak thought.

Within moments, a faint whine started up in the distance. Sounded like the man was in the Zodiac. If so, he had wasted no time and crawled back there in a big hurry. Not so stupid after all. He knew when to run. Novak kept the scope focused on the part of the Zodiac that he could see, but he couldn't get off a shot before the guy pulled it back behind the stern. Then Novak heard it roar to full life, and it was retreating at full speed in the opposite direction. The guy didn't know his enemy, couldn't ascertain how many there were or what kind of weaponry they had. He had made the right decision. Under those circumstances, Novak might have retreated. But that didn't mean the little killer wouldn't come back, loaded for bear, and with equally deadly reinforcements.

Novak edged the scope back down to the waves around where the girl had gone into the drink. He couldn't see her anymore, just dark, restless water, spotted with whitecaps as the wind picked up. The guy had just left a seriously injured woman out there to drown. She might be dead already, probably too weak to stay afloat. At best, she was unconscious, or soon to be. Whoever the hell the shooter had been, he was a cold-blooded bastard. Novak wished he'd gotten him with that bullet.

Novak stood up, keeping the rifle gripped tightly in his right fist as he took the helm at stern. If she was still alive, he had to fish her out. In any case, he needed to retrieve her body and take it in to the nearest authorities. She was somebody's wife or mother or daughter. So he weighed anchor, fired up the powerful engines, and steered the *Sweet Sarah* directly at the abandoned yacht. He increased his speed across the deep but kept his eyes glued on the dim light thrown off by the receding Zodiac, now far away to the west. Once he was sure the guy was not circling back, he estimated where the girl had taken the plunge. Wasn't easy, not in the dark, not on choppy seas. Not out in the middle of nowhere at midnight. He didn't have much time to find her, either, before she sank to the bottom and became shark bait.

Once he got closer, the boat's name became legible, painted across the stern escutcheon in big black letters: *Orion's Trident. Cancun, Mexico.* He motored to the port side of the vessel where she'd gone overboard. He cut the engines. He grabbed the laser spotlight and swept it back and forth across the water's surface. The killer's boat was now just a speck of light, heading away as fast as he could make it go. He wasn't coming back. Not now, in any case. It took Novak several more minutes to find the girl—way too long, he feared, but then a big wave crested over her, and he caught sight of her head bobbing in the water. Looked like she might still be alive. Yes, weak as hell, but now she was flailing her arms, trying to keep her face above water. Maybe twenty yards out from him. He focused the spotlight on her. Blood was all over her face. The head injuries were bad—he could tell that from where he stood. She wasn't going to last much longer. He brought the *Sweet Sarah* up as close to her as he safely could, cut the engines, and then tossed out a roped life buoy. She just bobbed up and down and seemed oblivious to it.

"Pull it down over your head!" he shouted to her, his voice reverberating out over the water. He was pretty sure he was going to have to go in and get her. He kicked off his canvas boat shoes, but then, somehow, she seemed to come out of her stupor enough to grab the life ring. She clung to it with both arms for dear life. Relieved, Novak slowly started towing her in, hand over hand on the rope, careful not to jerk it out of her grasp. She was too weak to hold on much longer. When he got her up against the hull, he dropped to his stomach and reached down as far as he could. He managed to grab her shirt, then got up on his knees and hauled her bodily up out of the water and onto his deck. She was conscious, but barely. She was groaning and strangling and coughing and choking. Novak laid her out flat on her back and knelt down beside her. She was bleeding heavily. He found two deep gouges, one at the top of her forehead, the other on her right temple. Her nose was bleeding, too, and the blood kept running down into her mouth and causing her to choke. She kept gasping for air and groaning, but that lasted only seconds before her eyes rolled back into her head, and she was out for the count.

Novak quickly turned her onto her side so she could breathe better. He put his mouth down close to her ear. "I'm not gonna hurt you. I'm trying to help you. Can you hear me? You're safe now. He's gone."

She must have heard his voice because her eyelids fluttered slightly in response. Then they closed again, and she didn't move. Out like a light. Novak stood up and scanned the surrounding water for the killer. He didn't want the guy turning around and flanking him. The guy who beat her up had shown a modicum of smarts. But as far as Novak could tell, the boat was gone for good, completely out of sight now. Her assailant had left her to drown, all right. His plan had been to kill her and the man who had been with her, and dump their bodies out in the middle of the ocean, with nowhere to go but down. No witnesses. Then sail away on a nice new hijacked yacht. But this time, the killer had hit a snag he hadn't expected. He didn't get the yacht he'd boarded or whatever booty was inside. But he probably wasn't acting alone. He probably had cohorts somewhere in the area. Armed men he was calling together right now.

Once Novak was sure the woman's airways were open, he positioned her head so that the blood was draining onto the deck and not down her throat. She was a small girl, looked pretty young, didn't weigh much—really skinny, in fact. Probably not much over a hundred pounds, if that. A buck ten at most. She was bruised up pretty bad, too, and not just from the blows he'd seen her take. There were other bruises, some old, some new, some black and blue and pretty damn awful. She had been beaten, no doubt about that.

Her hair appeared to be dark brown under the dim deck lights, black maybe, and she wore it in a long braid that hung down her back, almost to her waist. Lots of strands had pulled loose during the struggle and were plastered against her cheeks and neck. She had on a white oversize oxford shirt, a man's shirt, it looked like, long sleeves rolled up, dirty, bloody, ripped and torn, most of the buttons gone. She had on tight black nylon shorts and black boat shoes similar to his. She was a lot younger than he had first thought. Just a kid. Maybe even a teenager.

Novak pulled his T-shirt off over his head and wrapped it around her wounds, and then he slid an arm under her shoulders and another under her knees. He scooped her up, and she felt as limp as a boiled egg noodle. He carried her belowdecks to the fore cabin and laid her down on her side. Fetching his first-aid kit from the head, he brought it and a wet cloth back to the bed. She was sopping wet, and blood was still oozing out of the two-inch gash at her hairline. Both wounds were deep and ugly. He cleaned them out with some Betadine, pulled them together with butterfly bandages, and covered them with sterile white gauze. Then he washed a lot of the blood off her face and neck. She did not move a muscle the whole time. Her eyelashes did not twitch. She was not going to wake up anytime soon.

Leaving her lying on the bunk, he climbed the companionway to the aft deck. He took a few minutes to search the horizon with the night scope. Nothing anywhere. No lights. No roaring motors. Just the endless rocking of the boat on the cresting waves. The night was quiet, stars still glittering in their icy white splendor. They were alone. The two of them, two complete strangers, out in the middle of nowhere. He had no idea who she was, why she was with those guys, what the hell was going on. Great, that was just great, damn it. Exactly what he needed. Some helpless girl to worry about.

Once Novak was certain that the killer wasn't coming back, he went below and stood in the threshold and stared at the young woman for a few minutes. Then he went inside, leaned down close, and tried to shake her awake. She did not move. A long slender gold chain hung around her neck. He pulled it out. A beautiful gold crucifix gleamed in the overhead light. Appeared that she might be a Catholic. He picked up her wrist and felt for a pulse. He found one, slow, but halfway steady. Her skin felt like ice.

So Novak stripped off her wet clothes, down to her underwear, and wrapped her up in some warm blankets. Her body looked wasted, impossibly thin, and sported bruises just about everywhere. After she was settled, he walked to the head and washed his hands and splashed cold water on his face. He was almost completely sober now, the dregs of the booze chased away by the adrenaline of the armed encounter. He needed to shake off the rest of it in a hurry, just in case her captor came back to claim her boat. The spike in his blood pressure was coming down, too, slowly but surely, his heartbeat returning to its normal pace. He stared at his reflection in the mirror. God, he looked like crap. He looked worse than crap. Two weeks of dark beard, bloodshot eyes from the booze, face and chest sunburned from weeks spent alone at sea. He looked like a bum.

Novak was a big man, six inches over six feet, with wide shoulders and thick muscles and a tendency to intimidate most people who met up with him. He was a scary looking guy at the best of times, and he knew it. The girl lying unconscious in that bunk was sure as hell going to wake up and panic when she saw him looking as unkempt and dangerous as he looked right now. That would not be good. Not after what she'd just gone through. On the other hand, she had already been in some very bad company before Novak had come along and saved the day, which might act to make him come off a mite better once she got the story straight.

The big white-and-black yacht was still bobbing nearby, and he went back top decks and brought the *Sweet Sarah* up close, sent a grappling hook across the bow, and tied in to her. He looked at the yacht's name again. *Orion's Trident*. He ought to be able to find its owner on the registry in Cancun. The dead guy was still where he'd breathed his last, on his back, his face and most of his head pretty much gone. Novak sidestepped the blood and brain matter, took a knee, and searched the guy for ID. No luck with that. No driver's license, no wallet, no nothing. After that, Novak went below and tossed the boat slowly and methodically, searching for proof of ownership, a name, mail addressed to the owner, anything, but could find no identifying papers, not even a ship's log.

All of which was highly irregular. That told him that there had probably been some kind of illegal operation going on aboard the *Orion's Trident*. Drug smuggling, maybe. Or something worse. Then he found a torture chamber located down in the bilge and knew it was something worse. Inside, he found steel rings attached to the wall and heavy chains lying unlocked in the shallow water covering the bottom of the hull. The girl had been a captive, all right, and so had the guy who had tried to protect her, it looked like. They must have gotten loose somehow and attempted to run for it, a decision that had turned out badly for both of them.

Novak was careful not to touch anything that he didn't have to. He wiped off his prints when he did touch something. He didn't want any of this illegal operation to come back on him. He found some women's clothes and tennis shoes that looked like they might fit the skinny girl he'd rescued, so he stuffed them into a plastic bag. After that, he took some medical supplies and pain medications he'd found in the head, and then he went topside and leaped back aboard his own boat. He stopped again, carefully searching a full 360 degrees around the horizon. The guy was long gone. On the other hand, hijackers were not wont to give up an expensive boat they'd captured, not without a fight. That was fine by Novak. They could have the *Orion's Trident* and the murdered guy on its deck. They could bring on a fight with him, too, but he wasn't going to hang around and wait for it.

Novak took the controls of the *Sweet Sarah*, maneuvered her away from the yacht's hull, and took off back to the reef where he'd been anchored. He considered heading directly to the nearest hospital but nixed that idea almost at once. They were out in the middle of nowhere. The closest ER would probably be a three- or four-day sail, at the very least. He could call in help on the sat phone, but it would be too long a distance to ask a medical chopper to fly, even if they would even consider coming so far out to sea to pick up one girl with relatively minor injuries. She was in bad shape at the moment, but her wounds were nowhere near catastrophic. The worst-case scenario might be a concussion from the blows to her head. Novak had the training and medical supplies to doctor her himself for a day or two and wait for her to regain consciousness and tell him what had happened, who had attacked her, and where she lived. After that, he could take her home and let her family deal with her. On top of all that, he had a feeling she was involved in something criminal, and he didn't want to get pulled into a legal mess because of her. His course of action now decided, Novak swung the boat east and headed for a protected cove that he had used a couple of nights before. It could act as a temporary stop until she came to and could tell him what the hell had gone on aboard that yacht.

The anchorage he sought was on the far edge of a protected coral reef where nobody could sneak up on him. He had learned to be careful the hard way. He had been a Navy SEAL, and that training had paid off in lots of ways. He was fairly certain that he had stepped into something pretty damn ugly and something that could decrease his chances of living a long and healthy life. Oh yeah, something dark was gonna come back and bite him in the ass for this little Good Samaritan act. Time would tell, but that time was gonna be spent a good long way away from that abandoned yacht. Once Novak brought the injured girl aboard, the die had been cast, whether he liked it or not. And he didn't like it.

On the other hand, Will Novak had never been a man to turn his back on trouble, or on standing up for people who couldn't fight for themselves. Truth was, he liked to fight—especially with dirtbags who deserved to die and die hard. He liked to win too, even better. And he usually did win. That guy who had fled and left the woman to drown was apparently a murderer, a torturer, and a kidnapper. He had turned tail and run like hell when somebody with equal fire-power had challenged him. Novak wouldn't mind teaching him a lesson. In fact, he'd get off on it. Maybe he'd go after him when the time was right, hunt him down and let him go up against a man, instead of a weak and injured woman. Right now, he had the unconscious girl to worry about, and that was plenty.

Chapter Two

While the girl was bandaged up and still unconscious, Novak spent the next few hours making tracks. When he got to the giant reef, he felt better. Here, he could stay out of sight but still see and hear any boat coming at him from any direction. After he was anchored and saw that the coast remained clear, he cleaned himself up some, showered, trimmed his shaggy dark blond hair close, and shaved his two-week beard. Pulling on a clean white T-shirt and khaki shorts, he felt a hell of a lot better. Like a human being again. Felt better than he had since he'd left the States two weeks ago. Up top again, he checked out the water in every direction, saw no boat, heard no motor, so he descended back down to the galley and sat at the dining table. From his seat on the bench, he could see the fore cabin. The sliding door was open, and the unknown, unconscious young woman was still struggling to breathe out of what sounded like a broken nose. A nose that had probably been straight and attractive a day ago but was going to be crooked from this day forward, unless somebody fixed it.

The girl wasn't moving, but she wasn't shivering anymore, either. She was just so damn young. Turned out to be much more a child than an adult. Eighteen, nineteen, maybe even in her early twenties, but that was pushing it, by the looks of her. So young that she made him nervous, made him feel like a lecher messing with some captured kid. Other than her bruises, she looked healthy enough, just a normal kid before the abuse and hard blows began. Some jerk had worked her over pretty good. She did not look physically fit. Looked like the skinniest kid he'd ever seen.

She was thin to a ridiculous degree. Anorexia was the new look du jour, it seemed. Each bone in her rib cage had been readily apparent when he'd undressed her. Hell, he could have counted her ribs if he hadn't been so eager to get her covered up and warm again. She had either dieted to the size of a walking stick or had been starved into skeletal proportions. Very dark tan, though, like his, but with bikini tan lines, probably from days spent out at sea under the tropical sun. Long, lean legs. She had fought for her life, despite her thinness. He was more interested in her background than her physical appearance, and he wanted to know more about her, especially how and when and why she'd gotten herself into the kind of jam that put her up against a brutal thug like the one Novak had dealt with.

Who the hell was she? Who was the guy in the Zodiac? And the other guy he'd shot down in cold blood? Her husband, maybe? Her boyfriend? Whoever her captor had been, he had shown no compunction leaving her out in the middle of nowhere to drown. Or maybe she was the bad news in this little scenario, only getting her due punishment for some terrible act she had committed. Stranger things had happened. He'd known a few evil women in his day. That didn't seem likely to him, though. Not with this kid. Nothing made sense. He could ferret out her story easily enough. He just had to be patient, and he was a patient man. Always had been.

After about an hour spent inside the salon in the silent boat, studying nautical maps, trying to locate the nearest hospital in case she turned out to need one, he rolled up the maps and put them in their waterproof tubes and stowed them away. Then he just sat there, waiting and listening to her gasping and snorting and sputtering out of a once-attractive nose that was bent out of shape, and in the literal sense, so dysfunctional that it impeded her breathing to a dangerous point. After listening to her struggle to take in air for a while, Novak stood up and walked back to the bunk. He stood for a moment, looking down at her, and then he reached down and placed his thumb on one side of her nose and two fingers on the other side. He felt for the break in the cartilage, and then with one quick jerk, he put her nose back into place. Battleground first aid. Something he'd had to do to himself a time or two, and for an injured buddy once in a while, usually after some knock-down, drag-out fight, either in the desert in Iraq or in some seedy Asian brothel. The girl didn't move when he snapped it, didn't groan, didn't react, but she sure as hell started breathing better. Her nose had stopped bleeding, but she was lucky she was unconscious. Novak went top decks every quarter hour, checked for interlopers and encroaching enemies, found none, and came back down and waited for his new, unwanted, uninvited, injured guest to come to.

That didn't happen until mid-morning the following day. What happened at that point was not a pretty sight. She awoke abruptly and without giving him any warning. Novak's mystery guest came up off the mattress like a bat out of hell, screeching and flailing and kicking and fighting, terrified the hell out of her skull. Novak had gotten enough shut-eye through the night, basically dozing in his aft cabin and starting awake every half hour to check on her and scan the horizon. He now sat in the galley at the breakfast table, his empty plate still in front of him, watching the girl go nuts while he sipped his third mug of his favorite and very strong Jamaican coffee. He watched calmly as her fear ratcheted up a couple of levels to pretty much batshit crazy, figuring she'd have to calm down and act rational sooner or later. He wasn't going to get himself kicked and scratched up trying to fight her initial hysteria. She deserved some kind of outlet for her terror, anyhow. She had been mistreated horribly. Chained, beaten, and God only knew what else. He didn't like to think about what else. But she would be thinking about what else. For the rest of her life.

The panicked girl finally scrambled down off the bunk and headed for the galley. When she saw him sitting at the table, she froze in her tracks. When he offered no reaction, just stared silently at her, she realized she was nearly naked. Shivering all over, her nose bleeding a little, she grabbed a towel off the bench, wrapped it around herself, and then inched around on the other side of the galley as far from him as she could get. Then, eyes still on him, she fled helter-skelter up the companionway to the aft deck. Novak just sat there and drank more coffee and listened to her footsteps pattering around up top, running down the gangway to the bow and back. If he followed her, it would only scare her more, so he just sat and waited for her to calm down, tire out, and think coherently. She wasn't going anywhere; nowhere to go. They were anchored out in the middle of the Caribbean Sea. Not even an island for miles around. The good news was that she didn't appear to be too bad off physically, not the way she was getting around.

His selected course of inaction went well enough for a time, up until the moment he heard some doors bang open and realized it was the cabinet where he stowed his own small Zodiac.

Lucky for Novak, the girl wasn't familiar with the Zodiac's controls, because she already had the craft lowered down to the water by the time he reached her. She jumped down into it but was pretty much hysterical and kept killing the motor. The woman was clearly not a conditioned sailor. Not any kind of sailor. Novak stood back, leaned his palms against the wire, and called out that he wasn't going to hurt her. Tried to sound harmless. She didn't seem to think so and continued to try the ignition. After a few minutes, Novak got tired of it all, reached down, and grabbed her arm. She fought him in a panicked kind of frenzy, using her fingernails and teeth and anything else she could think of—scratching and hitting and biting and yelling and big-time getting on Novak's nerves. He got her out of the small boat and hoisted her back up over the rail without too much effort. She weighed next to nothing. She was trying her best to kick him in the groin, but that wasn't going to happen.

When she wouldn't stop fighting, he jerked her around until her back was pressed firmly against his chest, immobilizing her there with his forearm around her neck and his other arm clenching her arms and waist tightly against him. She kicked desperately and struggled and fought his hold, but he kept her immobile without a lot of trouble. She finally tired herself out and simply hung against him, limp and done. She had to be weak from loss of blood, so it hadn't taken long to take the fight out of her.

"I'm not going to hurt you, kid," he told her calmly, relaxing his grip a bit.

That caused another fit of fighting, but she tired quickly. Novak figured her head was pounding like the devil now. Her wounds were probably bleeding again. She would not be able to struggle much longer. She would not be able to do much of anything much longer. When she hung in front of him, panting and shivering, he tried to reason with her, keeping his voice low and soothing and unthreatening.

"I'll let you go as soon as you settle down and quit fighting me.

Like I told you before, I don't want to hurt you. I don't want anything from you. I'm trying to help you get out of whatever jam you got yourself into. For what it's worth, if I hadn't pulled you out of the water last night, you'd be at the bottom of the sea right now."

After that, the girl stood quietly and just leaned her head back against his chest, either thinking about what he'd said or planning how to kill him. He guessed the latter. She was also looking around the boat now, at the calm, glittering royal blue sea surrounding them, while waves rocked the *Sweet Sarah* in a gentle swaying motion. Not a single boat or human being was in sight. The yacht from which she'd come was now far away and adrift, unless her attacker had come back with reinforcements to claim it. So, okay, they were alone in the middle of nowhere, and he could hold her immobile for the next two days if he had to. No problem for him, but she wouldn't like it much. Neither would he. He'd like it less than she would. After a long stint of heavy breathing and silent consideration, she took a deep breath and held her body stiffly.

"Okay. I get it. You can let me go now."

Novak had not been expecting cooperation. Nope, and he wondered if her capitulation was a ruse designed to throw him off. But he let go of her anyway and stepped back away from her, not stupid. He expected her to dart away again, make a run for the bow, maybe, or try to knock the hell out of him with both fists. Less likely, she might jump overboard in a dramatic show of bravado. But that would just be silly and self-defeating on her part, and his gut told him that she wasn't a stupid girl, despite the fact that she'd somehow gotten herself tangled up with some low-life criminals who had beaten her and left her for dead.

To his surprise, she did not respond in panic. Instead, she backed slowly away from him until her retreat was stopped by the gunwale opposite him. It was only then that she seemed to realize she was nearly naked again, the towel left behind down in the Zodiac. She crossed her arms over her breasts.

"Where are my clothes? Give them back to me!"

She spoke educated English with a thick Spanish accent, breathless as hell at the moment. She looked Hispanic, Mexican, probably. Her eyes were not brown but darker than that, huge and thickly lashed and so black that they gave off a silver sheen from the sun's bright glare. She wasn't particularly pretty, nowhere near as beautiful as his wife had been, but she looked fairly good under such unfortunate circumstances. Surprised by her newfound courage, he watched her without comment. She watched him back. A wary standoff on both their parts, big-time.

"Your clothes were wet and bloody and ripped up. You came out of the water as cold as ice. I took them off you, right after I saved you from drowning, and wrapped you up in warm blankets. Your stuff is probably dry by now, if you would like to put it back on. I laid the clothes out in the sun, up there on the foredeck. I also brought some clothes off that boat you were on. Don't know if they're yours or not, but they looked about your size."

Novak pointed to where the black shorts and oxford shirt were spread out on the roof of the cabin. She shielded her eyes to see them, and then she gazed back at him. Their eyes locked hard for a long moment. She was sizing him up. He was sizing her up, too. His eyes remained steadfastly on hers. Hers looked big and confused and distrustful. Then they started darting around like crazy, looking for a way out of the terrible mess in which she'd found herself. She was hovering right on the edge of a panic precipice, swaying there, not sure yet what to do. Novak couldn't say he blamed her. She was in one hell of an ugly predicament. She didn't know who the hell he was. She didn't know if he was a good guy or a bad guy or a really bad guy. And she didn't know what he planned to do to her, way out there in the middle of the ocean, all alone, no other human being in sight to help her.

"Who are you?"

The girl hadn't asked him that—she had demanded the answer. Her ebony eyes had narrowed down now into suspicious slits. She had voiced the question imperiously, as if she was used to giving orders and expecting them to be followed without question. As if she was used to waving manicured and beringed fingers and things would be done for her. She was one of the privileged few, all right. She had reacted as the spoiled princess of a rich and doting family would behave. Only problem was, he didn't dote on her. And he didn't like spoiled princesses, or rich parents.

"Who are you?" he countered, crossing his arms over his chest.

Novak watched her wet her dry lips, and then she seemed to taste the blood on her mouth and reacted to it with a dark frown. She appeared somewhat startled by his question. She eyeballed him for a long moment and slowly shook her head. The slight movement obviously started her head to pounding, or maybe she just hadn't noticed the headache until then. She grabbed both sides of her head with her open palms and groaned out loud. When she looked back at him, her expression revealed visible shock. Her words came very low, distressed.

"I don't know. I don't know who I am. Tell me."

Oh yeah, right, Novak thought. She must think him a moron. Or born yesterday. He was neither. "Sure you do. Think harder."

"I don't know! I swear I don't!" She paused, glancing around, frantic all of a sudden. "Look, mister, I don't remember anything until I woke up down there without my clothes on. I swear, I swear."

"You don't remember a thing, huh? You don't remember being on a white yacht named *Orion's Trident*? I suppose you don't remember being chased by some guy who slugged you in the face with a gun and then knocked you overboard? None of that rings a bell?"

"No! I don't understand any of this! Who are you? Tell me!" Now her voice quavered a bit, her eyes getting wide and watery with distress that appeared legit enough. She put her fingertips against the bandage around her forehead, as if she'd just become aware of it. Oh man, if she was lying, putting on a show, she was laying it on nice and thick. And Novak would bet his life she was lying, and that meant she was damn good at it. Professional caliber, maybe. Which would be a good thing for him to keep in mind. However, she looked so small and beaten and victimized that it was hard to ignore her vulnerability. Novak's gut told him she wasn't nearly as innocent as she was letting on. Pure instinct, but his instincts had always been damn good.

It was much more likely that she remembered everything that had happened last night, and quite clearly. She just didn't want to tell him for her own reasons. Self-preservation, probably, at its finest. Maybe everybody aboard that yacht had been a criminal, including her. Maybe it was some kind of heroin- or coke-running operation out of Cancun. Maybe she had provoked the guys she was working with, stolen from them or tried to take them out and pocket their shares. That didn't much stand to reason, either, but nothing much did stand to reason at this point. Not in Novak's estimation, and skeptical was his middle name.

Still, there was that one room aboard the *Orion's Trident*, the one with the shackles and bloodstains. And there were the dark bruises on her wrists and ankles, blue-black and ugly and painful. She had been somebody's prisoner, no doubt in Novak's mind, but that didn't mean she was a Girl Scout, either. He didn't say anything, curious to see what she'd do next.

"You're telling me that you pulled me out of the ocean and put this bandage on my head and saved my life. Is that what you're saying?"

"Yep, that's what I'm saying. And you're welcome."

"Why? What were you doing out there all by yourself? What do you want with me? Why are you holding me captive?"

Novak just gazed at her. She was beginning to annoy him. "What difference does that make? Just so you know, though, I don't want a damn thing from you."

"You look all . . ." she floundered around for a suitable description, "scruffy and . . . not good."

Scruffy and not good? So much for cleaning himself up. "Well, you don't look so hot yourself, kid. But you do look a good sight better than you did last night when I dragged you aboard my boat. I had to mop up a pint of blood you left on my deck. So you're welcome for that, too."

She frowned some more. It seemed to hurt her headache. "This is just too much. I can't even think straight. I can't believe this is happening to me."

"No kidding."

Silence. She peered out to sea again. Looked in every direction. Frowned some more. The sun glinted on those black eyes. It was hot, probably ninety degrees. She was sweating. So was he.

Novak got fed up with the conversation, or lack thereof. "Look, why don't you just tell me who you are and where you live so I can get you the hell off my boat and get back to my own life. I've got things to do and places to go. You're an inconvenience that I don't want to have to deal with right now."

"Like what?"

Novak scowled down at her. "Like what *what?*"

"Like what do you have to do?"

"You tell me who you are. Then I'll regale you with the story of my life."

She shut her eyes and gave a heavy, put-upon sigh, quite the dramatic young gal. She wavered on her feet and clasped her fingers around the rail. "Oh no, oh, my God, I feel funny . . . oh, I think . . . I think I'm going to faint . . ."

And then her eyes rolled back into her head, and she did faint, damn it. It wasn't any act, either, Novak was pretty sure, although he had an idea that she might be quite the actress whenever the moment called for it. Not this time, though, not as hard as the back of her head cracked on his shiny teak deck. And not unless she was Cate Blanchett in disguise, acting the hell out of a swoon scene in some costume drama. He crossed over to her, squatted down and lifted her eyelid, found that she really was out cold. From the look of her body, it was more likely from lack of nourishment and hydration than from loss of blood. He cursed under his breath again, swung her up in his arms, and carried her below. Novak was not happy. No, he was definitely not happy. Now he supposed he was stuck babysitting an unknown, theatrical girl until her memory came back and/or she decided to quit playing games and level with him.

On the other hand, he guessed taking care of her until he could get her to somewhere safe was a good sight better than getting stinking drunk every night in order to drown out all those scared little voices of everybody he loved, endlessly calling inside his head. Time would tell on that, too, he guessed. Because he was fairly certain now that he was stuck with this frightened young woman, whoever the hell she was, and that she was not telling him everything, and that whatever she wasn't telling him now was gonna be very bad news for him later on.

Chapter Three

Although Novak felt a modicum of sympathy for the girl he'd rescued, he also felt like she was going to be a gigantic pain in the ass. Yeah, he had a pretty good suspicion that his delicate little mystery girl, who had demonstrated that she could fight like the devil and probably had a few dirty tricks up her sleeve that she could only have learned by experience and/or tutelage, was not an amnesiac. She was playing the role fairly well, he had to give her that. She awoke the second time in the evening after about three hours spent on the bunk unconscious. Or pretending to be.

Novak had checked on her several times to make sure she wasn't bleeding from the head or nose again, but she had been lying on her back, her chest rising and falling evenly. She was making little snorts and snores like his old beagle named Banjo used to do during Novak's formative years spent down at his father's sheep ranch in Queensland, Australia. To this day, he still missed that good old dog. Novak was fixing himself some supper in the galley when he heard the girl stirring around in the fore cabin. Lots of storage cabinets clicking open and shut. She was searching the boat, probably for a weapon. He heard the hatch above her bunk raise up, the one that led out onto the bow. Damn nosy girl, despite his hospitality. He had a feeling she might know how to use a gun—just instinctive self-preservation on his part. She wouldn't find one. He kept them locked up and well hidden in secret compartments. He wasn't overly worried that she would take off in the Zodiac again, either, not when she was aware there was exactly nowhere to flee. Besides that, he had it secured to the stern with knots she could never untie.

About ten minutes passed before she showed up in the door of

the galley. Looking hangdog and pitiful now, she stayed right there
and stared at him. Novak glanced over at her and then returned his
attention to the stovetop. His new boat had a great galley setup. He'd
designed it himself to accommodate his height. Sailboats weren't designed for big men his size; no boats were. All the most modern
conveniences and appliances were installed in the galley, with plenty
of room still left to turn around. He loved the *Sweet Sarah*, loved
everything about her. He probably valued her more highly than anything else he had. She was his sanctuary in bad times and his home
in good times, and he rarely invited anybody on board. This time,
he'd made an exception.

Forking up a fillet of flounder sizzling in the skillet, he flipped it
over. He'd put yesterday's catch on ice before all hell had broken out
in the guise of a skinny kid. The grease popped and smoked. The
cornmeal-crusted fish smelled good. His stomach growled. He was
hungry. She looked even hungrier. She looked like some kind of
homeless refugee from Somalia, or someplace. She was skin and
bones. Today's Hollywood producers would love her.

After flipping the other fillet over to brown, Novak turned to her.
"Want something to eat, kid?"

"Yes, please. Oh, thank you. Maybe that's why I fainted up there.
I don't usually pass out like that." Her words came out fast and
sounded über-conciliatory to Novak, and pretty damn phony, too,
maybe—but then, he was always highly suspicious of everybody.
Always had been, always would be. That particular idiosyncrasy had
served him well in his long and violent career. He nurtured it and
kept it alive. She stood watching his every move as if she expected
him to whip around and charge her using the spatula in his hand as
a weapon. Not gonna happen. She had on the black shorts she'd worn
when he'd pulled her out of the sea. He'd brought the dry garments
down and laid them on the bunk beside her while she slept. She had
also helped herself to one of Novak's 3X Extra Long white cotton
T-shirts that he kept folded in the fore lockers. Guess she didn't like
the clothes he'd brought off the *Orion's Trident*. His shirt hung on
her, as big as a jib sail, reaching well past her knees. When she saw
his interest in the T-shirt, she hastily explained, "Uh, I'm sorry, but
I borrowed this shirt. Hope you don't mind. I found it in the cabinet.
My blouse was all ripped up and had blood on it and stuff."

All that came out in rapid Spanish, but somehow sounding like a typical American teenager all the same. Maybe she'd gone to school in the States. He shrugged. "I don't care. Wear whatever you can find. It's a little baggy on you. The clothes in that bag I put on the bunk will probably fit you better."

Novak engendered a small smile, designed to disarm her, but he wasn't good at smiling or disarming, not with pleasant looks, anyhow. Especially not now. He didn't want her aboard his boat any more than she wanted to be there. She just looked down, as if embarrassed. He returned his efforts to cooking his meal, but he made sure he knew where she was and what she was doing. At the moment, she was inching around behind him. She sat down in the booth at the dining table. He had his .45 handgun, a Kimber 1911, stuck down the back of his waistband, just in case she was planning to attack him with a table knife. He had set out two plates and glasses, figuring she'd be hungry as hell when she settled down and became rational. But she didn't ask for anything, just sat silently and watched him work at the stove.

Novak didn't look at her again. He lifted the glass lid off the wild rice, cut off half a stick of butter and dropped it on top, and then pulled the pan off the burner. He replaced the lid so the rice would steam. He pulled out a cutting board and sawed off a couple of pieces of thick Italian bread. He fixed her a generous plate of food and set it down on the table in front of her. She just stared at it, her eyes downcast. It appeared to Novak that she was about to burst into tears again. He hoped to hell not.

"Well, go ahead. Eat. The food's good. I didn't put anything in it."

Novak went back to the fridge, got out a couple of Dixie beers, placed them on the table, and then he filled up his own plate. By now the girl had begun to eat, all right, wolfing down the grub as fast as she could get it in her mouth. He wasn't sure she was even chewing it. Maybe she really was starving. Maybe those guys who held her captive hadn't fed her anything the entire time she was on board. Maybe he should cut her some slack and quit being so tough on her.

Then again, he didn't know her from a hole in the ground, and he didn't particularly like the temperament she'd shown him so far. He sat down across from her at the table and pushed a bottle of beer close to her plate. She kept shoveling food into her mouth, looking down at the plate as she ate and not at him. He ate, too. His manners came off a hell of a lot better than hers. Neither of them said a word for the entire meal, just concentrated on the food. He finished first because she wanted more than he did. He filled up her plate again. Then he got himself a second beer and sat down across from her and watched her partake.

"Those guys didn't give you much to eat, I take it?"

"What guys?"

"Don't start with me, kid."

After that, she looked more scared than conniving. She stopped eating and laid down her fork. She propped the head of it on the edge of her plate. Her knife was lying across the top edge. She had placed a paper napkin down on her lap and had been dabbing the corners of her mouth. Once she got past the initial hunger pangs and slowed down, she had begun to show good table etiquette. Looked like she was a well-mannered young woman, even when half starved. He wished he could tamp down his wariness of her, but it hadn't happened yet. She had to prove herself trustworthy first.

"So, tell me. You remember your name yet?"

"No, sir."

"You can stop with the *sir*. No need. Call me Novak."

She was a Mexican national, Novak was almost certain. He knew lots of people from that country and she looked the part and sounded the part, except for some U.S. syntax and slang. He was pretty sure now about her being schooled in the States. Maybe she was a Mexican American. Second or third generation. He took a swig of beer, observing her while he did it. He just wasn't so sure about her yet. She seemed okay now, just a poor kid who had gotten herself into trouble with some bad people. Unfortunately, his gut kept insisting just the opposite. "Tell me what you do remember."

"I told you. I don't remember a thing. It's all just a great big black bunch of nothing."

Well, the alliteration was good. "Where are you from?"

She just shook her head, looked upset about his questioning. She started fiddling with the napkin, tearing off pieces and putting them on her plate. He watched her do that for a few moments.

"Let's talk about your name again. Think hard. Try to remember. See if it'll come back."

The girl tossed her head and swirled her long dark hair around her shoulders. It was thick and nearly waist length. She wouldn't look at him now. The bridge of her nose had a gash across it but was no longer bleeding. Then she latched those intense obsidian eyes on him. "Listen, señor, I told you I don't know. I wish I did. It's scary not knowing anything. Not even my own name."

"Know what, kid? I've been around the block a couple of times. I know something about lying, and I think you're lying to me right now."

"No, I'm not! Please believe me. You saved my life, or I guess you did. You said you did. I'm grateful for that. Really, I am. You didn't have to. You didn't even know me."

Novak considered her and considered her to still be lying through her teeth. "Okay, let's go through this together. One step at a time. I'll get you started. You were on a big white yacht with a black stripe down the side. Called the *Orion's Trident*. Registered out of Cancun. There were two men on board with you. One tall guy, one short guy. You were screaming for help, and then the tall one tried to rescue you. Got himself killed for the trouble. The other guy knocked you around some and then you went over the rail and into the water. Then he took potshots at you, wanting you dead, for damn sure. I warned him off with my rifle, and then he panicked because he couldn't see me. He roared off in a small boat, looked like a Zodiac to me, maybe, similar to mine but larger. Then I motored over to see what the hell was going on and if you were dead or alive. Any or all of that ring a bell for you?"

"No, sir. It's just all gone blank. Until I woke up here and saw you. I thought you were going to hurt me. I thought you were bad." She was staying with the accented English now.

"Okay, you don't remember a thing. Well, that's just great. So where do you suggest we go from here?"

She bit her bottom lip and puckered up as if ready to dissolve into some giant angst and bawl out her frustration. Alas, and again, no tears showed up. Novak took note of that, as he did her carefully sorrowful expression. She was a pretty young girl, but there was something else in her eyes, too. Something very adult back there hovering around in those jet-black depths. Some kind of gauging and conniving going on, for sure. He would bet his life on it. She must have sensed his distrust.

"I'm truly sorry. I'd tell you if I knew something. Maybe it'll all come back to me soon. Maybe I'm in shock? Could that be it? You know, from getting knocked in the head."

"Yeah, maybe. Could be a mild concussion, but you couldn't eat that much food if you were in really bad shape. Not without throwing it back up. But you did take a couple of hard knocks to the head. So you better take it easy from now on. Nix the fighting and running around."

"Did you really shoot at somebody, just to save my life?"

Novak scoffed at the question. "Yeah. I have a tendency to intervene when I see a murder about to go down."

"Really? You've saved lives before like that?" Her eyes looked huge and glinted in the soft light flooding down through the long and narrow porthole above the table. "Well, thank you so much, I mean it. For saving me. Maybe I'll remember something soon. Maybe I'll find a way to repay you."

"Yeah, well, thanks, but I don't want to be repaid. Let's just hope you figure out who you are." He observed her silently for another moment. "So, tell me. What am I supposed to do with you until then?"

She looked down at her hands and then she picked up the crucifix around her neck and held it in one fist, the absolute picture of abject misery now. She gave a helpless shrug. Her voice came back small and penitent. "I'm sorry I'm causing you so much trouble. I wish I could tell you everything you wish to know. I feel terrible that I cannot. I will pray to the Virgin Mary for my memory to return."

Oh, brother, Novak thought. Now she's a nun. He had tried his best to be patient, but this girl, there was just something wrong about her. He felt a twinge of aggravation. Couldn't help it. She was making *him* feel responsible for her, and he didn't like it. Didn't want to take on that kind of responsibility, didn't want her to remain on his boat, didn't want the complication of having to find her husband or parents, or anything else about her. "Well, I sure as hell can't adopt you."

That surprised her. Her expressions were easy to read at times. Other times, not so much. She gave a soft little laugh, all sweet and girly and musical. Cut it off pretty quick, true, but it relieved some of the tension looming up between them. Novak finished his beer and watched her. She looked a lot better, but that wouldn't take much. Color had come back into her cheeks a bit, put a pink bloom under the tan. She had dark skin anyway, further proof that she was Mexican. She absently touched her hair where it flowed down over her shoulders. It looked thick and soft and was the deep, rich color of fine ebony hardwood. It had waves from where the plaits had been pulled tight.

"Do you want anything else to eat?"

"I can get things for myself. You don't have to wait on me. You've done enough already."

So Novak sat there and watched her get more food for herself. He took that time to observe the bruises on her bare arms and legs and around her throat. The ones on her wrists and ankles weren't as bad as he'd first thought. She had been bound at some time or another, looked like rope burns, maybe. That indicated she had been a captive, as did the ropes and shackles he'd found belowdecks on the *Orion's Trident*.

The girl polished off another portion of food in nothing flat, and Novak hoped she wasn't making herself sick. "Okay, I think you've had enough now. Why don't you go lie down and rest awhile and let me think about what I'm going to do with you? How about I call you something? What name should I use?"

"I don't know my name. I don't care. You don't have to call me anything."

"I need to call you something."

"Then call me Friday, like in *Robinson Crusoe*, I guess." She smiled, but it was brief and tentative and seemed out of place under the circumstances. This girl was strange.

Novak studied her face. "You remember the name of that book but not your own name?"

"I guess so. I do remember that story. About the shipwreck and all that."

"How about I just call you Jane? Like Jane Doe?"

She just nodded, not very interested in what he called her, it seemed. "You want me to wash up the dishes? Since you cooked supper and all? I will. I will be glad to."

"Nope. I can handle it."

She nodded, and then she stood up, wiggled out of the booth, and headed back to the fore cabin. He heard her climb into the wedge berth and then slide the door shut behind her. The lock clicked. So much for trusting his intentions. He couldn't blame her.

Novak took the aft companionway top decks and scanned the horizon again, still expecting trouble. It was past twilight, well into the gloaming, sunset faded away, but a lovely, peaceful time on the ocean. He'd checked for interlopers about fifty times already. Because trouble was incoming and soon, no doubt about it. There were no boats approaching his position yet. Nothing in sight all around, only mile after endless mile of restless seas under quickly encroaching darkness. But he had that feeling he got sometimes, that little niggling worry that usually showed up when things were getting ready to come down hard on him. He moved back into the stern, fired up the engines, and headed her due east, away from the Mexican coast, setting a course in the general direction of the Cayman Islands. He guessed his best option was to take the kid back to his plantation house in Louisiana. Turn her over to the Lafourche Parish sheriff's office and let them figure out who she was and how she had gotten herself into this big mess. But that idea didn't sit well with him. Not until he knew who she was. She could be anybody. Anybody at all. And anybody at all could be a disaster for him, because if he'd learned anything in his life, it was that good things could turn into bad things very fast.

On the other hand, Will Novak had been a private investigator by trade since he'd left the military. He could find out the girl's identity himself, maybe. Possibly even from the computer equipment he had on board, but not without a name or birth date or anything else to go on. He could take her picture and send it to his partner. Claire Morgan was a hell of a good investigator, whom he trusted implicitly and could call upon night and day. Yeah, Claire was quite a woman, all right. She never gave up on her cases or on anything else. And that was putting it mildly. Actually, all he might need to do was check the girl's fingerprints. That alone might solve the mystery, if she had a criminal background. He didn't have a fingerprinting kit on board, but he might get something halfway usable with computer ink. Then he could e-mail the prints out to Claire and she could run them through AFIS for him. Quick and easy. Same went for her picture, especially if this kid turned out to be bad news. As innocent and pristine as newly fallen snow she was not, he would bet on it. But she could be the victim she purported herself to be. He could take her to a battered women's shelter in the islands and let them figure it out. It was a long voyage back to Louisiana. But for some reason, he didn't really want to cast the kid off somewhere—not quite yet. Just in case her life really was in danger.

Unfortunately, his damn protective instinct was beginning to kick in, and against his better judgment. He steered the boat out into the deep blue expanse of water stretching out in front of him, eager to put distance between him and the guy who had been killing people on the yacht the night before. Maybe, with a stroke of good fortune, the poor young girl with whom he was now saddled would simply remember her name and address and telephone number, and Novak could sail her right back home and be rid of her for good. Not likely, but it was a happy thought.

Nothing remotely like that happened. Not that night; not the next day. His guest remained in her cabin by herself most of the time, quiet as a mouse, not moving around much, not from what he could hear. Probably just lying on the bed, either asleep or trying to re-member her name and hometown zip code. She only came out where Novak was when she smelled food cooking. That went on until she climbed up on deck and sat down on the padded banquette across from him. Novak was fishing for their supper off the starboard side and pretty much ignored her.

"I remembered something, Mr. Novak."

That got Novak's attention quickly enough. He swiveled his seat around and stared at her. "Well, great. Tell me."

"I think my name might be Isabella."

"Nice name. You remember your last name, too?"

She got the usual flash of fright on her face and shrugged and changed her facial expression on cue to *I'm-just-so-damn-sad-and-pitiful*. A studied "feel sorry for me" look, oh yeah.

"Remember anything else?"

"No, sir." She glanced around and then she said, "I really am sorry for causing you all this trouble."

"Those guys were holding you prisoner. No doubt about it. You have rope burns where they tied you up. You were their captive. You don't remember why they were holding you?"

"Vaguely, I think. I faintly recall getting hit in the face. I remem-ber the taste of blood. It gagged me. I remember being really scared."

Novak observed her a moment and then placed his rod aside. "Do you have any tattoos?"

"Not that I can see."

Novak hadn't seen any, either. And he'd seen a lot of her. "Birthmarks?"

"I don't think so."

"I could take your picture with my cell phone and e-mail it to a friend of mine. Let her put it out to the U.S. media. Maybe the networks would pick it up and screen it nationwide. Maybe it would get coverage in some other countries, too."

Novak waited for her reaction to his suggestion. If she wasn't hiding anything, if she really was suffering from amnesia, she wouldn't mind putting her photo out. She would welcome any way to find out who she was. If she was wanted by the law, she wouldn't be so thrilled to have her image flashed around the world and hung up on police station bulletin boards. He waited some more.

"What if that bad man you told me about sees my picture and comes after me again?"

"He'll find me instead. I won't let him get to you. I'll make sure he doesn't."

"Why would you do that? You could get hurt. Shot. You said he was really bad."

"Because he's a damn coward who beat up a woman and left her to drown. He ran away when somebody who could fight back showed up. Don't worry about me. I can take care of myself. And I can protect you." Novak thought of Mariah, his sister-in-law, and how he'd promised her his protection, too, and only weeks ago. But now she was dead, and he hadn't been able to prevent it. Guilt ate into his gut every time he thought about her and the way she died. He tried to block out those thoughts and kept his attention leveled on the girl's face.

"Why?" she asked him again. "Why are you doing this?"

"Because you need help. And I've got what it takes to help you."

Her eyes filled up. No tears fell this time, either—again, something he definitely needed to take note of. Cate Blanchett, she was not. "Thank you," she told him, all teary-eyed and teary-voiced and touched and clogged up in her throat. Then she said, "I don't even know your first name."

"It's Will. Will Novak."

"Thank you, sir. Mr. Novak."

"Okay. And again, stop with the *sir* stuff. I mean it." Then he asked her in Spanish, "Is Spanish your first language?"

"I understand it. I guess it is."

"I've got some magazines and newspapers aboard. Maybe if we looked at pictures, something would jog your memory. I've got some maps of Mexico and Central and South America. Maybe you'll recognize something. A name or a place."

"I'll do whatever you want me to."

She was awfully agreeable all of a sudden, but why wouldn't she be? He just couldn't quite bring himself to trust her. Not even a little bit. There was something about her; something he couldn't quite put his finger on. She was hiding something. He simply knew it. He was astute most of the time. Read people well. He'd been an investigator too long to be taken in by a seemingly innocent face and a pack of lies.

"Tell me what you're hiding. I know you're hiding something."

Isabella's eyes reacted at that question, quick and alarmed, and then they slid down to the left and away from his searching gaze. He was right. She was hiding something, all right.

"Okay. I know you know more than you're telling me. Either spit it out or I'm just going to drop you off at the nearest marina and be done with you. You understand me?"

The newly designated Isabella suddenly got very still. Then she started in with more of the anxious hand-wringing. Nervous as hell. But she began to talk. "I'm afraid to tell you. I'm afraid you'll leave me somewhere by myself and that man will get me again."

"You're right. I will. Unless you tell me the truth. What do you remember? Or have you been lying to me all along?"

"I don't know if I can trust you."

"Ditto, kid."

The girl wouldn't look at him.

"What's it gonna take for you to catch on, Isabella? Have I hurt you? Have I mistreated you? Have I given you any reason to fear me?"

She inhaled a long breath, deep and bracing, blew it out, and then locked eyes with him. "Okay. I'll tell you. I was kidnapped. Out of a hotel resort in Cancun. They've been holding me on that boat for almost a month."

Novak said nothing—just waited. Not sure yet. Not surprised, not anything. This girl was something else. He was sure of that, but that was all he was sure about.

"My real name is Isabella Maria Martinez. My father . . . well, he's rich, very rich, and they wanted a lot of money from him before they'd give me back. But he said no, and so they said they were going to kill me and dump me in the ocean. And they did. I mean, they tried. I'd be dead now if it were not for you."

A little dramatic, but could be true. "Who were your kidnappers? Why you?"

"I don't know."

"How did they get you?"

She was picking at her fingernails, nails that were perfectly manicured and painted a pale pink. "I was on holiday at the resort with my boyfriend. We were at the Moon Palace outside Cancun. You know, it's that big place on the beach, real nice. I think he betrayed me to them." She appeared terribly distressed by that realization and moaned a little.

"Why would he do that to you?"

"I don't know. I thought he loved me. I guess he wanted the money. And now he's dead. That terrible man just shot him in the head."

This time she started to cry for real. No doubt about it. Sobs and wet cheeks, sniffling, the whole weepy shebang. She probably had loved the guy.

"Did you know the man who took you and held you on that boat? The little guy who took off?"

She shook her head and wiped her eyes on the hem of his T-shirt. "He was a really bad man." Her voice dropped low, so low that it was almost unintelligible. "He . . . tied me up . . . and then he . . . raped me." Then lower still, she said, "A bunch of times."

Novak felt the inner rage rising up again from deep down inside him, igniting like fire, flaming up into the red, raw anger that could overwhelm his emotions in a hurry. He felt his face grow warm, felt his jaw lock down hard. She was weeping for real now, her face hidden inside her open hands. Novak reached out and put his hand on her shoulder. She jerked away from his touch and gave a little startled cry. Then she jumped to her feet and rushed straight to him. She buried her face against his chest, crying hard, both her fists clutching the front of his shirt. She felt slight and weak and young against him. He put his arms around her, but there was still that little spark of doubt that she was not what she appeared to be—enough to worry his mind and eat at his resolve to keep her aboard. He did feel for her, especially if what she had just told him was true. But his brain was telling him that something was wrong with that story, that she was lying through her teeth, about most of it or all of it. And there was no way she could prove what she said was true. Or that he could disprove it.

Once she settled down and backed away from him, she acted embarrassed at her show of emotion. She wiped at her tears with her fingers, nose running, eyes red and swollen. Novak needed more information to put his mind at ease. "Should I take you back to your father, then?"

That got through her misery quickly enough. "No! No, he wouldn't even pay the ransom for me. He just let them have me and didn't care that they hurt me. I hate him. I really do. Really, I hate him so much."

"What about your mother?"

"She's afraid of him, too. He hits her, too. She'd tell him if I called her. She'd be afraid not to."

"Anybody else you can turn to? Uncles, aunts, grandparents, friends?"

"They're all afraid of him. Everybody's afraid of him."

"Why?"

"Because he's rich and powerful and can make people do whatever he says."

"How does he do that? Is he a criminal?"

She hesitated a long time. "No."

"What's his name?"

More hesitation. More fearful looks out to sea. She finally told him, but in a whisper. "His name is Henrique Martinez."

Novak sat up straighter. He knew all about Henrique Martinez, all right. Last he'd heard, the guy was a powerful general working his way up in the Mexican military. A dirty guy, brutal and deadly. On the take, and had been for decades. Novak had heard of him when he was on missions in Mexico. Now things were getting damn serious, and fast. No wonder the kidnapper dumped Isabella in the ocean and left her to die. He was already a dead man walking for daring to take Martinez's daughter. So was Novak, as soon as Martinez found out that his daughter was on his boat.

After that tidbit of information, Novak decided it wise to head back home to Bonne Terre as fast as his boat would take him. They would be safer on American soil, and on his home turf. It would take days to get there, and the girl was getting more and more anxious about not having a passport and ID—apparently, a tad savvier about travel documents than she had first admitted. As it turned out, however, they didn't have to worry about her passport. The bad guys caught up with them about sixty miles off Cozumel.

Chapter Four

Novak's first clue that they were in for a hard day came the moment he heard the slow, steady thumps coming his way. He knew the sound. He recognized it instantly—helicopter rotors beating their way out over the water and straight at him. He grabbed a pair of binoculars and searched the sky until he picked out the helo, a lone dark spot on the blue sky, about the size of a mosquito. Isabella jumped up from her seat under the canopy and watched the bird approach them, flying low and flying fast. She looked two degrees from terrified.

"Who are they?" Novak asked her, pretty sure she knew. Pretty sure she had known all along that this wasn't over, that they would be pursued to the ends of the earth, if necessary.

"I don't know," she called back. "I promise! I swear it! You've got to believe me! Please believe me!"

Way too hysterical with the protestations. Novak didn't believe her. Except for the fear. Novak grabbed the rifle, sure as hell ready to defend his boat. He didn't know who the guys in the copter were yet, but they weren't going take his boat. Not without a fight. He kept the weapon pressed to his shoulder, his eye at the scope, and aimed at the copter's rotors. The bird was flying in low at them from the starboard bow. Novak kept the throttle at full speed ahead as the sleek aircraft performed a wide banking circle around the boat and then roared back to hover about fifty yards off his port side.

Novak knew exactly what they were doing, too. He'd been on birds that had done similar maneuvers. They were hovering up there, relaying his location to reinforcements. Boats already in the water. The *Sweet Sarah*'s GPS reading was going out right now to their men, and that meant more dangerous company was on its way. It also told him that whoever was in that chopper had military training. That took everything up a notch. Now his as-yet-unknown enemy was up close and personal and hazardous to his health, and he did not know how or why or what the hell was going on. That also meant the girl might be a highly important asset to somebody somewhere, so she would probably live through the coming assault on his boat. Novak didn't put himself in the "valuable" category. He just might end up dead in a matter of minutes.

Taking careful aim at the stationary helicopter, he squeezed off a couple of warning rounds just under it. The pilot banked the aircraft hard right and quickly put a hundred more yards of distance between them. Then they stayed right with him, circling the sky just out of his gun range. When they decided to come in low again, Novak squeezed off two more warning shots. After that, he picked up the sat phone and put in a quick SOS to the U.S. Coast Guard, relaying his GPS coordinates and telling them to make it quick, that he was under attack. But he didn't have much hope, not this far south of U.S. waters. Then he hung up and confronted Isabella Martinez.

"If the Coast Guard doesn't get here fast enough, and there's probably not a snowball's chance in hell that they will, we are going to be boarded, searched, robbed maybe, my boat hijacked, and you will be taken prisoner again. This is your last chance to level with me about who these people really are and what they want with you. I'm not kidding around anymore. Level with me. Now."

"I don't know who they are! I don't think Papi would've sent them after me! He didn't want to pay off Diego, so he doesn't even care about me anymore."

Novak scowled down at her, wishing to God that he'd never laid eyes on her. "Can you shoot a gun?"

She shook her head. "No sir, I've never even held a gun in my hand. Not ever."

"Okay, just get below and hide somewhere. Don't make a sound. Don't come out, no matter what. Maybe it's not you they're after. Maybe it's just some band of Mexican thieves, out here to shake us down for money and steal my boat. They've been warning sailors down here about those kinds of attacks for several months now. They mean business and they're willing to kill, so don't get cute with them. Let me try to reason with them. But once they see you, they're gonna take you for ransom."

"I'm sorry, Señor Novak! This is all my fault!"

Tell me about it, Novak thought. She was scared and he wasn't going to badger her, not now. Later? That was a distinct possibility. "Just find a good place to hide and don't show yourself unless I call and tell you to come up. If they do board us and we manage to make it to shore alive without them finding you, wait until dark and then try to slip into the water without being heard after they tie up this boat. That's the only way you'll get away from them unharmed. Understand me, kid? It won't go well for you, not if they figure out who you are and that your daddy's got a lot of money."

Isabella gave him her usual terrified look. This time the fear looked quite genuine, and she ought to be frightened. If these guys were the kind of low-life scum he thought they were, she would be mistreated, and that was putting it mildly. He'd heard about these modern pirates, been warned daily by Coast Guard alerts that these bands of miscreants were boarding ships and holding Americans for ransom. Novak watched Isabella run down the steps and disappear belowdecks. Then he sat down at the helm, throttle on full speed ahead and holding the high-powered rifle at the ready. He didn't have a chance against them and he knew it, especially after he saw four big boats speeding toward him. They were moving fast and in a perfect chevron formation. More army finesse. If they caught him out here in the middle of nowhere, there would be no escape. He and Isabella both would be at their mercy.

So he resigned himself to impending capture and kept the sailboat heading north without letting up on his speed. Even with sails down and the engines running close to full-out, it was only a matter of minutes now. They'd catch up to him, unless the Coast Guard showed, and they were nowhere to be seen. That meant he was either gonna be dead or held for ransom, right alongside the girl. When that happened, it wouldn't matter anymore who she really was. Because the more Novak had considered her story, the less he believed she was the daughter of some crooked general. Something didn't smell right about her story. But too late now. It was out of his hands.

The sea bandits had matching boats—big fast racing boats. Boats that cut the water like blades and leaped high into the waves. Within minutes, they had eaten up the distance and encircled the *Sweet Sarah*. The helicopter ventured closer, right over Novak's head, sending a stiff wash of wind down on him. He could see a gunner strapped in at the open door, an AR15 assault rifle pointed down at him. The bird was painted jungle green and was no private aircraft. This was a military operation, or at the very least, a paramilitary one. Probably the latter. Maybe even a renegade bunch out of the Mexican army. If the gunner opened up on Novak, he would be dead in seconds. Things were not going to turn out well for him, no matter how the capture went down or who they were.

Minutes later, the gunner opened up and stitched a row of warning shots across the aft deck, not a yard in front of Novak. Cursing the damage done to his new boat, Novak let up on the throttle and played their game. Then the *Sweet Sarah* lost steam and eventually floated dead in the water. Novak was not stupid enough to make a run for it against four well-armed swift enemy boats and an armed helicopter.

Novak stayed in place at the helm and watched and waited. The attack boats approached him from all sides, two easing in and tying up at port and starboard. A pretty good operation, well done, well ordered. Novak kept his own rifle lying across his knees, his finger lightly on the trigger, a prudent move for self-preservation. He was outgunned, but if they decided to kill him on the spot, he'd be damned if he'd go down without taking some of them along with him. Still, he didn't kid himself. This was serious business. If found, Isabella was in for one horrific ordeal with these guys. She would be the prize in this takedown, and animals like these would pass her around like a bag of popcorn at a Saturday night movie.

The first man who swung aboard looked like a Nazi Gestapo officer. He was dressed all in black: T-shirt, pants, leather combat boots, cap with a shiny black visor, and Kevlar vest. Aviator sunglasses. The expensive kind. Mirrored. He was carrying a big and very capable AK-47. He stopped about four feet away from Novak, pointed his weapon at Novak's chest, and took stock of the situation. He was the one in charge of the boats. No doubt about it.

Four other guys scrambled up and spread out behind their boss. They looked Hispanic and were dressed the same as their leader, all in black, wearing Kevlar and pointing four more AK-47s at him. They all wore the black hats and expensive mirrored sunglasses.

Novak could see five small images of himself and his rifle reflected back at him. Yeah, a matched set of modern-day pirates. Walking the walk, looking the look. Nobody moved for several moments, all of them staring down the barrel of Novak's rifle. He kept his weapon aimed steadfastly at the leader's head.

"What is this?" he asked the guy in Spanish. "Whatever the hell it is, are you willing to die for it?"

Their weapons remained locked on him, and a quick glance told him the other guys on the surrounding boats were standing up with their weapons pointed at him. Not good odds. Zero odds, in fact.

"Please don't do anything stupid, sir. Put down your gun. Obey my commands or die where you stand. My men don't mind killing you, trust me." Well, surprise, surprise, this guy was a Brit and spoke in perfectly clipped U.K. English, an aristocrat straight out of the House of Lords, in Novak's judgment. Every word had been awash with haughty inflection. Novak had not been expecting that. His guess? This guy was a former MI6 officer with experience in covert operations. He'd gone over to the dark side to match his clothes.

He spoke again, his words slightly apologetic. "I don't mind them killing you, you understand. Shoot me, and you'll die, too. Your choice."

The leader was a serious guy, not nervous, not anxious, just matter of fact. Do it or die. He had been well trained. When Novak didn't react, he tried again. "I am expendable, you understand. My orders are to take you and your fine vessel, whatever the cost. Believe me when I say that it will go much easier for you if you cooperate with us. So stand down and be taken, sir. There is no dishonor in surrender when facing overwhelming odds."

Now that was a man who obeyed without question. That he was willing to die for pirate booty seemed a little much to Novak. "Who are you? What do you want? Why me? Why my boat?"

"Actually, I guess you'd say that we're pirates, as you probably have already ascertained. More sophisticated, disciplined, and organized than our counterparts of old. We are commandeering this boat, sir. And we want you, too, of course, as a hostage. We make our largest profits in ransoming U.S. citizens."

The guy was a polite pirate. No *argh, ahoy matey* crap being bantered about. More of a *tallyho, chap, please surrender or I will put a bullet in your head* vibe. Polished, well spoken, and highly educated. Truth be told? They had hit the jackpot and just didn't know it. They weren't going to find out, either. Novak had a ton of money in his name, most of it stashed away in banks all over the world—millions, in fact—all inherited from his mother and her wealthy French family on the day he was born. He also held the title to her ancient plantation called Bonne Terre, deep in the bayous of Lafourche Parish, where he still lived, also worth a small fortune. But he wasn't going to tell them that. He wasn't going to tell them a damn thing, not even his real name. "You won't get much out of me. I'm a boat bum. The *Sweet Sarah* here? She's all I've got."

"Not anymore. We lay claim to her right now. She's a sweet little prize, almost new by the looks of her. You keep her up very well. Probably worth a keen $50,000, $80,000 on the black market, I'd wager. Certainly worth the time it took to chase you down." He glanced down the companionway. "We'll get even more for that cute little bird you're hiding down below. You would not believe what a young girl like that is worth to her parents. Or, an even more lucrative asset to buyers from the Middle East. Call her up here. Save us the trouble and it will go easier for you."

Novak just stared at him. "What girl?"

"Please, sir, don't be stupid and die to protect her. Our people in the helo saw her clearly. Described her to me in detail. Said she was quite young. Women are fine commodities in the places where we deal. I know you want her to stay that way, so tell her to come up here and give herself up. Then all will end well. Otherwise, we'll drag her up here and shoot you down, and then she'll be ours anyway."

"What girl?" Novak repeated.

Four rifles ratcheted around him. Barrels beaded on him. Novak kept his weapon right where it was. If the Brit was ready to die, Novak could oblige him. "You will bite it, too. You do understand that? Last warning I'm gonna give you."

"No, no! I'm right here! Don't shoot him! He's just trying to take me home! That's all. Please don't hurt him!"

Isabella flew up the steps and out onto the deck between them, ready to save Novak's bacon. Novak cursed inside. Damnation, what the hell was she doing? Isabella stood there in the bright sunlight and blinked from the sun's glare. She had both hands up high over her head. She had on one of his oversize black T-shirts, tied in a knot at her waist this time, and her black shorts and her black boat shoes. She looked very young and very small and very vulnerable.

The Brit looked at Novak and grinned knowingly. He was short, stood about five feet nine inches, maybe. His teeth looked white in his tanned face. He showed them to Novak for a long moment. "Well, this is just brilliant. Now, this behavior is so much more civilized than aiming guns at one another. You are smart to cooperate with us, young lady. Smarter than your big friend here, it appears. And now, thanks to you, nobody gets hurt. Everybody lives another day. We will take you both captive, and you will go free as soon as your family pays your ransom. There you have it. We all come out winners in the end."

If the guy said tallyho or anything akin to it, Novak was going to shoot him. And they hadn't come out winners. They'd both be dead before the money order came through. Novak didn't move a muscle, or the direction of his rifle barrel. Sat like stone. So did all the pirates. Silence reigned for a few moments. The boat rocked forcefully on the waves. Nobody lost their footing. The helo had come in closer now, and the rotors were sending a raging wind down over them.

As it turned out, Isabella decided that she was a professional mediator. She looked at Novak and smiled sweetly. "Come on, please, Mr. Novak, don't get yourself shot down on my account. You've done enough to help me. Just surrender and we'll be okay. I know it. He said we would."

Shit, there went the false name and identity he'd been planning to give them, a designated signal that dinged the computer of an old army buddy of Novak's and gave him a heads-up that Novak was in trouble anytime the name was researched on the Internet. God, he was so damn sorry he had ever pulled that girl out of the sea. She walked forward to the Brit, hands still held high, and was quickly taken captive by two of the men behind him. They roughed her up a little, jerked her around, pushed her, because they were bad guys and wanted everybody to know it. They forced her down on a banquette in the shade of the canopy. Novak's jaw locked. When they aimed their guns at her head, Novak laid down his weapon. Just as they knew he would.

Novak was quickly surrounded, his hands bound in front of him with silver duct tape. He tensed his hands when they taped them and held them slightly apart and hoped his captors were too green to notice. They were. Good, he could get out of the tape in a matter of seconds. When the time was right. So, okay, he was taken. He had to accept it. Didn't like it, hell no he didn't like it, but it was only for the moment. Not for long. Other than the Brit, the lot of them appeared to be the usual greedy thug types. That would probably buy him time until they found out nobody was going to ransom him. But enough time.

Novak was prodded over to the girl with a gun barrel in his back. He could take them down, maybe, at a different time and in a different place. Subdue one or two of them, capture a weapon, and let loose on the others. That would not be a problem. He'd done it before, was trained to do it. But not here. Too many, too close to him. He couldn't do it, not with an innocent young girl's life at stake. Most of the foot soldiers in the boats looked young, teenagers probably, a few black guys, mostly Mexican nationals—poor, uneducated kids hired by the Brit in some seedy port city. Out of the slums, into the cool black bad-guy uniforms, big loud guns to carry, and ready to kill for a miniscule portion of the take. They were, to a kid, small, wiry, probably many of Indian derivation, Mayan, maybe. They looked quick and strong, and uncomfortable carrying deadly weapons. Likely had very little training in weaponry. All he had to do was bide his time and wait for the opportune moment.

As soon as Novak's hands were taped, they forced him to sit down on the banquette close beside the girl. Then they taped her hands up in the same way. Wrists together, in front of her body. They left their feet unfettered. Bad mistake, that. Yep, they were definitely inexperienced goons. He could get away. No doubt about it. Isabella kept talking nonstop, telling Novak over and over that she was sorry, so sorry, she didn't mean to get him in trouble. He pretty much ignored her. He could not let them think that she meant anything to him, or it would go worse for both of them. He could take care of himself, but she couldn't make it three yards on her own. Too young, too timid, too weak, too stupid. Not a chance in hell could she get away.

After a while, she just sat silently beside him, her face stoic, but her entire body was trembling. The young men in black hats had noticed her, too, and were making obscene gestures about her breasts and other body parts, laughing and regaling each other with what they were going to do to her when they got her back to camp. Novak didn't doubt a word they said. He just sat there and said nothing.

Stared straight ahead. Didn't look at them. Didn't act as if he heard them. They would pay for the disrespect soon enough.

After they were secured, with the Brit at the helm and another guard watching them, two of the Mexican kids sat at the helm, also watching them. The other pirates returned to their boats. The helo turned, banking in one last wide circle of the area, no doubt looking for military gunboats. Then it headed home, flying due south. The *Sweet Sarah* followed suit. Novak and Isabella sat there at gunpoint, saying nothing, another guard watching them from the bench directly across from where they were held. No sign of the Coast Guard. The cavalry was way too far away and way too slow this time. Novak was going to have to bide his time and get the two of them out of this mess on his own. When Novak saw the nearest guard glance out to sea at the speeding boats riding herd on them, he leaned up close to the girl.

"Listen to me, Isabella. Don't say anything. They're going to question you eventually. Don't go with the amnesia story, whether it's true or not. Don't tell them who your father really is, either. If you do, they'll think you're lying and try to beat the truth out of you. Make up a name, anything, some kind of background that makes sense. Somebody you know something about. Use their identity. I'm gonna get us out of this. Don't worry about that. Just hang on and don't say anything until I make my move."

"No talking! Shut up! You, big guy! Stop talking!" The guard leaned forward and pressed the long gun against Novak's forehead. Novak just stared up at him. He was going to enjoy taking these guys down. First opportunity that came along. But he could be patient when he had to. And he had to.

After that, they cruised along on calm blue seas, sun hot as Hades, wind-chased clouds scudding fast. Novak sat and fumed and got angrier with every passing minute. They had stolen his boat, damn it. He spent a lot of money having her custom designed for his size. Nobody was just going to take her away from him, especially not a bunch of young morons. Not without some serious blowback. He glanced to port and watched one of the speedboats. Another was on the starboard side. The third and fourth were following in the *Sweet Sarah*'s wake.

Fortunately, Novak knew both the Gulf of Mexico and the Caribbean Sea like the back of his hand. He'd sailed these waters often and for years. He knew the islands, the reefs, the atolls, the places to hide. He knew how to navigate with instruments and strictly by the stars. So he had already figured out basically where they were most likely headed. The Mexican coastline would be his initial and most generic assumption. More specifically, the southern Yucatan, where thick jungles provided the cover needed for this kind of operation. This type of outfit would have a camp, and it would be under the jungle canopy along the coast. He'd bet on it. He'd heard the stories of captives being held there, much like they were in Colombia and in some Central American countries, in makeshift camps—dirty, remote, hard to spot from the air. Most active pirates in this day and age were poor and uneducated, like the ones he'd taken down on a Somalian beach once upon a time, the guys who had left an ugly scar down the left side of Novak's face but had not lived long enough to brag about it. These men were foot soldiers, told what to do and what to think by their superiors. Maybe the ones in this group might be a little smarter, but not much, from what he'd seen so far. Whoever ran this operation had a helicopter for surveillance, which was unusual, so they had been receiving lots of ransom money from somebody. Or their major source of income could be drug smuggling—heroin, probably.

After a couple of hours, night fell. Dropped down like a black curtain plummeting to earth on all sides, quick and hard and dark. The sea became a dense wash of ink. Bright moonlight now and then. No stars to be seen. Storm clouds hung low and threatening, one hell of an ugly downpour going on somewhere out on the horizon. Lightning flashed, faraway thunder rumbled. A storm was coming their way, for sure. But no Coast Guard cutter waving the Stars and Stripes. He and the kid were definitely on their own. As they moved along at a swift clip, the guards began to act a little undisciplined. Not good, that.

The Brit in charge had taken over steering the boat now. Novak did not like the way he was handling it. The *Sweet Sarah* was Novak's baby, his most precious possession, and they weren't treating her with respect. Their plan was to barter her off to other criminal gangs for drugs and weapons or sell her on the black market for half her worth, so he had to break free and steal her back. Novak was not going to let them get away with this. No way in hell. He started planning his escape, going over every scenario, everything that he could do, everything that might go wrong. He wished Isabella was not his problem. She was one giant complication that he didn't want to worry about. But he was stuck with her, and he wasn't going to leave her to the unthinkable fate these vile cretins had in store for her.

They sailed onward for hours. The sea gradually became rougher, big swells pounding against the prow. Novak set navigational markers by the stars he could see. Most were still hidden by the massive rain clouds. He knew they were heading for the east coast of Mexico. They had veered a little more south now, so he estimated they would hit landfall somewhere down the coastline, near the Belize border. Maybe these men were Nicaraguans or Guatemalans. Isabella had remained quiet and dozed off a time or two. Then she'd start up and realize where she was and what was going to happen to her. That's when she'd push herself up against Novak's shoulder. He understood her trepidation. He was it, as far as she was concerned. The only positive that she had in her corner. She was terrified. Wasn't showing much courage anymore. He had the distinct feeling that she had experienced little adversity in her life, but it was now hitting her in an avalanche. A Disney princess down on her luck and with no handsome prince galloping her way. He hoped she could step up and do her part when the time was right.

Lights finally began to appear, far out in the pitch black in front of them. A land mass, had to be, still miles away but glowing dimly, stretched out like a string of tiny lights over an outdoor cafe. He watched the shore come closer, trying to pick out a landmark he recognized. Didn't see anything familiar. Just the pale hue of a strip of beach at the edge of the water, and what looked like a huge dark mass behind it. The jungle.

They eventually headed into a deep, sheltered cove, the curve of the beach wide and long. They headed for a lighted pier that stretched far out into the deep water. As they got closer, he realized there were two piers, and the light was coming from flaming torches set every ten or twelve feet along the edges. Looked like the piers reached about forty or fifty yards out into the water. He could make out the outlines of several other vessels tied up along them, probably other hijacked boats.

As they came closer, he could read their names: *Lucia Annie.*

Dolphin Dive. Two Kings. He wondered if their owners were already dead and buried or, most likely, fed to the sharks. They probably were dead, unless their families had coughed up some serious cash. Most families tried to scrape enough money together. Sometimes the bad guys took what they could get and let the owners go home. But they always kept the vessels for sale on the black market. The *Sweet Sarah* would be lashed to one of those piers soon. Once Novak got his feet planted on dry land, he could make his move. He was eager for the right time to come along, champing at the bit—anxious, in fact—to put some of these guys down.

When the *Sweet Sarah* bumped against the tires lining the dockage at the far end, out in the deeper water, several men came running down toward them. These guys looked more like native Caribs, judging by the dreadlocks and headscarves. They spoke in fluent Spanish, though, not the island dialects. They were talking together about the girl, saying she was *muy bonita* and arguing who'd get her first. That's when Isabella started up with the trembling and shivering again, because she understood every word. Novak whispered softly, telling her to act docile and afraid, but to fight them off as soon as she had to. She nodded, but she didn't look like the sort of girl who could fight them very hard or very long. She looked ready to pass out.

Novak watched a different man come striding down the dock to meet them. He was tall and thin, dressed in a white linen shirt and white pants and smoking a cigar. All he needed was a white panama hat and an overseer's whip. He stopped at the stern and stood looking down at Novak and Isabella. In the flicker of the torch, he appeared to be around fifty, maybe a little older, small eyes darting around the boat, estimating its worth. Didn't seem the Brit answered to him, because he climbed up onto the pier and strode off toward the beach without a word to the prisoners or the man with the cigar. This new guy was a real hoodlum, Novak was sure of it. He couldn't judge yet if he was more dangerous than the others. Novak didn't see a weapon on him, but it could be hidden under his loose shirttail. He cut short the crew's lascivious chitchat about all the atrocities they were going to carry out on the pretty girl. He cursed and told them she'd be worth more money than the boat they'd captured. So hands off, he said, in rapid-fire Spanish, until they found out who wanted her back and how much they'd pay.

After that, Isabella relaxed some, and so did Novak. But not much. Their captors became quiet and herded them at gunpoint up onto the beach and across about thirty yards of deep dry sand. They were flanked there by two more men and two more guns, and then marched up off the beach toward a thick copse of palm trees, the long dry fronds high above and tossing wildly in the incoming storm gusts, rattling like crazy.

The camp was a hell of a lot larger and more organized than Novak had expected. The criminals had a complicated operation and apparently made a lot of money. This was not as much of a ragtag, uneducated bunch of guys as Novak had first thought. At least, the people in charge weren't. About thirty yards off the beach, he made out a cluster of maybe half a dozen prefab huts with tin roofs, all scattered around under the towering palms. Two long buildings lay at one end of the beach, farther back from the water. Barracks, or housing for the helicopter, maybe. Armed guards were posted here and there.

As they were prodded up through the thick trunks of the palm trees, Novak saw a couple of men come out of a hut. He hoped they didn't separate captives. If they did, Novak knew the reason, and it wasn't something he liked to think about. Fortunately, as it turned out he and Isabella remained together, at least temporarily. They were pushed into a hut, fairly far from the water. Inside, there was a sand floor and nothing else. On one wall, a sturdy wood beam had been bolted into place. Two sets of shackles hung from an iron ring. The guards wasted no time chaining them up. Novak got extra-rough treatment, probably because he was bigger than they were and they felt intimidated. They pushed him down on the ground and shackled his feet, and then they did the same to Isabella. Novak didn't protest, because they made a big mistake by leaving only the duct tape binding his wrists together. Once she was shackled, the girl cowered in the corner and held the length of heavy chain in her lap. She kept her eyes squeezed shut. If she couldn't see it, it wasn't happening.

The guards went back outside and spoke softly to each other. Novak sat still, watched silently, and waited for their footsteps to recede. These guys were definitely not Mexican army, and thank

God for that. He needed to find the brains of the bunch and put him down first. The rest would probably scatter once there was no one telling them what to do. He had a feeling he would meet the head guy soon. So he settled back and pretended to be docile until it was time to act. But it wasn't easy. He had the overwhelming desire to hurt these guys. He believed in payback, and he was going to make that happen.

Chapter Five

The hut was roughly twelve by twelve, the prefab walls the color of gunmetal. It was dark inside, except for one electric lantern on the floor to the right of the door. The room smelled like a latrine, as if hostages had sweated and urinated or been left to rot inside it. Isabella pulled up the hem of her shirt and held it over her mouth and nose. Novak sat and waited for the guards to leave the hut and their voices to fade into the distance. He wasn't sure if there was a guy left outside the door. Probably was. Novak would have left a guard out there if he had secured prisoners inside.

Novak squatted down in front of the bolt hammered into the wall and tested the strength of the chain. It stretched out about four feet, not quite to the door but long enough to reach the bucket sitting in the corner for physical needs. Smelled like it was already full of excrement. He could pull the chain loose, maybe. The duct tape on his wrists was not a problem. He knew how to get out of most bindings. These guards were rank amateurs but well-armed. There were plenty of weapons to be had once he was free. All he had to do was put down the first guard he encountered and he'd have a weapon. Again, however, Isabella was Novak's problem. He had a feeling she'd panic at the least provocation, and that would do him in, too.

So Novak ignored her sobbing and listened again for nearby voices. Figured not more than two men would be outside. He looked at his watch. Surprisingly, they had neglected to take it or Isabella's crucifix when they patted them down. Three o'clock in the morning. Most likely the pirates who'd captured them would be tired, maybe green enough to doze off on duty, if Novak got lucky. After a while, he heard nothing except the night calls of birds and the buzz of nocturnal insects. He heard no movements outside and smelled no acrid cigarette smoke, of which most of their guards had reeked. He wanted to get both of them out of the hut and well away or the girl was going to completely lose it. He couldn't blame her, wished he had the time to console her, but they would probably have one chance to get out of this thing alive and that would be it.

Novak considered for a moment and decided it was too soon yet to make a break. The whole compound would be on high alert for the first hour, and then they would probably decide that Novak was not going to make trouble. So he settled down to wait—relaxed his tense muscles, tried to calm his mind, went over precisely what he was going to do. Usually not a problem for him, but this time the initial wait seemed like an eternity. He wanted out of that hut before anything worse went down with the girl.

As it turned out, he wasn't given time to be patient. About thirty minutes after they were chained up, two men ducked back inside the hut. These guys said nothing, but they were different from the men he'd seen so far. Better dressed for their mission. Matching uniforms. Jungle camouflage, like American troops wore in Vietnam. They said nothing, not to each other, and not to him. Oh yeah, these two were much better trained than the ones sent out to commandeer boats with lots of guns and lots of backup. Both these men were older than the others by a decade at least, and were trained in military doctrine and procedure. One guy knelt down and quickly unchained the girl, and the other one released Novak. They left the duct tape binding their wrists. They both stood back while their prisoners stretched their backs and legs, and then got impatient and prodded them to move outside into the warm tropical night. Things were happening a whole lot faster than Novak had anticipated.

Such prompt attention probably meant one of two things: The powers that be in this outfit had deemed Novak and Isabella unworthy of suitable ransom demands, and they would now be hustled out into the dark jungle, summarily forced to their knees, and bullets placed in the backs of their heads. Or, they were now considered high-end value hostages and needed further questioning for contact information. Novak inhaled a deep breath of the salty sea air and searched their surroundings for landmarks. They were being taken somewhere else, and he needed to be able to find his way back to the beach and his boat. Thirty yards in front of him, waves rolled in, gently, rhythmically, endlessly, and that's where his boat was, still tied up at the end of the nearest long pier. He was going to get the *Sweet Sarah* back. Tonight. The wind had picked up considerably now, rattling and scraping the dry palm fronds, bending them inland. He could smell rain in the air. The storm was moving closer, still fairly far out, but coming, nevertheless. It would hit the beach with lashing winds and high breakers. But that was good. That would give the guards something else to think about.

Far away, out in the bay, he heard somebody shout. Novak's guards took note and turned to look out toward the cry. But the yell died away, and nothing else happened. They got back to business. One of them, the taller man, shoved Isabella so hard in the back that she stumbled hard into Novak's chest. He caught her before she fell and held her steady on her feet, but he kept his eyes latched on the two armed men.

"You okay?" he whispered to her.

Isabella did not look okay, not anymore. She looked worse than she had when they'd tied up at the pier less than an hour ago. She was at the end of her rope, and it seemed to be slipping out of her hands. Not good. He needed her to be alert and cognizant and brave enough to do what he said, and do it immediately, without any hesitation.

So they stumbled through the night, pushed at gunpoint deep into the jungle, veering onto a narrow dirt path that led straight out into the darkness—the nonvisual kind of darkness, the kind only encountered in the hush of a natural habitat. Quiet. Only the continuous buzzing of insects. As long as he didn't hear the low growl of a jaguar up in the trees, Novak was good with everything else they might encounter. He'd been in jungle terrain before. So they walked on. The rushing surge of the sea gradually grew faint and distant. They were marched along single file, zigzagging between giant acacias and every kind of palm, the trees covered with vines, the guards, front and back, both swinging high-powered flashlights from side to side. Every fifteen yards or so, there would be an oil-burning torch. They walked for a long time, maybe thirty or forty minutes. The lead guard preceded Isabella, with Novak right behind her and the second guard bringing up the rear. The guy in front was the tall one who pushed Isabella. He was lean and quick, moved like a college football player. Novak assumed he was nervous, because now and then the cone of light from his flashlight quivered when he tried to hold it steady. The other guy was bulky and squat and breathing hard from the physical activity. He would be the first to go when Novak got the chance.

Novak glanced up at the sky, looking for stars. Couldn't see any. In the dim reflected glow from the flashlights and torches, he could see that the vines and heavily branched trees grew together above them, their foliage creating a closed, impenetrable canopy. Somebody had picked the right place to conceal their illegal operations. From the air, the cove would appear as any other inhabited cove with a dock. Police helicopters and search planes would be practically useless to zero in on what went on under the cover of the jungle. Flitting bugs and a myriad of biting insects swarmed up from the bushes and badgered them, and Novak swatted them away from his ears and mouth. It was miserable going.

To Novak's relief, Isabella was holding up fairly well, at least so far. But the farther they walked, the more she began to falter. The pace was swift, too much so for her. Novak had on running sneakers, but she was wearing the thin boat shoes designed for decks, not stubborn jungle vines and roots. She struggled along, tripping and stumbling, until Novak stepped up and held her elbow with his bound hands. He pretty much kept her up on her feet after that. The guards didn't object, but the one bringing up the rear was alert to every move Novak made, the barrel of his rifle aimed at Novak's center spine.

Novak wasn't stupid enough to make a move at that point, not with his hands bound and two armed guards, front and back and halfway vigilant. He knew when he could and should strike. Besides, he wanted to know where they were headed. Maybe they were taking them to some kind of settlement where they could find a car or jeep. Maybe even into a town or village with a road that offered a way to escape. That would be the best scenario he could hope for. That's what he needed. Finally, after a long, hot trek, attacked by biting flies and gnats, they stumbled into a clearing surrounded by densely tangled jungle. Incongruously, a big white house sat right in the middle, one of Caribbean design, with a wide, airy breezeway dissecting the middle, and two levels of open verandas. Quite a step up from the makeshift huts on the beach. Bright lights shone from nearly every window, throwing elongated rectangles out onto the porches and the dirt ground below.

Three other men lounged around on the lower veranda. Two of them were sitting on the front steps. The other was standing by the front door, leaning back against the wall. All three had Springfield semiautomatic rifles slung over their shoulders. All three guys were smoking—pungent cigarettes and a Cuban cigar. Hot and sweaty and weary, Novak and the girl were pushed up the steps, through the door, and into a wide central hallway. The guards outside made crude remarks about Isabella's sweet young body. The air inside was much cooler, maybe even air-conditioned. That meant generators and that somebody powerful liked to be comfortable.

Four big fanback tan wicker chairs sat along the walls facing each other, two on each side. The place looked bright and clean, the walls painted the color of pumpkins. The floor was covered with oversize terra-cotta tiles. This pristine palace in the jungle had cost somebody some big bucks. Piracy appeared to be a lucrative endeavor in the Caribbean Sea.

Three more guards stood inside, the trained kind, one on either side of the front door and another man beside a closed door in the middle of the hall, all wearing green and brown jungle camo. Personal bodyguards for the Big Boss, whoever the hell he turned out to be. Novak had a feeling he was about to find out. They were forced ahead, down the hall, where one guy knocked softly on a closed louvered door. A voice inside called out, and the guard opened the door and stood back to allow Novak and Isabella to enter the lion's den.

They stepped inside and stopped. It was a giant room. Four sets of French doors opened to the muted, raucous insect sounds still going on out in the dark. Big white fans were rotating in each corner. Large moths and other insects batted themselves against the screens, trying to get inside where it was cool. Novak studied the person sitting behind a big white wicker-and-glass desk at the far end of the room. He'd been expecting a man, the ranking alpha male of the pack, a big intimidating guy and supreme leader of men. But it wasn't a man. It was a woman, small and calm and utterly beautiful.

She sat behind that elegant desk, erect, her back held straight. An eighteen-inch Dell laptop sat in front of her. The top was open, the glow of the screen reflecting on her face. A multifunction printer sat to one side of the laptop. There was a satellite phone on the other side of the desk. Novak would keep that in mind. The woman appeared to be around thirty, but early thirties. Certainly no older than that. Asian descent, most definitely. She had some of the blackest, straightest hair Novak had ever seen, even darker than his wife's had been, and hers had looked like midnight on the bayou. This woman's hair was longer, unbound and reaching to her waist. Blunt-cut bangs over her eyes, long enough to cover her eyebrows. He noticed right off the sweet, shiny little chrome Sig Sauer positioned beside the printer and close to her right hand. A bejeweled dagger lay beside the gun, winking with rubies and emeralds. No scabbard. The blade gleamed in the spotlight that shone down from high above her head, and was honed to the sharpness of a razor. Her eyes were slightly slanted, which was exaggerated by thick black eyeliner and a ton of mascara and eye shadow. She looked exotic and seductive as hell. Oh yeah, this woman was something to behold.

Novak felt something move inside him. Maybe it was the dangerous kind of attraction he'd felt a couple of other times in his life. Maybe it was just wariness, and the knowledge that she could pick up that gun and shoot him in the face. Maybe it was a shiver of the unknown. He wasn't sure. He did believe with a fair amount of confidence that this woman would and could slice and dice a man to strips if he stared at her too long or said the wrong thing. She looked completely lethal, that's how she looked. He had a feeling most men would roll over and do whatever she wanted, at once and without argument. He also had a gut feeling that she was the devil incarnate. Not good. Just like the sexual appeal, he could almost feel the essence of cruelty wafting off her in unsettling warm and pulsating waves, like a blur of heat rising off an Iraqi desert highway.

"Please sit down," the woman invited them.

She spoke in English, low and breathy and enticing. She had a faint accent that was too muted for Novak to put his finger on. But he thought it might be pure Mandarin, so he felt certain that she was Chinese. She looked more Chinese than anything else. She lifted one small hand and gestured at the two high-backed peacock chairs sitting directly in front of her desk. The chair cushions were made of crimson brocade embroidered with golden dragons fighting each other. Her hands looked soft and small, and she had extremely long fingernails painted scarlet. The woman was inordinately beautiful.

Her stately posture added to her regal appearance despite her slight build. She was probably not more than five one or two. Imperious-looking, though, with the expression of the favored wife of an emperor. But a modern emperor, one in charge of a well-organized pirate band that ransomed human beings for cash.

Novak and Isabella sat down as instructed and awaited the woman's pleasure, which would probably not be something they would particularly enjoy. Novak knew that much already. This was not the development Novak had hoped for. From past unpleasant encounters, he knew full well that some of the meanest, cruelest snakes alive were hidden under soft, touchable hair and smooth, flawless skin, and breathlessly beautiful faces. Fair ladies, maybe, but never fair in any other way. And this woman looked like she would fit that bill better than most. She would smile like an angel and be the most treacherous and heartless and deadly bitch alive. Count on it. Novak watched her and hid his wariness about what was coming next.

Silence descended, with only the sounds of insects beating on the screens. She stared silently at the screen of her laptop and typed with fast, nimble fingers. No pecking with index fingers for her. Then she glanced up, and black, intelligent eyes laser-latched onto Novak's face. "Your name, please, sir."

Polite, oh, so polite. Her eyes returned to the keyboard as she waited, but her tone brooked no resistance. Novak wasn't ready to resist yet. So he told her. "Will Novak. And you are?"

She glanced up and stared silently at him. Surprisingly, she deigned to answer him. "My name is Li Liu."

"Nice to meet you, Li." Pretty generic Chinese name. Probably false. Women with her talents had lots of aliases.

"You are American, are you not?" she asked, holding his gaze.

"Through and through. Red, white, and blue. God bless America."

Novak made his assessment. Okay, this woman came off as highly educated, probably schooled somewhere in America, as well as in Beijing, perhaps—maybe even by the Chinese military. His guess was that she was well versed in several languages. She would be a worthy adversary. But right now? She held all the cards.

"Your passport, please?"

"Your goons took it when they stole my boat. Ask them where it is." That was a lie. His passport and all his other valuables were hidden in a special waterproof compartment in the hull of his boat, and well below the waterline.

Her eyes found him again and held him in a steady gaze. "My *goons,* as you say, are very well trained soldiers, Mr. Novak." She emphasized the word goons, all very sarcastic. Maybe she knew English better than he had thought. But she was wrong; most of her men were goons. Untrained, uneducated, unprincipled. Her body-guards were better, but not much. But he received her message loud and clear. You will obey. Or you will die. He'd heard that message before, in other jungles, in other hemispheres. But she didn't know that, didn't know a thing about him, and that was a good thing. "So, Mr. Novak, if you are sitting there planning an escape with your little girlfriend here, you will end up dead and so will she. It won't be a pleasant demise, I can assure you. You can trust my word. I do not give second chances to anyone."

Yep, she was fluent in English, all right. "Now I'm really upset."

Again, a long, silent eye lock. Then she picked up the gun, put her finger on the trigger, and aimed it straight at Isabella's face. She held the weapon correctly and very steady and maintained a calm, unconcerned expression. "Will you be more upset if I make an example of your little girl sitting there? Just to attain your attention?"

Novak watched her trigger finger. His eyes jerked in surprise when she suddenly pulled the trigger. The chamber clicked. Empty. Novak breathed easier, but she had gotten his attention, all right. Isabella started crying.

Li Liu smiled and looked quite lovely doing so. She opened a drawer and took out a loaded magazine. Seventeen deadly Parabellum slugs. She shoved it into the Sig and racked a bullet. Locked and loaded. "Next time I will shoot her in the face. I will not hesitate. Do you understand me now, Mr. Novak? Are you convinced that I mean business here?"

"She didn't do anything. Why threaten her? She's just a kid."

The woman put her finger on the trigger. Now she pointed it at Novak's chest. "Because I sense you are somewhat of a gentleman perhaps, the kind who likes to protect frightened young girls. True? Are you not that? You have no doubt sworn to protect her virtue. Am I correct, Mr. Novak?"

"You got a problem with protective men? Or just men in general?"

"I like to kill men and women equally well, Mr. Novak." She

smiled and placed the Sig back down on the desk but kept it close enough to shoot anybody who made a sudden move. The two guards stood a good distance behind them, on either side of the hall door, watching and waiting, obviously thinking their mistress could handle herself if Novak should be stupid. "Shall we continue with our interview, Mr. Novak? Or would you like to waste my time for a while longer?"

"By all means, continue. I'm pretty much a captive audience here. What would you like to know?"

"That you are, Mr. Novak. You are my captive, most definitely. I would advise you to remember that before you do something else incredibly stupid and experience some uncomfortable treatment from my men. They are very good at teaching recalcitrant hostages lessons in good manners. But I am fairly certain that you would behave yourself much better if I took my dagger and slashed up your lady's pretty face."

Novak said nothing else. She was right about that. And her accent was Mandarin, for sure. With a tinge of the American Northwest. Schooled in Seattle, maybe. In any case, she was a hell of a long way from home.

Li Liu typed for a while and then looked up at him again. "Well, well, Mr. Novak, you have quite a résumé. You are not the ne'er-do-well that you purport. Google is quite helpful to us, you see. You are older now than in this photograph. Your hair is longer now and you are not quite as clean-shaven as before. Blond hair. Blue eyes. Oh my, you stand six feet six inches tall and weigh two hundred and forty pounds. Very impressive." She gauged his body, looking him up and down, and then she smiled. "That appears about right. You spent time in the American military, I see. The army, and also in law enforcement in New York City. My, my, look at the commendations for bravery. Seems you were in the U.S. military, a Navy SEAL by the time you left for civilian life, I see, and just look at all that classified, redacted information in your file. Perhaps you have many military secrets you could share with us." She smiled at him. "Furthermore, you are no longer in the service, and you reside in the southern state of Louisiana. We have our ways, Mr. Novak. It appears that you are not quite the bum that you say you are."

Novak stared back. Some of his history was available on the

Internet, which happened to piss him off, but the military had classified most of it. He said nothing.

"Do you have a bank account, Mr. Novak? Perhaps good pensions from all that honorable work you've done?"

He watched her, but he'd already thought out his story. "Hell, I wish I did. Got kicked off the NYPD for drinking on the job and then drank away my military retirement savings. That sailboat out there? That's all I've got to my name. And you already took that, so I guess I'm dead broke."

"You will never see that boat again."

Yeah, well, that's what she thought. "Then I guess I've got nothing worth stealing. Just the clothes on my back, if you want those. Everything else I own is on the *Sweet Sarah*."

She eyed his body again. "Tempting, I must say. But do keep your clothes on." They stared at each other some more. "Do you have family members who might love you a little bit? Who might think that you're swell and would be keen on keeping you alive?"

Novak found her wording amusing. *Swell*? *Keen*? How did she learn her English? Watching Olivia Newton-John and John Travolta in *Grease*? "They all would think I'm keen, I suspect. If they weren't all dead and buried."

"Oh dear. My condolences. *If* I believed a word you have said to me. You are not a convincing liar, Mr. Novak."

"I'm better than you know."

The woman appeared to be patient. So far, she had been indulgent, but that fact might be the only good thing going down at the moment. He knew acting afraid of her wasn't a good move. It remained to be seen how far he could push her. She sighed audibly and caught his gaze again. "We do have ways of finding out everything about you, Mr. Novak. We are very good at such things. We have contacts in governments all around the world. I have been trained long and well. You can continue to play your childish word games with me, if you wish, but that will only get you or your young lady much pain and, yes, broken bones, if I deem it necessary. You may think me patient, but that will only last until I become bored with your annoying tough-guy attitude and have you shot down and thrown into the jungle to rot." She paused, observed him some more. "Nobody knows where you are, that I can believe. I also believe that we have a good chance of obtaining ransom for you. Because I think you are lying to me. Other than your name, I believe every single word that you've said so far is false. If you stop your deceit and tell me what I wish to know, things will go much easier for you and this girl that you seem to want to protect."

She wasn't kidding, all right. Novak decided it was time to spin out a better pack of lies. "Why would I lie? That would be stupid. Like I told you, I live on that boat. I've worked in the past, sure, but now it's the good life, beach bum all day long, every day, and drunk all night long, every night. Fish for my food. Do odd jobs now and then in ports of call that keep my gas tanks filled up. You know, handyman, bartender, that kind of stuff. I like it that way. Free to roam the seas. No ties. No home. No problems. So. You took my boat; that's it for my net worth. You got everything I own now. Congratulations."

"Of course, you know full well that I don't believe a single word you say. But nice try." Then she totally ignored Novak and swiveled her attention to the girl. Novak did, too. As soon as Li Liu focused those evil dark eyes on Isabella, the young girl started trembling. This was not going to go down well.

"What is your name?" the woman asked her.

"Isabella."

"Last name?"

"Ricardo."

Novak was impressed. She was savvy enough to lie. Good sign, that. He hoped she lied well. For both their sakes.

"Where do you live, Isabella?"

"I live in Jamaica, but Mr. Novak picked me up in Kingston at the bar where he worked part-time and asked me if I wanted to take off on his boat with him for a while. Said we'd cruise over to Cancun and stay gone for a whole month. We're lovers now. I love him. And he loves me."

The woman eyed her passively. So did Novak. He was shocked by her remarks. He couldn't believe she'd actually said that. He kept his expression neutral but it wasn't easy. The girl had made up a story off the top of her head that sounded halfway credible. The lover part was stupid.

"Lovers, you say? You and this big tough man here? How sweet. Is Mr. Novak a good lover, Isabella?"

Isabella had calmed down considerably now, apparently under the impression that she was fooling somebody. She smiled at Li Liu, almost conspiratorially, tilting her head like a flirt. "What do you think?"

The two women smiled at each other. What the hell? He didn't much like the way this thing was going. Isabella suddenly seemed fearless.

Li Liu smiled. "I do think you've got good taste, Isabella. That scar on his face is very sexy, is it not? I must say, however, that he appears to be intellectually slow. His lies are so clumsy." That was evil woman trying for jocularity. It didn't come off. Nobody laughed.

"Isabella's just a kid. Why don't you leave her alone?"

"My, my, you are so protective. Do you think your girlfriend is a good lover, Mr. Novak? She certainly seems pleased with your virility."

Novak said nothing.

Li Liu did some more typing, watched the screen intently. "Tell me her real name. She's obviously lying. You are not lovers. That is not her real name. I am growing weary of you both."

"Her name is Isabella. I did meet her in Jamaica. But as you've already guessed, we're not lovers. She's just a friend, a new one. I just met her. But she's still a nice girl, like a little sister, and I feel responsible for getting her into this mess. If I hadn't invited her aboard, she'd be safe in Kingston. Of more interest to you, she's dirt poor. She doesn't have any more money than I do. She was waiting tables for tips when I met her. That tell you anything about her bottom line?"

"What that tells me is that she's expendable."

Novak said nothing. But Isabella picked up on the woman's threat, loud and clear. She started crying into her hands. A habit of hers. Or she could be faking. She was damn full of surprises tonight.

"Look, see what you did?" Novak said. "You got her all upset."

Novak and Liu stared silently at each other some more. Then she said, "That's all for now. Neither of you are being cooperative. And that is very stupid. I'll interview you again tomorrow night. Maybe that long without food or water will help you remember your bank account number."

Novak had plenty of bank account numbers, all right, big fat ones that he rarely used. He'd be damned if she'd get her hooks in any of them. So he said nothing. Just gazed back at her. He and the girl would be gone by then. Li Liu picked up her cell phone and snapped his picture. She did the same with Isabella. Very smart, that. She would probably run them through a photo ID database, if she had people on her payroll inside U.S. law enforcement as she'd indicated. Or more likely, the Mexican Federales.

Then she called out a man's name. Emilio. One of the guards rushed over. She gestured for him to take Novak and Isabella away, and then she returned her concentration to the laptop. She was uploading their photos. Not good. Now time was of the essence, and Novak knew it.

Outside, they were led back behind the big house to a small hut built fairly far out in the jungle. Novak moved along, cooperating and acting docile, but he didn't have much time to make his move. He had to get out of there with the girl before they were shot or moved deeper into the jungle for safekeeping.

This time the guards did put them into separate huts. Novak was well aware of what that meant. The guards wanted Isabella alone and for their own sexual enjoyment. They would assault her, both of them or all of them, which was an act no doubt endorsed by Li Liu as an added perk for their loyalty and brutality. Female prisoners were fair game and available to all. Enjoy.

The bigger of the two guards shoved Novak into a hut, squatted down, and started cuffing him to a chain attached to an iron ring like the one at the beach hut. The chain was long enough to let him move around but wouldn't allow him to reach the door. He could hear Isabella now, somewhere nearby, her voice muffled but sounding like she was trying to scream. Novak didn't waste any more time. The attack on her was going down right now and he wasn't going to let it happen. He moved quickly and grabbed the guard by the front of his shirt. He jerked him down low and slammed his forehead against the guy's nose. Blood spurted, and the man staggered backward when Novak let him go. He tried to fight back but was too woozy. Novak had knocked the absolute hell out of him. He picked up his chain and looped it around the guy's neck. He twisted it tight, putting his whole body into the leverage. It took about six seconds before the guard went limp. Novak dropped him to the dirt and took the keys from the guard's belt. He quickly unlocked the shackles and then raised his hands over his head and swung them down hard and out to either side. The duct tape split apart, and Novak exerted pressure on the ring with all his strength until it finally came apart. He wound the length of chain around his fist a couple of times. Every bit as good as brass knuckles, maybe even better. Then he edged to the door and darted a quick look outside.

Nobody in sight. All quiet except for Isabella's brutal assault going on somewhere nearby. He ducked outside and found another electric lantern hanging on a post just outside the door. He turned it off and hunkered down low. He put a knee on the ground and listened, trying to pinpoint where Isabella's muffled cries were coming from. Then he heard her attackers laughing. Sounded like several men. He heard her begging them to stop, sobbing, until her voice suddenly was cut off. He followed the sickening sounds of an assault in progress. It took him about two minutes to find them.

The hut where they had dragged her was about twenty yards deeper into the jungle than the one Novak had been put into. Probably the designated rape hut. Maybe used for torture, as well. He pushed his back against the wall beside the door, concealed in deep shadows. Before he could duck inside, a guard exited right beside him. He carried an AR rifle in one fist. Novak didn't hesitate, darting forward fast before the guy sensed his presence. He sent the steel-wrapped fist hard against the man's temple, about as brutal a punch as he had ever thrown. The force of Novak's weight and size slammed the guy so hard he was knocked completely off his feet. When he hit the dirt on his back, Novak went down on top of him, his hands around his throat, but the guy didn't move again. Probably never would.

Novak jerked up the rifle, checked it over. It was loaded and ready. He eased inside the hut. There were three guys trying to assault Isabella. Two were concentrating on holding her down. They didn't look up to see who was joining the party. Big mistake. One guy was kneeling between her legs, pulling at her clothes. She was struggling desperately, giving them everything she had—which wasn't much, given how weakened she was. None of them saw Novak. Too bad for them. He took two steps forward and sent the rifle butt slamming against the back of the would-be rapist's head. It knocked him forward onto the girl's chest. She screamed when the hand pressed over her mouth let up, and Novak clubbed the second man in the forehead so violently that it took a chunk out of his skull. Number three was up on his feet now, scratching at the handgun strapped in the holster at his waist. Isabella scrambled away on her hands and knees, trying to cover her nakedness.

Novak ducked to one side before the guy could get to the pistol, and charged him, driving a shoulder into the man's gut. The guard doubled over, breath knocked out, and Novak brought up his knee and smashed it into his face. Blood spurted, cartilage crunched, and then Novak brought the rifle butt down on the back of his head, hard and final. The guy was done after that. Novak went down on one knee and pulled the Ruger out of the guard's holster and then stuck it down into his back waistband. The girl had retreated to the corner, kneeling, with her back to Novak, trying to pull her clothes back on. Novak took the rifle and listened at the door. He heard nothing outside, except for the distant roar of the ocean and the squawk of a bird startled off its nest by something in the night.

Quickly searching the men's pockets, he found lots of goodies that he was going to need, including a couple of cigarette lighters, Mexican and American currency, and last but not least, two more Ruger handguns with full magazines. Two flashlights and a razor-sharp machete lay on the floor of the hut. A jackpot of weapons, oh yeah. And that's all he needed. He stuffed most of the loot into his jeans pockets and left what he couldn't carry. He armed himself with another Ruger, the machete, and a flashlight. Then he turned his attention back to the girl. She was in pretty bad shape, pulling her shirt back on over her head, but she wasn't crying. That surprised him, but good, she had to suck it up now, and suck it up fast.

Kneeling beside her, he put his hand on her shoulder and spoke softly and in as gentle a tone as he could take time to muster, but he made his words count. "Okay, listen up, Isabella. Listen to me. You've been through something pretty damn bad just now, but you got to swallow it down, okay? Right now. You got to pull yourself together and help me get you out of here. Can you do that?"

She stared up at him, but her eyes looked dull. Shocked, maybe. Or angry, which would be better. He hoped she was as angry as hell, because he was. He breathed a sigh of relief when she pushed herself up, the rest of her clothes in her hands. Maybe she had more grit inside her than he figured. That was good. She was going to need it.

Chapter Six

Novak waited at the door for her while she finished putting on her clothes. Nobody in sight outside. Nobody had heard him take down the guards. Nobody had come running. Which didn't make much sense to him. Men had been stationed at intervals throughout the camp. Somebody should have heard the scuffle that went down. Why hadn't they?

The guards he'd put down wouldn't get up anytime soon, if at all. Once certain that all was clear, Novak stepped outside and found everything unnaturally quiet. Through the tangle of the jungle, he could see the lights burning inside Li Liu's house, but he couldn't see anyone anywhere. Somewhere far away in the distance he heard a man laugh. So guards were around, just not in sight.

Novak had ascertained already that the compound was run pretty much like a paramilitary unit. Not a top-notch one, certainly not like a U.S. Special Forces camp, but certainly with trained mercenaries in command. There had to be somebody besides Li Liu involved, someone above her in rank. Right now, Novak needed to put as much distance between them and the bad guys as he could. The only illumination was the bright circles thrown across the footpath by the torches. The jungle around them was dense to the point of being impenetrable and would be difficult to navigate. But it was their only chance. No way could they walk blithely down the path and back to the beach and reclaim his boat. So he pushed hard into the tangled vines and bushes, with Isabella stumbling along right behind him. He hacked at the thick woody trees with the machete, having to fight his way through. He needed to find a game trail or a rain gulley that would lead them back to the ocean. He swept the ground in front of them with the flashlight beam, aware of coral snakes and pit vipers and poisonous spiders and other lethal creatures lurking underfoot or in the brush. They were there somewhere, all right, and he did not want to step on them. He kept the beam low on the ground directly in front of him, sweeping his path.

So Novak hacked and sawed and jerked down vines and pushed his way through spiny thorns and waist-high stinging plants, stopping often to listen for a call to arms or the thrashing of pursuers coming hard behind them. Isabella held on to the back of his shirt and actually kept up with him pretty well for a time. After a while, though, she just stopped and leaned up against a tree trunk to rest. Novak switched off the flashlight and stopped too, but he didn't want to. His goal was to get them back aboard the *Sweet Sarah* and somehow take her out into the open ocean. On a dark night, they just might have a chance, but they had to keep moving. He was outnumbered big-time, and the girl had proven useless to help him. He'd have to do it himself, and it wasn't gonna be easy. But not much he'd done since he'd met Isabella had been easy.

After a couple of minutes of rest, he whispered for her to keep up and then headed out again. This time she kept close behind him. The vines on the ground were tangled and tough, some as thick around as his wrist. Isabella kept tripping over root wads and falling down, and Novak had to pull her back up to her feet. But they were getting closer to the beach, so he switched off the flashlight and forged ahead. He had no other choice. It was only a matter of time before they were discovered missing. Isabella was exhausted, emotionally shaky, staggering along and breathing hard, but he couldn't worry about that. Their headlong flight was hampered further by mosquitoes and gnats that rose up off the ground and swarmed them like living auras—biting bugs, tiny gnats that buzzed and flitted and got into their eyes and noses and mouths. It was miserable going, and both of them were covered with bites and scratches before they'd gone twenty feet. Novak doggedly kept his eyes on the prize. Reaching his boat and getting the hell off that beach was the only thing he could think about. The piers would be guarded, but probably by only a couple of guys, who wouldn't be expecting anyone to attack from the beach. If the pirates were halfway efficient, they wouldn't wait long to get his boat out of the camp and to some black-market port where it could be auctioned off to the highest bidder. They dealt in stolen goods, and most likely had contacts in the Caribbean who looked upon criminal activities as job opportunities. The *Sweet Sarah* would probably be advertised on the dark Internet or sold off to a criminal or terrorist organization for smuggling drugs. Novak still had a slice of time, a narrow slice that was dwindling fast, but he meant to take advantage of it. If he waited too long, he and Isabella would be dead before the sun came up.

Novak stopped again, sweating profusely, panting with exertion. Except for the insects, everything remained still around them, way too quiet. Something was wrong. He could feel it. Voices, shouts, laughter, snapped orders—some of the sounds they'd heard when they'd arrived—all of those things should be filtering off the beach because they were now within earshot. But there was none of that. He heard no human beings. There were way too many people around for such an eerie silence, even in the middle of the night. Isabella was no longer pulling on the back of his shirt. She was just trudging onward behind him, showing more guts than he had expected out of her. But she was young and privileged and had probably never faced adversity in her life, not until the last few weeks. Well, she was facing it now and would have to show some gumption or end up dead or sold to a Brazilian brothel.

Pushing ahead again, he angled his path toward the beach, guided by the distant sound of the surf. They were getting close now. The going was grueling, slow and difficult, but he counted himself lucky that they'd made it this far without detection. He raised the machete to hack some vines in his path and then froze as the most horrendous shriek of agony shattered the stillness of the jungle. Novak dropped to his haunches, instantly on guard, and the girl ducked down close to him. The scream had come from behind them, probably from the big house. It had been a female voice. Li Liu's voice, he was almost certain.

Before he could decide what to do, a second cry echoed out through the trees. Several birds were startled off their roosts with loud squawks and fluttering wings. The cry had been caused by the infliction of pain. Somebody was doing something terrible to that woman. Somebody was torturing her. It had to be that. Novak had heard screams of torture victims before, and it was not something a man could ever forget. He sure as hell wouldn't. The woman's next shriek was so shrill that it raised goose bumps on his skin and set off the kind of fear inside him that could quickly spiral into panic if not checked. Novak checked it and waited, remaining squatted down right where he was, not sure what was going down. Li Liu had been running the entire operation less than an hour ago, armed with both gun and knife, confidently surrounded by heavily armed guards who answered only to her. What the hell had happened?

Novak tensed up further when the next horrific shriek started up and shattered the stillness. Then came another and another, each one worse than the last. Then there were some long and awful cries that sounded like Li Liu was begging for mercy. Novak stayed hunched down, listening and waiting. Isabella was now pressed up tightly against his back. She had her hands clamped over her ears. Li Liu's men had to have turned on her for some reason. That was the only explanation that Novak could come up with. That didn't make much sense, either. Novak had watched her give orders, and they were obeyed without question.

All of a sudden, the screaming and begging stopped, right in the middle of a long and terrible shriek, as if her windpipe had been severed and that ended the cry. The night grew quiet around them, the raucous noise of insects and croak of tree frogs starting up again and building back into a cacophony. Novak had heard enough to be spooked. He pulled the girl up and pushed ahead through the brush, this time going as fast as he could. Somebody was out there with them, somebody who had taken his time murdering a very dangerous, well-armed woman. The guy liked a knife, too. If Novak guessed correctly, the killer had been slicing off patches of her skin. Most likely skinning her alive, slowly and cruelly. He kept up his struggle to get to his boat. In time, the jungle thinned out a bit, began to get sandy underfoot, and they made better time. The girl was still on her feet and holding her own, no doubt as creeped out as he was by the woman's excruciating cries. Li Liu was dead now. No doubt about it.

The soft wash of waves sliding up on the sand grew loud, and then Novak spotted the line of torches set periodically down the beach. He could see the path that led inland to the house, the darkness dotted with torches that he could just barely detect, located a good distance off to his left. He squatted down again. Listened. All he heard now was Isabella behind him, trying to catch her breath. She had to be exhausted, physically and mentally. No sounds anywhere, just the sea. No voices. No movement. There was apparently nobody at all out there. No one calling orders. No one leaning against a tree smoking. No one eating or drinking. No one on duty. More important, no one came running, concerned by the banshee shrieks filtering out from the jungle canopy. Novak's instincts told him that he was getting ready to face something very bad. Something evil was right on his heels, running fast, bloody knife still in its hand.

Novak stopped at the point where the beach met the jungle growth. They crept along together, just off the sand, keeping down low, making no sounds. Now Isabella had a grip on his shirt as if she'd never let go. She was terrified. She knew, too. Something terrible was coming. Nobody screamed like that and came out alive. But Isabella was trying to hold it together. So Novak kept his rifle up and ready for anything, slowly moving it from side to side, searching the dark night, not sure where the danger was coming from or what the danger was. The horrific screaming had thrown him off, big-time, thrown off his theory of how the camp was run. He liked to know his enemy, and he didn't know anymore. He did not want to venture out onto the open beach. He hunkered down and watched. For what, he wasn't sure. Nobody showed up. Nobody moved. Nothing. Novak started crawling again on his hands and knees, laterally, but inside the jungle, headed for the long piers and the *Sweet Sarah*. A few yards farther along, he found out why the night had become so quiet.

The first body lay at the side of the trail leading back to Li Liu's big house. It was the guy in the white linen shirt who had met them out on the pier. Except that he was dead now. He was lying on his back, arms and legs out spread-eagle. His cigar was beside his right hand, and a flashlight lay on the ground next to him, still switched on. The handle was half buried in the sand. The beam angled up and lit the swaying palm fronds high above, causing swinging shadows over their heads. The man's throat was a bloody mess, sliced through almost down to the spine with a deep horizontal gash across his gullet. The top of his head was sheared off. It looked like raw meat, still dripping blood. Scalped to the bone. A macabre calling card. It took a very sharp knife to do the things that were done to that poor guy.

The minute Isabella saw the gore, she fell on her knees and then down on her stomach and covered her mouth with both her hands.

She was retching and moaning into her palms. Novak pulled her over to him and got his hand over her mouth, muffling the sick sounds she was making. He put his mouth close to her ear. "You can't do this, or he's gonna find us, too. Be quiet, you hear me?" Isabella nodded. She understood, but she kept her eyes squeezed tight and a forceful grip on his forearm. Novak searched the man's pockets and took everything he thought they could use—more Mexican money and a pocketknife, but no weapon. The killer must have disarmed him. Novak kept his eyes moving constantly, darting from side to side, and listened for footfalls. Nothing at all, pure silence, except for the crashing surf. No human beings anywhere to be seen. Maybe they were all dead now. Maybe they had been invaded by a competing band of thieves, a deadly force that had swept in from the sea with murder in their hearts. Whoever had killed the man bleeding out beside Novak was a practiced pro, most likely a paid assassin. Otherwise, his victim would have put up some kind of fight, and he had not. No interruption in the smooth sand, no footprints, no indication that anyone had been there. Like a phantom. The killer had not seen fit to empty his victim's pockets or steal his cash. All he took was the weapon. So he had a different motive. This guy was highly trained and struck fast and hard and without pity. Novak was pretty damn sure that this wasn't the only body they would find. He waited a few minutes, then pushed Isabella farther back into the jungle cover.

"You stay here. Stay put, understand? Don't move and don't make a sound and don't wander around looking for me. I'll be back. If this guy sees you, you're dead. I'm going to check out the beach and come back for you. If you're not right here, waiting for me, I'm leaving without you. Do you understand what I'm saying?"

Isabella nodded, but she wouldn't let go of his arm. Novak pulled away and told her to get down and lie still and wait for him, that she'd be all right. He was surprised when she stretched out on her stomach and hid her face in her folded arms. She wouldn't venture off on her own this time, no way. She'd heard those awful screams. She'd seen what a scalped man looked like. So Novak left her in deep cover and moved down low and just inside the undergrowth. He was careful, stopped often and listened. This guy, whoever he was, was good at what he did. He would be hunkered down and listening, too. Listening for his next victim to make a sound. For Novak to make a sound.

Novak crouched low, moving swiftly through the palm trees until he was just above the piers. The beach looked deserted. All the activity around the captured boats had disappeared. Flaming torches still lit up the docks, spots of light glowing every twelve feet or so, their images reflected in the dark water. Enough light for Novak to see all the dead bodies, laid out in various poses of death. Some had died at their guard posts, others lost their lives on the sand, some floated facedown in the water, their corpses pushed and rolled farther toward the beach with each incoming wave. It looked as if the killer had moved among them and dropped them where they stood, one by one, stealthily, mercilessly—some kind of ghostly apparition, unseen, unheard, inhuman. Looked like each corpse had been scalped, the same as the first guy, the sand stained red under the heads. The killer liked souvenirs. Or maybe it was just a warning to anyone left alive, like Novak. Run fast or die. Novak got the message, loud and clear. He felt a cold chill rise up inside him, because he didn't know his enemy, didn't know who he was or what he wanted. Maybe this overkill was an act of vengeance, payback a thousand times over. This assassin could be Death personified out reaping in the jungle. And Novak had a feeling that this guy enjoyed what he was doing.

By the time Novak made it across the deep sand to the edge of the water, he had counted seven bodies, all killed the same way. Jugulars severed. Probably surprised from behind. Scalped and bloody. This guy did not take prisoners.

No longer willing to wait, Novak ran down to the end of the pier where they'd tied up the *Sweet Sarah*. She was still there, thank God. As he neared the boat, he stopped in his tracks, shocked, and just stared. No, she had been scuttled, her deck and hull underwater, only the mainmast and riggings visible above the surface. He looked around. All the captured boats were on the bottom. Cursing, he looked back at his own boat, trying to figure out why it had been done. The pirates would never have done it. Those vessels were worth big money to them. He scanned the water. The cove lay black and deep and quiet. What the hell was going down?

Eerie silence had descended over the grisly murder scene like a heavy bank of fog. Novak brushed off his anger because he didn't have time for it. Okay, no escape by sea. His boat was gone. The assassin/serial killer/vengeful ghost was on the loose and probably headed back to the beach after torturing Li Liu to death. Novak remained hidden in the deep shadows at the end of the pier and tried to reason what his best move would be. All he knew was that he had to get out of there, and get out fast. The killer was most likely winding up his death spree at the jungle house. Novak didn't have time to worry about who this killer was or what his motives were. Not right now. This guy apparently moved like a wraith in the mist, killed at will, and took down everyone he encountered, and that already meant lots of armed men.

Novak started running back down the length of the dock, knocking the torches off into the water. The dark was now his friend. The killer had to have come in to the beach somehow. Had to have come in on a boat, but there were no new boats and the captured ones were nonoperational. Novak kept down and shone the flashlight into the water along the side of the pier, thinking maybe the killer had come on a small Zodiac—anything that would provide him an escape when he was finished annihilating everything in his path. Novak was in such a hurry that he almost missed it. Half hidden under the pilings, close to the sand, he saw a black aluminum canoe bobbing and rocking in the shallows. He dropped to his stomach, reached down, and pulled it out from under the pier. It was tied up, and there was a paddle and a small black knapsack in the bow. The killer's boat, it had to be. It was nearly invisible in the dark.

Novak eased off the pier and lowered himself into waist-deep water, got a good hold on the side of the canoe, and jerked it up until it scraped onto the sand. Then he squatted down and waited there, on edge now, watching the beach for any kind of movement. Nothing—just the swaying royal palms and the flickering torches blown sideways by the incoming wind. The other pier and the beach were empty, so he took off at a hard run up to the tree line, rifle ready, finger near the trigger, knocking down one torch after another as he went.

Isabella had not moved a muscle. He grabbed her up onto her knees, told her to keep down, run fast, and stay quiet. He watched the edge of the jungle again, fairly certain the killer was out there waiting for them to move, or headed their way after finishing his bloody work at the house. They took off together, avoiding any remaining torches, and Isabella kept up with him. They made it back to the water without being attacked, but Novak did not take chances. The killer was somewhere close by, maybe even watching them already. When he appeared, he would come out of nowhere and strike without warning. The dead bodies scattered around were enough evidence for Novak.

Novak sloshed into the water, pulled the girl after him, and then shoved her up and into the prow of the canoe. It rocked precariously, but he stepped quickly into the stern, almost overturning it in his haste. It was too small for a man his size, but he grabbed the paddle and dug it deep into the water. He kept looking over his shoulder as he put down hard and steady strokes that sent them skimming alongside the dock toward the open cove. The killer would return for his canoe.

Halfway across the cove and well hidden in the night, Novak caught sight of the ghost. He was a small guy, compact build, dressed all in black like a Japanese ninja warrior. Maybe that was just what he was. He was running lightly across the sand toward where he'd stashed the canoe, down along the waterline under the torches. He had some kind of a knife in one hand. Novak held the paddle on his lap and watched him for a moment. Unless the killer had night goggles, he wouldn't spot them. And if he did have them, they were probably in the knapsack he'd left in the canoe. Novak dipped the paddle again but kept his eyes on the killer, who moved swiftly down the beach, bent almost to the ground. The man was closing in on the pier now. When he passed near the next torch, Novak saw the scalps hanging off his belt. This guy was a psychopath. The killer wasn't looking around, not even at the dead bodies he'd left mutilated and scattered across the sand. Apparently, he wasn't worried about anybody attacking him. Maybe he thought he'd gotten everyone. Maybe he didn't know about Novak and Isabella.

The little guy was now splashing through the shallows. When he found the canoe gone, he stopped as if stunned and stared down into the water. Then he turned and gazed out over the cove. Novak ducked instinctively, even though he knew the guy couldn't see him. A second later, the killer was running hard toward the end of the pier. He had a high-powered flashlight in his hand and had it up and sweeping the dark water. Novak plunged the paddle down harder, propelling them swiftly toward the open mouth of the inlet. The guy couldn't catch them now, not without a boat. But Novak was pretty sure he wouldn't stop. He'd be hot on their trail before it got cold. Then he would kill them. In fact, killing them might have been his mission all along. But how could he have known that Novak and the girl were there? Novak couldn't worry about that at the moment. He had worse problems. He had to get the hell out of there and find a good place to hide until he figured out who this guy was and what the hell was going on. No matter what else, now that Novak had stolen his canoe, this guy would be out for blood.

Chapter Seven

Paddling the black canoe through the dark was like sliding swiftly through a vat of black ink. No moon at all to light Novak's course. Cloud cover everywhere, with the heavy scent of impending rain. Great; all Novak needed now was a thunderstorm. But the bad weather had been threatening all day, and now the first cold drops were speckling his head. Once they hit the big breakers, Novak struggled desperately to propel the canoe far enough out to prevent it from being pushed back to shore. Gusts of rain sprayed the canoe and kept pushing it sideways. The paddle was a good one, but too short for Novak's wingspan, which tired him more, but the canoe had been engineered to cut through water swiftly and efficiently. Whoever had designed the craft definitely knew his stuff. All Novak thought about now was getting out to sea and putting miles between him and the murderous little guy in black.

Novak plied the water with deep and steady strokes, never letting up, never giving up. Once he got over the breakers and out on calmer water, he got the hang of the rhythm, and the canoe flew over the restless waves. Instead of his grueling physical effort, he tried to think about what had gone down back at the camp and why. He was pretty sure now that he was dealing with a professional assassin, a good one, who had been hired to take out a specific target. Someone in that camp had been the target—probably Li Liu, because she had paid dearly at the killer's hands. The dead guards must have been collateral damage—overkill, for sure, because if the assassin had the ability to sneak up and dispatch that many men, he could have easily bypassed the guards with his stealth and zeroed in on the woman. But he hadn't. He had wanted them all dead for some reason. That puzzled Novak. Assassins didn't usually mess around with dramatic flourishes like that. They went in, did the job, and got out. They didn't leave a string of mutilated corpses with possible evidence for the authorities to find. The confiscated boats weren't sunk by the pirates, no way; that would be stupid on their part. The assassin had done that, too, Novak would bet on it, taking away his victims' means of escape and/or pursuit while he was busy killing everybody. The guy was a sicko, all right.

Another possibility was that the assassin had been after Novak. God knows he had plenty of enemies, made in the military as well as through his investigative work. More than one man wanted him dead. Maybe somebody was tracking him, had been for a while. Still, that seemed unlikely out in the middle of the Caribbean. He was usually home at Bonne Terre, a stationary target and a much easier killing ground. Last but not least, there was little Isabella to consider. Maybe she was the one the ninja was after. The guy on *Orion's Trident* had tried to kill her and had been unsuccessful. Maybe he was back with a vengeance. He was the most likely person to know where they were. Nobody else would have a clue. Very little time had passed since Novak and the girl had been captured. It had to be Isabella.

Novak kept paddling. He had a few old enemies still living in Mexico who remembered him with no love in their hearts, men adversely affected by the covert missions he'd carried out in the past. They had long memories, just like Novak did. He had some good buddies down here, too, undercover and hard to find. But who could have tracked him? He had sailed down the Gulf and into the Caribbean with no specific destination in mind, a totally unplanned, unmapped voyage. He had anchored whenever and wherever he fancied and had followed no exact agenda. Nobody could track him, not easily, in any case. Hell, he himself hadn't known where he'd end up day to day. The whole scenario seemed bizarre and unlikely. But it had happened. Now he had to figure it out before something else bad landed on their heads.

Not right now, though. Now he needed to find a good place to hole up.

Isabella was still huddled down in the prow, had been the whole time, no doubt freaked out by the scalped victims strewn around the beach. Not a pretty sight for anyone to see. She was curled up in a fetal position, not moving a muscle, not saying a word. Her weight, as slight as it was, helped stabilize the narrow craft and guide it through waves whipped up by the incoming storm. What Novak needed to do was to find a protected cove or inlet, where they could gain temporary shelter and wait out the brunt of the storm. Fortunately, bad weather would slow down the killer, too. Best-case scenario: the killer was long gone, getting the hell away from his mass-murder scene. Novak's gut told him different, told him the guy did not leave witnesses. He would be a man who tied up loose ends, and Novak and Isabella were definitely loose ends.

Novak kept thrusting the paddle into the water, gritting his teeth, putting his back into it, and increasing the distance between them and the pirate camp. He had sailed out alone to grieve for his sister-in-law and deal with the horror of losing his family, and had ended up in a life-and-death struggle with what appeared to be a homicidal maniac. He never should have gotten involved, never should have fished that damn kid out of the water, much less kept her aboard his boat. He should've dumped her in a hospital or taken her to an island police station as fast as he could get her there. Let the professionals take care of her. But he had not done that. If he was honest with himself, he probably wouldn't have had the heart to leave her alone and helpless in a strange place anyway. Now he was just royally pissed off about her, about his boat sitting under-water, and the whole damn thing. The little psycho had scuttled the *Sweet Sarah*, Novak was sure of it. Taken his brand-new prized pos-session, a boat he'd named after his wife, and put her on the bottom of the inlet. Novak became angrier about that with every stroke of the paddle he put down.

Novak propelled the canoe onward, skimming the water and keep-ing about fifty yards out from the beach. His arms were rock-hard with the constant effort; his biceps burned like fire. He was in good shape, kept fit with his own daily workouts, but this was grueling beyond belief. His legs were cramped up under him in the narrow confines of the canoe. His thighs felt numb, but he had to keep going. He had to find a good place to put in and weather the storm. He could barely see the beachfront now that the rain was pelting them harder. No lights anywhere, not on shore and not out at sea. The strip of sand on his left was a mere pale glow now, with surf rushing in, appearing in uneven silver lines that eventually crested and crashed against the beach in the darkness.

Novak needed to find a river, any kind of stream or creek that would take him into the interior of what he now believed was Mexico. A lot of small freshwater creeks and at least one big river emptied out of the Yucatan Peninsula into the Caribbean Sea. He'd seen them on prior voyages. He'd even sailed up the big ones from time to time. He had to find one now, but he was closing in on exhaustion, physically and mentally spent, his body straining from the rigid balance he had to maintain to keep the narrow vessel from capsizing or being swamped by the big waves. They were fairly far out, and he started angling in, trying to avoid the riptides rushing back out to sea. That method worked pretty well, because the ocean was still relatively calm near shore. But a downpour was coming soon, and that would flip the canoe like a toy boat. He had to make landfall.

After what seemed like an eternity, Novak stopped paddling, sat up straight, and stretched his arms and back. Now the rain was beginning to come down hard. He had to find a place to beach. He wasn't as worried about the assassin now. The storm was his immediate threat. The killer was stranded at the camp with all his bloody handiwork. He had sunk the vessels along the pier and thereby left himself without a ride home. But this guy, whoever the hell he was, seemed pretty damned resourceful. He'd have a backup plan for sure, just like Novak always had one. Maybe a partner was working with him, or possibly a team, allies he could summon to pick him up at the beach.

The more Novak thought about it, the more he considered that to be the likely scenario. The killer couldn't have gone far in this canoe, not out into the open ocean by any stretch of the imagination. It was stealthy and quick and the perfect craft to glide into the beach at night undetected. If the guy was smart, he would've first anchored a nice big boat somewhere nearby and launched the canoe from there. And this guy was definitely smart. Maybe he'd anchored a boat within swimming distance of the camp. That's what Novak would have done. Novak liked to work alone, too. No need to worry about other people's mistakes.

Novak picked up the paddle again, trying not to think about the pain gripping his body. He was tired, had to get some rest soon.

Isabella still lay silent and unmoving, oblivious to the rain pouring down on her. She had to get hold of her fear and show him some guts. Because she was going to die if she didn't. She had been through a lot, granted, but she still was a pampered little princess out of her comfort zone. She said stupid things at the wrong times, like telling Li Liu they were lovers. He took into account her age and what she'd been through. Hell, the girl was damn lucky to be alive.

Novak finally glimpsed a break in the beach, still some distance away, but it appeared to be the mouth of a stream, his route off the ocean and into the heart of what he hoped was the southern Yucatan Peninsula. That meant small towns and people and telephones and vehicles. It also meant nosy police and eyewitnesses. He headed straight for the freshwater gushing into the ocean. He was used to this kind of approach, often in the dead of night. But he'd had a crack Special Forces team supporting him at sea. He preferred to approach the enemy straight off the water, go in silent and quick and hard, hit whatever target was assigned, and then get the hell out without incident. Just like the killer who was now probably hot on his trail.

Closer in, the surf was deafening, crashing and smashing onto shore. The breakers in front of him were big and forceful. The wind blowing at his back gained him lots of speed, and he redoubled his efforts with the paddle, working hard against the current flooding out of the river delta. He finally brought the canoe in over the roiling waves, and the water grew calmer. The river remained about thirty yards across, and he guided the canoe inland and kept her close to the bank. He began to relax a bit as he skimmed over the rippling water. When they rounded a bend, the river narrowed some. Not exactly the Mississippi, but he could probably reach some kind of civilization eventually if he continued heading inland. He kept glancing back, not underestimating the killer, but he saw nothing coming after him, no spotlights searching the jungle hugging the banks. Nothing. Novak had to stop soon. He needed to rest, even for half an hour. Sleep a bit, if he could. Just enough to keep his mind functioning so he wouldn't start making stupid mistakes. Now he felt a little better about things. If the girl didn't panic and go nuts, they just might make it out of this mess alive.

When he finally located a good spot, he guided the boat in toward the bank. Isabella sat up and looked around. "Where are we going?"

Novak kept dipping the paddle. "Hell if I know. Keep your voice down. Sound travels over water."

Isabella collapsed back down into the prow and didn't move. Novak ignored her and breathed easier when the stream grew calm. The water was sluggish, moving downstream in slow swirling currents. He was headed toward civilization now, he knew that much. He hoped they'd hit a village, or better yet, a city with a road that led straight to a U.S. embassy and/or an international airport. Maybe that wasn't going to happen, but a landline telephone would do the trick, if he could find one. Once he got out of the jungle and made sure the killer wasn't tailing them, he knew what to do. He had contacts who could help him. Right now, he was just too damn exhausted to think straight.

The sandbar he'd chosen had loomed up in the dark off to the right. He hesitated, not wanting to stop yet, but knowing he had to. He placed the paddle across his lap and tried to relax his aching shoulders. "Okay, Isabella, listen up. We've got to stop a little while and let me get some rest. You need to stay calm and do what I tell you."

She raised herself up, twisted around, and stared at him. He could barely see her in the gloom, but he knew her clothes were torn, the T-shirt she had on ripped and filthy. She looked dirty and wet and miserable and cold, and then the rain came down harder, in an absolute deluge, and beat the water around them into a maelstrom. Her hair straggled down over her face. Then she just groaned and slumped down again.

In time, Novak managed to beach the canoe and stepped out into the shallows. He pulled the canoe up farther onto the wet sand with the girl still inside, and then he walked around some, back and forth on the sand, trying to get some feeling back into his cramped legs. They felt numb. So did his arms. He loosened up some after a few minutes, and then he peered downriver but did not see a pursuer. But he couldn't see much else, either, not in the drenching downpour. He told Isabella to get out of the boat, and then he pulled it, empty, across the sand and into a lush growth of ferns and vines tangling the trees growing behind the sand. He motioned to her. She dragged herself over to him and stood watching as he brushed away the telltale groove, dug into the sand when he'd pulled the canoe in to cover, as well as their footprints. Another quick search of the river and then he'd had all he could take. He crawled under the protection of the thick bushes overhanging the bank, lay down behind the canoe with the rifle in his hand, and shut his eyes. A moment later, he felt the girl lie down and press herself up close against him. She was moaning.

He didn't open his eyes. "Get some sleep, Isabella. We're moving out again soon."

No answer. She was trembling all over, both from fear and from the frigid rain pouring down on them, no doubt. The storm was loud and punishing, the rain clattering on the leaves and drumming atop the water. Lightning flashed now and then.

"I'm gonna get you out of here, kid. Right now, you gotta be quiet and let me get some rest."

She didn't answer, but she snagged her fingers in his shirt and didn't let go. That was the last thing Novak remembered, until he heard something that brought him back awake—something he knew didn't fit with their circumstances. Sounded like a little silvery chime of bells, soft but insistent. He sat up quickly and then pushed himself up to standing. Dawn was trying to infiltrate the dark clouds, but the rain had stopped completely. Isabella jumped up too, alarmed, and hung onto his arm.

"I hear a phone ringing," she said. "Inside that knapsack."

That brought Novak's sense of danger rocketing up big-time. He grabbed the knapsack and jerked open the top. He had been so eager to get the hell away from the killer that he hadn't thought to search the bag. It was an amateurish mistake that might get him killed. As it turned out, the knapsack held a treasure trove of goodies: energy bars, bottles of water, waterproof maps of Mexico and Central America, waterproof matches, and lots of magazines full of Parabellums to go with the sweet little Glock 17 held in a black nylon holster with a gun belt wrapped around it. Right now, Novak was more interested in the sat phone. He picked it up, wary as hell, and pretty damn sure who was calling. Novak considered his options, but not for long, and then he checked the phone, found it unlocked, and punched on. He didn't say anything.

"Hello, Mr. Novak." Soft voice, speaking in Spanish. A man. The killer. It had to be.

Novak said nothing.

"You should not have taken my canoe. Maybe you'll lose your hair because of that mistake."

"Maybe you don't have so long to live anymore, you murdering bastard. Maybe I'm gonna get you first."

The killer was silent and then he said, "I doubt that. Listen carefully. That girl with you? She is not who you think she is. Turn her over to me and you can go on your way, free and clear, with no more trouble. I have no need to harm you. I only want her."

"Okay, your turn to listen. I'm going to take you out. You'll never know I'm there until the knife slides in."

Silence, and then an audible sigh. "You would be stupid to trust her. You will end up dead. You have no idea who you're up against."

"Ditto."

"I'm right behind you. Coming hard and fast. You have nowhere to go and nowhere to hide. You should've destroyed that phone in your hand. That was a stupid mistake. Maybe you're an amateur, after all."

Novak jerked the battery out of the phone and smashed it under his heel. Then he destroyed the phone and hurled all the pieces as far out into the river as he could throw them. The killer had been tracking them with the phone's GPS. They had to get out of there.

"Let's go, Isabella! He's been tracking us with that phone."

"Was that him? The one who killed those men and did that to their heads? What did he say?"

Novak grabbed the knapsack and stared down at her. "He told me not to trust you. That you were not who you seemed to be. Got any idea why he'd say something like that?"

Isabella shook her head and appeared terrified. "I think he's the man who knocked me in the water. He came out here to kill me, didn't he? I don't know why he'd tell you that about me! I haven't done anything. He killed Diego and then he tried to kill me. I didn't do anything to him."

Novak watched her face. If deceit was there, he couldn't see it. All he could see was the fear. It looked real. "You sure he's the one who attacked you that night?"

"No, I don't know for sure. I haven't seen him up close this time, but I saw his face on the boat when he beat me. He's not going to stop until he gets me! I don't know who he is, Mr. Novak. Or what he wants, but he's lying about me. He just wants you to turn me over to him. I swear, I swear! I haven't done anything. They had me tied up! You saw my bruises. You saw what they did to me."

Isabella was verging on hysteria and it was coming off legitimate. She was so scared she could barely get out the words. Something was going on, something she and the killer knew about but Novak didn't. This bastard wanted her, probably because she was an eyewitness to Diego's murder and could identify him. Novak was the only thing stopping him. Now he was getting close, and they better move out fast and keep going.

Novak got a good grip on the canoe and pushed it back into the water. He ordered the girl back into the prow and told her to stay down, and then he shoved off and maneuvered them to midstream. Then he worked the paddle like hell, pretty sure the guy wasn't kidding. He was not far behind them. Novak's gut told him that, and he always followed his instincts. There had to be a village or town along this river somewhere. Novak had to find it, and quick.

Chapter Eight

Wisps of mist, the color and texture of gray gauze, clung to the surface of the river. The sun was having trouble defeating the gloom of the jungle terrain, as if they were deep inside the Amazon rainforest. The river was running quiet. Novak's canoe cut through the swirling moisture and sent curls of fog trailing behind them. He estimated another hour or so and maybe they'd see the sun. He wasn't in a hurry now because of the fog cover. Once the sun lit up the river, Novak would be a sitting duck for anybody with a rifle. Novak paused long enough to grab an energy bar and drink a bottle of water. He tried the cell phones he'd taken from the guards, but none of them could pick up signals. Their batteries were almost dead anyway, damn it. He broke them up and tossed them into the river, not at all sure somebody else wasn't tracing their GPS location with those phones. Who? He didn't have a clue, but everything else that had happened was pretty damn bizarre and unlikely, so he wouldn't be surprised by that, either. After that, he returned to the steady, relentless, workaday paddling. He wanted to put miles behind him, far from the sandbar, far from the sea, and far from the psychopathic killer stalking them.

Novak's plan was to ditch the canoe soon and continue on foot. The narrow craft could carry a small and compact figure like the killer. It was lightweight, designed for speed and stealth, not for long distances or a man who stood six feet six inches. The killer had a second boat, Novak was certain of that now. Logic told him it was probably a big, powerful oceangoing vessel that was now speeding up the river behind them. It would be fast and sleek. It would catch the canoe if Novak didn't get off the water and onto land soon.

Novak had been thinking about the killer. He struck Novak as a solitary operator, a lone wolf who enjoyed killing, enjoyed the slashing and mutilating and bloodletting. Now that Novak had gotten some sleep, he felt revived enough to think things through more logically. His gut told him the girl was the key, of course. The killer admitted it in so many words. He had been aboard the *Orion's Trident* that night and he had tried to murder Isabella. No doubt he had reasons for hunting her down, and he sure as hell was going to a lot of trouble to get her at the moment. He just hadn't expected her to hook up with somebody strong enough to protect her. She was in serious peril now. This guy was not going to stop until she was dead.

Novak had suspected from the get-go that there was more to innocent-looking little Isabella Martinez than she was telling him. Her tale of abduction and imprisonment at sea had been a little bit on the sketchy side from the start, and with enough inconsistencies to give Novak pause. She was not what she appeared to be, that was for damn certain. As soon as he found a safe haven, he intended to force the truth out of her.

At the moment, his best bet was to find a village or a good-sized town where they could disappear long enough for Novak to call in some help. He knew he was somewhere along the coast, traveling upriver into the Yucatan jungle. They had no supplies to speak of, just what he'd found in the knapsack. Once they reached civilization, the Mexican police would get wind of a gringo traveling with an innocent young girl who looked scared to death. Novak was a big guy, a stranger, who looked tough and like he just might turn out to be trouble. He would be noticed, all right, and he would be reported to the authorities, especially if the massacre at Li Liu's camp was discovered anytime soon. The cops would suspect him of the murders, too, if he was picked up wandering around in close proximity to the crime scene without his passport or visa. If the killer coming after them was as smart as Novak believed, he might even contact the Federales himself and accuse Novak of kidnapping the girl. Some officers just might be corrupt enough to be paid off. Novak could not go to them or trust in them. Contacting any Mexican or local authorities was out of the question. He had to get out of this thing on his own. And he could, if he just had a little bit of luck.

Seeking help from local villagers wasn't a great move, either.

They would most likely be dirt poor and turn him in for a few pesos. More likely, they'd be petrified to help an American that mysteriously walked out of the jungle out in the middle of nowhere. But he did have one advantage—the best one possible. He had an old friend in the area. A good friend. At least, he hoped to hell his contact was still viable. Better be, because that was probably his only chance to escape the killer.

The morning finally dawned, the sun like a laser beam slicing into his tired eyes. He kept paddling up the river. Soon the sun was bright and hot, broiling down, burning into Novak's bare head. Isabella had pretty much stayed curled up on the bottom of the canoe, still terrified, or at least that was what she wanted him to think. At the moment, she was nothing but a giant albatross hanging around his neck, a dead weight slowing him down and complicating his every move. Their pursuer said he was after her; just turn her over and all would be well. Yeah, right. Novak had no illusions about the outcome of that scenario. The killer would take him out, too, the minute he got the opportunity. Truth was, Isabella, or whoever the hell she really was, held the key to everything that had gone down since Novak had laid eyes on her.

The banks along the stream began to rise higher, with some rock cliffs appearing, everything, everywhere, thick with dark green vegetation and mountains of vines smothering the tree limbs. The water ran deeper now, with swift, swirling currents out in the middle. A town had to crop up soon, he was pretty sure. Half an hour later, he picked up the sound of traffic passing along a road. Then they slid around a hairpin bend in the river, and there it was. Civilization. Up ahead maybe half a mile was a nice modern bridge. A car was passing over it, an old Nissan sedan, white, dirty, and moving slow. It passed a small gray Dodge minivan going in the opposite direction.

Scanning the right bank for a suitable place to beach the canoe, he brought them in close, anxious to get off the water for good and blend in to the thick bushes before they were noticed by the locals. A weedy slough showed up at one edge of a sandbar, and he paddled the canoe straight into it until it slid to a stop on the sand. He wasn't kidding himself. He looked rough now, face covered with dark stubble, clothes ripped and filthy and wet, arms and face scratched up and dirty and insect-bitten, eyes bloodshot from lack of sleep.

Isabella looked worse. All that, plus she appeared scared and ill. The two of them together would stick out to any onlooker, and he would especially cause concern. His height alone was a problem, along with the girl's obvious terror at anything and everything that moved. People would think she was his captive, and that would get him thrown in jail. So he had to proceed with caution. Nothing looked good. Nothing was going to get much better, either.

Novak helped the girl out of the canoe, glad she wasn't crying anymore. But she looked awful, like a young, pitiful waif, and that wouldn't do, not when traveling with him. She instantly crumpled down on her knees in the wet sand and watched him drag the canoe back into the bushes. He held the rifle in one hand, loath to leave any firepower behind. But he would definitely be noticed if he was carrying a long gun around with them. Authorities would be called, for sure. He had the fully loaded Ruger and the Glock that he could carry concealed. Reluctantly, he placed the rifle in the bottom of the canoe and quickly covered it with tree branches and debris. He had a feeling the killer would know the best places to beach a canoe, every bit as well as Novak did. He grabbed the killer's knapsack and hunkered down beside the girl. She looked up at him and tried to look brave. Didn't come off so well. She looked sick. He hoped she wasn't.

"Okay, listen, Isabella. You're doing just fine. But we've got to keep moving now, and you've got to try to forget what happened to you last night. If we run into anybody, you've got to act like nothing's wrong. If you can't do that, I'm gonna have to leave you out here with the canoe and come back for you . . ."

"No! No, please, don't leave me out here alone! I'll do better, I promise. I'm okay, I am." She pushed up on wobbly feet to prove it.

"Okay, good. But you have to do exactly what I say, because we're gonna start running into people and they're gonna think you're my victim, that I kidnapped you or abused you, or something bad like that. You start crying and acting all terrified, it's over. Can you pull it together, or not?"

Isabella nodded, enough so that Novak halfway believed her.

"First off, we both need to clean up a little bit. Get as much of this dirt and mud off us as we can. I'm going to give you my shirt to hide your bruises, because whoever sees us will sure as hell think I've been beating you up."

"I'll tell them you didn't! I'll make them believe me!"

"No. I don't want you to say anything. Just stay quiet and follow my lead. I'm going to have to come up with a story that fits our situation, okay? You smile when I smile. Frown if I frown. Can you do that? Say nothing, and try not to look afraid."

"Okay."

"Are you sure you can do that? Tell me if you think you're going to go to pieces."

She nodded firmly enough for him to believe she would probably try her best and fail miserably. But he had no choice. Despite what he'd told her, he couldn't leave her out on the riverbank. Not alone, that was for damn sure. Even if he left her a weapon, she wouldn't last ten minutes, not if she was accosted by a practiced killer.

Novak looked around, scoped out the river, and made sure the coast was clear. Then they waded out into the stream, knee deep, and washed their faces and arms as best they could. Novak pulled his shirt off over his head and handed it to her. The white T-shirt he had on underneath had noticeable bloodstains, so he tried to wash the blood out and then left it hanging out over his pants to hide his weapons. He watched her slip the T-shirt over her head and poke her arms through the sleeves. She stood up and it hung past her knees. But it did hide most of the bruises and scratches. She finger-combed her hair and braided it tight again, and began to look fairly okay. She looked very young and vulnerable without any makeup on her face. They started down a footpath that skirted the river. Novak was headed up to the road, where a couple more cars had passed over the bridge.

The bridge looked relatively new. It seemed familiar to him. He stared at it, and after a moment, he was pretty sure he knew where they were. Novak had crossed over that bridge several times, and once, a long time ago, at night, seriously wounded, and hidden in the back of a truck. If he wasn't mistaken, he now believed that they had just come up the Rio Hondo, which was the river that formed the border between Mexico and Belize. That would put them on the Mexican side. That would also mean there were border stations on either side of the bridge, something he needed to avoid. So he moved away from the riverbank and led Isabella through the more dense jungle terrain, past where he estimated the border station would be. They climbed up a rocky, litter-strewn hill and found right off that

the road did not lead to some little village. It led to a large, busy
Yucatan city. Novak figured it must be the city called Chetumal.
Heartened at his first stroke of good luck all day, Novak breathed in
relief. This was the best news Novak had gotten since he had awoken
from his own troubled nightmare and gotten himself involved in Isabella's real-life one. They took off down the side of the tarmac road
toward loud traffic sounds, their path shaded by some big banyan
trees.

Novak did not want to be noticed, but he would be. He always
was. Whoever the killer behind them really was, he would no doubt
be intelligent enough to figure that Novak would head to the nearest
town and lose himself in the hustle and bustle there. The man would
also know they would head there to find help or report his crimes.
They kept walking. After twenty minutes, they happened upon a
black metal road sign that read CHETUMAL, POBLACIÓN: 150,000.
He'd been right. The bigger the city, the better he could hide. He
knew Chetumal fairly well, had been there several months at one
time. It was at the extreme southern tip of Quintana Roo province
and situated on the sea: more excellent news. As was the fact that
American cruise ships docked there, so Americans would be a regular sight walking on the streets, tall and short, big and little. So all
he needed now was a place to hide out, a phone that worked, and his
friend being willing and available to pick them up and give them
shelter.

Once up on the main road, Novak kept a close eye on the passing
cars, glad that traffic was sparse. He finally saw what he'd been looking for, a slow tourist bus rattling down the road behind them. It was
packed with people, probably visitors and shoppers coming up from
Belize. Two young boys rode on the roof, holding on to the luggage
racks. Novak walked out to the side of the road. The bus began to
slow about thirty yards short of them, braked with a low squeal, and
stopped dead in the road. A few moments later, the driver released
the brake and rolled toward them.

Novak turned to Isabella. "When he gets here, let me do the talking. If he lets us get on board, don't say anything to anybody. Don't
look at anybody. I'm going to tell him that our boat capsized on the
river and we're trying to get back to our hotel."

"I'll do good. I promise."

Novak didn't place much credence in her promises, but he

watched the bus ease up and stop, with the passenger doors right in front of them. The driver operated the lever and the door slid open. "Hey, thanks for stopping. Think we can get a ride back to our hotel, señor? Our boat capsized back there on the river, and we lost everything. I've got money. I can pay."

The driver looked Novak over pretty good. He was an older man, hard to tell what age he was. Maybe late sixties or early seventies, but he looked more like ninety-nine. His face was wizened, sun-browned to a deep reddish bronze, and heavily lined. He wore a white Houston Astros baseball cap with a silver logo. Long gray hair secured in a ponytail stuck out through the back of the cap. He had on a blue-and-orange plaid island shirt covered with orchids and umbrellas and flamingoes. Looked like he'd come from Miami.

The driver shrugged and motioned them aboard. A trusting sort. Isabella suddenly decided to assume a different and sunshiny persona. No more sobs, no poor-me moans, no more looking as if she was going to faint any second. It was all replaced by a bright and noticeably phony smile. On the other hand, she looked young and helpless and innocent, a kid who needed to be picked up by a nice old bus driver and let off at her hotel, not the least bit threatening to anybody. Novak, on the other hand, looked exactly like what he was, a big tough guy who just might beat the crap out of the old man and steal the bus. He smiled and tried to look friendly.

Isabella climbed inside and found them a seat near the front. There were lots of people along the aisle. Most of them held shopping bags and luggage on their laps and on the floor between the seats. The bus rolled off again, with a series of creaks and squeaky brakes. Isabella stared out the window as if enraptured by the jungle's beauty.

They were off the river, and thank God for that. They sped along on the road, and the passengers behind them chattered in Spanish and laughed and had a good time, unaware that a serial killer could stop the bus at any moment and kill them all. The bus drove on. Novak watched the road behind them, not sure what he was looking for. As they neared some little town on the outskirts, the driver turned off onto a four-lane highway. Now they were headed into the city of Chetumal. It had an airport, which might come in handy, and lots of American businesses, including Walmart and Sam's Club and

McDonald's. It was a pretty place. Novak had halfway enjoyed his time there but had never been back.

Novak kept his eyes peeled for a good place for them to lay low and wait for the cavalry to arrive. After a while, they passed a square concrete-block building painted orange-red, like it was operated by demons from hell. The sign read MORAN HOTEL. Reminded him of an old Clint Eastwood movie he'd seen once, where Clint had made some cowardly townsfolk paint the whole town red, every single building. Then he called the place Hell. Novak couldn't recall the name of the movie. Novak liked Eastwood. But there was no real cover at the Moran, so he bided his time.

A little farther down the road, in the distance, he caught sight of a place that might be more suitable. The sign said THE HOTEL LAGUNA ENCANTADA. It was built very close to the road, the door almost opening on to the street. It was a long, rectangular white concrete building with a row of arched windows across the front. It looked severe and plain, like a giant German D-Day bunker with fancy windows. They passed a sign advertising another hotel right next to it but with a slightly different name: HOTEL LAGOON. Or maybe it was all the same place. Novak couldn't tell.

There was a curved decorative wall with a nice sign on the right side of the bunker hotel. Both backed up to a big lake called the Lagoon Encantada. He liked the idea of the walled courtyard surrounding the Hotel Lagoon. Some sort of Mexican party was going on inside. The bus windows gave him a mere glimpse of the festivities, but he could see people dressed in native costumes, women twirling around in brightly colored skirts, children running wild, and he could hear a mariachi band playing. It looked crowded, and maybe a little bit drunken. The tequila was flowing in there, no doubt about it, but that sounded damn good to Novak. He missed being drunk at the moment. More important, everybody there was concentrating on having a fun day and would not notice a stranger and his bedraggled young companion.

"This is it," he called out to the driver as they reached the road that led back into the Lagoon Hotel. He slid out of the seat and stepped back and allowed Isabella to precede him to the front door. Isabella stepped down in front of him, and Novak stopped beside the driver and dug out way too many of the pesos that he'd stolen from the dead guards. The driver seemed pleased at the overpayment, no doubt thinking the stupid American didn't understand the currency.

Once they were standing on the side of the road opposite the hotel, the bus rumbled off. Nobody else had gotten off, everybody headed into the city for fun and games. Novak scanned the road behind them. The killer was coming. Getting closer all the time. Long-nurtured instincts told Novak to burrow in somewhere and keep his head down.

Isabella stood quietly at his side, listening to the loud singing and music coming over the wall of the hotel. They could hear the guitars and violins and people laughing. Then she actually looked up at Novak and smiled happily, as if they hadn't just trekked through bloody corpses and evaded the assassin from hell. "Hey, Señor Novak, maybe we could go back there where the music is and have some fun, no?"

"No. Hell, no. We're going in there but we're not gonna have fun."

Isabella pouted. Disappointed. Thought he was an old fogy. He guessed she wanted to kick up her heels while waiting to get her throat cut from ear to ear. Novak wondered if she maybe had a little mental deficiency, had been slow in school, maybe. Then he wondered where all her heartfelt terror had gone. Now she acted downright comfortable with their state of affairs and at peace with the world. Maybe she thought they were home free now that they were out of the jungle and among people again. But they weren't. Nowhere close.

Novak was more concerned with her quicksilver turns of personality. Hell, he was still on edge, and he'd worked covert missions for years. His distrust of the girl ballooned into full-fledged wariness. This young woman was not who she said she was. He felt it in his gut, and had from the beginning. He also had a feeling that whatever she wasn't telling him was going to get him killed. His only hope was that he could reach his contact and get the hell out of the country. So he had to bide his time and keep a close eye on Isabella. Novak took her by the arm and led her across the street. They walked through the gate into the Hotel Lagoon. Novak was more than worried about what she was hiding and if he would end up on a slab at the morgue before he found out.

Novak tried to get his bearings. He knew they had climbed aboard the bus right before it turned onto the four-lane paved highway, called Avenida Mexico con Calle Heroes, and that had brought them this far. If he recalled, the highway would take them into the suburbs and then into the city center of Chetumal. The other time, he'd been taken to a safe house, sick and shot up, but he'd gotten help and had been nursed back to health before he was extracted for his next mission. That's how he had known about the customs checkpoints on both sides of the Hondo. Chetumal was big and modern, a busy seaport, and one hell of a good place to disappear. He hadn't wanted to take a bus all the way into the city. The distant outskirts were a better bet: sparsely populated, sporadic buildings (many of which looked abandoned and ramshackle and ready to fall down), scrub trees, trashy vacant lots amid the ever-encroaching jungle. Some homes with clotheslines hung with freshly washed garments, small children playing in the yards who stopped and watched the traffic roll on by to better places. Not far back, they'd passed a hamburger joint, of all things, and a small Catholic church. He had seen a sign pointing down a side road to a grocery store. So they had definitely reached the land of the living again.

Inside the walls, the festival got louder. Novak just wanted to get inside the hotel, unseen and unnoticed. It was a small place back by the lagoon, and he hoped there was a room available. He took hold of Isabella again and avoided the lobby. He led her instead through a paved courtyard with a fountain. It was deserted, everybody out at the festival, living the good life. He wanted a room facing the party and a view of the incoming road.

The fountain tinkled prettily and the shade felt good to his burned skin. He headed for the side door. He found a dusky back hallway just inside, with a terra-cotta tile floor and the smell of enchiladas hanging in the air. Smelled good to Novak. He was hungry. They walked down the hall and found a wood counter with a short man standing behind it, watching the dancers through the window. He was smoking a brown cigarette that smelled terrible. When he turned, Novak looked at the name embroidered on his white shirt. Antonio.

Novak inquired in Spanish if he and his daughter could possibly rent a room, one that overlooked the dancers, adding they'd just need it overnight. Isabella kept nodding along with everything Novak said, giving Meryl Streep a run for her money.

Antonio apparently appreciated the wad of money in Novak's hand. "*Sí, señor*. Your daughter, she is *muy bonita*."

Isabella dropped her eyes and tried to look demure but didn't carry it off—not well, anyway. Maybe it was the mosquito bites puffing up her face. The clerk laughed and handed Novak a big iron key. Novak handed him pesos worth about thirty American dollars plus a big tip, which was probably high for what they would find upstairs. Ten minutes later, they were on the second floor and entering a room that was not exactly Hilton quality. The ceiling plaster was cracked in places, the dresser dusty, and the bedspread wrinkled from where somebody had done something on it. Novak didn't want to know who did what there. On the other hand, there was a fairly modern bathroom, with pink fixtures circa 1980, maybe. But it offered running hot water and a showerhead and a toilet and sink. Clean towels on the racks. Good enough. They wouldn't be there long enough to get comfortable. It beat fighting their way through jungle vines in the dark with a stolen machete.

Best of all, there was a very old black rotary phone on the bedside table, the kind Novak hadn't seen since he was a boy. The girl immediately fled into the bathroom and turned on the shower, as most any woman who had been dragged through the jungle all night would do. Novak threw open the balcony doors and found no real balcony, just a waist-high black wrought-iron grille across the opening. Fine by him. He wasn't going to loll around on a balcony and let the killer spot him. He stood back in the shadows of the white cotton curtains and observed the party going on below, watching for a little ninja maniac dressed all in black and scalping his way through the crowd. He didn't see him. Nobody down below looked suspicious. No *policía* in sight, either. Just regular folks, laughing and talking. Young children chased around and stole fruit and candy off the tables. Men sat on benches and tossed back jiggers of tequila. It was Novak's kind of place. Maybe he'd come back someday.

Relieved to be out of sight for a change, Novak sat down on the edge of the bed. He pulled up a number from deep inside his psyche, a long-ago memory that he'd never forgotten. He dialed and listened to it ring at the other end. He let it ring five times, and then he hung up and called back again. It rang once this time, and he hung up. Waited exactly two more minutes and then redialed. Any other arrangement of calls, any variation, and nobody would pick up. Novak counted the final rings and hoped the code was the same as the last time he had used it.

Somebody picked up at the other end. A voice said, "How may I help you?"

At the sound of Jenn's voice, Novak smiled. Couldn't help himself. That deep southern drawl that she tried so hard to disguise but couldn't. She hailed from the great state of Mississippi, and was southern through and through, and proud of it. Novak felt himself relax a little for the first time since he realized that Isabella was probably going to get him killed. He had hoped Jenn would still be on the job.

"It's me," he said.

Apparently, she recognized Novak's voice right off, too, because she said, "I should just hang up on you right now, you bastard."

"I'm in big trouble, Jenn."

"When aren't you?"

"I need an extraction."

"You're not in the military anymore."

"I paid my dues. I need help. Please, Jenn. I'm desperate."

Silence for a few seconds. "Out of Mexico?"

"On Avenida Mexico, outskirts of Chetumal."

"Crap, Novak. I'm busy."

"This is life or death."

"Of course it is. When isn't it with you?"

"I'm sorry about before. I had to take off that way. I didn't want to."

"Oh, sure, right."

Then they were quiet. "You gonna come?"

"Well, don't I always?"

Novak grinned, very glad to hear that. He hadn't been sure what she'd do. "I'm gonna need some clothes. Something that won't stand out. Big and loose fitting to hide my weapons." He hesitated, glancing at the bathroom door. He could still hear the water running. "And bring some women's clothing, too. About size six, I guess. I don't know. Might need smaller than that. She's the skinniest girl I've ever seen."

"Are you serious? You've got a woman with you? You want me to dress your girlfriend? Good God, Novak. You take the damn cake."

"It's not like that. She's just a kid. She's in trouble. I'm trying to help her out and it's getting sticky."

"What kid?"

Novak stiffened when he heard a soft click on the telephone line. He spoke quickly. "Our canoe capsized in the river and we're stuck here so hurry, please. We lost almost everything. My daughter's exhausted."

Then Antonio's voice broke in, speaking in rapid Spanish. "Extra charge for using the phone, señor."

"Okay, no problem," Novak said tightly. The guy hung up.

"Where are you, exactly?" Jenn asked.

"The Hotel Lagoon, the smaller one behind the arched sign. Not too far over the border on Avenida Mexico?"

"I know the hotel. Sit tight. You're lucky that I'm working up here in Chetumal. I can be there in twenty minutes."

Jenn clicked off without saying another word. Her home base was a beach bungalow near Belize City several hours away, but she frequently drove north to check on the covert safe houses that she operated in Chetumal. It was a stroke of good luck that she was working in the city today. About time fortune smiled on him. Novak replaced the receiver in the cradle. He sat there and inhaled deeply, then blew it out, big-time relieved. Jenn was still ticked off at him, and she had a right to be. But she would come through for them. She always came through. She was the best at her job that he'd ever run across. Now, after he'd spoken with her, he was eager to see her again. Truthfully, he had never expected to meet up with her again, not after he'd taken off almost five years ago. It should be an interesting reunion. If she didn't slap the shit out of him.

Chapter Nine

Jennifer Ryman arrived in just under thirty minutes. She was a pro, through and through. Not only was she a covert military procurer and facilitator, she expertly ran CIA safe houses all the way from Merida to Panama City. She supplied her people with whatever they needed, whenever they needed it, and with no time wasted on conversation or red tape. Years ago, when he was injured on a mission in Nicaragua, Novak had been forced into hiding. He'd made it up to Mexico but he'd been seriously wounded, and she'd personally nursed him back to health. He'd stayed with her for well over a month on medical leave, and then spent another much more pleasurable month with her before he had been ordered back to the United States. Unfortunately, she had been in Merida delivering an asset to the airport when the car arrived with orders for Novak to leave immediately. He had gone with them without saying goodbye. Jenn hadn't liked that much and for good reason. She also hadn't kept in touch or reached out to him at any time since. Nor had he reached out to her. So he was understandably wary.

When a low double tap sounded on the door followed by three more in rapid succession, Novak picked up the Ruger and checked the chamber. He gestured for Isabella to get inside the closet. She ran to obey. As soon as the doors clicked shut behind her, he crossed the room and stood with his back against the wall on the right side of the door. He waited a moment to see if another knock sounded. Jenn would not do that. She always went strictly by the procedure codes. "Yeah?"

"It's me. Open the door."

The low, husky timbre of Jenn's voice made Novak want to smile.

He'd heard that voice plenty of times, over the telephone, across the little dining table in her house on the beach, and in Jenn's big soft bed, her whispers warm and throaty and sexy against his mouth. She was one hell of a desirable woman. She knew that, of course, and used it well to her advantage, both at work and in her free time. He hadn't minded in the least. He had wanted her, too. She was a woman any man would desire. But she was a hothead at times and gave him pretty much everything he could handle and more, and he better remember that. He swung open the door, not sure what to expect.

Jenn didn't look at him, just pushed past him without a word. Novak checked out the hallway, found no one around, and then shut and locked the door. When he turned around and faced Jenn, she pushed the Ruger to one side with the back of her hand. "I ought to knock you on your back for ducking out on me like that."

Nothing like getting right to the point. "That was a long time ago, Jenn."

"So?"

Novak didn't want to argue with her. He'd lose. "Yeah, you should hate me. I deserve it."

"Oh yeah, you sure do."

Novak frowned. "I'm sorry, Jenn. I'm not good at goodbyes."

"Not good at hellos, either, are you?"

"I was under orders to return to duty immediately. Emergency deployment. Time was of the essence."

Jenn didn't answer that. She planted her hands on her hips and glanced around the room. "Quite a dump you've got here. Where's the girl?"

"In the closet."

"Oh, that's gentlemanly. Why am I not surprised?"

"You don't know her."

Their gazes locked for a few seconds. Jenn was a tall woman, almost six feet, maybe five foot eleven. She still had to look up at him, and she didn't like that much. She was a tough woman and she could be as stubborn as any woman he'd ever met. Her hair was very curly, a pale blond the color of sunshine, held back at the moment in a long and silky ponytail. She had dyed her hair a coppery red the last time they'd spent their time together and had worn her hair quite short. She changed her hair color and appearance as often as she changed her clothes. A real chameleon. That idiosyncrasy had kept her alive during some hazardous situations. But she was back to her natural blond today, and that's the way Novak liked her best. She had on tight black jeans that showed off her lithe figure and a pink and coral tank top with shiny silver seashells all across the front. She was lean and muscular and fit and looked as sexy as hell. She had on black Nike tennis shoes without socks. She was carrying a large brown leather bag, and a blue duffel bag was slung over one shoulder.

"You brought the sat phone, right?" Novak was really glad to see her, and not just because she was saving his skin. He realized with some surprise that he had missed her.

"I'm a procurer, remember? That's my job. Of course I've got it. I've got everything you'll need and more. Most of it's still down in the RV. I parked out back in the alley. Figured you'd not want to make a production out of sneaking your girlfriend out of here."

"God, Jenn, I am so glad to see you."

"Don't tell me you missed me or I'll slug you one."

"Okay."

They studied each other for another moment. She didn't look much older than before. Maybe a few lines around those big and luminous brown eyes of hers. She looked really good. Her beauty had been the downfall of many a bad guy. Well trained in martial arts, she was capable of knocking Novak on his back if he was the least bit careless. He liked that about her, too. He liked a lot of things about her. He liked the way her breasts were straining against the tight tank, making the shells round out and look real. He shifted his eyes. Better get a grip on that, and right now. Stay on point, because she was going to.

"We've got serious trouble, Jenn. Thank you for coming. I mean it."

Jenn glanced over at the closet door. "I think it's safe to let the poor girl out of there now, don't you? I'd like to get a look at the poor kid."

"Yeah, sure." He glanced at the louvered doors. "Come on out, Isabella. It's safe."

The door cracked open, and then Isabella peeked out. "Isabella, this is my good friend Jenn. Jenn, Isabella Martinez."

Isabella stepped all the way out and looked highly uncomfortable in the presence of the other woman. Jenn stared at her a long moment, and then she looked back at Novak. Novak had seen that look before. She looked incredulous. Then she looked concerned. Then she shook her head.

Novak frowned. "What?"

"You don't know? Really? You've got to be kidding me."

"What?"

"That girl over there? The one you call Isabella? I'm not sure that's who she is. She looks a damn sight like Marisol Ruiz, who just happens to be the only daughter of Arturo Ruiz, the most brutal drug lord in Mexico. She was kidnapped out of a convent exactly six days ago. Everybody south of Barrow, Alaska, knows about it, including me. Good God, Novak. If it is her, you are in some deep shit here. Please tell me you didn't kidnap this kid."

Novak's jaw dropped. That didn't happen often. That didn't happen ever. Ruiz was a drug lord, known far and wide for his cruel, inhuman treatment of enemies and minions who betrayed him. The Mexican government was afraid to cross him. He was also suspected of multiple beheadings to send a message, sometimes a dozen innocent victims at a time, their bodies laid out across a busy highway to increase terror in the townspeople. It usually worked. He was known to cut down anybody who got in his way, and probably had at least half of the Mexican police force in his pocket. He made El Chapo look like a schoolyard bully. Novak's shock faded pretty damn fast. He turned on the girl. "That true? Your name is Marisol Ruiz? You've been lyin' to me about everything?"

Isabella, a.k.a. Marisol, a.k.a. who the hell knew who she really was looked contrite and hung her head and regressed before his eyes to about twelve years old. "I'm sorry, Señor Novak. I had to lie to you. I really did."

"Bullshit."

Her true identity complicated things big-time, and he didn't like where it left him: holding the bag, pretty much, and number one on a Mexican mafioso's hit list.

Jenn was not very understanding. "Are you out of your mind, Novak? I can't get involved in something like this. This is serious trouble."

"I didn't have a clue what her name was. I fished her out of the ocean, and she's been telling me a pack of lies ever since. I knew she was lying, but I didn't expect anything like this."

Ticked off in a big way, Novak turned to the newly designated Marisol. "Why the hell didn't you tell me the truth from the beginning?"

Marisol Ruiz dissolved into her usual pitiful-me act. "I was afraid to! I didn't know you. I didn't know if you'd take me back home to him. I don't want him to find me."

"So you ran away from home? Is that what you're telling us? The kidnapping was a hoax?" That was Jenn. She looked upset now. Angry. Her voice was hard and her jaw was set.

Furious, too, Novak crossed the room and pulled Marisol over to the bed. He pushed her down and glared at her. "Start talking, dammit. And tell me the truth, for a change. From the beginning. I've had it with you, Marisol, if that's your name. Got that? I've had it. One more lie and I am out of here for good."

Jenn leaned back against the desk and watched. His show. She wouldn't interfere. Novak paced away and looked through the open louvers of the balcony doors, focusing his attention down on the people eating and dancing and laughing. "Okay, we're waiting. Talk, kid. And it better be good."

Marisol Ruiz didn't want to tell them anything. That was pretty damn evident. She was putting on a fairly good show of being frightened. Wringing her hands and doing a lot of fast thinking, no doubt. But he'd seen her adapt her character to meet the situation before. She was probably concocting a new script full of lies.

"What do you want me to say? Most of what I said is true. Just not my father's name. I was afraid to tell you that. But I was kidnapped by Diego. He took me out on the *Orion's Trident* and tied me up while he demanded ransom. Then the other guy, you know, the guy after us, he sneaked aboard one night. He shot my boyfriend and then he tried to kill me. All that's true. You saw it happen, remember? If you hadn't come and got me out of the water, I would be dead." She hesitated after that, considering, and then she said. "That guy who takes the scalps? Okay, he works for Papi. He's like a son to him. He'll do anything Papi asks him to."

"Papi meaning Arturo Ruiz?"

She nodded, looked down at the floor.

"If he works for your father, why would he leave you out there in the ocean to die?"

"I don't know. Maybe Papi told him to. Papi beats me. He beats my mama. Maybe he's tired of me running away and wants to get rid of me. I wouldn't be surprised. He orders lots of murders for people who cross him. He's a bad man. That's why I wanted to get away from him. I'm scared of him and what he does to me."

"So you do know this guy who's chasing us?"

Marisol had the decency to look guilty. "Yes, of course. He works for Papi. You know, like a lieutenant."

"Well, who the hell is he?"

"I don't know his real name. Papi always calls him the Mayan."

Jenn and Novak looked at each other. Neither of them believed her, not everything she had said, anyway. Something was not on the up-and-up in this new scenario, either. Marisol had proven herself to be a liar, a fair actress, and a con woman. Why should they believe her now?

"Very nice story on short notice," Novak said to her. "Now, how about telling us the truth?"

Marisol attempted a mightily shocked expression. "That's the honest truth. I swear it, I do. I swear it on the Blessed Virgin. That's what happened. If you hadn't found me and pulled me out of the water, I'd be dead right now. I'd be eaten up by a shark, maybe. Nobody would have known I drowned out there. I was half conscious when you found me. You know I was. You saved my life. I'll always be grateful to you for that."

Jenn stood up. She looked highly peeved. Jenn was also one hell of a good interrogator. After that little spiel of self-serving crap, Novak let Jenn take over. He just stood behind the louvers and searched the crowd below in case the Mayan decided to show up.

"How did the kidnappers get to you?" Jenn asked her. "Tell me. Start from the beginning and don't leave anything out."

"I met this guy at a nightclub in Merida. He was really cute and looked just like Adam Levine, you know, the singer in Maroon 5. He was just gorgeous. He had all these cool tats and was real sweet to me. Paid me lots of attention and bought my drinks. Then we drove to Cancun and partied there for a while. I liked him a lot. I still like him. I wish he wasn't dead."

Apparently, that remark might possibly be true, because big fat tears welled up in her eyes. She let the sobs burst forth. Looked fairly real, too. Novak watched the tears roll down her cheeks, not particularly impressed. She was good at concocting sob stories. She was

good at sobbing. He had listened to more of that than he ever wanted
to remember. Somehow, though, now he was leaning toward believing her. Bad thing was, he had gotten himself in one hell of a mess
because of her, and now he'd brought Jenn in on it, too. Not good.

Jenn wasn't finished. Didn't look like she believed her, either.
"What's his name?"

"Diego."

"How long did the two of you date?"

"A couple of months, maybe three." Marisol wiped the wetness
off her cheeks with her fingers. "I thought he loved me. He said he
did. I loved him. I loved him a lot. He was sweet and he was really
nice to me." She stared up at them, eyes shining with loss. Maybe
the tears were real. Maybe not. Probably not.

"Did your father know about this boyfriend?" Novak asked her.
"Is that why he sent this Mayan guy after you?"

"I guess, I don't know. Papi hates me. So does the Mayan. I ran
away a couple of times before I even met Diego. I'm so scared of
Papi. You don't know him. He just gets mad and explodes and does
terrible things to people. I've seen him. He goes berserk and sometimes just kills somebody for some little thing that doesn't amount
to anything." She stopped there and sniffled around and wept some
more. Then she started up again, all trembling voice and quivering
lips. "I was too scared to go back home or to call Mama. I thought
she'd tell on me. I thought I could run off with Diego and we could
disappear and be together forever and I'd never have to see my family
again. Papi said he was going to put me in a convent for good if I
didn't behave. He thinks I should be this little angel that never does
anything wrong. He said I couldn't drink or smoke or go to parties
or wear short skirts. He said I had to be a nun."

Novak scoffed at that. So did Jenn. Marisol pouted because they
didn't believe her.

"Diego couldn't have loved you much if he asked your father
to ransom you."

"I thought he loved me. He said he did. So when he invited me to
go on a cruise on his father's yacht, I said yes. He kept telling me he
loved me, and I believed him. He was kind. Then when the Mayan
found us and sneaked aboard, Diego tried to save me. That's when
the Mayan shot him dead." She turned to Novak. "You saw that. You
saw how he shot him down. That's when I ran and he chased me."

"Yeah, old Diego was just one hell of a great guy, wasn't he? But he betrayed you for money and now he's dead." Novak returned his gaze to the dancers below his window. "For God's sake, what the hell's the matter with you? This Diego guy kidnapped you. How the hell could you love him after that?"

"Well, he had a good reason. He probably needed money so we could run off together. I understand that. He probably wouldn't have turned me over to Papi once he got the money. Not if I didn't want to go. But I don't care! He didn't deserve to die like that, shot in the face, just because he took me out on his boat. I understood why he did it. I would've gone with him anyway, if he'd just asked. I told him that."

Novak turned to look at her. "What about those bruises on your wrists and ankles? How'd you get those if you two were such lovebirds?"

Marisol hesitated, looked down at her hands a moment. "He told me what he was doing. Said he had to tie me up so it would look real. He said he'd turn me over, and then he'd come back and meet me somewhere and we'd take the ransom money and run away and never come back to Mexico. And then the Mayan showed up and chained us down in the bilge. He kept coming down and hitting us. Then Diego got loose and we tried to get away, but the Mayan killed him."

Jenn sighed. Not happy, either. "Is that his real name? Diego? Diego what?"

"Diego Ortiz. He was really sweet. And he did love me. I know he did. You can't tell me that he didn't."

Jenn was not gentle. "Grow up, Marisol. Quit acting like a naive little girl. The guy was probably going to kill you after he got the money. He used you and got killed doing it. You're lucky you're not dead because of him."

"He would never hurt me."

"What about the bruises? That didn't hurt?"

She was quiet for a moment, sitting there and rubbing her wrists. "Like I said, Diego didn't want to tie me up but he had to make it look real."

"And you actually believed that?" Jenn said.

Marisol stared at Jenn a moment and then swiveled her gaze to Novak. She turned on the waterworks again. The absolute picture of misery. And she sure as the devil had made Novak's life miserable, right along with hers. His lingering sympathy for the kid was eroding fast. All he wanted now was to get rid of her and go back home.

Jenn looked at Novak. "So now what? You plan to keep babysitting this kid? That your plan?"

"I hope you mean 'we'?"

"Hell no, I don't mean 'we.' I mean you. Trust me on that. I want nothing to do with this girl. She's a little liar, and she's lying to you now. I thought you had better instincts than this, Novak. I cannot believe you bought this little crybaby act of hers. She's going to get you killed. Wait and see."

Jenn meant every word. Jenn always meant everything she said, and she was usually right on. He'd had his doubts, all right, but the kid had been young enough and pitiful enough that he had felt the need to help her. "Yeah, but you haven't heard the entire story. She's been telling lies, but that's not the real problem. We've got that assassin coming right behind us. The Mayan. He wants to kill her. And he wants to kill me, and you, if you get involved."

"Yes, I'd say that's a problem, all right. My take? Leave her right here in this room and let me extract you out of Mexico, while you're still alive and in one piece."

Novak hesitated. Jenn was right, of course. He was tempted to take off and let the kid fend for herself. But Jenn hadn't seen the carnage left on that beach by the Mayan. She didn't know his brutal ruthlessness. The Mayan wanted Marisol back, or probably just dead, and he most likely had a large paycheck riding on it. He would slit her throat and take the long braid of hers home to her daddy as proof. Daughter disposed of. Novak didn't like Marisol much, not at all right now, but he couldn't bring himself to simply abandon her. Not with that psycho following them. No matter how much the kid had lied to Novak, the fact was she did not have a chance against this Mayan guy. Maybe Jenn could get them both to the States. Once there, Novak could hand Marisol Ruiz over to the FBI and wash his hands of her for good. They'd probably be glad to get a mafioso's daughter in their custody. Then Novak could salvage his damn boat and get on with his life.

Jenn slung the heavy backpack up onto the bed and flipped it open. She had stuffed clothes inside, lots of them, packed neatly, garments that would fit Novak and Marisol, as well as everything else she assumed they were going to need. Novak was more interested in the food. He was hungry, hadn't had much to eat since their capture. Neither had Marisol. He took out a couple of bananas and tossed one to the girl.

"Go change into these clothes," Jenn ordered Marisol, handing her a pair of faded denim jeans, a light blue chambray shirt, and a St. Louis Cardinals baseball cap. "I guess we better cut your hair if you hang around very long. That braid's going to identify you right off the bat. Maybe you could pass for a boy until we get you back to the safe house."

"But I like my hair long," whined Marisol.

"Tough shit," Jenn told her. "Unless you want us to call your Papi and tell him to come pick you up."

Marisol puckered up but didn't cry anymore. Maybe she'd met her match. She took the clothes and walked into the bathroom. Once the door was shut, Jenn didn't hold back. "Every word that comes out her mouth is a damn lie, Novak."

"No kidding."

"Okay, so now the Mexican police are probably after you, too, on top of Daddy the drug lord. This is not good news, Novak. God knows who else is looking for her. And they'll keep coming until they get her or until we can cross into the U.S."

Novak grabbed a tan canvas shirt and black ball cap out of the bag and put them on, but he kept his gaze on the crowd. The mariachi band was still playing. Some couples were dancing now. The women were swirling full red skirts, the men clicking their heels and clapping their hands. People were standing in a ring and watching them, clapping along. Having a good time. Happy. Must be nice. "Or both of us could hide out in your safe house until things cool off." He spoke without looking at Jenn.

When he glanced back at her, Jenn did not look thrilled at the idea. "And let's not forget her daddy's cartel. You know, the one full of murdering, cold-blooded henchmen who behead people just for the hell of it. Know how he sends out warnings, Novak? With headless dead bodies. Sometimes he sends the heads to the family. Sometimes he sends the bodies. So you tell me, what are they gonna do to us if they catch us helping her?"

"They'll kill us before they ask a single question and then take their boss's baby girl home to Daddy. Or they'll just kill her on his orders and dump her body." Novak hesitated. "There's something else you need to know."

"Oh my God. Now what? This cannot get any worse."

"Oh, it can. Trust me." Novak caught Jenn's full attention and held it. "This guy. The one she calls the Mayan? He's not just one of Ruiz's employees and not just an adopted son, or whatever. He's a highly trained assassin. He sure as hell knows what he's doing. His MO is to cut the throat and then take the scalp as a souvenir. He's already killed at least ten or twelve people. I saw the bodies."

Jenn stared at him. "He's a professional assassin?"

"I think so. A brutal, deadly little guy. He takes scalps."

Jenn sank down on the bed. "My God, Will. I can't believe you just walked into something like this. You know better."

She had reverted to calling him Will. A good sign. "He's going to kill us, too, if he finds us first, and he's damn good at it," Novak said. "That's why we need to get to a safe house and get there quick."

"He's horrible, Jenn! He just skins off people's hair and leaves their head all bloody and gory." That came from Marisol, from behind the bathroom door. Eavesdropping. They ignored her. Silence reigned for several minutes.

"Okay, now that you've dragged me into this, I guess I'm in. Tell me again, everything that happened."

So Novak told Jenn the whole sordid story. He told her how things went down out on the ocean, how he'd gotten the girl out of the water, how they'd been taken by the Asian woman and her men, how the assassin had shown up, all of it. It sounded even worse in the telling.

"After listening to all that, I'd say this guy is most definitely a paid killer, and the girl's daddy put out a cartel hit on his own daughter, and there's probably one on you, too. At the very least, if he thinks you've got his kid, there's probably one hell of a giant reward for anybody who brings your head to him inside a brown paper bag. That's another fun thing the cartels down here like to do."

"Thanks for pointing that out."

"What the hell, Novak? You know better than to get caught up in something like this. Are you losing your touch?"

Novak felt something closely akin to embarrassment. He felt ashamed, somehow. She was right. He had been gullible and careless. "They stole my boat. I want it back."

"Your boat. Of course. That's the important thing in all this. Why didn't I think of that?"

Novak got defensive. "I just tried to help a kid who I thought was in trouble. She was out in the water, floundering around and bleeding from head injuries, drowning. What would you have me do? You would've done the same thing I did. I know you that well."

Jenn didn't deny it. She couldn't. They commenced with another long considering look that revealed mutual annoyance. Then Jenn suddenly smiled and transformed her face into an incredibly beautiful thing. "We better watch it, Novak. We do lose control when we get angry."

That remark brought back a flood of memories of some wild nights spent in her bed. Their lovemaking had never been the tender, sweet kind, not like it had been with his wife, not like with Sarah. Nobody could be like Sarah. He and Jenn? They'd brought out other kinds of emotions in each other: lust and anger and passion and aggression. It had been a turn-on for both of them.

His expression made Jenn laugh. "Yeah, I remember all that, too. Oh yes, all was good until the day you walked out and never came back."

Novak thought it wise to return his attention to the fiesta. She was never going to forgive him for that affront. Jenn went about unpacking the portable satellite dish and set it up in front of the open balcony doors. He was lucky she had shown up. She was an ally, a trusted friend, a professional, and that's what he needed at the moment. It was good to see her, good to hear her voice again.

"Okay, I guess I have no choice but to help you out," Jenn told him. "Let's get out of here while there's still a distraction going on outside."

"You need to know about this guy coming after us. You cannot take him for granted. Those men he killed? They were armed and dangerous. He got them all with no alarm being set off. Then he tortured a woman to death. We heard her screaming, and I've never heard anything quite like it. So I stole his canoe and got away or he would've killed me and the girl, too. He is not going to leave any survivors."

"I doubt very much if he could've gotten you. You're too good. Even if you were softhearted enough and dumb enough to believe that girl's cockamamie story."

"He's good. Well trained. Deadly."

"So are you."

They stood there and stared at each other.

"Then we need to go. Now," Jenn said again.

It didn't take long. Jenn hastily repacked the gear and then banged her fist on the bathroom door. Marisol opened it, now dressed in the clothes Jenn had given her and with all her hair stuffed up into the ball cap she had pulled down over her face. Jenn hustled her out into the corridor and then downstairs. Jenn had come in a small white Winnebago. Novak pushed the girl toward the side door of the RV and told Jenn to get them the hell out of town. Then he boarded after Marisol and sat down beside the back window with the loaded Ruger on his lap. Marisol sat across from him on the seat beside the door, eyes wide, hands clasped tightly in her lap. She'd seen the Mayan's handiwork, and she'd never forget it. Nobody would.

Their best bet was to hole up in one of Jenn's safe houses until they figured out how to get out of Mexico alive. It wasn't a good plan, not by a long shot, but it would have to do, at least until Novak had a chance to get rid of the Mayan for good.

Chapter Ten

Jenn should have been a driver at the Indianapolis Speedway. She got them out on the highway, hung a left, and headed down into the city. Novak and Marisol sat in the back and said nothing to each other. They drove in virtual silence for a long time, and then they hit the busier Highway 186, and the rural country landscape began to fade away. Lots of businesses, motels, and restaurants started to show up. Not much later, Jenn turned onto the Avenida Insurgentes, which Novak knew ran across a good portion of the city before curving southward to the Boulevard Bahia, which ran along the beaches.

Novak watched the cars out the back window, still expecting to be followed. How, he couldn't figure, but the guy had shown himself capable of almost anything. The traffic had increased, and their surroundings looked like any other big tropical city: shopping malls, parks, schools, hotels, private homes, and lots of churches, palm trees and flowering plants everywhere. They drove past a zoo and a planetarium, with plenty of people milling around. Chetumal was the capital of the Quintana Roo state of Mexico, with clean, beautiful beaches, museums, and state government buildings down close to the sea.

Busy day-to-day hubbub and lots of hole-in-the-wall hiding places for a man on the run to choose from, Novak thought. He knew that Jenn had several safe houses both inside and outside the city environs. That was her job and the reason they'd met in the first place. She liked to locate her houses next to busy highways or the sea, for the accessibility, so that extraction would be easier. She was driving fast and handling the Winnebago as if she had driven it over the Sierra Madre, which she just might have done.

Traffic became snarled while they were on Insurgentes, but Novak was beginning to get his bearings. He felt himself finally beginning to relax a bit. Across from him, Marisol sat gripping the armrests of her seat and looking awfully nervous. When she saw him watching, she shut her eyes and tried for sympathy. Novak pretty much ignored her after that. He returned his attention to the road behind them. There was heavy traffic now, and they inched along the city streets with other cars and trucks and buses, past strip malls and a McDonald's and an Applebee's. Place didn't look much different than any American suburb, except the signs were all in Spanish and the Mexican tricolor flag was fluttering everywhere. Jenn drove on with expert control, remained quiet, and concentrated on getting them somewhere safe. Her loaded Glock sat beside her on the middle console. As usual, she was as steady as a rock when things got dicey. She would get them to wherever she was going—no problem, no worries, sit back and relax.

Now they were hitting stoplights, braking at every intersection. Lines of traffic honked and crawled along in both directions. But Novak viewed that as good news. Nobody would notice the old Winnebago in this kind of traffic jam. It had to be ten or twelve years old. Even so, Jenn would have it souped up like brand-new.

So they drove on with very little said. Novak was glad he hadn't picked up a tail behind them. The farther they got into the city, the better he felt. At least, he did until Jenn slowed down at the next stop sign. That's when he heard Marisol's swivel chair squeak. He twisted around to look at her, but before he could move, she had thrown open the door, jumped out, and was fleeing the vehicle on foot. She took off running through the traffic, darting in and out between cars and trucks. Then she nearly got herself hit by a taxi, followed by a lot of honking horns and angry drivers yelling at her.

"What's she doing?" Jenn cried out from the driver's seat.

"She's running, damn it. I guess I'm gonna have to go get her. She's dead if he finds her. Where's the safe house? We'll meet you there."

Jenn told him the address. He knew the place, had stayed there a couple of times with her. "Be careful, Novak!"

Novak stepped down onto the road and slammed the door, just as the light turned to green. Jenn pulled away and made a sharp right at the next corner. Novak headed across the street after Marisol, not running but walking swiftly so as not to draw attention. Once he stepped up on the opposite curb, however, he hurried faster and kept his eyes glued on Marisol's back. She was running down the sidewalk in front of him. She turned right at the next corner and disappeared from sight. He started jogging, avoiding other shoppers on the sidewalk. When he got to the corner, he caught sight of her again, rushing headlong down the sidewalk, weaving in and out of pedestrians and heading toward a crowd of people at a band concert going on inside a large median in the middle of the street. He slowed to a walk and kept the Ruger hidden in his waistband.

Furious, Novak cursed to himself. The little fool was going to get herself killed. He lost sight of her for a moment but got a glimpse of her almost at once, pushing through a crowd of laughing children in front of an ice cream shop. He peered up the block in front of her. The only thing he saw that she could be going for was a public telephone. Then he saw another girl, with blond hair and wearing big sunglasses, about two blocks up the street. It looked like she was waving for Marisol to hurry. She was standing in the open door of a gray Nissan, parked and headed in the opposite direction. Marisol saw her, too, and took off running toward her.

Novak had to stop and wait for cars to pass so he could get across the street. That's when he saw him. The Mayan. Small, black shirt, driving a new white Subaru Outback. The killer himself, right there, only yards away. At first, Novak just froze where he stood. How could the guy have found them so fast? It wasn't possible. At least, Novak thought it was the killer. Maybe not. Surely not. He hoped to hell not. About that time, the man in the car caught sight of Novak and threw on his brakes. It was him, all right.

Novak ducked quickly behind a group of people heading for the band concert, and then darted down the next alley. He ran hard toward the end of the block, wanting to cut off Marisol before she met up with the other girl. He was pretty sure the Mayan hadn't seen Marisol yet. He had been driving along the street slowly in the opposite direction, glancing side to side, searching the crowded sidewalks. Somewhere behind him, Novak heard a car pull into the alley. He glanced back. The Subaru was coming at him fast. Novak took an abrupt left and headed down a narrow back passage between two ancient brick buildings, avoiding the trash cans and dumpsters. He took another abrupt turn into a different alley. Above him on both sides, old-fashioned iron fire escapes clung to the buildings, stopping about fifteen feet off the ground. But the ladders were pulled up and secured on the second floor. Novak glanced behind him again. The Mayan was on foot now, running down the alley behind him. Novak could hear the thud of his feet on the cracked pavement.

Novak made it to the far end of the block, trying to judge where he could come out between Marisol and the unknown girl beckoning to her. It was a rendezvous, no question. Who was the girl? He burst out into the street, right in front of Marisol, and she skidded to a stop. Novak grabbed her and looked up the street. The other girl must have seen him intercept Marisol, because she jumped in the Nissan and took off. Marisol jerked and twisted, trying to pull free, so Novak grabbed her bodily from behind and clapped his hand over her mouth. Then he backed her into a recessed doorway that led into a crumbling stucco apartment building. Marisol kept trying to punch him, and Novak cursed and put his mouth to her ear.

"The Mayan's right behind me, damn it. He found us already, and you're the one he wants, not me. If you want to stay here alone and let him get you, fine by me. I'll be glad to let you go. That what you want? Better make up your mind fast because he's coming hard."

Marisol sagged against him, her fight gone. Novak took his hand off her mouth. "I don't think he made the street in time to see us. How the hell did he find us so fast, Marisol? And who the hell was that girl you were waving at? Tell me the truth, damn it. Did you contact somebody? How did you do it?"

Marisol became immediately distressed. "No, I swear, I didn't call him. I don't know any girl around here. But he wants to kill me. I'm sorry, I'm sorry! Please, help me get away from him. I got scared and ran, that's all! I thought I could disappear in the crowds and he'd never find me."

"Who's the blonde? I saw her up the street waving to you, Marisol. Tell me who she is, or I'm going to let him have you."

"I don't know any blonde. She couldn't have been waving at me. I don't know anybody in this town. I've never been here. Please, let's just go. I'm scared!"

Novak cursed under his breath. She was lying. He knew she was. "Just do what I tell you to do from now on. If you try another stunt like this, you're on your own. You get that, Marisol? I'll wash my hands of you for good."

"Let's go, let's go, before he gets me."

Grimacing, the Ruger in hand now, Novak took her elbow and pulled her into the lobby of the crumbling apartment building. Inside, it appeared to have once been a grand lobby, the walls covered with colorful murals of Mexican dancers with a backdrop of volcanic mountains, but the artist's paint had long ago faded to pastels, and parts of the murals were dark with grime. A staircase lay off to his right and he headed straight to it. He kept a tight grip on Marisol's arm as he took the steps to the second floor. The place was in major ill repair. The yellow paint on the walls was peeling, and some ceiling plaster lay scattered on the intricate brown mosaic floor tiles. The halls were pretty dark, just one window at each end, and most of the ornate brass sconces were not working. The whole building smelled of cooking grease.

Novak pulled Marisol along with him, holding on to her wrist, angry as hell, wondering why he kept rescuing her. She didn't deserve a second chance, much less a third or fourth. He should have stayed in the motor home with Jenn and left Marisol to whatever horrible fate befell her. They made it down the length of the hall in a matter of seconds and took a turn into the adjacent corridor that ran toward the front of the building. When Novak heard somebody clattering up the steps far behind them, he started trying doorknobs along the hall. Most of the doors were locked up tight, but he finally found one that opened under his hand. He pushed Marisol inside in front of him, shut the door quietly, locked it, and placed his back up against it. He listened, his weapon up and ready, well aware the Mayan wouldn't give up.

Then he saw the two small children standing at the other end of the hall. He hid the weapon down behind his right leg. The little boy looked about four, maybe, and the girl was probably eight or so. They were both still dressed in pajamas. Matching red ones. They just stared at him and Marisol. Novak lowered his voice and spoke to them in Spanish, trying to sound friendly.

"Hello there. Sorry to bother you, but we're trying to find our way out of the building. Could we use your fire escape, maybe?"

The girl had long black plaits twisted up and pinned atop her head. She just pointed down the hall, never taking her big brown eyes off him. Novak headed that way, pulling Marisol along with him. She was cooperating, for a change. The hallway led into a large kitchen where an old woman sat at a white kitchen table, shucking ears of corn into a bright orange bowl. She stopped in mid-motion, the ear of corn suspended in her hands. She stared silently at him.

"We're lost, señora. Mind if we use your fire escape?"

The woman blinked once, and then she pointed at the window across the room. Novak moved there in a hurry and glanced down into the alley below. The apartment faced the street on the far side of the building, away from the foot traffic and band concert. He didn't see anybody down there. Not in the alley, not in the adjacent street. Everything looked pretty much deserted. So he climbed out the window onto the iron balcony and then helped Marisol out behind him. The woman started stripping off husks again as if nothing had happened.

"Okay, we're gonna get to street level and we're going down fast. Can you jump down when we get to the bottom?"

Marisol nodded, breathing hard. "Yes, yes, let's just do it. He's going to get me!"

Novak was going to find out how the guy found them so fast later, but right now they had to get out of there. So they started down in a hurry, their feet thundering on the iron rungs, the sound ringing out like gunfire. On the second floor, Novak sat down on the fire escape edge, grabbed the ladder, put one foot on the bottom rung, and rode it down toward the ground. It stopped about six feet off the pavement, and he jumped down the rest of the way. The girl was right behind him. She swung off the bottom rung like it was a trapeze, and he caught her when she let go. They took off running again. Novak headed for the vacant lot across the street. They didn't slow down, crossing one yard after another at a full run, ducking under clotheslines filled with fluttering sheets and children's clothing. Marisol kept up with him.

Winding their way through back alleys, they walked now, but ducked in and out of yards and between houses. Novak flagged down the first taxi that drove into sight, pushed the girl into the backseat, and gave the driver the name of an area that he knew ran along the harbor. Fifteen minutes later, they left the cab at a stone wall that separated the street from a beach full of tourists. Novak paid the guy with more stolen pesos.

The Boulevard Bahia skirted the curve of the sea. The sidewalk in front of them had public viewing binoculars attached to stands, the kind people used to watch ships far out on the ocean. Marisol trailed along with him, acting docile, but constantly looking around. He had a feeling she was looking for the unknown blond girl that she denied knowing. Novak knew better. She had a lot to answer for, but he didn't have time to force the truth out of her, not now.

Ten minutes later, after walking swiftly down the sidewalk, Novak hailed a new taxi and told the driver to head for the airport. If the killer was on their trail and somehow identified the cabs they'd taken through his own secret sources, which had proved pretty damn on the mark so far, he might assume they had flown out. But they weren't catching a plane anywhere. Going through customs without a passport would flag him and Marisol, and he didn't want to give up the Ruger. What he wanted was to get out of the public eye.

Once they were mingling in the busy line of people waiting at the baggage curb for Delta Air Lines, Novak watched their taxi disappear into traffic. Then he led Marisol to the first taxi in the cab line. He gave the driver the name of a public park he knew, one located about three blocks from Jenn's safe house down on the coast. The ride there took twenty minutes, but Novak was fairly certain they'd lost the Mayan. The blonde, too, if she was following them. What Novak wanted to find were some answers.

The park was large and shady and crowded with local picnickers, which was encouraging. Maybe for once Novak was going to catch a freaking break. There was a big party, looked like some kind of family reunion, with maybe twenty or thirty family members, all having a hell of a good time under a large covered pavilion. Other people were spread out around it under the trees, sitting on blankets, and laughing and talking in small groups. He mingled among them for a while, holding tight to Marisol's arm, hoping they appeared to be out on a stroll but all the while gradually making his way across the grass to the other side of the park. They passed a big swimming pool surrounded by a chain-link fence, and then four tennis courts, all busy with people swatting the ball and shouting out scores. Also good. Nobody watched them. Nobody cared what they were doing.

Not long after that, Novak heard the distant sounds of the sea. The beachfront was about two or three short blocks south of them. Jenn had chosen this safe house in a popular beach area that had several international hotels and plenty of families milling around. He could see the tops of the high-rises from where he stood. It was a good choice. American tourists came here and went home on a regular basis, tourists that nobody in the neighborhood knew or wanted to know. Another stranger entering a rental house would set off no alarms, and it would be easy to mingle on crowded beaches if one needed to escape in a hurry.

Jenn's street was the next one over, and Novak slowed to a casual walk and held Marisol's hand, hoping to portray a couple on their way back to some hotel. He hoped nobody saw her bruises and called the cops on him. The girl was behaving herself now, so they walked down the quiet, shady sidewalk to the two-story house that looked pretty much like any other house in any other beach community in the world. There was a dirt driveway that led back along the side of the house and down a small slope to where Novak could see a closed garage, one big enough to hide the Winnebago and Jenn's other vehicles. Jenn was good at choosing perfect sites. Jenn was good at everything she did.

Novak kept a tight hold on Marisol and strode up to the door. He spotted the cameras up high on the porch, hidden well, but he knew where to look. He pushed the doorbell and waited. There were trellises, thick with beautiful pink bougainvilleas, the flowers shielding the front porch from the street. Lots of plants in terra-cotta pots sat around on the front porch, filled to overflowing with verbena and lilies and miniature roses and pansies, all lush and fragrant and well cared for. There was a galvanized iron watering can beside a spigot and a red surfboard leaning up against the wall. Several beach towels hung from hooks for show but had probably never seen the water. Jenn had a green thumb, along with all her other virtues. All her safe places had plants everywhere, and lots of those plants had microphones and cameras hidden inside the foliage. He'd been holed up inside places like this one way too many times not to recognize the signs.

"Where are we?" Marisol's voice sounded tentative.

Novak ignored her. He stared up into the eye of the camera above the door until he heard the soft click of the door latch. Then two other locks slid back. He turned the knob. Novak shut the door behind them and all the automatic locks slid back into place. They were standing inside a dark hall, no windows, no lights at all, three closed doors at the far end. There were cameras mounted on the ceiling, focused on whoever entered the front door.

"Where are we?" Marisol whispered again.

"A safe place, at least for the moment. C'mon."

He let her precede him, because he wasn't stupid and she wasn't above slugging him in the head and making another run for it. He'd never trust her again. At the end of the hall, the middle door opened, and Jenn appeared in the threshold.

"About time, Novak. I thought I was going to have to come looking for you and save your hide again."

"We took the scenic route. Where's the hold?"

"Good, you've finally come to your senses."

Novak gave her a dead-eyed stare.

Jenn took the hint. "In the back. Red steel door. Like always."

Novak took Marisol's arm and pulled her along. She was not resisting, but her muscles were all tensed up. Probably thought he was going to shoot her. That sounded pretty good to him. He opened the heavy red door and put his hand on the small of the girl's back and shoved her inside.

"Wait, don't leave me here!"

"You've got a bathroom in there and a comfortable bed and everything else you need. Food and bottled water in the fridge. No windows, no phone, no nothing. You can't escape, so don't even try. And it's completely soundproofed, like the rest of this house, so yelling for help is not going to do you any good, either. Take a nap and relax. You're not going anywhere."

Marisol stared back at him. "Okay. I'm going to do everything you say from now on, Mr. Novak. I promise."

"Yeah, you sure are, kid. Trust me."

Novak closed the door in her face and slid three outside bolt locks, and then he sought out Jenn. He found her in the kitchen, pouring herself a cup of coffee.

"Want some?" she asked him.

"You bet. Got anything good to eat?"

"Don't expect me to wait on you, Novak. I haven't forgiven you yet for slinking off in the middle of the night like a damn coward." But then she smiled. Novak did like her smile. And the *yet* she'd used was an encouraging sign. It looked as if she had gotten back home in time to take a shower. Her hair was damp, and she had on tight

red capris under an oversize black silk shirt that buttoned up the
front. Red Nike sandals with tiny mirrors on the straps. Toenails
painted fire engine red. She didn't have on anything under the shirt,
except maybe her weapon at her waist. He could smell some flowery
shampoo, the scent of roses, maybe. Brought back some good memories. Made him want her again. He looked away, getting ahead of
himself. She held grudges forever, so romance probably wasn't in
the picture.

Novak pulled out a chair at the kitchen table, sat down, and retrieved the Ruger and the Glock. He started with the Ruger. He
released the clip and checked everything over while Jenn poured
him a red mug full of hot black coffee. She retrieved a platter of ham
sandwiches from the fridge and a bag of Lay's potato chips and
placed them down on the table in front of him with the mug. Then
she took her coffee and sat down across from him. "I figured you'd
be hungry. You usually are, in the best of times."

"I've been on the run from a paid serial killer. Makes a guy
hungry. Couldn't stop for tacos."

One corner of Jenn's mouth curved up a little. She took a sip of
coffee. "Okay, tell me where you found her. And everything else
again. Don't leave anything out this time. There's more to this than
you've told me. You have stepped into something really nasty this
time."

"No kidding." Novak took a bite out of the sandwich and continued to eat while he spilled out the entire story, in detail and from the
beginning.

Jenn sat and listened, and watched him over the rim of her mug.
"That's not much to go on."

"I want to know who that girl in there really is and why these
people want her."

"All I know is what the TV reports and newspapers say. They're
saying now that she was kidnapped out of some convent up in the
Sierra Madres. So was some other girl. Nothing much is being said
about the second girl yet. Actually, not much is being said about
either of them, not anything that'll help you. No IDs. No pictures of
them. No rewards offered. But word on the street is that Marisol
is the daughter of a drug lord and is one of the girls who was kidnapped. Believe me, Novak, if he wants his daughter kept out of the
news media, it will be. It's said that he didn't want photos of her

taken, didn't want to worry about abductions for ransom. Nobody in this country wants to cross him. He's said to be as cold-blooded as anybody in Mexico. I suspect he's warned the cops off because he wants to find her himself and punish the abductors. I vaguely remember her face because I keep an eye on what the drug traffickers are doing around here. I saw Ruiz and his daughter, not too long ago on a surveillance video. They were leaving Mass at a cathedral in Mexico City. Nice clear shot. I think that girl in the hold looks a whole hell of a lot like the girl I saw. Maybe not, but chances are good that she is, considering the rumors going around. And if she is, she is definitely worth a lot of money to her father. He will want her back and he'll have his goons out looking for her, you can bet on it. Don't know if this Mayan freak is one of them. Maybe he's after a reward, but then again, he's already attempted to kill her once, right?"

"Yeah. He left her for dead out in the middle of the ocean. She's not innocent, no way, but she's hard to figure. She comes off so lost sometimes, yet I know she's been playing me. Worse than that? That guy she calls the Mayan? He almost got us today. I mean he was right there, right behind us, Jenn. On the same damn street, looking for us. He's got to be tracking us everywhere we run. I thought it was the sat phone he left in his canoe, but apparently it's not. And now I think there's a girl after her, too. She denies it but I saw a woman beckoning to her with my own eyes."

"Who was she? Maybe she's the girl who went missing with Marisol?"

"Wish I knew. She wants Marisol, had a car waiting to pick her up."

"How'd she manage that?"

"I think Marisol is signaling people somehow."

"How?"

Novak shrugged. "I intend to find out."

Jenn thought about it. "You think she knows what this Mayan guy wants with her?"

"He wants her dead, that's what he wants with her. And she knows it. She's been lying her head off since I got involved in this whole freaking mess. I think she's in there thinking up more lies as we speak. I think she's an expert at it. I think she knows exactly who this guy is and why he wants her out of the picture, but it's not for the reason she told me. I'm going to have to get it out of her before we leave here."

"And how do you plan to do that?"

"I'm going to ask her politely, and then I'm going to make sure she knows she's got no choice but to tell me."

"Want me to play bad cop?"

"I look more the part."

"You're just a big teddy bear. Especially around defenseless women like Marisol. She'll play you like a fiddle."

Novak glanced at her. "In the beginning she did, maybe. Not now. She's beginning to get on my nerves."

"Don't give me that. You've got this soft spot for vulnerable women. It's in your genetic makeup. It always happens. If she had been some young guy, you'd have forced her to come clean a long time ago." Jenn was smiling, teasing him, like she used to. Softened her face like crazy when she played around like that. "We are two hard-asses, aren't we?"

"Trained to be. Not smart not to be," Novak said.

"But not so much with a scared little teenage gal, huh?"

"Nothing's wrong with being scared. From what I've seen, she needs to be scared. She needs to come clean with us and talk, because we are all now directly in this guy's crosshairs. He gets her, he gets us. She's telling us some of the truth, maybe, but not the why and how."

"Okay, go ahead, eat. I've got apple pie warming in the oven."

"Yeah, I can smell it. So you bake now?"

"No, but Mrs. Smith does. I've got ten boxes of her pies stored in the freezer."

Novak smiled as Jenn continued. "I'm gonna bring that girl out here, let her chow down, let her get nice and comfortable, and then we'll scare the hell out of her."

"Sounds like a plan."

Chapter Eleven

Jenn sat silently and watched Novak eat. She didn't partake. Neither of them said much else that meant anything. It seemed odd to be around her again, after so many years had gone by. She didn't look much different. Sexy as ever. Especially in what she had on. There had always been a strong connection between them, a deep friendship as well as the kind of sexual energy and electricity that burned and shot sparks when they were alone and safe and making love. There was some sexual awareness going on now, too, crackling between them, and Novak was finding it hard to ignore.

Novak had met Jenn ten years after his wife had died, and Jenn knew he didn't love her and probably never would. Not like he had loved Sarah and their kids. That had been okay with Jenn. They had been lovers and happy enough together, for a while, anyway. He looked away from her and studiously got a grip on his libido. It wasn't the time or the place to think about things like that, and it wasn't smart on his part. He wasn't sure he wanted to get anything started again, even if she did.

"I know that look in your eye, Novak. I saw it plenty of times up until you took off. Relax. Have I ever made demands of you?"

"I said I was sorry, Jenn."

"Truth? I forgave you a long time ago. Have to say, I never thought I'd see you again. Not down here inside this house."

Nothing else was said. Novak ate a piece of pie with a scoop of vanilla ice cream. She watched him eat it. They were comfortable enough together to sit in silence. When he was finished, he wiped his mouth on a napkin, finished his third cup of coffee, and put down the mug.

"How about I do some research about this Mayan guy?" Jenn said. "He's got to have left tracks behind somewhere. Unless he's government connected and his files are wiped."

"Only thing I know for sure about him is that he's good at what he does. I've got a feeling he's left a trail of bodies ten miles long and not a single clue left to incriminate him."

Jenn retrieved her Apple laptop and set it down on the table. She opened the top and started typing. She stared down at the screen, concentrating on the task, a small dent between her eyebrows. Novak admired her while she worked the keyboard.

"Okay, CIA has a file on somebody that sounds like him. Calls him the Mayan, so that matches. Looks like he was active for years, 1980s on, up until about ten years ago when he dropped out of sight. Murders just stopped, and groupthink is that he's dead or locked up in prison under an alias."

"Does it give the MO? Anything in there about scalping victims?"

"Not that." Her fine eyes lifted and locked on his face. "Says here he cut out the hearts of his victims a time or two. Was thought to be following the rituals of ancient Mayan priests. Apparently, that's what they did with war captives. Plus, those priests liked to toss captives' heads to the crowds and let the warriors play soccer with them, or something resembling soccer. No mention of the Mayan beheading anybody. Says here he scared the hell out of his enemies. He hit fast and without warning. Nobody ever saw him go in or come out, just found the bloody crime scenes he left behind. Sounds like a lot of this is hearsay and rumor. No clear evidence."

"Does it mention any connection between him and Arturo Ruiz?"

"Just rumors that he worked for Ruiz as an assassin. His victims were usually drug traffickers or drug mules who'd cheated Ruiz. Pretty much concentrated on taking out bad guys and doing hits for hire. Nothing political that I could find."

"Ruiz cleaning out the competition, maybe? How about a picture of the Mayan? Background info?"

"No photo. Nobody ever sees him, except for you, I guess. This says he's like a shadow, dresses in black, goes in and out in the dead of night, leaving everybody dead and mutilated behind him. Says he uses a special knife made out of green obsidian, some kind of legitimate Mayan artifact he got hold of somehow. The kind those same Mayan priests used centuries ago. Doesn't say how he got it or what it's supposed to mean ritualistically. They assumed he was a Mexican national or maybe from somewhere in Central America. Most of his jobs were in this area, though, around the Yucatan. A few others thought to be his jobs were in Africa. About ten assassinations were perpetrated in the Middle East. Specifically, in Turkey and Syria."

"Probably used the obsidian because it's hard enough to cut through a man's breastbone."

"He's a sick guy. They've got crime scene pictures of the mutilations. Want to see them?"

"Not particularly. I've seen his handiwork up close. It's not pretty."

"There's a list here of people they think he murdered by contract. They never caught him, never came close. Accounts say he's too careful. Gets rid of all witnesses. Which I suspect means you and that girl in there, at the moment. Glad I haven't seen him yet. When his signature killings stopped, they figured he was dead and the file went cold. Nothing tied to him for the last decade."

"Until now. I saw him myself. Or somebody impersonating him. Anything else?"

"No, but I'll keep looking. I've got access to all the databases, as you know."

"How about Ruiz? If that girl in there really is his daughter, he's waist-deep in this whole thing."

"I told you what I know. Let me see what else I can find."

There followed a few seconds of typing and intense concentration. Then her face relaxed visibly. She looked at him and then swiveled the laptop around to face him. The photograph was grainy and taken from a distance. A young girl in a Catholic school uniform. A blue blazer and plaid pleated skirt and white knee socks. "Meet Marisol Ruiz, Novak. Looks like our girl to me."

"Is that the best picture you've got?"

"I haven't found any others except the one I already showed you. I think it looks a lot like your girlfriend in there. Same long dark hair. Thin as a rail. I would say it's her, maybe."

"Sort of looks like her. Sort of not."

"She looks around eleven or twelve in this picture."

"Does it give anything else on her?"

Jenn pulled the screen back around. "Only child. Her mother died at Marisol's birth. This says she's almost twenty now." She scrolled down some more. "Okay, I just hit pay dirt. This article says she's got a tattoo. A tiny blue butterfly on her lower abdomen, just under her bikini line." She looked questioningly at Novak. "You seen that yet, Novak?"

"I haven't looked under her bikini line, Jenn. Give me a break."

"Just asking. That might be all the proof we need. If it's true."

"You're gonna do the looking. I want nothing to do with that."

Jenn just smiled at him and then returned her attention to the screen.

Novak said, "If that's true about her mother, she's been lying to us about that, too. She told me Ruiz abused her mother."

"Says here she's reported to be a pretty girl, intelligent, good grades, but very headstrong and rebellious. Says she's run away a bunch of times and had to be tracked down by her father. Wow, listen to this. She's got an arrest record in Mexico City for petty theft and drunkenness and drug use. Cocaine and weed. Never did time. Daddy dearest bailed her out, I presume. Probably got some of the cops in his pocket, not to mention a few high-ranking Federales. Most drug lords down here collude with the rotten apples."

"Marisol told me she's run away before, but her father always finds her. That's when he supposedly beats her and locks her up under house arrest."

Jenn sighed. "Says she made it out of his compound one time and was gone almost six months. That happened a few years back, before his men found her and dragged her back home. Apparently, that compelled her daddy to stick her up in that mountain convent. Wanted to make a nun out of her. Probably so he could get some sleep."

"Fat chance. Not that girl in there. You heard her story. Says she got involved with Diego Ortiz, who ended up holding her for ransom out on that boat. What about the other girl who was kidnapped? Say anything about her?"

"Nope. News articles concentrate on Marisol, with very little other info. They say the other girl was younger. No mention of name or family or history. That's a bit strange, don't you think? She could be the girl you saw today. The blonde?"

"Maybe. I'm sure they knew each other, but Marisol denies it. Still, why would Ruiz send his personal assassin-slash-adopted son to kill her and everybody else who touches her?"

"None of it makes sense. Maybe he got tired of trying to reason with her and wants to get rid of her. Maybe she became a thorn in his side."

"She's that, all right."

"That girl in there? Trust me, Novak, she knows exactly what's been going on. Telling us the truth, that's a whole different ball game."

They stared at each other a moment, thinking about options.

"So? You ready to go at her? Let me check out that tattoo?" Jenn asked him.

"Yeah. Let's do it."

Jenn put away the laptop and left the room. A minute later she was back in the kitchen, Marisol in tow. Jenn was the picture of concern now, very sweet and attentive to the girl's comfort. She sat Marisol down at the table directly across from Novak. Then she moved to the kitchen counter and fixed the kid a plate of food. She put it down in front of Marisol and sat down beside her. Nobody said anything.

"Aren't you going to eat?" Marisol asked them, looking from one to the other, stiff and wary.

"We already ate, sweetie," Jenn told her.

Marisol looked relieved, and Novak could almost see her relax. Probably thought they were stupid and was already planning her next escape.

So Marisol ate her sandwich in total silence while the other two stared unblinkingly at her. After a while, she began to look uncomfortable. Then she tried to ignore them but without any luck. She took her time eating, though, finishing everything and then pushing the plate away. She dabbed at the corners of her mouth with a white paper napkin and drank the Coke that Jenn had provided. The table manners showing up again. She wasn't gonna belch out loud and laugh about it. Other kinds of good manners hadn't cropped up in her all that much. Just lies upon lies. Honesty had not been taught at the convent as a virtue worth developing.

"Thank you," she said, smiling at Jenn. "That tasted really good. I was starving."

"Okay, you ready now?" Novak asked her.

Marisol looked confused, or pretended to be. "Ready for what?"

"Ready for us to interrogate you."

Apparently, she wasn't ready, judging by the alarmed expression overtaking her face. "Interrogate me? What does that mean?"

"I think you know what it means. We want you to tell us everything that we want to know and we want you to tell us now."

"I did already! I did tell you everything, every single thing I could remember. I'm still confused and stuff. You know, I got hit in the head. Remember? I don't recall every single thing yet. Please, don't hurt me. Are you going to hurt me?"

Big tears welled up. Jenn wasn't having any of it.

"Don't pull that crybaby act on me, kid. I don't buy it. Tell me the truth. Novak's too nice a guy to get physical with girls like you, but it doesn't bother me, not at all. Believe me."

Marisol leaned away from her and assumed a look of abject terror. It looked legitimate to Novak, not so much to Jenn.

"Stop with the theatrics, kid," she continued. "I don't have that kind of patience. Not after the way you jumped out of the Winnebago and put us all in danger. I don't feel the least bit sorry for you. I don't know you but I don't like you much. I don't like having you in my house because you are trouble, and you're bringing it down on our heads, too."

No way would Jenn ever hurt the kid. Novak knew that. Marisol didn't, and Jenn looked tough. She was tough, but she didn't torture people. His threats certainly hadn't gotten through to Marisol. Let Jenn have a stab at it.

Novak pushed back his chair and stood up. "Okay, I'll leave her to you, Jenn. Maybe you can make her see reason. I'm gonna take a look around outside. Make sure we weren't followed."

"No! Mr. Novak, please! Don't leave me in here with her! Please, Mr. Novak, please don't go. She hates me!"

Novak sat back down. "Does that mean you're ready to tell us the truth?"

"Yes, yes, I will. I promise."

Novak and Jenn exchanged skeptical glances. This girl had proven herself a damn liar. It would be hard to believe anything that came out of her mouth. She had obviously told a ton of lies in her young life. Maybe she'd had to. Maybe she just liked to. Maybe she was a pathological liar and got off on it.

"I don't know, Marisol. I'm pretty damn sick and tired of asking you questions and finding out later that all your answers were lies.

I saved your skin, several times now, and you still won't come clean with me."

Marisol had been sitting there working herself up to some serious and tearful outrage. "I've been too frightened to! Don't you understand how terrifying all this has been for me? I've been through a lot of bad stuff. I don't know you, so I'm afraid of you. And her! I don't like her at all. She's mean. I don't like this place. I don't like being locked in that room and treated like a prisoner."

"Yeah? Well, I don't like your whining or anything else you've pulled on me."

Marisol fell hastily into a full-fledged sulk then and stared down at her empty plate.

"Okay, take off your shorts." That was Jenn.

Marisol looked genuinely shocked. "No! Why?"

"Because we know that Marisol Ruiz has a tattoo. Do you have a tattoo?"

She didn't hesitate. "Yes, of course, I do. But just one. It's down here." She pointed vaguely to a spot below her waist.

"What kind of tat?" Novak asked her.

"A little butterfly."

"What color?"

"Blue. Why?"

"Okay, pull down your pants," Jenn said. "I want to see it for myself."

"No way. You can't make me undress."

"Wanna bet?"

Marisol looked at both of them. "Okay, but I don't think it's right for you to make me do this. It's probably illegal and stuff."

Neither of them said anything, too disgusted with her for words. They waited.

The girl turned her back to Novak and pulled down the front waistband of her shorts. Jenn examined the tattoo and then nodded at Novak. So she was Marisol Ruiz. Good, at least now they knew that much, otherwise it would be one hell of a coincidence. Novak was more interested in everything else.

"How did you get on that boat? *Orion's Trident*?"

Marisol looked as if her brain was working on overdrive now, frantically assessing which lies would work and which would not. Trying to recall what she'd said before. That was the trouble with liars. They had to have a hell of a good memory. Novak was well acquainted with the signs of deceit, and Marisol was displaying all of them.

"It's time now for you to tell the truth, kid. If you don't trust our motives now, you never will. We might as well drop you off at a police station and let them drive you straight home to Papi."

Jenn stood up and moved around behind the girl. She put both hands on the girl's shoulders. She pressed her down in the chair. Mild intimidation. It usually worked. It did this time, too. Marisol's big dark eyes flashed in panic. "Please don't hurt me. I can't stand pain. I can't. It makes me throw up."

More tears. Tears that looked damn real. Wet to the touch, but lots of actresses cried on cue, and apparently so did little Marisol Ruiz. But she seemed to know about pain and what it did to her. Still, Novak was tired, and tired of her, and tired of wasting time.

"Who's the Mayan? What's he want with you? The truth now, all of it."

Marisol started sobbing, loud and sloppy enough to stop up her nose and make it run. She coughed, poor little thing. "He works for Papi. He kills people for Papi. Like I said before."

Novak believed that to be true. "You've already told us that. So he's your father's own personal assassin?"

"I guess so. I don't know him very well. I just saw him sometimes in my house. He's creepy and stuff. Papi didn't like me to be around him. They always went off alone in Papi's private office and talked."

"Do you really think your father would order a guy to hunt you down and murder you in cold blood?"

"*Sí*, he would do that! I'm telling you the truth. He doesn't care about me, not anymore. He doesn't care about anybody. He doesn't love me or my mama. He beats her up. And he ordered the Mayan to kill my brother, too."

Okay, lie one and lie two, coming in fast and furious now. This girl just didn't learn. He decided to let her continue. See if anything truthful came out of her mouth. "Why did he put a hit on your brother?"

"Because Francisco tried to get away from him. He tried to escape and flee up to the United States, to Texas, to Houston, but he didn't make it. So the Mayan caught him and killed him. He brought his scalp home to Mama and Mama fainted when she saw it . . ."

Novak just shook his head. She was not only a bald-faced liar, she was a damn imaginative one, too. He wondered if she sat around all day thinking up emergency sob stories. "What's the Mayan's real name?"

"I don't know," she cried out, with a great display of pseudo hysteria now, sobbing, phony tears streaming down her cheeks. "Papi just calls him the Mayan. Like I told you already. He's scary. He's killed so many people, so many. Hundreds, I bet. Ever since I was a little girl, I knew what he did. He's got all these rituals that I heard Papi talking about. He kills people with some kind of special knife. One made out of green obsidian or something. He got it down in Guatemala."

Okay, now she was throwing in some tidbits of truth to make the story sound better. "Why did he need a special knife?"

"Papi said it was so sharp it could split a single hair. He told me it was a knife that the ancient Mayans used for human sacrifices. To cut out people's hearts. A real one, an artifact that somebody dug up in an archaeology excavation. Papi said he gave it to him because the Mayan is descended from those priests."

"Then why is he not cutting out hearts now? Why did he scalp those men?"

Marisol looked trapped by the question. This time it took a while for her to come up with the right lie. She dropped the poor little mistreated girl routine and took on a whole different persona. Now she seemed quite calm and coolheaded. "Okay, I'll tell you everything. I guess I can trust you."

"Go right ahead. We're listening."

"I told you the truth about Diego and the kidnapping. What else do you want to know?"

"How is the Mayan tracking us?"

"I don't know that. I swear. I'd tell you if I knew. Do you think I want him to get me? We thought we were safe out there in the ocean, but he sneaked aboard somehow. We didn't hear him, we didn't see him coming. He was just there all of a sudden. You saw him shoot Diego. You saw him attack me. He left me for dead in the ocean. You know all of this already. You had to save me."

"It's the same guy, the one out on the boat and the one following you? This Mayan guy?" asked Jenn.

Marisol looked down, fearful again. "It was him. I think he thought

I would drown and be gone forever. But now he knows I'm alive, and he's coming to finish me off. I guess Papi told him to make sure I was dead." She wiped away a new tear. All serious now. "He'll find us and he'll kill me, then he'll kill you and cut off the tops of our heads like he did all those men on the beach. We'll all be dead soon."

Despite his misgivings, Novak was beginning to believe a lot of what she was saying. The tat itself was pretty good proof. But not infallible. The rest of her story was still suspect. But at least they knew who she was and why she was being stalked.

"We know you ran off once and disappeared for six months. Where'd you go?"

"I went to Florida and enrolled at the University of Miami. I wanted to go to school in America. Papi wouldn't let me. I like the United States, where everybody is free to do what they want. Where nobody knew me and wanted to kidnap me."

Novak took over the questioning. "What else can you tell us about the Mayan?"

"He kills for pleasure, I guess. Papi said he cuts out hearts and keeps them in special little black clay pots that he makes himself." She gave a little involuntary shiver.

Novak leaned back in his chair. "This Mayan guy found us way too fast. Zeroed right in on us. You've got to have an idea how he's doing it."

"I don't know. I keep telling you, I don't know. He's just good at finding people, I guess. I don't know him. I just know what Papi told me. I never talked to the Mayan or anything. I've always been afraid of him. He crept around our house when I was little, but Papi treated him like a member of our family. He said he was his adopted son."

"Why are you lying about your mother? We know she died the day you were born."

Marisol's face was easy to read. *Uh-oh, busted.* "I don't know why. I just did."

Novak blew out a frustrated breath. This girl could drive a man crazy. She needed serious psychological help. "Okay, that's enough for tonight. I'm taking you back to the hold, and I want you to get some sleep. Got that? Wash up, put on some clean clothes, and try to relax. Don't try to escape, or he'll probably find you and murder you. If you pull something stupid, I'm not coming after you again. No more. I'll let him have you." He stopped and let that sink in.

Looked like it might have this time. "Your best chance to stay alive is right here with us. Now, I want you to think about everything that's gone down. Tomorrow, you need to tell us everything you can remember about this killer. Especially how he tracks his victims. Try to recall everything you've heard about him. Because I want him, and I'm going to get him. Think long and hard. And no more lies. If I catch you in another lie, I'm going to dump you down the street at the beach and you can find your own way home, and good luck with that."

Marisol looked subdued. No more tears, no more arguments. Maybe she'd seen the light. He hoped to God she had. But he wouldn't bet on it. Jenn led the girl back to the hold and locked her in. Novak just sat there alone in the kitchen and tried to sort through what Jenn had uncovered and what Marisol had told them. Then he attempted to separate fact from fiction. It wasn't easy.

Chapter Twelve

While Jenn was securing Marisol for the night, Novak wandered over to the fridge and took out a couple of cold beers. Then he went exploring. Most of Jenn's safe houses were similar in setup. She had housed him in Belize at her own place on a private beach, but during his time with her, they had made several trips up into Mexico for maintenance and restocking of her covert sites. He had been to this very house once before for several days, remembered it well. It had a good floor plan that could meet any possible emergency or exigency. The architecture of her houses was usually different, but the hidey-holes and the escape hatches were not. He found the hidden door in the hallway and punched in the right code, holding the two icy bottles between his fingers as he climbed the steep, narrow steps that led up to the roof.

At the top of the stairs, he unlocked another heavy steel door and stepped out onto a private rooftop garden. Tall white lattice panels were erected all the way around, covered with more lush bougainvillea vines. More flowering plants were everywhere, of every type and hue, alongside palms and orange trees in giant pots. A glass-topped outdoor table with an orange market umbrella sat in the middle, strings of tiny solar lights attached under it. And there was the big double-wide hammock, an amenity that he and Jenn had used often and well while in the house, bodies entwined, gazing at the stars.

Novak placed the bottles down on the table and walked across to the east side that faced the ocean. Hinged doors in the lattice panels were always closed but could stand open to the breezes at night. He pulled them open and gazed out over the sea, blurry in the fading light, but gray and wild and restless, stretching all the way east to

Africa. Along the wide beach was a pedestrian boardwalk lit by a long line of lampposts that glowed like dinner tapers in the twilight. He wished he were out there in that inky dark sea. He wished he were still on his boat. He wished it wasn't sitting on the bottom of that cove. He missed it. He missed the swell of the waves under his feet. And that's what he was going to do, as soon as he got himself out of this god-awful mess he was in. Raise the *Sweet Sarah* and have her refitted.

The roof was a pleasant spot, cooled by soft ocean breezes, and a place where Novak knew Jenn spent her idle time. The safe house in which he'd lived for a time with Jenn also had a roof garden. Maybe different types of flowers, different furniture, different view, but basically the same. Both had nifty hidden retractable escape ladders that would get her and her asset down to the garage if the house was stormed from the front. Now, in the evening, the sea wind felt cool against his skin and the smell of the sea and Jenn's roses took over his senses.

"This always was your favorite spot, Novak. Especially at night."

Jenn was standing in the door, watching him. He sat down on the chaise longue and stretched out full length. It wasn't quite long enough for his legs. "Yeah. Fresh air and open spaces."

"Tell me about it. Not a man to be tied down."

Their gazes held, but not for long. Novak knew what she wanted to talk about so he changed the subject. "You still keep the motorcycles out there?"

Jenn sat down on the chair beside him. She leaned back and crossed those long, shapely bare legs of hers. She looked damn good doing it. Novak twisted the top off a beer and handed it to her. "Yes, I've still got them. Just two at the moment. My last asset took off on the small Suzuki. But the big Harley that you like so much? It's still here. They're all gassed up and ready to roll. Why? You taking off already?"

"I need to borrow one, the Harley, I guess. And I'm going to have to ask you for another big favor. Sorry."

"Okay, nothing I didn't expect. It's gonna get as dicey as ever with you back in the picture."

"You remember that resort area up the coast from Chetumal? The one off by itself with a couple of nice hotels? Near where the

American cruise ships dock and their passengers come ashore to swim and have beach parties?"

Jenn gave him a look. "What do you think? That's where I picked you up for extraction. You were lying out there on the sand, burning up with fever and a gunshot in the thigh. You looked half dead, Novak."

"Yes, I was half dead. Thanks again for saving my life."

"You're welcome."

"Look, I've been sitting here thinking about things and trying to second-guess this guy. He's onto us. We've already seen him here in the city. Pretty sure who he is now. Don't know why he's here, except that he wants that girl downstairs in the worst way. But he's coming at us and he's coming hard. Those hotels up there where you picked me up? I think that's where he'll put in. I think he's got some kind of big fast boat and that's how he got here so quickly."

"Why up there?"

"Because that's the place I picked for extraction. That's where I'd go if I were him. He's a pro. He'll know his boat won't be noticed there like it would be inside the city center. It's an inlet off the ocean, and I remember there's a ton of marinas where he could tie up and never be noticed. I think he's already docked there and rented a car at one of those hotels and found a way to track us. Maybe he's got satellite surveillance connections somewhere, somebody important helping him. Maybe even the Mexican government is in on this somehow. I don't know. I just know he shows up everywhere we go."

"I can see how he'd rather dock up there," Jenn said. "That strip runs a good three or four miles along the coast. Very Americanized. Lots of tourists, lots of bars and nightclubs and nightlife. Lots of noise and excitement. Crowded. Not many locals. So what do you have in mind?"

"I want you to go up there with me, pick a hotel, and get me a suite with at least two bedrooms. Has to have a good ocean view and a balcony. Top floor, if possible. Those marinas are spread out right in front of the hotels, all across the bay, if I recall. I want to set up surveillance. See if I can spot him. He's docked up there, I can feel it. Probably laying low after missing us today, and looking to locate us again. I'd book the room myself, but I'd stand out. People have a tendency to remember me because of my size. I don't want anybody to remember me. He's going to inquire around about me."

"Oh, you're memorable all right, Novak. But you're just guessing, right? You're not sure he's up there?"

Novak tipped the bottle up, took a sip. He focused his gaze out on the dark horizon. "Maybe he is. Maybe not. It's just a gut feeling, but I trust my gut, always have. This guy, this Mayan? Pretty sure now that he likes to travel by water. That's how he got into that pirate camp where we were being held. Paddled in with that canoe and spent the evening slitting the throats of every single man and woman he laid eyes on. I stopped counting corpses and concentrated on getting the hell out of there. We were damn lucky we didn't end up dead that night. If he'd found us when we were chained up in that hut, he would've finished us off."

Leaning back in her chair, Jenn got quiet. She just stared out over the ocean for a while. "You have always been lucky, Will. A dozen people plus dead, and you didn't hear any of it go down?"

"I heard nothing. Not until that Liu woman started screaming like you wouldn't believe. Awful, agonized shrieks that echoed through the jungle, shrill enough to raise the hair on my arms. So we moved faster and made it to the beach. That's where I saw the bodies scattered around, his fresh kills. All were young men, all armed, all guards at their posts. Yet he managed to get them, one at a time, slit their gullets and slice off their hair. The scalping thing doesn't fit, either. I can't figure why he'd take the time to do that. No need, as far as I can figure. Seemed like overkill, and too theatrical for a professional like he's supposed to be."

"Only you can get yourself into this kind of thing, Novak." Jenn sighed and took a drink.

Night was falling rapidly now. He could hear a bird squawking somewhere off behind them. Probably a big macaw, caged up and wishing it wasn't. He listened to the soft lull of the tide, washing up on the sand, receding into the whole again. The smell of the sea made him long to be back on the ocean again.

"So you believe her now?" Jenn asked. "That this guy is an assassin and he's after her because her father wants her dead? Can't imagine a father doing that, but he is a brutal son of a bitch, they say."

"The tattoo pretty much nailed it down for me. I'm not sure she's capable of telling the truth. I think she's been lying so long that she doesn't know how to tell the truth anymore. She came out of the water that night and woke up making up stories."

"And you're still dragging her around, because . . . ?"

"Initially, I just felt sorry for her. And obligated to help her. That guy knocked the hell out of her. She should've had a mild concussion, at the very least. Maybe she does have one and that's confusing her thoughts. I've been trying to figure her out and what I should believe. But she was a kid out there, alone and scared, with nowhere to turn. That's why I stepped in. For better or worse."

"For worse, I'd say." Jenn sighed again. "Ah, the softhearted knight returns. Might've been better if you'd turned her over to the authorities before this guy started trying to kill you. Let them deal with her."

"Don't think that didn't occur to me. I had pretty much decided to drop her off at a police station somewhere, when they commandeered my boat. Didn't have a clue that playing Good Samaritan was gonna turn into a life-and-death duel with a butcher. But it's done. Nothing I can do about it now."

Jenn watched him. "He's already here in Chetumal. You sure you lost him today? Should we move her to a different safe house?"

"I think we lost him. But he's damn good. You know that night he accosted those pirates? I figure he had a bigger boat anchored offshore somewhere but close to the cove, a small yacht, maybe. He launched his canoe from there. He had to have a boat to get up here this fast. No cars were on that beach, no roads to the interior that I saw. I think after I stole his canoe, he made his way back to the other vessel, maybe even swam out to it, and started tracking us. GPS coordinates, most likely. Thought I stopped that when I smashed up the phone we found in his knapsack. But he's got some way he's doing it now. We've got to figure out how or he'll dog us everywhere we go."

"Well, tell you one thing. I, for one, do not want to meet up with him. Ever. Can't say I want you to meet up with him, either. Or that girl downstairs, as far as that goes. So okay, we'll check out those marinas and hope you're right. And maybe you should burn that knapsack and everything inside it."

"Good idea. I'll do that." Novak looked over at her. "It's always busy up there along that strip, or used to be, anyway. Lots of boats coming in off the ocean and docking at the marinas for the big beach parties. The streets are crowded. The hotel balcony gives me a place where I can spot him before he spots me."

"Then what?"

"Then I'm going to steal his boat. That should slow him up a good bit."

"And if you're wrong about him being there?"

"Then I'll figure out where else he might be."

Jenn nodded. "Okay, but we've got to find out how he's finding us. This time was way too close for comfort. Do you think the girl is contacting him somehow? Working with him, maybe? And what about that other girl you saw? How does she fit in?"

"I don't have a clue. But I could have sworn she was signaling to Marisol. Maybe not. Maybe there was somebody else between them that she was waving at. Maybe I'm wrong. But he was already there, already had a car, and was searching the surrounding streets for us. It shocked me that he had found us that fast, that he was on the same block. My God, we had just gotten there ourselves. Marisol had run there at random, or so it seemed." He finished off the beer and turned to Jenn. "What about available cars?"

"I have vehicles stashed all over the city. Two right here, out back in that garage. A black Toyota Camry and a small dark blue Hyundai hatchback. Both suitably nondescript, legally licensed, and insured. I have six more in the area, some in storage garages. Plenty of weapons and other equipment, too. As you know from last time."

"Surveillance equipment?"

"The best made."

"You are mighty good at what you do, Jenn."

"I know. Glad you finally noticed."

Novak grinned. "Okay, you take the hatchback, and I'll take the Harley. You still got my jacket and helmet?"

Jenn nodded. "Oh yeah, with the bloodstains and everything. I kept them for sentimental value. Everything's out there with the bike. Nobody's gonna recognize you with the visor down."

"Which hotel's gonna be the best for surveillance?"

"One of them is about three stories tall, and the other is five floors, I think. The tall one's probably the most suitable. Called the Bahia del Sol. Nice place, top quality, luxury rating, probably four stars. It's the best bet for privacy. Usually crowded with Americans and Brits. Some other Europeans. And the balconies are big, covered, and give a panoramic view of those marinas you're so interested in."

"Perfect. That's what I thought." Novak felt better. He wanted to do something—go on the offensive. Tired of playing defense. The Mayan had been making the plays. Time to switch roles and shake the killer up a bit. "What about leaving the girl in the hold alone? Is that too risky, you think? Could he get to her here while we're gone?"

"I would normally say no, definitely no way, but this guy you've got chasing you? He's a damn bloodhound. If you really managed to lose him, she'll be fine here. I'll lock her in the hold and there's no way she can get out or he can get in. Not without blowing the door. Maybe he won't find us so fast this time. You took precautions when you came here, right? Hopefully, we can get you set up at the Bahia del Sol before he finds this house. As for Marisol, she's got enough of everything to survive for over a month. I'll be back in a matter of hours anyway. Unless you need me to stay up there and watch your back."

"I just need you to call in that reservation, go get me the key, and make sure you get the top floor. Use an untraceable credit card under one of your assumed names. Tell them that we're a married couple, in case they see us together."

"No problem."

"How far are we talking about? I can't remember."

"Thirty or forty minutes, depending on traffic. An hour from down here at the most."

"Okay, let's go. You can bet our Mayan friend isn't sitting still. He's trying to pick us up again right now."

It did take almost an hour. Jenn pulled up in front of the Bahia del Sol Hotel in a worn and dirty 2010 Hyundai hatchback and parked across the street. Novak left his cycle, crossed the road, and slid into the front seat beside her. There were people moving around everywhere, most of them dressed in shorts and T-shirts and skimpy bathing suits and flip flops. Crowds surrounded food carts along the main walkways, and the aroma of tamales and tacos was making Novak's stomach growl. Novak had arrived first on the Harley and had done a quick reconnoiter around the hotel before Jenn had gotten there.

It hadn't taken Novak long to locate a back entrance of a fairly isolated parking lot on the south side of the hotel. He had waited there for Jenn, sitting on the chopper under some impressive royal palms and watching the hotel's side door long enough to know that nobody much used it. It was accessible by swiping a hotel card key. Novak told Jenn to go do her stuff and watched her cross the busy street and enter the front lobby.

Once Novak found the coast clear, he got out, ran across to the Harley, fired her up, and then headed down south along the street hugging the beaches. He rode in heavy traffic for about a mile and then circled around through deserted back alleys toward the hotel. The area had been built up some since he had lain on that beach, bleeding and sweating and half delirious with fever. Lots more restaurants than there had been before, lots more clubs, lots more bars, and lots more people. Now, on a warm and pleasant night, everything was hopping. That was a good thing. Nobody even glanced at him.

By the time he returned to the hotel, there were a few more cars in the parking lot, but it looked like the weekend guests had already arrived, probably the night before, checked in, and settled in their rooms. He parked the bike under the same palm trees, half hidden by a stand of white azaleas. He waited there, leaning against the Harley, until he saw the hotel's side door push out and Jenn step into view. Novak stood up and walked swiftly toward her, zigzagging through the parked vehicles. She handed him the card key, the credit card, and a thick roll of cash. Then she picked up the satchel full of the equipment he had requested and handed it over.

"Be careful, Novak," she said. "This guy's a psycho of the highest degree."

"Don't I know it. You be careful, too. I'll call you as soon as I locate his boat. Keep your eyes open. Don't take chances. He might already be out there, tracking the kid somehow. Watch your back."

"I know what I'm doing."

True. She had never lost a prisoner, a witness, or an undercover operative, not to Novak's knowledge.

"Well, good luck," she said. "Hope you're right about the boat, but there are lots of marinas in Chetumal besides the ones up here. It's a long shot, if you ask me. But you've got good instincts. I know that better than most."

"I think I'm right about this. I feel it. But if he doesn't show, I'll move on to plan B."

Jenn nodded, turned, and walked swiftly down a sidewalk that led around the hotel's kidney-shaped swimming pool and eventually meandered through some flower gardens. There was another hotel exit at the other end of the sidewalk and it seemed to be the one that most of the guests preferred to use, probably because of its proximity to the pool and playground area. He watched Jenn out of sight and then didn't waste any more time. He swiped the key and stepped inside. Empty ground floor corridor. Completely quiet and cool. Nobody around. Lots of doors to lots of rooms, all closed. No guest elevators in sight, but there was a freight elevator sitting empty about ten yards down the adjacent hallway, so Novak boarded it in a hurry and rode up to the top floor. Hadn't seen a soul. Everybody out sightseeing and partying and eating burritos. Everybody but him. So far, so good.

The suite Jenn had reserved was at the south end of the hall, last room on the left, facing the sea. Novak swiped the key again and ducked inside. He breathed easier. As far as he could tell, nobody had seen him. Talk about a stroke of good luck. Nobody wanted to hang around inside a hotel room, not with a fun-filled tropical night just outside their doors. Not so good were the security cameras he'd seen in the hallways. None inside the freight elevator, so he'd continue to use it. If his luck held out, nobody but Jenn would know he was there.

Inside the spacious suite, it smelled like stale canned air. But it was cool enough. The suite looked pretty good. Large and luxurious. On the modern side, all white and black and gray. Big black sectional with a built-in recliner and an oversize chaise on one end. Modular white chairs. Modern art that looked like splashes of red and yellow paint dribbled down a white canvas. Two bedrooms with their own baths. A living area separating the bedrooms and replete with a big-screen TV and wet bar. A small galley kitchen with stainless steel appliances. Fancy. A lot more so than most hotels in rural Mexico, especially the Hotel Lagoon. Not the Ritz-Carlton, by any stretch of the imagination, but suitable for his purpose. He wasn't going to stay long, anyway.

The suite had two balconies facing in two different directions because it was located on a corner. Even better. The living room balcony overlooked the marinas; the other balcony was in the master bedroom and gave him a bird's-eye view of the grounds below, the swimming pool, and his Harley. He could gaze almost the entire length of the street that ran in front of the hotel. He could see at least four marinas in the bay just across the street, side by side, one after another. A myriad of tall masts looked like a leafless forest out on the water. He would check out every boat in every one of those marinas. This was where he'd put in if he were an assassin on the hunt. Totally anonymous. The assassin would be crazy to choose a dock inside the city center, where police patrolled the streets.

Novak placed Jenn's duffel bag down on the floor near the big French doors and pulled out the high-powered binoculars that she'd provided. Top-of-the-line, military quality, night vision—perfect for surveillance. God bless her little heart. He opened the balcony doors and stood there a moment, breathing in the sea and the warm night air. It smelled good; it tasted good. He didn't want to set up outside on the balcony where he could be spotted by a professional like the Mayan, but he really didn't need to. He just needed to set up a nice little surveillance station inside the doors, where he could watch for his prey undetected. He felt sure he was on the right track. His instincts were usually pretty good. It was worth a shot, in any case. He wanted to be the hunter for a change, not the hunted. The Mayan had taken the offense long enough.

Unfolding two tripods, he attached the field glasses to one and a digital camera with a powerful zoom lens to the other. Then he pulled up a dining room chair. Before he sat down, he stood there for several moments and eyeballed the wide bay spread out below. Lights spangled the road like a sparkling diamond necklace. The height of the hotel gave him a great vantage point. The bay was big, shaped almost like a heart, stretching out in both directions, maybe four city blocks wide. On the north curve of the arc that ran out to sea, there was an ocean break formed from large gray concrete blocks shaped like ginger jars. It closed off the shallow part of the inlet and left a deeper channel for large oceangoing vessels and private pleasure craft.

Directly in front of him, the docked boats were tied up on either side of long and narrow planked piers, across from each other. They looked like pigs feeding at floating troughs. Lots of them. A good place to hide a boat, any boat. The Mayan would know that. He had proven his merit already. Novak was pretty good himself, but he figured most of the Yucatan Peninsula was the Mayan's stomping grounds. He better remember what this guy was capable of, but he was going to get him. No doubt about it. Half a dozen large yachts were anchored off the far ends of the piers, out in the deeper water. The Mayan was out there somewhere, in that giant mass of masts. Novak felt it. He knew it. And he was going to find him.

Shrugging out of the leather jacket, he pulled out a bottle of ice-cold water from the mini fridge. He twisted the cap and drank about half of it, and then he put it aside and sat down, ready for a long, boring surveillance. He started sweeping the boats tied up right in front of him. The Mayan would not be registered in either hotel. He'd stay on his boat. Safer that way. That's what Novak would do under optimum conditions. More private, and all calibers of firepower hidden belowdecks, nice and handy and deadly. If the killer was smart, he'd also have his gangplank booby-trapped, in case anybody tried to surprise him while he slept. Novak had his own homemade alarm system on the *Sweet Sarah*.

If the killer had lost sight of them now, as Novak suspected, the guy just might hide himself in a busy marina while he nailed down his next move. He was ritualistic, it appeared. Who he really was and evidence of his nefarious deeds were likely inside that boat. Novak had a feeling he and the Mayan might have some instincts in common, as well as a strong sense of self-preservation. But time would tell.

Novak sat guard until the sun rose over the sea. Now it was quiet and deserted. People were still in bed. He took a break and drank more water, made himself coffee out of the little pot in the kitchen. Ate a small box of Nutter Butter cookies that he found in the mini-bar. Then he sat down and took up his post again. A lot of the boats below looked battened down and deserted. More time passed. Mid-morning and first day of vacation at a beautiful resort with a glorious turquoise sea waiting right outside their doors. Some boat owners were beginning to stir, others were probably sleeping off last night's drunk. Looked like some were opting for the big brunches offered by the hotels.

It was a gorgeous day, already warm, probably in the low eighties. Blue sky, not a cloud anywhere to be seen, just hot sun blazing down and making the water shine and glitter like a giant aquamarine slab.

A good day for tourists to do just about anything they wanted. If the Mayan was hunkered down in one of the boats out there, he'd have to show himself eventually. He would have to get up and go out and find Novak and the girl. His boat probably wouldn't be particularly big or fancy. It would just be a typical craft on the outside, just like any seafaring sailor would choose, but with a killer's deadly lair down below. Novak would soon see. Because he was going to sail it home to the bayous. That wouldn't stop the Mayan, but at least Novak would be on his home turf when the killer came to get it back.

So he sat there alone, in dead silence, the corridor outside quiet except for a door opening or closing now and then. He kept scanning the berths below, back and forth, stopping on any person who happened out on deck or walked toward the street. He settled himself in for a long and thorough, precise search of each boat, slow, careful, and rarely taking his eyes off the scene. After an hour passed, more people swarmed the street below. Boat owners began coming up on their decks and moving around. Ten o'clock. Up for the day. Ready for sightseeing or visiting ancient Spanish cathedrals or stretching out on the sandy beach at the south end of the boulevard. The Mayan wouldn't be doing any of that. He'd be lying in wait, just like Novak was, sharpening his green obsidian blade, no doubt. But it wasn't going to sever Novak's scalp, or Marisol's, either, and especially not Jenn's, not if things turned out the way Novak hoped.

So he sat there. Alone. Hours and hours, watching and waiting and searching. He got up several times and paced around, stretched his muscles, drank more water, ate a package of peanuts, and then he went back to work. Jenn had texted twice, telling him she got back fine and everything looked okay. Marisol had showered and was sleeping and cooperating. Behaving herself. Nobody had come calling, not yet, anyway.

Novak kept his attention on the marinas. He tried to get into the killer's mind. What kind of boat would he prefer to use for his deadly missions? Probably not a sailboat like Novak's. Probably something faster and sleeker, but not too fast and not too sleek. Nothing noticeable or memorable. He'd want something dependable, something with lots of horsepower, something that would get him away from his crime scenes in a hurry, without looking showy or remarkable. He would not draw attention to himself in any way. He would want to blend in, but he would need a home base large enough to stow his canoe and his weapons. And that place would be on his boat. Novak started searching below for vessels with clamps on the hull or stern designed to stow a canoe. Most likely, though, the guy would keep the canoe hidden under a tarp.

Novak watched until his eyes burned with fatigue. He was near exhaustion. Boaters were moving about everywhere now, sitting on their stern decks, some barbecuing, some having cocktails with friends. Novak dismissed any craft with more than one person aboard. The Mayan would work alone. No witnesses. No survivors. He would want to make sure nobody could describe him to the authorities. Might be the reason he was after the girl. She had seen him, up close and personal, when he had killed Diego Ortiz, attacked her, and knocked her into the sea. She could describe him. Novak could, too. He'd seen him in that car, would now recognize him anywhere. The Mayan was a phantom, a mystery to everybody. He would want to keep it that way. So Novak began skipping over the crowds and paying closer attention to the deserted craft or those with a single person on deck.

Two more hours passed, and Novak barely moved, not until he heard a soft tap on his door. Then he came out of his chair fast, the Ruger off the table and gripped in his hand. He moved to the door. He didn't peek out the eyehole, not with this guy. That might get him a bullet through the eyeball. It could be Jenn or it could be a maid. He pressed back on one side of the door. "Is that my steak?"

Jenn would know the appropriate response. Unless she was being forced to betray him, with a gun held to her head. That was unlikely, not with Jenn's skills, but Novak never took chances. Her voice came back, very low. "Yes, sir. Well done with sautéed onions."

Novak unhooked the chain, then the dead bolt, but he still held the gun on her as she entered. He closed the door and reset the locks.

"What the hell, Jenn? Did he come back?"

"No. I brought you that steak, onions and all." She grinned. "You haven't eaten anything, have you?"

"What about the kid?"

"She's fine. Watching Mexican soap operas. Happy as a lark. She was painting her toenails pink when I left."

"You shouldn't be here. It's too risky. Were you followed?"

Jenn scoffed. "Whatta you think, Novak?"

"I think you should've stayed in the safe house like I told you to."

"I don't answer to you. You came to me for help, so stow the caveman attitude. Besides, you need someone to spell you on surveillance or you'll get careless and miss your target. I had Marisol describe him to me in detail right before I came up here. I can watch while you get some sleep. And don't tell me you don't need sleep. Your eyes look shot all to hell."

Novak just stared down at her. She was right. He was dead on his feet, so tired he could barely think straight anymore. He needed to close his eyes, all right. He hadn't had much sleep—next to none, in fact. On the other hand, he needed to find that boat before the Mayan found him. "Okay, thanks, Jenn. Sorry I got you mixed up in this."

"It's my job to mix it up with bad guys. I'm ready and able to help you. Just like I was the last time. But I don't want a partner who's dead on his feet and making mistakes."

Novak stared at her some more. She looked good—fresh, beautiful, tough. She was one of the few women he'd gotten close to since Sarah had died. Jenn hadn't wanted anything from him back then, just some companionship, but no commitment. But they liked each other. She had known from the beginning how he felt about his dead wife. She hadn't made demands. That's the way she had wanted it five years ago. That's the way Novak still wanted it. He watched Jenn pull a white Styrofoam box out of a brown paper sack and place it down on the small table in front of the bar.

"Better eat this before it gets cold. Then get some shut-eye while you can. You look like crap, Novak. You need to clean yourself up and lie down and quit arguing with me. I brought you some shaving gear."

When she sat down in the chair he'd just vacated and placed her eyes to the binoculars, Novak did what she said. He was hungry now that he smelled the food, and he was dead on his feet. She was right about that, too. It felt like three months since this ordeal had begun. So he ate the T-bone steak and the baked potato smothered in butter and the salad and drank the double coffee, and then he got up and lay down on the couch near Jenn. He remained fully clothed and kept the gun right beside his hand. The Mayan was not a guy to underestimate. He might be figuring out that Novak's next move was stealing his boat. Novak would be stupid not to consider that. But he had to rest, even if for only a few minutes. Forcing himself to relax muscles that had been tense for hours wasn't so easy. He stretched out full length on the oversize sectional's chaise and lay still and stared up at the pale yellow stucco ceiling, listened to the air conditioner click on. The minute he shut his eyes, he slept.

Chapter Thirteen

Novak slept like a dead man for going on four hours. Jenn sat guard at the binoculars and glimpsed neither hide nor hair of the Mayan or anyone remotely resembling his description. As soon as Novak opened his eyes, he rolled off the chaise, wide awake and wary. Jenn glanced at him and then went back to watching the boats. He stood up, stretched his stiff muscles, and then walked into the bathroom, showered, washed his hair, brushed his teeth with the new toothbrush Jenn had provided, and got dressed in clean civilian clothes, also from Jenn. Dark blue denim shirt, 3X XLong, and a pair of faded jeans. Socks and a new pair of black Adidas running shoes. She thought of everything. He stared at the dark whiskers covering his jaw but didn't shave. He did not want to look like the photograph Li Liu had taken in the jungle camp, just in case the Mayan had found it and had enough smarts to put Novak's face on a wanted poster. Novak was on the run now.

When he got back to the living room, Jenn still sat motionlessly at the open balcony doors, attention glued on the marina below. "Thanks, Jenn. I mean it. I needed that break, if I'm going to outlast this guy."

"You were out for the count and it was beginning to show." Jenn stood up, swiveled her head around, and rolled her stiff shoulders. She stretched her arms up over her head. Her shirt hiked up and revealed her toned and tanned midriff. Novak knew her body well. He knew from experience how firm her flesh was, how soft her skin felt, how she tasted, how she smelled, and how she responded to his touch. He caught his thought process right there and averted his eyes.

No time for that, but he wished there was. He transferred his gaze out to the long piers and docked boats and kept it there.

"Unfortunately," said Jenn, "I didn't see anybody who looked remotely like the Mayan or any boat that looked the least bit suspicious. I did see, say, a thousand tourists all dressed alike and traipsing around everywhere. Not many men showed up walking by themselves. Couples, families, groups of girls—lots of them. Nothing out of the ordinary. Now that you're awake and fresh as a daisy and might be a functioning human being again, I'm going back home and make sure the little lying princess is behaving herself. She's probably scared by now and thinks we've abandoned her out there all by her lonesome. I'll take the Harley and leave you the Hyundai. You'll have better cover with it."

"Okay. Watch out for Marisol and her drama. Did you check out any of her story?"

"Found out that Marisol was registered at University of Miami for a semester. Left abruptly right before finals. Sounds like that part was true."

Novak hesitated for a second, but he went ahead and said it. "The last thing I want is for you to get hurt, Jenn. And not just because you're coming through for me."

"Why then?"

"You know why."

Jenn studied his face for a moment. "Well, ditto right back at you. But right now, we're stuck with her, and you know it. Who's gonna take her into their fold with a serial killer hot on her trail? Nobody but you, Novak. You just concentrate on being careful. And please, hurry up and get this guy. I can think of better things we could be doing."

Novak could, too. Maybe not the same ones she was thinking of. Probably not the same ones. "Just be careful," he said, "and keep the burner phone close. I've got the distinct feeling something's gonna happen and happen soon, and it's not gonna be good."

"Me too. But I'm always ready to move. You know that. Quit worrying about me and take that blasted SOB out. You've got the sniper rifle, right?"

"Yeah. Loaded and ready."

"Well, use it on him, for God's sake. This guy's got a whole string of cold-blooded murders to answer for. The death penalty's probably too good for him."

Then she grabbed her purse and left him standing there without saying goodbye. When the door closed behind her, Novak reset all the locks and sat down again in the chair in front of the binoculars. Night had fallen now, the sea black and impenetrable once more, the light posts along the piers and busy street blinking on. Novak was getting antsy. Maybe he had been wrong. Maybe the guy was anchored somewhere offshore like before. Maybe he had a second canoe to bring him ashore. Deep down, though, Novak trusted his instincts. The Mayan had gotten to a car and found them, and in record time. He had to have come by sea. Novak went by his hunches. He wasn't giving up on his gut, not yet.

So he sat in sheer silence, listening to the traffic passing on the street below.

He stared into the marina until his eyes crossed, scanning for men who walked alone or relaxed on a boat alone. If the killer didn't expect Novak to go after his boat, he would still consider himself the stalker, the one with the advantage. He probably wouldn't take undue precautions to secure it, either. He was here to find and kill Novak and the girl. He had seen them. He knew they were somewhere in the vicinity. The killer was probably salivating at the idea of obtaining a couple more scalps. Wouldn't get much with Novak's military cut. He didn't know the full extent of Novak's military past, probably only what he got off Li Liu's phone and computer. Therefore, it stood to reason that he didn't know who he was up against. That was a good thing.

Almost an hour later, a guy who looked a hell of a lot like the Mayan finally showed himself on the stern deck of a midsize ocean yacht in the third row of the hotel's marina, a few degrees to the right of Novak's vantage point. The guy was a good match: same height, same weight, same light tread. The stealthy way he moved was the giveaway.

The sea was calm. The evening was quiet, except for the crowd gathered at a beach party somewhere, their cheers and cries muted and far away. The tide was low. Novak clicked about a dozen photos of the guy as he walked to the foot of his gangplank and took some time searching the street above and the surrounding boats. He had a pair of binoculars, too. Novak's fingers itched with the desire to pick up the rifle propped beside him and put the assassin in his crosshairs, pull the trigger, and put him down for good. It took a minute or two to conquer that impulse. He wanted to know more about him first. He wanted to know who he answered to and why they wanted Marisol dead, so much so that they'd chase her all over the Caribbean. After about ten more minutes, the Mayan went below, stayed there about thirty minutes, and then came up top, crossed the gangplank, and jumped down on the floating dock. Then he headed at a swift clip up the pier toward the street.

Novak took a few more pictures of the boat and the killer. The yacht had its name painted in reflective letters: *Calakmul*. Novak wasn't familiar with the word, but it sure as hell sounded Mayan. Maybe Jenn could translate it. The boat claimed Cancun as its port city. A nice steady craft, but similar to dozens of other boats tied up around it. White with red stripes, a popular color choice; maybe a hundred other boats in the marinas pretty much matched it. But it was the exact type of boat Novak had figured the guy would choose. It looked fast and sleek and powerful enough to get somebody away from a bloody crime scene, all engines full steam ahead. It was bigger than the *Sweet Sarah* but not as large as most yachts. It would be comfortable for one or two people, maybe three, maybe even half a dozen, but Novak bet nobody still living and breathing had ever stepped aboard. A floating torture dungeon—that's what Novak would probably find when he got below on her. He was going to enjoy sending it to the bottom.

Relieved that he finally found his prey, Novak shoved the Ruger into his back waistband, settled his shirt down over it, and took off. He had to get down to the grounds before the Mayan made it to the parking lot. He wanted to see where he was going and he wanted to get a piece of him, up close and personal. If the killer had a home base nearby or a contact who was feeding him Marisol's coordinates, Novak was going to put them out of commission. He took the stairs down to the ground, three at a time, swinging around the landings at each floor and moving about as fast as he could move. He felt good, refreshed, and ready to roll. He had him now, and he wasn't going to lose him. He exited the hotel at the side door to the parking lot where Jenn had left the Hyundai. Cars were parked everywhere, giving him lots of cover, so he darted in between them, his attention focused across the street and latched onto the concrete steps up which the Mayan would have to climb to street level. He hadn't appeared yet, so Novak hightailed it to the car, fired it up, rolled it out of the parking space, and stopped at the end of the row. He idled there, half hidden in shadows, his eyes glued on the steps across the highway.

The Mayan reached street level a minute later. Novak lifted the binoculars and got his first good look at the guy's face when he passed under a light. He looked like a Mayan, all right. Novak was pretty sure he had ancestors who had come straight out of the ancient Yucatan jungles—Tulum, maybe, or Chichen Itza. He was small in stature, looked five feet five inches or so, light on his feet, wiry and strong, and probably as quick as he was stealthy. He had sneaked up on the guards and made short work of them in bloody, horrendous ways, without a single alarm sounded.

The guy walked at a casual pace now, not soliciting undue attention. He was dressed like any other tourist around, in stone-washed denim jeans and a plain black T-shirt. White sneakers. His hair was long and straight and black as the nocturnal ocean behind him, and held back at his nape. He had a small backpack slung over one shoulder, probably where he kept his ritualistic green obsidian blade and maybe a few bloody scalps. Novak had no doubt that this guy was a born psychopath, a stone-cold killer who enjoyed his work, went about it in a workaday fashion. Didn't matter who, didn't matter when, didn't matter where, and didn't matter if it was a man, a woman, or a child. Quiet, personified brutality. At that moment, Novak decided that he had to kill him. But first things first.

Novak needed to know where the guy was headed. His biggest fear was that the killer had already tracked the girl to Jenn's safe house. Once Novak got the two women out of the way and knew they were safe, he could get the Mayan at his leisure. Maybe he could catch him unawares on the boat and get a few answers out of him before he died. Somehow he didn't think so. Better bet might be to take his boat, pick up the women, and get the hell out of Mexican waters. He could come back for the Mayan on his own.

Novak watched the Mayan cross the street and stride down the marina's parking lot. Halfway to the back, he stopped and looked around and then headed at a fast clip for the back row. He stopped beside the same white Subaru Outback that Novak had last seen on the streets of Chetumal. He unlocked the car by clicking a keychain from some distance away, a brand-new vehicle, it looked like, probably leased under a false name. Novak watched the guy get in and start the motor. The lights flashed on, and he rolled out toward the highway.

The vehicle was plain, nothing out of the ordinary. This guy knew how to blend in like a native Mexican and do his deadly work like the ghost of a Mayan priest. And what he was doing was killing for hire. Not for long, not if Novak got his way. The women were safe for now, and Novak had all the time in the world to stalk his stalker and take his time taking the guy out.

The Outback pulled out into traffic and headed south toward the beach party. Novak wanted to find out if the Mayan was really employed by Arturo Ruiz. See if Marisol's story held up. He was having trouble believing any man would want to take out his own daughter. Novak was going to find out the truth. He waited until three cars had come between him and the Subaru, and then he pulled out and kept his eyes glued on the guy's taillights. He drove the speed limit, sure as hell not wanting to be picked up by the cops. So did the Mayan.

In time, the Mayan hung a right off the highway and pulled into a pharmacy parking lot. He parked in front, got out, shopped around five minutes or so, paid, and came back out carrying a large sack. Then he turned out onto the main drag until he got to the area with all the nightlife. It was crowded, everybody on the sidewalks laughing and having a good old time. Not long after, Novak watched him turn left into an Applebee's restaurant. The place had lots of customers coming and going. Novak drove past the entrance and turned around at a gasoline station down the street. He drove back and pulled into Applebee's by a different entrance.

Parking in the shadows along the street, Novak watched through the restaurant's big plate-glass windows as the killer chose a booth, one in which his back would be against a wall and from where he could see the Subaru. He ordered from the menu and then took some time punching numbers into a cell phone. He sat there for some time, staring down at the screen, and then put the phone down when his food arrived. He ate alone and quickly, staring down at his plate. Occasionally, he glanced out at the car. After he was done, he was given a sack of carry-out, after which he paid for the meal, left the building, and returned to the Outback. Just a normal tourist out for dinner.

Novak kept out of sight and waited. Maybe the guy had just been hungry and would now head back to the boat. That would be good. Maybe he didn't know where Marisol and Jenn were, after all. Or maybe he was going on the hunt again. Maybe he was waiting for coordinates from whoever was tracking Marisol.

The Mayan did not turn north and head back to the marina. He went south again, heading down the highway toward the northern suburbs of Chetumal. Novak pulled out and tailed him. They were passing lots of trendy restaurants and nightclubs and theaters, the party spots, mostly built up around American businesses. Lots of the tourists were off the cruise ships, no doubt about it. The sidewalks were thronged with mostly young people out on the town and strolling about in large groups, probably a lot of them up from the city. Novak could hear mariachi bands playing in the outdoor cafes. Maybe the killer liked the nightlife. Maybe he was going to pick up a hooker and take her back to the boat and scalp her. Maybe that was how he amused himself on his off hours.

The Mayan didn't do any of those things. He just kept driving, slowly and carefully, until he reached the city limits of Chetumal and stopped at a four-way intersection. Then he turned inland and headed up a ramp and onto the same four-lane highway that had brought Novak into town on the bus. Novak followed the car, staying thirty or forty yards behind the Subaru. Twenty minutes later, the guy took an off-ramp down onto another busy street, and then he circled back toward the ocean. By that time, Novak had begun to get a bad feeling. Because it now looked to him as if the Mayan was heading, in a roundabout way, for Jenn's safe house. Novak didn't wait to find out. They were about six city blocks from Jenn's street now. The traffic had cleared as they neared the beach communities and hotels.

Novak jerked out his phone and punched in Jenn's number. When she picked up, he said, "Get out, Jenn. Go out through the tunnel. He's headed straight for you right now. About a mile away. Get Marisol and get the hell out. I'll meet you where we had that picnic in the rain. You know it."

"Yes," she said, and then she hung up and got busy. She would get the girl out to the car that she kept gassed up and head out through the back alley. She had probably followed the same getaway procedure dozens of times during her career. Marisol would be okay.

But this meant that the Mayan knew exactly where she was. How the hell had he located her? How the devil was he tracking them? If he could track them with this kind of pinpoint accuracy, they would never get away from him.

Novak considered his options and then chose the best one. He picked up his phone again and dialed up the local police station. When a man answered at the other end, Novak spoke in Spanish. "There's a man out on Avenida Alvaro Obregon. Just past the intersection at Revolución. He's driving a white Subaru Outback. He's small and short and he's wearing a black T-shirt and jeans and a ponytail. He's got a gun and he's shooting at people out of the car window. He's already wounded a lady! Hurry, you got to help us! I think she's dead!"

"What's your name, sir?"

As if. "Hurry, please, she's dying. Now he's shooting again. Everybody's running. He's coming this way. Hurry, please!"

"Help is on the way, sir. Please give me your name—"

Novak hung up, and within three minutes, he heard a distant police siren coming his way. He braked and pulled over, and then he took the battery out of the cell phone, opened the door, and dropped it on the ground. He pulled out into traffic again, waited several minutes, then threw the phone out the window in front of an oncoming truck. A police car came into sight in his rearview mirror and then roared by him. Flashing lights were already visible ahead, where it looked like the cops were converging on the Outback. Maybe Novak would get lucky, after all. Maybe the Mayan had a cache of drugs hidden under the seat or a bag full of illegal weapons. Maybe he had some scalps in his backpack, or the green obsidian blade that he planned to use on Marisol. But for now, thank God, the killer had been waylaid by the Mexican authorities and would likely be tied up for some time. Novak had a window of opportunity to get to the women and figure out how the Mayan was tracking them.

Novak turned off about two side streets from the commotion ahead, and then he headed back toward the Parque Ecológico, where he and Jenn had their picnic so long ago. The park had very few visitors after dark. Jenn and Marisol would be hard for anybody but him to find out there in the darkness. He knew exactly where Jenn would be. He drove slowly and carefully, eyes on the rearview mirror, sure as hell not wanting to attract any undue attention.

Fortunately, the park looked pretty much deserted. Novak turned in to the nearest entrance and followed the meandering tarmac road. It was a nice place, and he had enjoyed it when Jenn showed him around. He had still been walking with a cane that day. He took the path to the right when the road forked. Jenn would get to the park first. Novak trusted her ability, especially when she was on her home turf and doing her thing. He came to a gravel utility road, one that led him back into a small copse of trees. Jenn's RV was parked on the shoulder about thirty yards in, almost invisible in the darkness.

Jenn got out of the driver's seat the minute his headlights hit her vehicle. She started walking swiftly toward his car. Novak killed the lights and got out.

"What the hell's going on, Novak? Nobody's ever found one of my safe houses before."

"I don't think he found it through any mistake we made. I think he found it through the girl."

Novak strode past her and opened the door of the motor home and then stepped up into the Winnebago. Jenn remained outside on watch, but held the door open. The light inside was on, and the girl was sitting in the same place she'd been before, right before she had jumped out and run off. "What the hell's going on, Marisol?"

Novak was damn pissed off now, because she had to have been the one who alerted the Mayan. She was going to tell him how she'd done it, and more important, why she'd done it. The girl pressed herself farther back into the chair, acting terrified. But she wasn't terrified. She was watching him and calculating how much she could get by with. "What's wrong? Why are you yelling at me? What did I do?"

"You're leading that guy straight to us. Tell me how you're doing it."

Man, the innocent look she could put on. "No, I'm not. Why would I do that? He's trying to kill me!"

"You tell me."

"I don't know what you're talking about."

"I followed him, Marisol, and he went shopping and had a quick little dinner and then he headed straight for Jenn's house. He had to have known somehow. You're the only one who could've alerted him. Do you have a cell phone on you? Did you call him?"

"No, I don't have a phone. I don't have anything."

"Who was the blond girl you were meeting on that street?"

"I don't know any girl. I can't believe you think I'd want him to find me. You saw how he hit me on the boat. He tried to kill me. He left me for dead."

Jenn glanced up at him and then turned to watch for incoming company. "Hurry it up, Novak. I want to get out of here."

"He's not coming after us anytime soon. I sicced the police on him. At least for now."

"I swear! I swear it!" Marisol was starting up with her weeping act, imploring him with clasped hands and woeful eyes. "I don't want him to find me. He's going to cut my throat, like he did to those men. He's going to cut off my hair."

Novak stared down at her and tried to think it through. His anger was making it difficult. "How many times have you run away?"

"Lots of times, but the longest was when I went to Miami."

"Did this Mayan guy find you that time?"

"Yes."

"What did he do when he found you?"

"He handcuffed me and took me back to my father's compound near Mexico City."

Novak felt his jaw clamp. She was still lying. She didn't know how to tell the truth. He turned to Jenn. "She's got to have an implanted chip in her body. That's the only way he could keep finding us. I don't know why I didn't think of it before. Every wealthy family in Mexico implants their children with GPS chips because of the kidnappings going on down here. Ruiz would definitely have it done to his own daughter."

Novak grabbed the girl up by her shoulders. "Did anybody ever inject you with anything?"

"No! Wait, I mean yes. They gave me a sedative when they brought me back from Miami. It made me sleep for hours."

"Where did they give it to you?"

"At Papi's compound."

"I mean where on your body, damn it!"

"In my hip."

"Let me see. Hurry it up."

For once, Marisol obeyed without complaint. She pulled her shorts down on one side, enough for him to see. Jenn stepped up and watched as Novak moved the tips of his fingers along the upper curve of her hip. He found the chip after about ten seconds.

"Give me your knife, Jenn."

Jenn pulled it off her waist and handed it over, hilt first.

"No, stop! Wait! What are you going to do? Don't cut me—"

That's as far as she got before Novak had the tip of the knife under her skin and was digging out the small black GPS chip.

"Ouch! Stop it!" she cried, trying to twist away. "Why would they put that in me?"

"Why do you think? They wanted to track you next time you took off."

While Novak examined the chip, Jenn stepped inside and pressed a towel down on the cut to stop the bleeding. A moment later, Novak smashed up the chip and hurled the pieces out the door. That chip answered a lot of Novak's questions. Marisol was sure as hell gonna answer the rest of them.

"Let's get out of here, Jenn. We'll go back to the hotel. Separately. Different routes. But you need to strip-search her in case there's another chip before we go anywhere else."

Jenn told Marisol to take off her clothes, and then she examined every inch of her body, while Novak stood outside the door and watched for cars. When she didn't find anything, they took off, one at a time, Novak first. At the entrance to the park, Novak turned right and headed back north to the Bahia del Sol. Okay, now a few more pieces of the puzzle fit into place. But there was more to it, and he had to get the answers. He'd find them on that boat, and that was where he was going right now.

Chapter Fourteen

Back at the Bahia del Sol, everything remained nice and calm. Novak arrived first and took the stairwell to the top floor. The late hour ensured that he wouldn't run into any nosy people. His surveillance equipment still sat in place, and he hastily swung the balcony doors open and sat down. The killer's boat was still out there, completely dark, and rocking slightly on incoming waves. No sign of life whatsoever. A quick scan of the parking lot below told him that the Mayan's Subaru Outback was nowhere to be seen. So he waited and watched, deciding pretty much right off the bat that he was going to steal that boat and he was going to do it tonight. Now that Marisol's GPS chip was destroyed, she and Jenn should be safe. He wanted them back at the hotel first, and then he was going in. Novak coveted that boat in the worst way. The thought of taking it right out from under the assassin's nose gave Novak supreme pleasure.

The two women showed up twenty minutes later. Jenn was wont to take the most circuitous route possible—her inbred evasion tactics. She reported that nobody had seen them enter at the back of the hotel. The grounds had been basically deserted, just one couple playing tennis on a lighted court on the far side of the dark pool area, night owls and/or insomniacs.

Novak sat Marisol down on the couch and demanded answers. The routine was getting old and tired. He knew already that she might spin a new pack of complicated lies. She was good at it, but the tattoo had done a lot to prove her real identity, so he rested a bit easier on that count. Still, he had doubts and probably would never trust her completely. The question was, why had she habitually lied to him?

So he asked her the same questions again, but nothing he said shook her innocent declaration of ignorance. She just sat there and looked pitiful. More denials and more trembling fears that the Mayan was going to get her. That he was coming after her. That he was going to scalp her. That nobody could stop him. Marisol was a pretty little liar and proved it endlessly. Still, she was a stupid young girl in mortal danger. Neither he nor Jenn were cruel enough to cast her out on the street and let the killer have her.

"Jenn, we need to talk. You stay right here," he told Marisol.

Marisol slunk down farther in the easy chair until she looked smaller, almost like a child. That kid really could win an Academy Award.

"So what now?" Jenn asked him. They stood just inside the master bedroom door. She stayed in the threshold, watching the girl. Marisol had moved now and was lying facedown on the couch. Quiet, for a change.

"We're never going to trust her motives," Novak said. "So, we need to concentrate on finding a safe place to drop her off. Let somebody else worry about her for a change. A police station, or a Catholic convent, maybe."

"I'd choose the convent. The police around here can be iffy. And the Mayan? What about him? He's not going to stop coming after us, is he?"

"Not until he finds us again and takes care of business. Won't be so easy now, without the GPS. And I'm taking his boat tonight and leaving him stranded here."

"You really think he's still coming?"

"Yeah. He wants to silence that kid in there. She's an eyewitness to the murder of her boyfriend as well as the attempt to murder her. I'm taking his boat to throw him off and put a crimp in his style. I think that boat is his command center and he'll be lost without it. At least for a while. It's sitting down there right now, deserted, ripe for the taking. With a little luck, I can find out his real name and report him to the authorities—Interpol, if he's got the Mexicans paid off. I need to get the boat out of here before the police release him. If they're working with him, it won't take him long to get out. If we're lucky, they won't release him until later tonight. Depends on how deep the bribery goes. I figure I've got a window of about an hour, maybe a little more, if they don't lock him up. That's plenty of time to get the boat and take her out to sea."

"What about us?"

"You stay here with the kid. Make sure you stay under the radar. You'll be safe enough up here. Just keep your weapon close."

"Well, don't get caught. We've got enough trouble without having to get you out of jail."

This time Novak actually smiled. "You're awfully agreeable all of a sudden."

"I can be agreeable at times. Think back."

Novak's eyes dropped to her mouth. It wasn't hard to recall those times.

Jenn smiled, but almost instantly sobered. "What do you want me to do?"

"Stay here and watch the parking lot. Keep the lights off. I'm going out to the boat and take a look around. I'll board her if it looks like a go. If he comes back, I'll have the element of surprise. If he doesn't, I'll get the boat started and take her out to sea. You and the kid can meet up with me later somewhere. Safer for you that way, in case I get caught. Got a good place where we could rendezvous?"

"Let's just meet up at my beach house on the coast south of Belize City. You remember where it is. It's safer down there, and I have more pull with the authorities. I've got to check on an asset I've got stashed down that way, anyway. I can take the Winnebago and get the girl through the border with a bribe. I know some of the border guards. You've been to my place. Meet you there sometime tomorrow."

"Think you can handle Marisol by yourself?"

She gave him a look. "What do you think, Novak?"

Jenn had an innate way of garnering cooperation. Marisol would toe the line around her. Then again, Marisol was a young and flighty girl who lied every time her lips moved. Sometimes fear shadowed her eyes, too, fear that Novak sensed was genuine. She was afraid of the killer but had tried to shake Novak anyway. Why? It didn't make sense. She was safer with him. She would already be dead if it weren't for Jenn and him. And then there was that blond girl that Marisol claimed not to know. Novak thought differently but couldn't figure how she fit into Marisol's drama. Or if she did at all.

"Okay, Jenn, stay on the binoculars. The Mayan's gonna come back here in a white Subaru Outback, unless he's been thrown in jail. Maybe they found illegal weapons or drugs in his possession, but I don't think he's stupid enough to be caught like that. Not with his track record. So he'll be back here eventually."

"Okay."

"I'll keep an eye on the windows. Keep the lights turned off. If you see him coming, switch them on. Don't use a cell. He'll hear it, even on vibrate. It's too quiet down there on the water at night."

"Sure you don't want some backup? I could handcuff Marisol to the bathroom sink."

"I can get down there, sight unseen, no problem. Two of us might be noticed."

"Just don't get caught, Novak."

When they left the bedroom, Marisol was still lying on the couch, either asleep or pretending to be. Jenn sat down in front of the binoculars. "It's dead down there. Better get going. Time's a-wasting."

Novak slipped a black sweatshirt over his shirt and snugged on the ball cap. When he stopped at the front door, Jenn glanced at him "Good luck. Don't take stupid chances. I like you better alive."

"Don't worry."

Novak let himself out, making sure that he heard the locks click and then the rattle of the security chain. He moved quickly down the hall and into the stairwell. It was very late now. Everybody in bed, he hoped. Nobody was taking the stairs, but nobody ever took the stairs, not since elevators had been invented. He ran down to the first floor, took a quick peek out into the hallway. Nothing stirring. He exited through the side door and tried to avoid the wavering reflections coming off the pool lights. It was quiet out in the rose garden. No cars were moving around in the parking lots. Nobody was out on the balconies, talking or smoking cigarettes. The tennis players were gone, the court now dark and deserted.

Remaining in the shadows, he cut through some shrubbery beds instead of taking the solar-lit pathways. He moved quickly down some steps that led to the sidewalk in front of the hotel, avoiding lampposts. On the other side of the street, the marina appeared tucked in for the night, the boats dark, the water still. The air smelled of fish and the sea and engine oil. The breeze had started to gust. The cool night air felt good on his skin. Palm fronds rattled and scraped above him. He crossed the thoroughfare at a fast walk that wouldn't draw undue attention and descended a shallow flight of steps to the main pier. Looming shadows protected him there. He waited a moment, found Jenn's suite on the top floor across the street. Lights were off. He was good to go. He couldn't see the parking lot where the Mayan had parked earlier from where he stood, but Jenn could.

There were half a dozen piers, all of which stretched fifty yards or so out into the water. The Mayan's boat was on a branch of the pier closest to the outlet into the ocean, chosen for a hasty escape, no doubt. Well, good. The docks were planked, some floating, with ropes stretching between posts along the way, and some with sturdy pilings. Each was about six feet wide, with berths lined up on each side, facing each other. Nearly every berth held a boat. Most lights were turned off. Somebody was having a party way off to Novak's right somewhere, in an adjacent marina. He could hear the music— Pharrell, singing "Happy." The people listening sounded happy as well. Novak wouldn't be happy until he got on that boat and had her miles away. He looked up at the suite again, found it dark, and then moved on, his sneakers silent on the planks. Halfway to the boat, he heard a television program coming from inside a big sailboat similar to the *Sweet Sarah*. Sounded like some late-night comedy with canned laughter, all in Spanish. A streak of anger flashed through him, thinking of his prized sailboat sitting on the bottom at the end of that pirate dock. But first things first.

The Mayan's boat was battened down, expertly done, nice and tight, dark and quiet. Novak hunkered down at the end of the gangplank and listened. This guy was stealthy, and Novak better remember that. Nobody ever seemed to hear him coming or live to tell about it. The TV he'd heard had been turned off now. Gentle waves lapped, and the boats bumped up against the rubber tires. Far away, deep in the suburbs somewhere, he heard the sound of a police siren, faint and strident, until it faded away. He glanced back up at the balcony. No lights.

After a moment spent searching the shadows, he made it across the gangplank and stepped down onto the starboard deck. He squatted there and waited. The boat was a real beauty, equipped for ocean voyages, three big outboards in the stern. Raised pilot's seat with double steering wheels. There was a line of lights built into the floor, just enough of a soft glow to guide his way. He proceeded cautiously, glancing often up at Jenn's surveillance point. He wasn't positive that he was alone on the boat. The Mayan could have made it back without them seeing him. Unlikely, but stranger things had happened. He broke the lock on the stern hatch, and then opened the doors and looked down the steps. It was like looking into a deep black well. Nothing. No lights. No sounds.

Novak listened a minute or two longer and then eased down inside. At the bottom, he switched on his flashlight. He was impressed. This boat was a top-of-the-line luxury vessel. The Mayan made good money with his deadly arts. Hired assassinations were expensive propositions. The interior looked like a layout in *Ladies' Home Journal*—yellow walls, flowered couches, scented candles, bouquets of artificial flowers. Maybe this guy had a grandma from Indiana decorate the boat, or maybe he had a girlfriend or a wife who liked frilly stuff. Or, maybe he had a feminine partner who killed right alongside him. Novak hoped to hell not.

After a few moments, he moved across the salon and into the narrow galley. The boat's interior was laid out similarly to his own boat. Larger, maybe. A little more powerful. A couple more staterooms. There were some round portholes, others high and rectangular, and a large window down low beside the galley's table. He moved there and looked up at the hotel again. No lights. Nobody coming. Then he opened the stateroom doors, one at a time, searching each cabin with his flashlight beam. Nobody aboard. He stopped again in the galley and listened. He found the head, one that was larger than most bathrooms aboard boats, and a small storage/engine room in the stern. He moved inside it and flashed his light around. Mayan spears and hatchets hung on the walls, colorful strings of beads hanging off the handles. Handwoven baskets on the floor. And some scalps. Maybe a dozen, inside the baskets. Good God, this guy was nuts. Probably hair that belonged to the unfortunate pirates that had taken Novak. One scalp had long black hair like Li Liu's. Novak swallowed down revulsion, pretty sure it was the woman's straight and silky hair, sliced off from the forehead back. A cold chill pebbled his arms, and he felt an odd twinge of fear, in a way that he rarely ever felt fear. He ignored it. He had been afraid before—in battle, in life-and-death altercations, and in firefights with the enemy. But this guy? This guy was different. This guy was a monster.

Novak moved back to the big window and looked up at the hotel. The light was on. Shit. Novak wasted no more time. He moved back quickly and climbed up through the stern hatch. He stopped, dropped to one knee in the darkness, and looked down the pier. He didn't see him yet. That meant Novak had some time. He pulled in the gang-plank and let it clatter down on the deck and then quickly untied the mooring lines and threw them off. Then he took the steps up to the helm. It took him about twenty seconds to hot-wire the engines. He reversed her slowly out of the berth, about the same time the Mayan emerged from the shadows at the other end of the pier. Too late now, buddy. Surprise, surprise.

Once he had the boat out, he got her turned around and idled her out past the warning buoys and into the open bay. There, he opened her up a little more and headed toward the ocean outlet. When he was about fifty yards out, he looked back. The Mayan had made it to the empty berth. When Novak saw the killer searching the water, he gave the guy a two-fingered salute. Your boat is mine now, my friend. Turnabout is fair play.

After that, Novak eased the throttle forward and increased his speed. He didn't have to worry about the killer calling the cops, not when he'd just got done tangling with them. But he did have to worry about him calling in some buddies from the Ruiz cartel, if that was who he was working for. Didn't matter. Novak would be long gone by then, well on his way down to Jenn's beach house in Belize. First and more importantly, though, he was taking the *Calakmul* out to open seas, far enough to feel safe, and then he was going to search the boat from stem to stern. Maybe, just maybe, he would uncover enough information to help him find out where the Mayan lived. Then he would pay him a call at his house some dark night and even up the score for good.

Chapter Fifteen

Once Novak reached the ocean, he turned the boat south and headed down the coast toward Belize. It wouldn't take him long to get there. After Jenn crossed the border over the Rio Hondo, it wouldn't take her long to get home, either. But he would have time enough to search the boat before he anchored off Jenn's beach. The Mayan was now stranded in Chetumal, but Novak wasn't stupid enough to stop worrying. The killer was no doubt already on the move. He was too well trained and methodical not to have alternatives in case of trouble. Novak sure as hell took him seriously. He tried to call Jenn on the sat phone to make sure they had gotten out of the hotel without problems. She didn't answer. That troubled him a bit, but she often didn't answer her phone when on the move with an asset, he knew that. Or maybe she was just out of range. He'd try again later.

Right now, he wanted to search the cabins below and see what he could find. About thirty miles offshore, he switched off the engines, climbed down to the stern, and scanned the horizon. He felt a bit paranoid. It was unlike him, but it paid to be paranoid with this guy. He didn't see any boats. Light had brightened the horizon, dawn trying to break through the gloom. Didn't see anything but whitecaps and cresting waves. Then he scanned the sky for black helicopters. He was never sure what might happen next, not on this trip. He had been cursed from the moment he awoke from his nightmare about Mariah. But the sky stretched out over him, slowly clearing to blue and empty of threats. He was alone on a vast expanse of salt water, and it felt good to be out there. In time, the rising sun burned down on his bare head, and the glare of the choppy dark blue water made his eyes ache. He poked on the sunglasses he'd found at the helm. Maybe, though—maybe—he was finally on the receiving end of a stroke of good luck.

The Mayan would be searching for him, but it would take time, even if the *Calakmul* had an embedded GPS tracking device hidden somewhere on board. And it probably did. Novak's boat did. Novak just had to find the device and disable it, because he did not want company. He kept his weapon close while he searched through all the cabinets and compartments above deck. All he found were life preservers, blankets, and lots of other navigation and safety equipment. Scanning the ocean to the west again, he was relieved to see nothing at all but gently surging waves. Then he headed down below and started tossing the girly-decorated salon and staterooms, one at a time, slowly and thoroughly. He found exactly zip in the way of additional condemning evidence. Certainly no smoking gun with a map to the Mayan's home address. The interior made the killer appear to be a regular kind of guy, not the insane serial killer that Novak knew him to be. No alcohol of any kind to be found, unfortunately. Novak could use a couple of stiff drinks. No drugs, no porn, no indication of vices or obsessions, other than that pesky habit of slitting throats and ripping off the tops of victims' heads.

This guy apparently lived aboard by himself and had zero personal interests. No mementos of family, no photographs, but lots of black clothes. No videos, no books, no newspapers, not much food in the galley. Nonperishable goods, for the most part: canned soup, rice, flour tortillas, crackers, lots of that kind of stuff. Bags and bags of miniature candy bars, the Hershey's kind, dark chocolate and milk chocolate and Krackle bars. The guy definitely had a sweet tooth. The staterooms were pristine, beds made, everything just so. Orderly as hell.

This guy was a killing machine. Novak examined the scalps and then looked around the boat again, thinking there might be some clue somewhere as to who the victims had been: a name, or a photo for the Mayan to caress and enjoy on his off-hours. Novak wondered if some of those scalps had been taken aboard this very boat, their owners' bodies disposed of at sea. Out in the middle of the ocean, the Mayan could weight them and watch them sink to the bottom, gone forever. But he hadn't been so fastidious at the hijackers' camp.

He had gone about the beach methodically slaughtering everybody in sight, leaving a conspicuous trail of corpses.

Novak returned to the small room in the stern. He stood in the middle of that macabre space and stared at all the bloody souvenirs designating agonizing deaths. It was chilling to consider how these people had suffered, while he stood alone in the dusky light from the one lone porthole. Novak decided the Mayan needed to breathe his last. If it took Novak forever, he would get him. No trial, no prison, no parole. This room was evidence enough for Novak that the Mayan deserved whatever he got.

Sickened by the foul odor of the rancid dried blood on the hair, Novak climbed back up to the deck, breathed in fresh sea air, and tried to reach Jenn again on the boat's sat phone. No answer. He felt another tingle of alarm, but Jenn had always been cautious. He wasn't really worried about her, maybe just spooked a bit by the trophy room he'd discovered below. He scanned the horizon again, found no boats approaching, and then he froze when he heard a low thud come from below. The Ruger was out of his waistband and in his hand in seconds. The sound came again, very faint. It sounded almost like something rolling around on the floor, far belowdecks.

Novak descended the steps again and stood motionlessly in the main salon, listening. Nothing. Just the soothing sway of the chop. After several minutes, another thud sounded, coming from under his feet. Novak followed the noise up toward the bow and found nothing. He felt along the walls, which were lined with compartments for stowing gear. On the floor in front of them, he finally found a small handhold in the teak floor. A trapdoor, one that led down into the bilge. He kept the gun in his right hand and placed it up against his shoulder. Then he pulled up the door, and a sickening smell of rank, stagnant water almost made him gag. It smelled like a sewer down there, stomach-turning and foul. Four shallow steps led down into the dark hole. He could hear seawater sloshing around. A thud came again, louder now.

Squatting there, he hesitated a moment, his weapon now pointed down into the darkness below, not sure what he might find. Maybe dead bodies. Whatever it was, it sure as hell wasn't going to be good. He waited, thinking it might be an ambush. But that didn't make sense. He heard nothing else. No voices, no breathing, nothing except the sloshing of water as waves rocked the boat. He took one step down and felt along the interior wall for a light switch. His fingers touched one. He flipped it on.

Ducking his head, he gazed around the dank, nasty hole. That's when he saw her—a little girl, maybe nine or ten years old. She was dressed in a short yellow nightgown with white daisies embroidered across the top. She was across the bilge from him, up against the hull, lying on some kind of a raised platform with a bed on top. It looked clean, with blankets and pillows, and was secured in place with ropes. One end had come loose and was bumping against the hull and making the sound he'd heard. Novak glanced around for the bilge pump, found it a few feet away, and switched it on. Then he stepped down into the water and waded over to her. It hit him ankle deep and felt slick and oily against his bare ankles.

The child was very small. She had long dark hair that was braided into pigtails. She looked as if she was drugged or unconscious, he wasn't sure which. The bed had a rail to keep her from falling out, and the sheets were bright white and sanitary. There was a pink teddy bear tucked under her right arm. The other arm stretched out to a metal ring on the hull where her wrist was attached with soft cotton ties, the kind hospitals use to restrain restless patients. She had been beaten. Both arms were bruised up pretty good, and she had a swollen black eye. A clean white gauze bandage had been wrapped around her forehead at her hairline. Novak cringed inside, his first thought being that she'd been partially scalped.

Novak held on to the hull and put his fingers against the side of her neck. He felt a pulse, a slow, weak one, but she was still breathing. He could see her chest rising and falling, and when he leaned down close, a low wheezing sound came from her open mouth. God, he hoped she didn't have a collapsed lung. Whatever it was, she looked in bad shape.

Novak searched the bilge and found nothing else of interest. It was warm down there, and would get warmer as the sun rose. He needed to get this little kid to a doctor. Right now, though, he just wanted to get her the hell out of that dank, dark hold. Who was she? The Mayan's current victim, left behind to finish off later? But why would he want her? She was little more than a baby. Why would he hurt her and then carefully doctor the wounds he had inflicted? Just to keep her alive for more vicious abuse? The bandages were clean and applied with some expertise. Her face and arms and hair looked clean. That probably meant she hadn't been with him very long. She could be the daughter of a victim, and he'd brought her aboard to hold for ransom. But that seemed messy for a pro. Maybe she was a young relative of Arturo Ruiz? Ruiz had sent the Mayan after Marisol. Maybe the child had been on his hit list, too. Or perhaps she was just a bargaining chip he was holding in case his relationship with Ruiz went sour. On the other hand, she could just be a witness that he hadn't had time to get rid of yet. It had to be something like that. Maybe he hadn't had the heart to cold-bloodedly kill a tiny child. Novak pretty much dismissed that idea. The Mayan was as ruthless and deadly as any man Novak had seen. He was keeping the child alive for his own selfish reasons. Whatever his motive, the little girl was now Novak's problem and lucky as hell that Novak had found her.

Novak untied the restraint, and then he carefully slid an arm under her shoulders and the other under her knees. It felt like she weighed nothing at all. Very frail and tiny. The most terrible surge of fury roiled up and overtook him, black and awful and nearly over-whelming. His heart thudded faster. He was angry to think that anyone could hurt a helpless child the way this little girl had been hurt. He fought down the churning rage, because that's not what the kid needed right now. She needed a doctor. He carried her up the steps and into the nearest stateroom. He lowered her onto the bed, got her under the covers, and tried to make her comfortable. He slid open a porthole above the bed and let in some fresh air and light. Then he found a towel, wet it, and dabbed the beads of sweat off her face and neck. She felt very hot to the touch, feverish, her face flushed. She was burning up with fever.

Novak cursed inside. How many victims of this guy was he going to have to rescue? First Marisol and then this little kid. He searched the boat for a medicine cabinet, wanting something to bring down her temperature, but found no painkillers, no antibiotics, no aspirin, nothing. He found ice trays in the fridge, wrapped some ice in a clean towel, and used it as an ice pack. He made up a couple more packs and tucked them around her body. That's when he saw the cuts on her arms and legs, lots of little slits about an inch long, as if some-one had sliced her over and over with a razor blade. This guy, this Mayan, was a devil on vacation from hell. It looked to Novak as if he had been toying with her, torturing her, maybe, or just frightening her to death. The wounds were superficial, but no less horrifying to a child feeling a blade slice into her skin again and again. Maybe the Mayan had been after information. But what would a little girl know that an assassin would be interested in? The whereabouts of her parents, maybe? Whatever the reason, this child had suffered greatly. Was still suffering.

Novak went back up top and checked again for unwelcome visitors. Still alone in the middle of the sea. Nobody in sight. He went back down to the stateroom and sat on the bed beside the girl. She was in a lot worse shape than Marisol had been. She was sick and unconscious, maybe even in a shallow coma. He touched her face with his fingertips to rouse her. Her eyelids did flutter slightly, but that was it. He raised her eyelids. Her pupils were dark and dilated. He couldn't tell what color they were. She had dark brown hair, with sun streaks the color of honey. The loose strands at her temples were stiff with dried blood. Just an innocent little kid, caught up in something horrible. He shook her arm gently, wanting her to awaken, but she only moaned softly and didn't open her eyes. He stared at her a moment, and then he loosened the bandage around her head and examined her wound. It wasn't an attempt to scalp her. She'd been struck with something. He saw a half-inch gash that had been doctored with Betadine and stitched up. Not by a doctor, though. Looked to Novak as if the Mayan had done it.

Novak just sat there beside her for a while, trying to control his anger. Every so often she would jerk her hand or her foot, as if dreaming. She never opened her eyes. She'd been treated medically somewhat, but what she really needed was a doctor and some antibiotics. Novak walked to the galley and filled a glass with water. She looked dehydrated, so thin and frail. No telling how long she'd been kept below in that dark hole. Her lips were dry, but she wasn't conscious enough to take a sip. He rubbed water on her lips with his finger and tried to ease a few drops into her mouth. After he'd done this a couple of times, she subconsciously licked at the drops with her tongue. That was a good sign.

Novak left her again and checked out the sea for enemies. Nothing. He had lucked out so far. Calm water, medium swells. A beautiful day. He tried Jenn again. This time she picked up. She didn't say anything, just waited.

"It's me."

"Where the hell are you? You said you'd be here waiting for us."

"I ran into trouble once I got the boat out on the water. There was a little girl tied up in the bilge." He hesitated. "I think that bastard tortured her."

"Oh, my God. Is she dead?"

"Still alive, but barely. She's got a fever, and I can't wake her up."

"Not good. Who is she? Do you know?"

"Don't have a clue. She's either drugged or unconscious. Dehydrated, and she looks like he might've starved her. I've got to get her to Doc before I come for you, or she's gonna die. Is Marisol behaving?"

"Timid as a mouse all day long. Which is a bit out of character."

"Don't take your eyes off her for a single second."

"Don't worry. Okay, let me think about this a minute."

Novak waited, but it didn't take Jenn a minute. "We'll be safe enough here at my house on the beach. Just hurry up and pick us up when you can."

"It might be as late as tomorrow night."

"That's okay. Just call me when you've got the girl taken care of. You can anchor off my beach and we can swim out. Or better yet, sink that damn boat and we can fly out of here until things settle down."

Flying the hell out sounded good to Novak. He had found himself a hell on earth south of the border, and he didn't like it. He'd had enough. "Okay. Doc can help this kid, whoever she is. She's in really bad shape."

"How is Doc?"

"Fine, I guess. I haven't seen him in about a year."

"If he's not drunk, he ought to fix her up."

"He's a better medic when he's drunk."

Jenn laughed softly. "Okay, just keep me posted. We'll dig in here and wait."

She clicked off. Novak felt pretty good. Jenn and Marisol were safe for the moment. All Jenn's houses were secure and well protected, especially her own personal residence at the edge of that beautiful beach. They'd be all right until he got there. He climbed to the helm, started the engines, and pushed the controls down, slowly increasing speed, constantly on the lookout for pursuers. Because the Mayan was coming, and Novak knew it. All around him, the ocean was wide and empty and deep, that same dark royal blue. It felt good to be out there. In time, he caught the distant blue blur of an island.

The *Calakmul*'s navigational equipment was top of the line, but Novak had been to Doc's home base more times than he could count. He knew the coordinates by heart. He set the boat on course, full speed ahead, and then went below to check on the child again. She was lying still, eyes closed. She looked terrible to him. He didn't know how bad off she was, but it didn't look good.

Novak spoon-fed her a few more drops of water and climbed back up to the helm. He sat there, watching the prow cut its way through the chop and thinking about what Jenn had said about flying back to the U.S. After a while, he picked up the sat phone and put in a call to his partner back in the States. Claire Morgan had been on her honeymoon the last time he'd seen her, but that hadn't stopped her from helping him out when he needed someone to watch his back. He was going to have to ask for her help again. She was one of the few people he trusted. If he had his choice, he would get his own boat lifted out of the water and cleaned up and then sail back home, but that wasn't going to happen. Right now, he was too deeply embroiled in Marisol's mess. He wasn't going anywhere. Not until this poor little girl was in Doc's hands and both Marisol and Jenn were safe with Novak.

Claire picked up on the third ring. "Hey, Novak. You still out rolling in the deep? Feeling sorry for yourself? Nobody else invited?"

"Listen, I don't have time to chat."

"What the hell, Novak? You called me." Slight pause. "What's wrong? You're in trouble, aren't you? Where are you?"

"Out in the middle of the Caribbean, southeast of Chetumal, Mexico, heading for a friend's private island."

"That's specific."

"I need you to do something for me."

"Name it."

"Are you still on Kauai?"

"Nope, we're back at Lake of the Ozarks and going over plans for my very own brand-new house that Black's building for me. He's still über-guilty that he got the old one blown up. But it's well on its way and gonna be a sight to behold, unless I put a bit in his mouth and hold him back. You know what a big spender he is. But it is looking pretty cool, I've got to admit."

"Can you get away?"

"For you? You bet. Just tell me where."

"I need you to come get me in Black's plane. If it's okay with him. I'd like him to come, too, if he can cut loose from his patients." But Novak already knew what Black would do. Pretty much everything was okay with Black where Claire was concerned.

Claire put her hand over the phone, and Novak heard her talking to somebody. Silence. One beat, two beats. Then she said, "Okay. Sounds good."

Novak had to grin. It felt good to hear a voice he could trust. He'd had little reason to smile since he'd met up with Marisol Ruiz. Fortunately for him, Claire was always pretty much up for anything at any time. Sometimes that penchant for action got her in trouble. Sometimes she got Novak into trouble. Sometimes it was the other way around.

"Any reason why you can't just sail back on the good ship *Sweet Sarah*?"

"Well, that's a long story."

"Your stories usually are."

"Some pirates hijacked my boat and then some psycho Mayan serial killer scuttled it and started trying to kill me."

"Come again?"

"You heard me. My brand-new, custom-designed Jeanneau Sun's now sitting on the bottom of a sheltered cove just south of Chetumal, Mexico, near the mouth of the Rio Hondo."

"Wow, Novak. Just wow."

"I'm serious."

"Yeah, I get that. Well, not to worry. We're on our way. Where exactly are you?"

"Out at sea, like I said. East of the Belize coast. There's a little airstrip you can land on. Take down these coordinates." He told her the GPS location. "It's near Belize City. A friend of mine runs it. Just mention my name and he'll let you set down."

"Somebody else from your past, huh?"

"Yeah. You can trust him."

"Okay, we'll locate it on my brand spanking new computer setup that Black had to buy me. He had to buy me new everything because he still blames himself for what happened. It's like Christmas around here, I'm telling you. Play your cards right and maybe you'll get a shiny new toy, too."

"Tell him to bring his medical bag."

"That sounds ominous. Okay, just a sec. Black's right here. He's already nodding. I've got you on speaker."

Novak waited a moment and then heard Black speaking in the background.

"He says we can be there in three to four hours, five at the most if we hit bad weather," Claire told him. "That gonna work for you?"

"Yeah. Hopefully, we'll be waiting for you at the airstrip."

"Figures. Do we need to bring our 50 calibers?"

Claire was kidding. Novak wasn't. "Yeah, if you've got them."

"Crap, Novak. Tell me what's going on down there. You're gonna be okay, right?"

"It's a long story that I don't have time to get into. You don't need to get involved any more than flying us out of here. Black's gonna hate me for involving you."

"Nah, not if he gets to tag along. You know what a sucker he is for this kind of stuff. All that Ranger training and covert ops and all that. Anyway, we've been off enjoying our own private paradise on earth for months now. It's time to put some serious adventure back into our lives."

"There are a couple of women I'm bringing, too. And a little girl, maybe."

"That's three more girls than you usually have around."

"One of them says the serial killer is after her. I'm not sure who the injured kid is. But Jenn's an old friend of mine. I want her to come out of this mess safe and sound. I'm going to make sure she's okay, right after I get this little kid to Doc."

"Black's the best doctor I know. Bring the kid with us, too. We've got plenty of room on the plane, and plenty of medical supplies we can load up."

"This girl can't wait four or five hours. Doc's closer."

"Thought you said your boat's on the bottom?"

"I did. The killer sank her. I'm going to get him before I come home. He doesn't deserve to live another day."

"I think I've heard this song before."

"Call Jack Holliday if you need more firepower."

"How many bad guys are you up against?"

"Most of them are already dead."

"You've been busy."

"The Mayan got most of them, and now he's after me for stealing his boat and rescuing the kid. His specialty is slitting throats and taking scalps."

"Damn, Novak. We better haul in a crate of M16s."

"Just be careful. This guy is like a shadow."

"So are you. It'll probably take me almost five seconds to persuade Black to do this. We'll take off as soon as we can get his plane gassed up, flight plan down, and then we're on our way."

"Like I said, be careful. You can't mess with this guy. He's deadly."

"Yeah, they usually are."

They hung up and Novak heaved a relieved breath, feeling a little better. He liked to do things himself, work alone, but this time he needed some help. Black and Claire were both as tough as they came. They knew what they were doing, and they were on their way. At the moment, he had to get the little kid into Doc's capable hands and then head for Jenn's beach house and get the women to that airstrip. At the moment, it seemed a doable situation. He just hoped his luck lasted a little longer this time.

Chapter Sixteen

About forty miles off the coast of Belize were the Hicks Cays. Northeast of the big island was the smaller Long Cay. Almost exactly between their northernmost shores was a tiny private island called Soledad Cay. It was owned by Doc Smithy, a guy like no other in Novak's book. Doc had bought that little slice of paradise and in the process given up most of his military earnings and retirement but had never regretted it. The isle had been a good investment, then and now. Novak had set the navigation by memory and was heading straight for his good friend's haven, hoping the brisk tailwinds whipping up and the cooperative currents would speed him along. The girl below was still unconscious, feverish—not doing so hot.

Doc had made himself a small, warm, sandy piece of heaven, all right, a destination that Novak always looked forward to visiting, mainly because of the absolute privacy. When he walked along those long tan beaches, he felt like nobody else existed in the world. That's the way Novak liked it. That's the way Doc liked it, too—maybe too many years spent in the military for both of them. Novak didn't blame the guy. Smithy had been one of Novak's compadres in the SEALs, a valiant medic who had saved the lives of countless wounded buddies without a care for his personal safety. He had been wounded half a dozen times, all while saving downed warriors. The guy had a boatload of Purple Hearts to show for his courage under fire. Novak had been one of those soldiers once upon a time, and he'd never forgotten what Doc had done for him. Novak trusted the guy with his life, had done so on several occasions. On the other hand, Doc was as eccentric as hell. Even he admitted his idiosyncrasies were world-class. A conspiracy theorist, he believed in and planned for invasion and world domination but had yet to decide who would be doing the invading and why.

Doc had built himself a big shady villa on the lee side of his island, sheltered in a protected cove. Novak had spent weeks at a time there and returned every chance he got when sailing this far south in the Caribbean. That's where Novak was headed now, and with a great deal of urgency. When he spotted the island's silhouette, he felt better, and then pretty much relaxed as he entered the cove. First thing he looked for was the American flag flying high off the top veranda. A small Marine Corps flag flapped in the wind just below it. The Marines flag had always been Doc's signal to friends that he was home and all was well. If the Marines flag was down, he either wasn't there or trouble was afoot. Trouble didn't find Doc much anymore, but those conspiracy theories made him a super-cautious guy. Today both flags were snapping proudly in the wind coming off the water.

Relieved, Novak steered the boat all the way to the dock, cut the engines, and jumped out to secure the lines. After that, he checked on the girl, found her about the same, so he climbed back up and crossed the dock to the beach. He headed across the sand toward a flight of tall winding steps leading up to the bungalow. He was almost to the bottom of the steps when a shot rang out and sent splinters of wood flying off the banister near him. Novak hit the ground, and then he took off his sunshades and ball cap and stood up slowly, his arms stretched high and wide to show he was unarmed. "It's me, Doc," he shouted up at the house. "Novak. I come in peace."

Far above him, on the second-story balcony, Doc stepped out from behind an elaborate bamboo screen, a big AR rifle still in his hands. He was smiling. "Sorry, my friend, I didn't recognize the boat. I thought you bought yourself a new sailboat!"

"Long story. Come on down here, and I'll tell you about it."

Moments later, Doc stood next to him. They embraced, slapped each other's backs, and then Doc pushed back and grinned up at Novak. He was a small man, five foot eight, maybe, but about as gutsy a soldier as any Novak had met. He was balding now, would look a lot like Friar Tuck with a thick ring of hair left over his ears if he didn't shave his head. He had dark skin, but now his body was burnished darker still by the intense tropical sun and a life spent on the beach and out on the sea in his catamaran. His cheeks were lined, deep commas bracketing his mouth from lots of laughter and hard drink. His eyes were always bloodshot, and were now, too, and he still wore his favored goatee and long Elvis sideburns.

Doc had earned all his ribbons and medals a thousand times over, and he had a ton of them packed away somewhere. He lived alone except for his Costa Rican wife, Auroria. She had now appeared up on the balcony and was waving to Novak and beckoning him to come up. Auroria was a little bitty thing, with dark hair and shiny black eyes that missed nothing, and probably the sweetest lady Novak had ever known. She treated Doc like a king and always had.

Novak shook the hand that Doc held out. "How the hell you been, Doc?"

"Good. You?"

"I'm in trouble."

"Okay. What happened?"

"I really stepped in it this time."

"That was your habit in days gone by, as I recall."

"I'm gonna need your help. That's why I'm here."

"You got it. I owe you, remember?"

Novak had dragged Doc out of a firefight once, after he had killed Doc's pursuer with a sniper bullet. They had been far up in the mountains of Afghanistan. Kunar Province. Doc had been hit, bad enough to cash out of the Marines, and afterward found this little isle and Auroria and made both of them his life. "Come aboard. There's a little girl below who needs medical attention. She's in bad shape, Doc."

As they walked out to the boat together, Doc asked Novak lots of questions that he couldn't answer. Once they were inside the girl's cabin, Doc walked to the bed and stared down at the child. She lay on her back, very still, bruised and small and pitiful.

"Good grief, Novak, what the hell? She's just a baby. What— eight, nine?"

"I don't know how old she is. I don't even know who she is. Not her name, not anything about her. I'm fairly confident that the guy who owns this boat sliced her up like this. I found her tied to a bed in the bilge, feverish and dehydrated."

"Who would do such a thing?"

"They call him the Mayan. Not sure who he really is. I've seen him, though. Nobody seems to know much about him. He moves like a ghost, I know that."

"How'd you end up with his boat?"

"I stole it. He scuttled the *Sweet Sarah*, so I'm gonna return the favor once I get this kid fixed up and some other stuff out of the way."

Doc frowned. "Why would someone want to hurt a little girl?"

"Maybe he was trying to pry information out of her. Maybe he's a pedophile or a sadist. Who knows why? It's complicated, and I haven't figured everything out yet."

Doc sat down on the bed and picked up the child's hand. He felt her pulse and then lifted her closed eyelids, one at a time. "The pupils are dilated. Looks like she might be in a shallow coma, probably because of the head injury. Has she moved or said anything?"

"She's moved around some, groaned—dreaming, I guess—but she hasn't said anything coherent, and she hasn't opened her eyes."

"I'll get a line of glucose and some antibiotics into her. Does she have internal injuries? Did he hit her in the kidneys?"

"I don't know. She's pretty bruised up, but it looks more like he slapped her around the head and body. He sliced her up some with a knife."

"My God, she's so little. How could he hurt her like this?"

"I've seen what he does to his victims, up close and personal. He's stealthy and quick, and takes people by surprise, kills them quickly, and then slices off their hair. The scalps are trophies, I guess. Who knows? He's crazy. He's got a few on display right here on this boat. Back in the engine room."

"Good God, Novak."

"He's an evil man. I'm going to put an end to him."

"And this is his boat. You stole it? Really?"

Novak nodded. "Yeah. I took it but didn't expect to find this sick little kid aboard. I don't know how long he's had her. Frankly, I'm surprised she's still breathing. He doesn't leave anybody alive."

"She's not doing well, but she'll live."

Novak stood back as Doc performed a more thorough medical examination. He pressed gently along the bones of the child's arms and legs, feeling for breaks. "Look how he slashed her. Not too deep, thankfully, or she'd be dead. Good thing you found her and doctored her up when you did."

"I didn't put those bandages on her. He must have."

Doc stood up, hands on his hips. "Why the hell would he cut her up and then bind the wounds?"

Novak shrugged. "Who knows? To make his fun last longer? He's a serial killer. He likes inflicting pain."

"I think her right wrist might be fractured. Not too bad, maybe a cracked bone. Trying to pull loose from the bindings, I bet. Let's get her up to the house. Auroria's one hell of a good nurse, and she loves children like nobody I've ever known. She'll baby this girl back to health, no matter how long it takes. You just watch."

Novak nodded, but was not exactly thrilled to have to ask his next question. "I've got another favor to ask of you, Doc. I hate like hell to put all this down on you, but do you think you could keep this kid out here for a while? I've got something else I've got to do. It's too important to wait. If you could just tend to her for a day or so, bind up her wounds, get her to feeling better, then I'll come back and figure out who she is and take her home. I won't be gone long. Maybe a day or two. Maybe less than that, if my luck improves."

"What's so important?"

"I've got Jenn waiting for me, and this girl I helped out, who was also kidnapped and abused by this same guy. They're at Jenn's beach house now. I don't know where the Mayan is or what he's planning to do next. I want to get both of them safely on a plane back to the States, and then I'll come back here and take the kid."

"You have a way to do that?"

"Yeah. My new partner's got access to a private jet. She's on her way to pick us up."

"You could have them land over here on my airstrip but I'm not sure it's suitable for a jet."

"Thanks, but it's all arranged."

"What the devil's going on, Novak? How's Jenn fit into all this?"

"I had to go to her for help. No choice. I was desperate. All I know is that somebody wants the two girls dead. Either the Mayan has some kind of grudge, or somebody hired him to assassinate them or hold them for ransom. Now that we've gotten ourselves involved, I'm pretty sure he's after Jenn and me, too. He'll go after you and Auroria if he finds me here. You need to know that before you get too deep in this."

Doc scoffed. "I've seen worse than this guy, trust me. Of course we'll take care of this little girl. I've got all kinds of meds and IV bags stored up at the house. You know that. I've bound up your wounds enough times." Doc grinned. "So you and Jenn are working together again, huh? I must say, I'm surprised to hear it. She was pretty damn pissed when you walked out on her."

"Yeah, I found that out. But I needed help and she came through for me. Just like you are."

"Don't worry about it. Getting a little dull out here, anyway. C'mon, let's get her up to the house. We'll clean her up some and settle her in the guest room. There's a bed for you, too, if you want to get some shut-eye before you take off."

"Thanks, but I've got to get over to the coast."

Almost an hour later, Auroria had bathed the girl and dressed her in one of her own clean nightgowns. Doc had set the child's broken wrist and hooked her up with glucose and antibiotics through an IV, and then his wife tucked her in to a bed made up with sheets line-dried outside and smelling of the sun. When Novak checked on the child, Auroria was sitting in a chair beside the bed, watching her. Novak knew she wouldn't take her eyes off the girl. He thanked Auroria and then walked out onto the upper balcony and sat down at a big wicker table beside Doc. Doc was drinking shots of tequila. Novak joined him in the next one. He sure as the devil needed a jolt to keep going.

"You think he knows you came here?"

"Not unless he's got a GPS embedded on that boat out there and can track it. Which he probably does. He doesn't leave much to chance, not that I've seen."

"Where'd he scuttle your boat?"

Novak told him about the hijacking and what had happened in the camp.

Doc whistled and observed Novak for a long moment. "This is serious shit. You are going to need backup, all right."

"Yeah, tell me about it."

"What about the *Sweet Sarah*?"

"I'll have her salvaged as soon as I can. I've got to get Jenn and Marisol out of his sights first."

"Where are you taking them?"

"I'd like to take them back to the States and turn the girl over to the FBI. I know Jenn won't want to leave here, but I'm going to try to make her go with us."

"Good luck with that."

"Yeah, I know. She's stubborn as hell."

"What about this Mayan guy?"

"He's not gonna stop coming. He wants his boat back and he wants those two girls who can ID him. I haven't figured it all out yet. Marisol keeps lying, and the little girl is in no shape to tell me anything. Marisol claims he's working for Arturo Ruiz. She also says she's Ruiz's daughter, and her father sent the Mayan to kill her. Any of that sound true to you?"

"Fathers generally don't assassinate their children. But I do know Ruiz has got a daughter. Rumors get out about them. They say he is utterly ruthless. Would kill his own mother, so maybe he would kill his own child if she crossed him, as hard as that is to believe. I know he's bad news and not somebody you want to mess around with. He's best known for beheading innocent civilians and anybody else that looks at him sideways. You don't know about him?"

"Jenn told me some stuff. You still have that satellite hookup?"

"Yeah, gotta get the episodes of *The Walking Dead*. That program creeps me out, but Auroria loves her zombies. We never miss it."

"You get the news, too?"

"Yeah."

"Seen anything about kidnapped girls, cartel assassins, anything like that?"

"I don't watch the news much, not anymore. I read. Pull down e-books off Amazon. When I get tired of that, I make love to Auroria in new and amazing ways. Then I go fishing for dinner."

Novak laughed and poured himself another shot. "Sounds like the good life to me."

Doc nodded. "Tell me about this new partner. Not like you to hook up with a woman, Will. Not at all. Or a man. You were a loner the day you were born."

"Claire's different. She's good. I trust her."

"Well, knock me over with a feather. She must be one hell of a looker."

Claire was indeed a very good-looking woman, but that wasn't what appealed to Novak. "Claire's married now. And she's differ-ent than the other women I've worked with. Gets herself in more trouble than I'm comfortable with, but always seems to come through relatively unscathed." Novak tossed down the tequila, set the glass aside, and leaned back in his chair. "She's been honeymooning in Hawaii, so I've been doing my own thing."

"Looks like your own thing might put you in the ground, if this Mayan guy gets to you."

"He's going to try." Novak set his gaze out over the calm inlet. "I want him dead, Doc. He doesn't deserve to live and breathe like the rest of us. Not after what he does to victims. Doesn't matter to him— man, woman, or a child like that little girl in there. But it matters to me."

"Well, good luck. If the Ruiz cartel is involved, the Federales probably are, too. At least some of them might be on the take, and that means you're shit outta luck, no matter what you do or where you turn."

"Thank you for the encouragement."

Doc only laughed and poured himself more tequila and held the bottle out to Novak. Novak shook his head. "Well, Novak, wish I could tag along, but Auroria would kill me. I mean that literally. I promised her that if she'd marry me and live on this island, I'd stay right here and be a good boy forever more."

"She needs to keep you in line. Nobody else can." Novak glanced down at the dock. "That little girl is gonna wake up in bad shape, you know. Bless Auroria for her kindness. The kid'll respond better to her than to me."

Doc sighed heavily and tossed back the drink. "Yeah, Auroria's an angel, all right. And dinner's almost ready. You need to stay. Fried fish and fried potatoes. She's one hell of a cook."

"Wish I could, but I better get out of here. You hit the jackpot with that woman, Doc."

"Yeah, I did, didn't I?" Doc smiled and then walked with Novak out to the boat.

Novak was damn lucky to have Doc as a friend. He had come through again. Now all Novak had to do was get Jenn and Marisol out of Belize and then he could go after the Mayan. That's what he hungered to do. The Mayan already had one foot in hell. Novak was going to throw the rest of him in.

Chapter Seventeen

Once Novak knew the child was in good hands, he headed out to sea on the *Calakmul*, his destination Jenn's beach house. He cleared the bay and went to full engines ahead out into open water. He didn't get far. Maybe twenty miles off Soledad Cay, he was spotted by a military gunboat, one flying a tricolor flag of green, white, and red. Mexico military. They were much faster than his boat and came up astern in a matter of minutes. They warned him by radio to kill his engines and allow his boat to be boarded for search.

Novak hesitated, not touching the throttle, unsure of what to do. He was not yet in Mexican waters, and that meant they had no business boarding him. He was damn positive that he didn't want the Mexican navy to search the killer's boat, not with the baskets of scalps down below. But he had little choice. The gunboat cruised along with a dozen armed men pointing M16s at him. This scenario was getting old, and fast. He could not catch a damn break no matter what he did.

The Browning M2 .50 caliber machine gun mounted on the other boat's prow made up his mind for him, the kind of weapon that would annihilate anything it hit, including him. He had to cooperate whether he wanted to or not. He pulled back the throttle, slowed down, and then killed the engines. The big yacht gradually settled down into the water. The gunboat maneuvered closer, ready to board. Novak picked up the sat phone and called Jenn. She didn't pick up, damn it. Probably on the move again. He left a voice mail telling her about his new dilemma and asking her to get her Washington contacts to intercede with the Mexican government. Then he put another call through to Claire Morgan's private cell

phone, and she didn't pick up, either. Damn it to hell. He left a brief
message for her, asking for help ASAP and giving the gunboat's reg-
istration number and description, explaining that he was probably
going to end up in a Mexican prison, which also meant he had a
good chance of meeting up with dirty officers on the payroll of the
Ruiz drug cartel. He pulled out the Ruger and the Glock, ejected
both mags, emptied both chambers, and placed the pieces down on
the pilot's seat. He stepped away and placed both palms on the top
of his head. Within minutes, he was going to go down to the ground
and go down hard. From what he remembered about Mexican
jails and Mexican interrogations, the next few days were not going
to be a barrel of laughs.

While the uniformed soldiers scrambled aboard, he slowly descended the steps to the aft deck, hands still on his head, and waited
to be taken prisoner. Mexican military types did not mess around,
did not believe in a kinder, gentler approach. Not the army and not
the navy—not anybody. They shot you down first if they deemed it
necessary and made up good excuses later. They weren't particularly
known for exemplary treatment of drug dealers and/or foreign nationals who gave them lip, either. They tied up at starboard. Four
guys in head-to-toe green camouflage jumped over the gunwales.
The first two men knew what they were doing. The second two
looked like new recruits who were copying the other two. If he had
to take them down, he was starting with the new guys.

Any other time, any other place, Novak would've given them a
run for their money. This time, out in the middle of the ocean, he
was outmanned, outgunned, and out of luck. Within seconds, he was
flat on his stomach on the deck, a black leather boot planted on his
spine. The officer in charge was barking out questions to him, speaking in rapid-fire Spanish. The guy's nameplate said Olmos. Captain
Olmos. Novak answered in kind and let him know right off that he
was an American citizen and demanded to speak to the American
ambassador in Mexico City and make a phone call to his congress-
man in Washington, D.C. Olmos didn't look impressed. None of
them looked as if they cared what Novak wanted. So he added
quickly that the boat wasn't his. That he'd found her floating abandoned at sea without a crew and that he was taking her to Chetumal
to turn her over to the proper authorities.

None of them believed a damn word of that, but he hadn't expected them to. It was an incredibly weak story. He didn't expect them to go easy on him, either. Damn it, why couldn't he catch a break? This whole trip to the Caribbean had been a disaster from beginning to end. He'd run into brick walls ever since he'd met up with Marisol Ruiz. Trying to look innocent, he kept his head down and watched more sailors swarm the deck and rush below to search out the illegal drugs he was transporting. He braced himself. The shit was about to hit the fan, all right. Any minute now. The officer ordered him onto his knees and told him to clasp his hands behind his head. Novak obeyed, because he wasn't stupid, and he had no other choice. That's when the questioning began in earnest, with a lot of yelling meant to intimidate him. Novak stuck to his story. The officer finally stopped talking and gave him a long, hard stare, his eyes caramel brown and hard as nails. He was nobody's fool. Novak's luck had run out for good this time. They maintained a silent stare-down until one of Olmos's lieutenants ran up from below, grasping a scalp in each hand. Then everybody got real excited, real fast.

"So we have finally gotten you, you filthy pig," Olmos ground out, up close to Novak's face. "You have haunted the Yucatan for the last two years with your bloody, cowardly acts. Now you will face the consequences of your crimes."

"You've got this all wrong, Captain Olmos."

"Then why did we get a tip that we would find the Mayan in this area of the sea on this very boat? Can you explain that to me?"

Okay, sounded like the Mayan knew how to play payback, alerting the police, as Novak had done to him. Turnabout is fair play. The guy was a clever adversary, all right. Novak remained silent, thinking fast but not fast enough. They had him. The police gathered around the scalps, handling them with distaste and looking at Novak in disgust. He decided it was time to change tactics.

"Okay, Olmos, listen up. I know this looks really bad for me, but you've got it all wrong. Want to know the truth?"

Olmos came over and stood in front of Novak, still holding some poor soul's hair in his hand. It was long and crusted hard with dried blood. "Go ahead, señor, talk. I will listen, but I will not believe."

That was putting his skepticism up front and on the table. Novak met his eyes, tried to appear honest. "All right, this is the gospel truth. This is exactly what happened. That Mayan guy you're talking about? He's after me. I guess there's a hit out on me. He boarded my boat one night when I was sleeping, a sailboat called the *Sweet Sarah*. Then he sunk her and took me prisoner at gunpoint. Brought me aboard this vessel and tied me up down in the bilge. Go down there yourself and take a look around. You'll see where he held me. There's a mattress down there where he kept me chained up. He's got a hook drilled into the hull that he tied me to."

Olmos gestured for a couple of men to check out Novak's story. His eyes never left Novak's face. "Please continue, señor."

Novak couldn't tell if the guy believed him or not. Wouldn't bet on it. "I managed to pull loose and surprise him when we were out on the water just east of here, near Long Cay. I got the better of him, managed to disarm him. I got his gun, that Ruger you found up at the helm, and turned it on him. He ran and jumped overboard when I fired at him. It was last night after dark, so I just left him out there and headed back to Mexico to report what happened, because his boat is registered in Cancun. I'm glad I ran into you out here. Saved me the trouble of trying to find you."

"And you left this man stranded out in the ocean?"

"It was dark. He was trying to kill me. Last I saw, he was swimming back toward Long Cay. We weren't far offshore. He probably made it there just fine. Put out word to the authorities over there if you don't believe me, and have them pick him up. You need to find him. He's your guy. Not me. He was hired to assassinate me. I'm lucky to be alive."

"What's your name?"

Novak decided it was in his best interest to tell the truth. Or some of it. "My name is Will Novak. Triple citizenship. I was born in America and grew up in Australia with my father. My mother was French. Now I live near New Orleans in the state of Louisiana. I was sailing by myself, not far from here, and he found me and sank my boat. He might've been planning to extort money from my family, for all I know. But I got the better of him, thank God."

"You got the better of the most deadly assassin in Mexican history?"

"Yeah, I guess so. I can take care of myself. I served in the U.S. military. Now I'm a private investigator. I've got a gun permit, but my own weapon went down with my boat. I'm investigating a bank heist in Belize City. Go ahead, check me out. I'm legit. I can give you a number in Washington D.C. to call, or you can call my private investigation partner."

The captain was considering his story. The military part might impress him. It usually impressed his counterparts in allied countries. But it was obvious from the guy's frown that he wasn't taking anything Novak said into serious consideration. A moment later, he turned to his adjutant and ordered Novak taken aboard the gunboat and locked up in the brig.

Novak didn't fight or try to escape; he knew better. He was in trouble again, big-time, and he wasn't sure he could get out of it. He couldn't win for losing on this trip. His fate depended on where he was taken now and who made the decision whether he should be given the benefit of the doubt. Novak cursed himself again for ever pulling that damn Ruiz girl out of the ocean. He would be on his way home right now if it weren't for Marisol Ruiz. Now his boat was underwater and he was no doubt headed to an overcrowded, filthy Mexican prison to stand trial for brutal murders he didn't commit.

On the bright side, which was fading to black at warp speed, he did have some powerful contacts, both in the American embassy in Mexico City and in D.C., and was owed favors by important people. He could probably worm his way out of this mess sooner or later, but he better come up with a better and more cohesive story and do it before he met a real police interrogator in some underground torture chamber.

The Mexican captain wasted no more time. Novak was prodded at gunpoint onto the military boat and then locked below in a cabin with nothing but a narrow cot and a toilet. No porthole. No way out. Novak lay down on the bunk and tried to rest. He had a feeling he was going to need it. He could sleep anywhere, and that held true this time, too. When he awoke again, it was when a gun barrel jabbed into his side.

Novak was escorted up top by a pair of guards and then into a motor launch that took him to shore at a pier in what looked like a small coastal military base. There, a green government helicopter waited in an open, grassy field to fly him to the capital city. Which was something Novak could live with. He'd take his chances with the diplomats over the Mexican military brass any day of the week. He cooperated fully with each new order, and the guards seemed happy to prod him along, mainly because he had to obey them and had no chance in hell to escape a full Mexican contingent. If they took him to their capital city and contacted the American ambassador, he would be able to talk himself out of trouble. That would not be a problem. So he wasn't too worried. He was more concerned about Jenn and Marisol. If the Mayan had put the gunboat onto Novak, he would now be hot on Jenn's trail.

Novak's peace of mind did not last long. He was flown to Mexico City, all right, low and fast, but not to be interviewed by the diplomatic corps. Instead, he was thrown into a cell in the basement of a building that had nothing to do with the military or government. He'd heard horror stories about the Mexican secret police and their methods of interrogation. He didn't know if any of it was true. But then it got worse. He was secured with nylon cords, hands behind his back, and tied to a chair in the middle of an empty concrete room. His feet were left free, which was their first mistake. Feet were weapons and should always be secured. Apparently, nobody in Mexico knew that. He had no illusions about what was coming next. They were preparing to torture him; probably thought he was an American spy. He had better steel himself and be ready to face whatever they threw at him. He could hold his own, but not forever. He had to make his move soon.

So he sat there and waited, working the cords loose, mentally preparing himself. An hour passed and stretched into two, and he was cold, uncomfortable, and angry that he'd allowed himself to get caught on that boat. He tried to remain calm, patiently working the cords and making slow but steady progress. It was only a matter of time before he got himself out of the restraints.

In time, a new guy showed up. Just one man, but Novak suspected that was because the guy didn't want witnesses to see what he was about to do. Maybe that was because the man carried a cattle prod in his hand. He was dressed in civilian clothes—tan polo shirt and khakis, nice leather loafers. Looked like a damn tax accountant. Short and compact, with a Y-shaped scar down the cheek of one well-used face that looked about fifty and was road-mapped with deep lines and pockmarks. His expression was not pleasant, set in hard, brutal, cruel lines. He had a nice corporate haircut, and there was a tattoo of a knife dripping blood on the side of his neck. Great. Maybe one of the Mayan's buddies.

On the far side of the room, there was a long rectangular table pushed against the wall with several sets of light switches and electrical outlets above it. The guy began laying out various instruments of torture in a precise and ritualistic order: knives, pliers, hatchet, all kinds of psychopathic goodies. A black telephone was attached to the wall beside the light switches. The little torturer busied himself for a time at the implement table, getting his jollies, whistling some Mexican ditty and trying to make Novak think long and hard about what was coming next. Then he turned around and gazed straight at Novak for a couple of seconds. Novak didn't blink and didn't worry, because he was now out of the ropes. They'd given him way too much time to free himself. His captor walked over and stood right in front of him. He squatted down and smiled. His teeth were pristine and white. Probably dentures.

"Hello, Mr. Novak. Or should I call you the Mayan?"

Novak said nothing. Just stared back. He flexed his fingers and then doubled both fists behind his back. Ready to go.

"You were caught with a lot of evidence that points to your being a multiple murderer. A hired assassin, in fact. They have counted a dozen scalps found aboard your boat. That tells me, and more importantly, tells my superiors, that you are a killer of innocent people. Are you ready to admit your crimes and suffer the appropriate punishment?"

Novak remained calm and waited. "You got the wrong guy. The Mayan took me captive. He was planning to kill me or hold me for ransom. I got away and he went into the water. Then I took off in his boat and headed to shore to alert you guys. That's the truth. That's what I told the authorities who picked me up. That's what I'm telling you."

"Your lies are not believable. Your story is false. The officers who picked you up did not believe a word of it, nor do their superior officers, nor my superiors, one of whom is headed here to meet you as we speak."

That means I've got to move now, Novak thought. "I'm telling you the truth. I'll answer all your questions. I've got no problem with that. But I want you to contact the American embassy and let them know I'm here and what you're charging me with."

The guy showed Novak his teeth some more. Real proud of those dentures. His eyes weren't smiling. They were bulging and restless.

He was waiting for Novak to show the first signs of terror, like all practiced torturers did. "We've been looking for you for years, you know, but our task forces failed to find you, and all that was long before I joined up. You've outsmarted us again and again, but this time? This time you are not getting away with your crimes."

"I didn't kill anybody. I'm not the Mayan—"

Novak's words were cut off as the guy thrust the cattle prod into his chest. Novak yelled and jerked spasmodically as the jolt went through him, like a current of lighting up his spinal column. When it was removed, he shook with reaction, gasping for breath.

"Now, señor," the little guy was saying, "if you please, tell me the truth. You are the Mayan, are you not?"

Novak heaved in a deep breath, got hold of his shaky muscles, and then rocketed out of the chair and rammed his right fist so hard into the guy's Adam's apple that he heard it crunch under his knuckles. The guy went over backward, gargling on his own blood, and Novak jerked him back up by the front of his shirt and brought his knee up and smashed it into his face. Blood spurted everywhere, and the guy went down. Novak stood there a moment, panting, still trembling in reaction to the shock, and then he left the guy on the concrete floor, barely breathing.

Novak grabbed a machete off the torture table and headed for the door. He stopped beside it and listened. No noise, no voices. He pulled it open and found two guards stationed outside. They were smoking and watching a soccer game through a window across the hall. He hit the first one so hard in the head that it knocked him completely off his feet. He heard the skull crack. The other guard was bringing up his rifle, but Novak got a good grip on it, jerked it out of his hands, and thrust the butt hard into the man's face. The guy went down to his knees. Novak kicked him in the face. Neither one of them moved again. Novak looked around and rubbed his sore wrists, and then he moved quickly down the corridor and found the steps leading up to the first floor.

That's where he met the other six armed guards. All of them raised their weapons and pointed them at him. Novak dropped the rifle and machete and raised his hands and went along with them. He'd never had this much bad luck in his life. Not in his missions with the SEALs, not in Iraq, not in Afghanistan, not anywhere. His chest still ached from the electric current, but these new guys seemed like a nicer bunch. They allowed him to walk between them, unbound and unfettered. Very sweet, but one great big mistake. He could take them out now, no problem. But he wanted to know where they were taking him. If it was upstairs to be interviewed by a top government official, maybe he'd get out of this mess alive after all. He hoped somebody had shown up from the American embassy and demanded to see him. Well, that didn't happen, either. His luck was not getting any better.

Instead, and to Novak's concern, they marched him straight out through a side door and shoved him into the backseat of a shiny black Lincoln Town Car. Very plush inside; very quiet and well-maintained. The driver wore green camouflage and didn't turn around when Novak got in. Too cool a guy to notice the new prisoner. Twin guards crowded in on either side of him and jerked a dark hood down over his head. Not good. Not good at all. All this drama was getting old. Or maybe he was too old for this kind of crap.

They drove for what he estimated to be an hour and a half or so. He listened to the sounds outside the car, dim but identifiable. They were in heavy traffic first, stopping at intersections, and then came lots of honking horns and braking automobiles and more frequent stoplights. A siren wailed now and then. Novak said nothing. The guards said nothing. The driver said nothing. A real lively bunch. So he sat there unmoving and figured that one of three things was going to happen next. One, they had found out his true credentials and would take him somewhere isolated and let him go before his capture got them in trouble with the U.S. government. Two, they would take him somewhere isolated and put a bullet in the back of his head. Or three, he was headed to the American consulate and freedom. He suspected it might be option two, but he wasn't going to let that happen. He was unshackled and sore as hell from the shock to his body, but it just made him angrier. He could still fight, and he sure as hell could take down these two guards and the cool-joe driver. He planned it out in his head in specific detail, trying to decide if he should make his move inside the car or wait until it stopped and they pulled him out. He decided on the latter. Being inside city environs with lots of witnesses and his captors wearing military garb might do more harm than good.

The drive continued for quite some time. Another hour, maybe. He could see at the bottom of the hood that daylight was fading.

More hours passed. Lots of time, just sitting between the guards with nobody saying a word. The drive went on for what seemed like most of the night. Where the hell were they taking him? Argentina? He could also tell they were gradually rising in elevation, going up into the hills. Winding roads, dead silence inside the car, silence outside the car; it was looking more to him like the *take him out and execute him* scenario. He waited, forcing himself to be calm now. The adrenaline had faded long ago, but he kept himself ready to strike. He had his plan, and handling the two guys in back should be easy. The third guy might be a problem since he was harder to reach, but he had a hunch the driver was the kind of guy who didn't like to mess up his hair. So he went through the steps inside his head and waited, and calmed his pulse, and tried to be patient. He had better chances here than he'd had in the torture chamber with that cattle prod.

Novak waited as they kept ascending curving roads. He could tell it was still night, but it had to be closing in on dawn soon. All the better. Once he made his escape, he could take the car and make a run for it. If he could find a phone somewhere, he could call Jenn and hole up in her nearest safe house. If not, he could dump the car and steal another one. He needed reinforcements, and he needed to find out what the hell was going on. Whatever it was, he was caught in the middle of it. He didn't like that. He didn't like anything that was happening. He was usually patient and methodical and even-tempered in this kind of situation, but enough was enough. He was sick of getting pushed around. Time to take charge and put a few more people down for good.

Chapter Eighteen

When the limo finally slowed to a stop, the driver's window slid down and somebody outside the car spoke in low, colloquial Spanish. Then the guy on Novak's right jerked the hood off his head. Novak blinked and squinted as the Lincoln rolled forward again and followed a paved driveway up a long and gradual hill. It looked like a private estate. Tall white stone walls, at least seven or eight feet high, protected inhabitants from intruders. Or perhaps from the police. It looked like the domain of a drug lord to Novak. And that meant Ruiz, which also meant the Mayan.

They drove for about fifty yards, up through a vast field of grass with a multitude of trees crowding the perimeter but very few inside the wall. Novak twisted around and found a panorama of a sprawling city spread out far away in the valley below. Ablaze with lights, Mexico City spread out for miles in the wide basin surrounded by ancient volcanic mountains. The estate was out in the middle of nowhere, where everyone was safe except for Novak. The actual mansion and outbuildings were protected by a second wall, a lower one of about five or six feet, with a wide and ornate metal gate fashioned with a huge stylized sunburst. A button sent it opening slowly inward. Another curved and beautifully landscaped road took them to the front of the Spanish Colonial–style mansion. A massive red double door set with black iron hinges faced a bricked plaza, and beautiful gardens surrounded the circular court, with flowering vines and tinkling fountains.

The house was gigantic, somewhat resembling the façade of the Alamo in Texas, but three times larger and with the studied kind of grandeur that occurs when modern man imitates historical landmarks. Stone Mayan gods stood on either side of the front door, and black iron balconies ran across the upstairs rooms. Twin bell towers on either side, tall and slender, with arched windows at the top, flanked the eight-foot front door. Up in the belfries, armed guards stood in the open arches and pointed automatic rifles down at Novak. Novak made no quick moves as he exited the car. This place was definitely not an army base. This was the home turf of Marisol's evil *papi*, and that meant Novak was in big trouble.

Novak was led across the bricked court to the front door. Politely, too. Any other time, he might have disarmed the guards escorting him, shot down as many of the guys on the roof as he could spot, and made a run for it. But the massive gates had closed up tight behind them, and they had to be miles from the nearest village. No wonder Marisol Ruiz felt like a prisoner in the place. Novak had no choice but to go along with whatever they threw at him, but the right moment would present itself. It always did, and until then he would take advantage of their hospitality. The gigantic door dwarfed him and was swung open from the inside by a maid wearing a crisp black uniform with a white apron, an older woman, maybe fifty or so, her gray hair pinned into a bun. Novak entered with his double guard and they all stood together in a quiet central hall. Large red terracotta tiles lined the floor, and there was Mayan art all over the place, most of which looked like priceless museum artifacts, as well as a few Spanish conquistador swords and iron helmets that must have been heisted from Mexico's National Museum of Anthropology. Novak was not interested in the decor. His attention latched onto the man descending the wide tiled staircase.

Okay, the head badman himself was making his appearance: Arturo Ruiz, Father of the Year reject. He turned out to be a big guy, almost as tall as Novak, maybe six feet three or four inches. Close to three hundred pounds, mostly muscle, except for a soft and flabby paunch that hung over the elastic waistband of his sweatpants. That was where Novak would hit him first. He was smoking a narrow Cuban cigar, a cheroot, maybe, one that left a distinct and somewhat pleasant odor hanging in the air. Mr. Mafioso was wearing a bathrobe, red velvet, with a white T-shirt and the stretchy black sweatpants under it. Probably not expecting to entertain any avowed enemies at bedtime. He smiled at Novak when Novak was pulled up in front of him, as if delighted to have a captive to abuse. He motioned with a toss of his head for the guards to escort Novak into the room at the far end of the hall. The guards stood back politely and allowed Novak to precede them.

Once they reached what turned out to be a big library, they shoved him down into a chair sitting in front of a wide Spanish desk, both made from teak and brass-studded leather. Not so polite anymore. Great mullioned windows rose up behind the desk, floor to ceiling and dwarfing everything else in the room. Novak could see the night sky, stars sparkling, but the hint of dawn was peeking over the distant horizon. The sky was slowly lightening to gray. They had come a long way from the city. Ruiz followed them inside, rounded the desk, and sat down in a crimson-cushioned chair that looked like something found in the royal throne room of the British monarchy. Then he stared at Novak, still smiling. Maybe he was a friendly guy.

"Welcome, Mr. Novak." His gracious greeting was spoken in English and in a deep, impressive voice that was very heavily accented.

"Somehow I don't feel so welcome. Maybe it's all these guns your guys keep jabbing into my back. And that hangman's hood they forced me to wear all the way up here."

"Your reputation precedes you, Mr. Novak." After that was said in English, he lapsed back into Spanish, obviously more comfortable in his native tongue. "We have taken the proper precautions for our safety and will continue to do so while you are a guest in my home. You have earned a reputation for killing people who annoy you. You have single-handedly injured three officers and put them all in the hospital this very day. Who could blame me for my caution?"

"I blame you for that, and for just about everything else that has happened to me since your friends in that gunboat accused me of murder."

"It was an unfortunate incident, but something that had to be done. You are a persistent man."

"Yeah, it seemed unfortunate to me."

"But then again, the *Calakmul* is not your boat. It is the boat of my dear friend."

"The Mayan, you mean? He sank my boat so I meant to return the favor. Didn't have time to sink it before your goons got to me."

Ruiz contemplated him. He lifted his face and blew a couple of excellent smoke rings. Novak hadn't seen anybody do that since he and his friends had sneaked behind the bleachers back in high school. He watched the smoke drift in little circles up to the big rafters. Then Ruiz waved his hand, and the guards backed off and retreated. They stopped at the door, rifles propped on their right shoulders like sentries in front of Buckingham Palace. This guy definitely had royal aspirations.

"Do you know what *Calakmul* refers to, señor?"

"It's been on my mind a lot lately."

Ruiz smiled. "It was the name of one of the greatest cities of the Mayan empire."

Novak just stared at him, trying to gauge what was coming next. He was not here for a geography lesson on the Mayans, or a meal of tamales and tacos. So he sat still and stared unblinkingly at the notorious crime boss. He didn't look so intimidating in that red velvet bathrobe and matching scuffs, but what man would?

"So, here we are, Ruiz. You went to a hell of a lot of trouble to get me here. I guess I should thank you for that. Never have liked cattle prods. So? What do you want with me?"

"I think we both know what I want."

"Maybe you know. Me? Not so sure. Maybe you should fill in the particulars so we can straighten all these misunderstandings out and I can get back home to Louisiana."

"You have been traveling with my daughter, Marisol, no? You have been helping her escape from me."

"I don't know what you're talking about. I don't know anybody named Marisol."

"I want to know why you took her and kept her from me. Why you tried to hide her so that I could not find her? She is my only child and very dear to me. You had no right to do that. You have caused me a great deal of grief and worry."

"Good luck with keeping your kid happy, but don't look at me. I don't know anybody named Marisol. I just got caught up in something out on the Gulf. Believe me, I'm sorry I did. Pirate types hijacked my boat and then all of them ended up dead with the tops of their heads sliced off. Maybe you've got the wrong man here. Maybe you need to talk to the Mayan."

"I have heard that you are ruthless, a man to be reckoned with. That you kill whenever it pleases you."

"Ditto. Hey, maybe you need to talk to that personal assassin of yours. See what he's been up to lately. Me, I just try to defend myself when necessary. Never go looking for trouble. Never have."

Ruiz took a drag on the cigar, blew more smoke, no rings this time. He sighed. Poor guy just couldn't catch a break with that crazy daughter of his. But he kept his eyes fixed on Novak's features. His expression had grown rock hard and unmoved.

"Look, Ruiz, I don't know what you're talking about. How about just letting me go and we'll call this thing even. I've never seen your daughter in my life. Like I just told you, I was out on my sailboat, minding my own business, when I was hijacked and taken to some jungle camp south of Chetumal."

"I have it on good authority that you have been traveling with my daughter, and I suspect that you have been trying to turn her against me. I want her back in this house, safe and sound. You have been interfering with my family, and I do not like it. I would prefer to kill you right now where you sit, stab you in the jugular and watch you bleed out. I'd do it if I thought that would get my Marisol to come back home and live with me."

"Man, you are not listening to a word I'm saying. You got the wrong guy this time. I was just fishing out there when those pirates showed up and took my boat. Then your own personal little ninja assassin killed those guys and tried to kill me. Guess I owe him a debt of gratitude for screwing that up, except he keeps following me around and trying to finish the job. Doesn't seem friendly of him, but I've always been a sensitive guy."

"Yes, my dear boy is quite thorough." Ruiz coughed into the back of his hand. Too many cigars, too many smoke rings. Novak just stared a hole through him. "I was told that you stole his boats from him. Not once, but twice."

Novak smiled. "Yeah, but I had to. I needed some transportation after he sank my sailboat. But look, Ruiz, I'm just a beach bum. That's it. I'm not interested in working anywhere for anybody. Hard work disagrees with me. So does killing, despite what you've heard. I like the peaceful life, doing nothing and enjoying it."

"You are tiresome. Tell me why you had my daughter with you. Were you paid to help her get away from me? If so, I need the name of the person responsible for this affront to my family. Please tell me so this does not become difficult."

"I have no idea what you're talking about."

"Tell me what you and Marisol were planning to do. I know she's been on your boat, as well as in Chetumal with you. Were the two of you trying to run away together? Elope? Is that what this is all about?"

"Why don't you tell me this? Why'd she run away from you if you have such a great relationship with her? Ever ask yourself the hard questions?"

"Because she is young and headstrong and immature. I refuse to let her do dangerous things or associate with undesirable people such as yourself. She resents my interference."

"Maybe you should just let her go off and do her thing. She's an adult now, isn't she? Maybe you'd both be better off."

Ruiz heaved a deep breath that lifted his massive chest. It fell again, a heavy, heartfelt sigh. "I want her safe. Here with me where I can protect her from herself. Not out on her own where she gets herself into trouble."

"Well, wish I could help you, but I don't have a clue where she is."

"My daughter is not much more than a child. I have enemies who might wish to harm her or use her against me. I cannot allow that to happen, my friend."

"I'm not your friend. And I'll say it again, I don't know her, I don't know where she is, and I don't know how to find her. I sure as hell never eloped with her. You are wasting your time hassling me."

"I know that you are lying."

About that moment, Novak picked up a tiny little blip in the night sky behind Ruiz. It was blinking and moving fast over the tree line at the bottom of the hill. He watched it approach the estate, pretty damn sure it was a helicopter coming straight at them and at a high rate of speed. Ruiz seemed unaware. He didn't turn around. He just watched Novak watch it. Novak frowned, not quite sure what was going on.

"You don't understand what happened to Marisol, do you, Mr. Novak?"

Since the man already seemed to know, Novak dropped the subterfuge. "I understand she's scared of you and thinks you're going to kill her the minute she steps foot back in this little Spanish palace of yours."

Ruiz compressed his lips in a tight line and then he shook his head. "All wrong. All lies. Marisol is headstrong and easily influenced. I have punished her, as any father punishes his child. I have been harsh with her at times, I readily admit it. I had no choice. Most of her life, I have been much too generous. I would never hurt her or any other member of my family. She is all I have now. She means everything to me."

"So what then? You order your little Mayan buddy to teach her a lesson or just get rid of her for you?"

Ruiz frowned. "What do you mean?"

"Come on, Ruiz. You remember him? The guy who slits throats and takes scalps? Real nice guy. The one with the boats. The one you sent to murder your own daughter."

"He was sent to find her. He would never hurt her."

"Yeah? Think again."

"He's like a son to me and a brother to Marisol. He would never hurt her."

Novak just stared at him. Okay, this whole conversation was more than a bit off-kilter. Ruiz seemed genuinely puzzled now. Novak halfway believed him, but not all the way. But it could be that Papi was clueless. He didn't know squat about what was going on. The Mayan was playing Ruiz for a fool.

The helicopter had arrived outside and was hovering over the long expanse of grassy lawn, its rotors beating hard. The sky was getting blue now, the sun peeking over the horizon. Novak said nothing else, just watched the chopper. It was white. The racket was deafening. *Thut, thut, thut.* It hovered for a time and then it set down, slowly and expertly, a good way behind the house in an open field of grass. The rotors continued to turn. Nobody got out.

"Looks like you've got company back there. Maybe the authorities coming in to arrest you."

"That is not possible."

"Paid off, huh?"

Ruiz smiled, damn indulgent where Novak was concerned, it seemed. "Actually, the chopper is here to pick you up."

Novak went immediately wary. Didn't sound right to him. Didn't sound good, either. They probably intended to take him up to ten thousand feet and push him out the door. That sounded more within the realm of Ruiz law.

"Come, Mr. Novak, we don't want to make them wait."

Ruiz stood up and gestured expansively for Novak to step through the French doors that opened to the outside terrace. Novak walked out into the cool, fresh air. He was on edge now, big-time, and for good reason. Maybe they were going to shoot him and let the chopper act as a flying garbage disposal. On the other hand, he'd been in their custody a long time now. If they wanted him dead, they would've killed him already. Also strange was the fact that he still was not bound, not in any way. Maybe they considered escape impossible, given the compound walls and rugged mountainous terrain, miles from the city.

Outside, there was a long flight of concrete steps that led down to a rectangular swimming pool and large pool house, also built in the same elegant Spanish architectural style. Lots of statues of the Virgin Mary holding baby Jesus down there, along with other religious icons along the pathways. Ruiz stood at the top of the stairs and gazed out over his kingly domain.

"I never have understood why Marisol fights me so. I have given her everything she ever wanted. She has been my whole life, my only family, since my wife died giving birth to her. And yet she flees from me and worries me to distraction."

"Could be your tendency to, you know, murder people and traffic drugs and send assassins to kill her."

"Don't be ridiculous. I keep my business dealings away from her. It is her young friends who have corrupted her. She was a sweet child, just a little angel, until she went off to college in your country."

"Yeah, college is always a bitch for mafioso kids."

Ruiz ignored him after that, his eyes latched on the helicopter. He started down the steps. Novak walked a little behind him. He felt like a prisoner heading to the scaffold, one who thought he had been reprieved but was instead the subject of a cruel joke. In any case, he wasn't going down easy. They had made a mistake keeping him unfettered.

Muscles tense but ready to move, he stepped a few feet away from Ruiz when they reached the long patio at the bottom of the steps. The pool lay on a separate terrace below them. The helicopter was still out in the vast yard at ground level, rotors spinning. Ruiz started down to the pool. Novak followed again, wary as hell. Something was about to happen. He just wasn't sure what.

They strode along the edge of the pool that shone now under the slanted rays of the morning sun peaking over the mountains in the distance. More steps took them down to the grassy lawn, lots of flower gardens and low stucco walls all around them. Deadly drug lords lived high on the hog in Mexico. Ruiz didn't stop walking until they were about twenty feet out onto the grass. That put somewhere around fifty yards between them and the helicopter. It was just sitting there, ready to take off at a moment's notice. Ruiz stopped at the spot where about twelve of his armed men stood, spread out on either side of him and Novak. They all had rifles pointed at the helicopter instead of at Novak. So that meant the chopper was not friendly to Ruiz. First good news all night.

Not sure yet what was going to happen, Novak focused his eyes on the helicopter, just like everyone else. The rotors were moving faster now, the light still flashing on top, all in all making one hell of a racket. Ruiz raised his arm in a sort of wave. A few minutes passed, and then the passenger-side door of the chopper swung open. A woman got out and stood beside the door.

Novak's heart nearly stopped. It was Claire Morgan. God bless every hair on her head, it was his partner. She had come through big-time. She was carrying a semiautomatic rifle and had it zeroed in on Ruiz's massive chest. Along the line of armed men beside Novak, all their rifle barrels moved a fraction of an inch and beaded on Claire. Claire's odds weren't so good at the moment. But that was Claire. She had guts like nobody he'd ever seen. He just hoped she hadn't walked into a trap, because that's what it looked like to Novak.

Novak kept his eyes riveted on her. Somebody else climbed down out of the chopper, another woman. He didn't recognize her at first. A tall blonde. Thin, tan, dressed in white shorts and an orange tank top. She had a white bandage on her upper arm. She stepped out beside Claire, and she looked a lot like the woman Novak had seen the day he was chasing Marisol through the streets of Chetumal. What the hell was going on? He couldn't see the pilot because of the glare of the sun behind the chopper, but it had to be Nicholas Black. Novak was glad to see some friendly faces for a change.

"You see, I am a fair man, Mr. Novak. You are free to leave with your friends," Ruiz was telling him. "We negotiated a trade last night. My daughter for you. The terms were that simple. I do hope your friends in that helicopter don't renege on the deal, because you are totally outnumbered, both in men and firepower."

"Wouldn't be wise to underestimate us," Novak told him.

"Oh, I am not. I've read newspaper accounts of your friends out there. But Nicky Black is the one that I know personally. He and his brother, Jacques Montenegro. They must think a great deal of you, because Jacques and his people intervened quite forcefully for your release."

Novak frowned. Maybe so. Maybe all that was true. But the unknown woman, whoever the hell she was, would be the sacrificial lamb, once Ruiz realized she wasn't his daughter. Her father hadn't seemed to notice that yet, but all hell was going to break loose when he did.

Ruiz was smiling and shielding his eyes from the blinding rays of the sun. "I love my daughter, Mr. Novak. She has caused me more grief than you could ever imagine, but she is my only child. I want her here with me."

Novak said nothing. Then Ruiz got personal. "Are you blessed with children, Mr. Novak?"

Novak felt himself stiffen. He didn't talk about his children to anybody, not since they died when the south tower came down. Not ever. He didn't answer Ruiz's question. Ruiz didn't seem to notice.

"If and when you do, you will understand a father's love for his daughter. The protective instincts are embedded inside us at the very moment they come into the world. Marisol is vulnerable, being my daughter and very much an easy target for my enemies to exploit. Others wish to use her to extort money from me. She is not safe from harm anywhere in this world except here on my compound. That's the reason I always bring her back."

Novak could understand that. "Well, good for you. You captured her again."

"It would be unwise for you to return here."

"I get that."

Novak watched the blonde start walking slowly toward them. He knew how hostage exchanges went down, so he headed out across the grass to meet her. He moved a lot faster than she did, because he expected bullets to punch into his back at any minute. No reason for them not to finish him off. They were holding all the cards. If it hadn't been for Ruiz's fear of Jacques Montenegro, Novak would probably already be dead on the ground.

The young woman met him about twenty yards from the chopper.

She was a pretty girl. Looked a whole lot like Marisol except for the blond hair, which was bleached. Dark roots showed down the middle part. She appeared quite calm and collected about walking into a lion's den. She didn't look at him at first, but then she stopped walking and turned to face him. Her smile was strange and somehow knowing.

"So we meet at last, Mr. Novak."

"Who the hell are you?"

"Jenn and your little Marisol will explain everything to you. Jenn told me to tell you not to worry about them. They are both safe and sound at her beach house. She said they'll wait for you there until you can come back and pick them up."

That relieved Novak a hell of a lot. "Who are you?"

"Jenn will tell you everything. She's waiting for you."

"Why are you taking this kind of chance? You don't know what you're getting into. Ruiz is going to kill you the minute he realizes you aren't Marisol."

That made her smile. "But you're wrong, Mr. Novak. I am Marisol Ruiz. I am Arturo's daughter."

Novak could only stare at her. She'd managed to shock him, and he didn't shock easily.

She glanced down the length of the grassy field at her father and then turned back to Novak. "Enough people have been hurt because I wanted to be out from under my father's control. All of this is my own fault. It is time for me to return home and face my father's anger."

Novak wasn't buying it, not for a minute. "If you're Marisol Ruiz, who's the kid I've been dragging around for days?"

"Go to the beach house and let them explain it all to you. They are quite well and waiting for you. The Mayan will not waste his time on them now that I am home. He is more interested in finding that little girl that you found hidden on the *Calakmul*."

"How do you know about that?"

"You better get out of here while you still can," she told him. Then she started walking slowly toward Ruiz and his armed guards. Novak looked back at Ruiz. The big man stood in the same spot, waiting, his eyes on the blonde, his cigar forgotten in his hand. All his men swiveled their weapons to Novak's head.

Frowning, confused at the weird turn of events, Novak ran toward the chopper. When he was about ten yards out, Claire Morgan yelled at him. "Hurry the hell up, Novak! Before they start shooting!"

Novak ducked under the rotors, the wind whipping his shirt, but he paused at the copter's door. Ruiz and the girl now stood about six feet apart. It didn't look like the warmest reunion he'd ever seen. He was having trouble believing that she was really Marisol Ruiz. It had to be a trick, but if it was, Ruiz was buying it. Novak climbed into the backseat, and Claire jumped in the front and slammed the door. Nicholas Black told them to buckle the hell up. Claire obeyed, but she kept the rifle beaded on Ruiz. Black lifted slowly off the ground and banked left in a gradual turn toward the sea. Once they were out of range of the compound, Claire turned to Novak and said, "What the devil? You trying to get yourself killed?"

Novak was more than glad to see her. He was glad, too, to get out of the Ruiz compound in one piece. But there was that one little snag. He put on the headphones that Claire handed him and spoke into the microphone.

"I hate to tell you this, but we've got a problem."

"Oh great. What now?" Claire asked, twisting around to look at him.

Novak glanced back at the small figures standing at the edge of the pool, as Black swept the copter around and headed back to the city. Father and self-proclaimed daughter had not embraced, but he hadn't ordered the young woman shot, either. "That girl down there? She's not the Marisol Ruiz I know. So who the hell is she?"

Claire's jaw dropped. "She told us that she was Marisol Ruiz. She's the one who showed up at the airstrip after Jenn and I set up her exchange for you."

"Well, I've never seen her before."

Claire shook her head and turned back around. Novak frowned some more and tried to figure out how he was being played and why, without much success.

"How did you know Ruiz had me?" Novak asked them a moment later.

"You called me, remember? Said you were being taken prisoner and the Ruiz cartel might be involved."

Black spoke up. "My brother knows Ruiz. He negotiated your

release. You made an impression on him when you helped us last summer in Sicily."

Novak knew all about Nicholas Black's brother. Jacques Montenegro was a well-known, powerful mob boss out of New Orleans. Black was not a part of his brother's business and never had been. Novak also knew Montenegro played a major role in a bigger syndicate, with lots of mob contacts all over the world. Jacques had used his illicit business relationships in Sicily to gain his brother's release and now had used them again in the mountains of Mexico. He was turning out to be a good friend to have.

"So you're welcome," Claire said.

"You talked to Jenn yourself?"

Claire turned around again. "Yeah, she got hold of me somehow, and we put the exchange in motion. That girl we just let out back there? She showed up at the airstrip in a white Winnebago and told us that she was Marisol Ruiz and Jenn had sent her out to us. She said Jenn was okay and would wait for you at the beach house. You don't know her, really?"

"I have no idea who she is. But she's connected with the girl I've been protecting because I saw her on the street when the kid with us tried to take off. I think they've been in contact somehow, maybe by cell phone or something. Maybe the girl back there at the compound is the real Marisol Ruiz. Maybe the two of them had some kind of ruse going on. Ruiz didn't shoot her down the minute she got close to him. That tells me that she probably is his daughter."

"Jenn told me that Marisol had agreed to go back home to her father. She said once the girl was with us, Jenn would wait for you at the beach house. Everything seemed fine then. She was worried about that child you told us about. She thinks the killer's going to go after the little girl instead of us, especially once Ruiz gets his daughter back into the fold."

Novak felt a prickle of fear slither down his nerves. The blond Marisol had told him that Jenn and the other girl were waiting at the beach house. And that made as little sense as everything else that was going on. If the Mayan had been out to kill Marisol, and he had been, he just lost out on his paycheck. But Ruiz told Novak that the Mayan had been instructed to find her, not to kill her. So who was the girl that Novak had been protecting for days, the one with the same blue butterfly tattoo that Marisol was supposed to have? And why did the Mayan want her if she wasn't Marisol? The killer couldn't get to her now, wouldn't be able to find her, not since Novak had dug out the GPS chip, so she was safe with Jenn. And he couldn't get the real Marisol; she was under her father's protection and inside that fortified compound. But the child could definitely identify him as the man who had abducted and tortured her, and he might be able to get to her out at Doc's. So they better get back there quick and get her out. And that meant that Doc and Auroria were in danger, too. The Mayan left no witnesses.

"Let me have your cell," Novak said to Claire.

She handed it back to him, and he tried to call Doc. Nobody answered. Shit. Something bad had gone down; Novak knew it. "I think he's going after the little girl I found on his boat, too. I think he's found out where she is and is probably headed there, if he's not there already."

"Good God, Novak, what the heck is going on down here?"

So Novak told them the whole sordid story. Neither Claire nor Black commented, just listened intently.

"I've never heard of an assassin called the Mayan until now." Claire looked at Black. "Have you?"

"Not by that name. I know there are assassins for hire all across Central America. Some pretty bad guys. The scalping thing is new to me."

"I'm going to get him," Novak said.

"That'll probably get you a standing ovation from all concerned," Claire said.

"He's on a killing spree, and he's coming after me next, if I don't get him first. And he tortured that poor little kid. She's probably eight years old, maybe even younger. He beat her and slashed her up with a knife."

Claire looked horrified. "Oh my God."

Black said, "Then you need to get him."

"I want to know who the girl is, the one who's been telling me she's Marisol all this time. I want to know why she lied to Jenn and me. She could have gotten us killed. Did Jenn say the girl was with her at the beach?"

"She just said she had agreed to go home. I assumed she meant the blonde who showed up."

Black glanced back at Novak. "Is there a place I can put down near where the child is? If the killer knows how to get to her, we better get her out of there first. Jenn seems capable of taking care of herself. The little girl is a sitting duck."

"Where'd you leave her, Novak?" Claire asked.

"With a good friend of mine. A Marine medic who's taking care of her. I think she knows something that the Mayan wants to know, and that's why he's keeping her alive."

"Maybe she saw him commit a murder," said Black.

"Well, let's go get her and then get Jenn and the other girl you're talking about. I want to get out of here," Claire told him. "We'll all be safe back in the States. We can figure out how to bring down the killer after we get them up there."

"Where'd you land the plane?"

"At the airport in Belize City. We leased the helo there."

Right now, Novak didn't know who he was more worried about, Doc and his wife and the child or Jenn and the girl pretending to be Marisol Ruiz. The Mayan seemed to know his way around and appeared to have lots of access to lots of pertinent intelligence. Novak just had to figure out how to counter the killer's next move. Not a whole lot else was making sense at the moment.

Novak dialed up Jenn's private line. He let it ring according to the arranged code. No answer. Then he called back and let it ring ten times. Nothing. Then he tried a second number. Nothing there, either. Then he sat back and felt sick to his stomach. She should have answered, should have been waiting for his call. Claire and the blonde had both said she was safe at the beach house. Maybe she had a good reason for not answering. Maybe the phone was dead. Maybe she'd left the cell in the car or lost it somewhere. He kept telling himself these things as they reached the coast and sped out over the ocean. But he was worried. Now he had a bad feeling in the pit of his stomach, about everything and everybody.

Chapter Nineteen

Once Nicholas Black got the helicopter out over the water, it didn't take him long to get them to Soledad Cay. They flew very fast, skimming the water, the sound of the rotors' beating relentless. Nobody said much else. Novak sat there and continued to worry about Jenn. Down deep, he couldn't believe she'd let anybody get within a hundred feet of her and the girl. She was just too damn good at what she did. But he was anxious to get to that beach house and find out what the hell was going on.

Then he thought of the tortured little girl he'd left at Doc's house. He felt certain the Mayan would go after her first. It stood to reason. He had kept her alive and on board his boat. He had tortured her. He would want to finish her off before he again went after the woman masquerading as Marisol, whoever she was. Novak was at a loss as to what her role was in all of this. Why had she stayed with Novak and insisted she was Ruiz's daughter? What was her connection with the real Marisol, if the blonde even really was Marisol? It appeared to Novak that she had to be. Once the two of them had stood face-to-face, her father had accepted her. Maybe one of the other girls, either the one still with Jenn or the little child, was the other kidnap victim who'd disappeared from the convent along with Marisol. Maybe the Mayan knew the little girl's family and wanted to take her and hold her for ransom. Maybe she'd seen him take Marisol and had to be silenced. Or maybe he had just liked the looks of her and that's all it took. Who knew the inner workings of that maniac's mind? The whole damn thing was bizarre. Novak would feel better when he had the Mayan in his crosshairs and could slowly tug back on the trigger and be done with him for good. Right now, however, he did not have all the facts and was not quite sure what was going on.

When they finally arrived at the turquoise waters off Doc's cove, Novak leaned forward and looked for the flags. The Marine Corps flag was gone. Crap. That meant trouble, and that probably also meant the Mayan had been there. Black took the copter down low and hovered over the boat dock, pushing fast-moving concentric rings out across the water.

"Doc's not in there."

"How do you know?" Claire asked.

"He signals with the flags. He's not in there, but I know where he is. He's got a bunker out on his airstrip. If he gets spooked, he gets the hell out on his Cessna. If he doesn't have time to fly out, he holes up in that bunker."

"Good. That probably means they got away, if that guy showed up here," Claire was telling him. "They're probably safe and sound and hidden away inside that bunker, so quit looking like something horrible has happened. You don't know that yet." She was trying to cheer him up, but she didn't know the Mayan, hadn't seen his work. But Novak knew Doc. Doc was nobody's fool. If he'd had any advance warning at all, any inkling of incoming danger, he would've gotten his wife and the little girl on that plane or inside that bunker. He'd never take a chance on Auroria's life. Novak just hoped he'd had some kind of forewarning.

"Where's the airstrip?" Black asked, glancing back at him.

"Straight behind the house, about a mile and a half, I guess."

Black took the helicopter up over the house, and Novak leaned his forehead against the back window, his eyes glued on the dark green jungle rushing past below, waiting for the terrain to clear and reveal the dirt airstrip.

"There it is. Up ahead. See it, Nick?" Novak said.

"Okay, I got it."

They slowly circled the field. It looked deserted. "That's Doc's Cessna, there under the camouflage netting. So they didn't get away on the plane. If he's still here, he's in the bunker. Land this thing and let's hope they're in there."

Black took the helo a good distance away from the airplane under the netting, then hovered for a few minutes, watching the jungle perimeter for attack, just in case. The Mayan could be there, and they all knew it. After several minutes, Black touched the chopper gently down onto the ground.

"Stay here. Be ready to get the hell out," Novak told them, as he pulled the door lever and stepped down onto the ground.

Ducking low, he ran out. He stopped a few yards outside the wind draft and waited, watching the camouflaged netting, his arms held up and out to his sides. If Doc was in there, he would be watching them. Nothing happened. The roar of the helo was deafening, and then, thank God, he caught some movement under the Cessna's wing. Seconds later, Doc stepped into view, armed with a rifle. He waved Novak toward him. Novak turned and gestured for Black to turn off the rotors.

Novak ran across the grassy field and met Doc at the nose of the plane. "Thank God, Doc. You had me worried there for a minute."

"Yeah, it was pretty damn tense for a while. I didn't hear him coming until it was almost too late to get out. Good thing he didn't know about this place."

"Is Auroria okay? And the kid?"

"Yeah. They're both down in the bunker."

Novak nodded. "Sorry I brought that guy down on you. Did you see him?"

"I heard the boat coming. Then the motor stopped somewhere outside the bay, and I figured he was gonna try to sneak in on us, like you said he did to that pirate camp. I didn't wait, just got Auroria and the kid the hell out. I would have tried to shoot him myself if I hadn't had to worry about them. Guess it was about two or three o'clock in the morning. I've got to say that you spooked me when you told me how he operated. I wanted nothing to do with that animal. How'd he find us?"

"I don't know. Probably had the GPS location where the Mexicans picked me up on the *Calakmul*. He seems to have his ways to find people. They got me before I was too far from here. I think he was the one who put them on to me. I guess I led him right to you. God, Doc, I'm sorry."

"Think he'll come back?"

"No, I think he would've tracked you out here to the bunker and killed all three of you if he'd known about it."

"That's why I built it. You're not the only one with old enemies."

"C'mon, let's get Auroria and the girl out of here."

Doc had built the bunker himself, underground, constructed of timber and concrete, ventilated with fresh air, but not made for any kind of siege. It was a temporary hiding place, well hidden in the jungle undergrowth beneath some of the netting. Hard to see from the air, or from a few feet away, it was a two-room fortified cabin of sorts, with enough weapons and ammunition to fight off a small army.

"I need a place like this on Bonne Terre," Novak told him, looking around. "Look, Doc, my friends out there in the helicopter can take you over to Jenn's. She can put you up in a safe house for as long as you need until I get him. We're headed there right now."

Doc shook his head. "No, we're okay here. Maybe I'll fly us over to Costa Rica for a few weeks. My wife has family there. They'll put us up, and she's been on me to take her to visit them."

"You'll be safer with me," Novak said.

"You really think so?" Doc searched his face, and Novak knew he was probably right. He wouldn't be safe with Novak, not right now. Nobody was.

"Okay, but don't waste time getting out of here. Get going now. I'll call you when I get him."

Doc nodded. "Just get that child to a hospital stat. I think she'll be all right, given some time. She's a lot better off now than she was when she got here."

"Has she said anything?"

"No. She mumbles occasionally and tries to open her eyes. Hasn't made it all the way awake yet, though. The antibiotics are helping. She's breathing easier and the fever's gone. She'll be okay when she comes to, and I think that'll be soon. She probably doesn't want to wake up, not after what she's been through."

The child was lying on a couch at the back of the bunker. Auroria was holding the girl's head on her lap. Very gently, Novak lifted her into his arms. He carried her out to the helicopter, and Claire and Black got out and started walking toward him. Black was a doctor, a psychiatrist, but he could help her. He'd know exactly what to do.

"My God, she's so little. Just tiny." That was Claire.

Black stepped up and felt her pulse and examined the splint on her wrist. "Yeah, she needs to be in a hospital. Come on, let's go. Tell Doc and his wife to hurry."

"They're going to stay with her family for a while. Doc says they'll be safe there."

Within minutes, Black and Claire were back in the front seat and Black was lifting off and heading out over the jungle again. Novak sat in back, the little girl stretched across the seats. He stared down at her bruised face, at her frail body, and made plans for what he was going to do to the Mayan when he got his hands on him. He thought about that all the way back to the coast of Belize.

The closer they got to Jenn's beach house, the more worried Novak became. She was still not answering any of her cell phones. She always answered eventually. Maybe she wouldn't if she was transitioning an asset, but she would return the call as soon as she could. Something was wrong, he knew it, and he feared the worst. The Mayan knew how to find people. He had found Jenn; Novak was sure of it. And if that was the case, Jenn was dead. Novak could not stand the thought of it.

Black set the chopper down on the wide dirt road that led down to Jenn's beach. Her house was small, with big airy porches and a widow's walk on the roof. Everything looked okay, untouched, just the way he remembered it. He pulled out his gun. "Wait here. I'm going in."

"No way, Novak. We're going with you."

Claire had that look on her face, the one he'd come to know that he couldn't argue with. "I've got a bad feeling about this, Claire. I brought Jenn into this crap, and I'm going in alone. I'm afraid he got to her."

"No, you are not going in alone. You got us down here, and we are going to help you. Somebody's got to."

Novak didn't have time to argue with her. He just nodded and started out toward the house. They left the child safely locked in the backseat and followed, spreading out on either side of him, keeping about ten yards' distance between them. Novak stopped at the edge of the beach. "You guys circle around to the front. I'll take the back. Stay outside until I clear the house."

They moved off and then angled around toward the ocean. Novak made his way up to the back deck, climbed the steps, and stood silently beside the kitchen slider. A gray Nissan was parked on the side of the house. It was the car he'd seen the blonde driving in Chetumal. She had been here, all right. Jenn should have seen him by now and opened the door—unless they were walking into a trap. The Mayan could still be inside, holding the women captive. Maybe it was a good thing Claire and Black had come along, after all. He pushed on the door handle. It slid easily to one side, so he pushed it open enough to edge inside. Everything looked the same as it had the last time he'd been there. Brown wicker furniture, white walls, white cabinets and countertops, but everything else awash with bright primary colors.

The first thing that hit him was the smell. Sick, horrible, stomach-turning. The smell of spilled blood. Novak knew then that Jenn was dead. His heart twisted. Every instinct told him to prepare himself for the worst, that he would find her dead and butchered any minute. He listened. Heard nothing but the low roar and ebb of waves sliding in over the hard-packed sand outside the front of the house. The camera over the refrigerator was tracking him. If Jenn was alive, she would have been watching and would have already shown herself.

Novak took a deep breath and covered his nose and mouth with the tail of his shirt. Then he moved across the kitchen, down low and slow. The light was shadowy inside, all the plantation shutters closed against the hot sun. That was normal. Jenn always kept them drawn to keep the place cool. A big bamboo ceiling fan rotated in the kitchen. Novak could feel the draft on top of his head. The smell was almost overwhelming. He moved past the kitchen table where he had eaten so many meals with Jenn, where he had made love to her once. He stopped at the door to the kitchen and kept his gun ready. He thrust the door open and the sickening odor intensified.

The living room was a mess. A big-time struggle had gone down. Jenn had fought her attacker tooth and nail. The glass coffee table was broken, Jenn's books scattered all over the floor. A vase of fresh daisies was overturned, the blossoms wilted now. All the security cameras had been taken down and smashed. Near the front door, he found the most blood—lots of it—a big puddle that had oozed under a wicker rocker and pooled against the white wall behind it. A river of red. Somebody had been murdered right there, not a foot in front of him. He stepped around the couch and looked down at so much blood that Novak could hardly believe it. Too much blood loss for any human being to survive. The Mayan had gotten her in the jugular. Or maybe he had gotten the woman he thought of as Marisol, who hadn't known how to fight back.

He checked all the rooms and found no sign of Jenn's body or evidence of another murder. He still had hopes of finding her alive. It was hard for him to believe that anyone had gotten the jump on her. Then he moved to the front slider. That's where he found Jenn's shoe—one of the sandals she had been wearing the morning she'd taken off with Marisol, the red ones with tiny little mirrors on the straps. It lay on its side in a pool of blood. Jenn's blood. Had to be. More blood was smeared across the floor and on the bottom of the door. The Mayan must have stabbed her right here while she was fighting for her life. No body, but again, this massive amount of blood could mean only one thing. Both women had been killed inside this room. There were no footprints in the blood leading away from the altercation.

Novak's heart started squeezing in upon itself. It got so tight for a moment that he couldn't breathe. He had been the one who had signed Jenn's death warrant, and Marisol's, whoever she had been. If he hadn't sought Jenn out, if he hadn't put her in this guy's cross-hairs, she'd be right here, alive and playing her favorite Sting CDs, or lying in the shade in the hammock, or taking care of her beloved plants. He tried to shake off the pain, the guilt. But he hadn't found her body. Maybe he was wrong. Maybe she was alive somewhere. Hiding. He searched the house again. Went up to the widow's walk. Nothing. Everything else looked in order.

Novak opened the slider and stepped out onto the covered front porch. That's when he saw another lake of blood, right outside the door. It had turned black now from the heat. It was sticky, like a pool of tar, with a stench that made him gag. Too much blood to have survived.

Claire and Black stood out in the front yard, waiting, looking as grim as he felt. They'd seen the blood, too, and knew what it meant.

"I think he killed Marisol first. Inside the house," he told them. "I think Jenn made it outside. I think he cut her throat right here. Right here in front of me."

"We found a trail of blood leading down to the beach." Claire pointed toward the low sand dunes between the house and the sea.

Blood spatter speckled the front steps, too, and great swaths of smeared blood. Novak found Jenn's other red sandal at the bottom of the steps. The Mayan had dragged her body down to the ocean. It looked as if she might have still been alive then, struggling for her life. Or maybe she had made a run for it after having been stabbed. He followed the blood spoor out over the soft warm sand. The Mayan had made no effort to cover it up. At the top of the dunes, it looked as if a body had lain in the tall seagrass. The grass was pressed down, and then shallow grooves in the sand revealed drag marks. Novak walked to the edge of the waves. The trail ended there. No more blood. No bodies. He had disposed of the bodies in the ocean. Maybe the tide had taken them out. Maybe he had put them in a boat and dumped them far out past the breakers.

Novak stared out over the beautiful turquoise sea that blended gradually into azure shadings with a strip of deep cobalt blue at the horizon. God, Jenn was dead. She had been surprised, even as careful as she was, and then murdered by a monster. Novak locked his gaze on the incoming waves and let his heart grow hard. Let his jaw lock down. Let the internal rage erupt and flood white-hot through his bloodstream.

Novak had always been methodical. He went about his business in a pedestrian fashion, got the job done, did whatever it took. He pursued bad people, some worse than others, all deserving of what they got. This time it was different. This time it was Jenn. She was special, and she had died a terrible death at the hands of a brutal serial killer. He was going to find the Mayan bastard and put him in the ground. Because the house, the beach, the blood, all were his calling cards. He had wanted the girl pretending to be Marisol, and he had finally gotten her. Novak didn't even know why the Mayan wanted the girl dead. Jenn had been collateral damage. And Jenn had been there because of Novak.

Novak turned abruptly and walked back to the helicopter, already planning how he would obtain his pound of flesh. Claire and Black followed him, both silent, aware of his anger and anguish, and respecting it. They knew what he had to do now, and they were going to let him do it. And they would help him, if he wanted them to. All he had to do was ask.

Chapter Twenty

On their way back to Goldson International Airport in Belize City, Novak listened to everything Claire and Black had to say, but he already knew what his next move would be. The Mayan was going to die. Claire was insisting on taking the sick child back to her place in Missouri. Black agreed that the girl would be safest there, far away from everything bad that had happened to her and from the assassin still hunting her.

"What do you think, Novak? C'mon now, snap out of it already. Talk to us," Claire was saying.

"Can we get her through customs?" Novak asked, staring down at the sleeping child. She looked so innocent lying there. Just a little kid, caught up in a nightmare.

"I can take care of that. No problem." That was Black. He didn't elaborate, but Black never overestimated anything and was cautious to a fault, so Novak took him at his word.

"We've got top security at the lake," Claire was telling Novak now, "both at Cedar Bend Lodge and at my cabin. Good grief, you should see the security systems Black put in at my new house. I mean, he got me a safe room and everything. The house isn't quite finished yet, but finished enough to make do. It's got its own private cove and private gated road. You've seen it yourself, Novak. We'd see this guy coming a mile away. Please, I don't want to leave her down here where that guy might find her. Black can take care of her medical needs. He's a doctor. There's just not a downside to taking her home with us."

Novak didn't resist. "Okay. I'll go along with you and get her settled. Then I'm coming back and finishing this thing."

Claire and Black glanced at each other but knew better than to object. Novak would do what he had to do. They couldn't stop him. They wouldn't even try.

Black's fancy new Gulfstream jet was waiting for them inside a hangar, gassed up, flight plan ready, all systems go. They took off for the United States half an hour later. Black's regular pilots manned the cockpit, so the three friends sat down together in the main salon and discussed their plans. Which didn't amount to much—not yet, anyway. Truth be told, they sat around pretty much in silence and contemplated how bad things were. Black had settled the child in the bedroom at the back of the plane and checked on her often. He said she was doing fine. Novak finally lay down on a long couch in the main compartment and forced himself to quit envisioning Jenn in death, how she must have looked after the killer had slit her throat, how she must have looked sinking down under the waves off the coast of the home that she loved so much. He had to make himself get some sleep. He was going to need it.

Novak had been in Missouri at Claire's beloved Lake of the Ozarks a couple of times, and both times had been for her weddings. The first one hadn't panned out, through no fault of her own. The second try had come off without a hitch. Back in late July when they'd finally wed, Black's posh lake resort had been the height of luxury and elegance. Claire's little A-frame on the lake had been just the opposite, small and cozy and comfortable. Novak had liked her place better, mainly because of its privacy, until it had been completely destroyed in an explosion. So he wasn't quite sure what to expect when Black set the helicopter down at the Cedar Bend Lodge helipad. The weather was unusually mild and sunny. The hotel was crowded with lots of guests everywhere, enjoying the indoor pools and golf course and tennis courts. Other people flocked to his casual cafes and posh five-star restaurant.

As soon as the rotors slowed, Novak caught sight of a small boy racing toward them with a tiny white poodle right on his heels. He had to smile, happy to see the kid again. The boy's name was Rico, ten years old or so, and the bravest boy Novak had ever known. He wasn't Claire and Black's son, but he was currently living with them. He seemed overjoyed to see them back home and jumped eagerly up into Claire's arms the minute she stepped out of the helicopter. She laughed and hugged him, and then he ran around and hugged

Black's legs. Claire scooped up the excited poodle and baby-talked it. Novak remembered the dog's name was Jules Verne. It was a happy homecoming. At least, it was for them.

Uneasy, Novak looked around, really examining their surroundings. This many innocent civilians rushing around everywhere made him damn nervous. The big resort would provide cover for a bad guy stalking a child. The Mayan would know that. Novak wanted to get the little girl inside a safe place and keep her there. Very gently, he lifted her into his arms. She had awakened on the flight home. But she hadn't said a word, just staring up at him out of big brown eyes full of fear. Hell, he didn't blame her. She didn't know who they were or what they were going to do to her. He spoke softly to her in Spanish, telling her that it was all right, that she was safe, and trying to explain where they were and what they were trying to do for her.

"Nobody's going to hurt you, I promise," he had whispered. "We're here to protect you. Nobody's going to hurt you anymore."

The child had closed her eyes after that but her body remained tense. He needed her to talk to him. He needed her to tell him who the Mayan was and why he'd held her captive. More importantly, Novak wanted to know where he could find the bloodthirsty bastard. But she wasn't going to tell him anything, not anytime soon. She wasn't going to trust them, either, not for one single second. Even more surprising, she cowered away from Claire and hid her face whenever Claire tried to talk to her. The child seemed more comfortable with Black than with anyone else. He knew what he was doing. When he talked to her, he leaned down close, his voice soft, and placed a gentle hand on her hair. If she would grow to trust any of them, it would be Nicholas Black.

Novak carried the child across the hotel grounds toward the private elevator that went up to Black's penthouse apartment. Rico was running alongside them, very happy to see Novak, too, but even more interested in the little girl. He kept demanding to know what was wrong with her. She had her eyes shut tight now and wouldn't look at anybody. Tears squeezed out from under her lids and slid down her cheeks.

"C'mon Rico, back off, you're scaring her," Claire told him. She grabbed his hand and knelt down in front of him. "Tell me what you've been up to. You been good and minded Harve?"

"Harve's teaching me to play chess. It's fun. I almost beat him last night."

"Good for you. Is he upstairs?"

"Yes, he's been waiting for you to get here. He got that hospital bed all fixed up with clean sheets the way you asked, you know, all that stuff."

"Good job, Rico."

Once they were inside the elevator, Novak felt a bit better about being there. He trusted these people. The child would be safe enough, now that they had her inside. Safe enough for him to return to Mexico and finish the job. On the other hand, the killer appeared desperate to get the girl back. He had wanted her enough to hold her captive on his boat, which wasn't even close to his usual MO. The way Novak saw it, the assassin just murdered anybody who got in his way. Novak felt that this kid was the key to everything that had happened. His gut was telling him the Mayan would come for her. She needed to let them know what was going on, so they could prepare, but she wouldn't, not until she trusted them. So it was up to him to get Claire and Black on board with the plan he'd come up with during the flight home. They would agree, he wasn't worried about that, not now that they knew what had been done to the defenseless child.

Once they had the girl back in bed with her own private RN sitting beside her, the rest of them moved off down the hall to Black's vast living room. Huge windows looked out over the beautiful blue lake. Sailboats were out, scooting along under brisk winds. Novak felt another quick burn of anger over the loss of his boat. One more loose end that he had to take care of. He sat back and watched the others reunite and was glad for them. They had become almost like a happy little family. Even Harve, Claire's old partner at the LAPD, was part of it. He had been paralyzed in the line of duty years ago and was confined to a wheelchair, but it didn't stop him from living his life. He absolutely adored Rico, and spent most of his time with him. The boy reciprocated his love. It didn't take long for them to take off again, this time on a fishing trip at the hotel's dock. Harve promised them an old-fashioned fish fry when they got back with a stringer of bass.

Once Harve and Rico disappeared into Black's private elevator, Claire sat down on the couch beside Novak. "I told Black I wanted my cabin back, you know, exactly the way it was. So guess what he did?"

"I did exactly what you asked me to," Black interjected, taking a chair directly across from them. "It's practically a duplicate of the old one."

"Oh yeah, except you made it about ten times its original size."

"That's exaggerating it. Anyway, your place was cramped. I needed room to stretch out my legs when we stay out there."

These two, Claire and Black, they were quite a couple. They were happy together. Almost as happy as Novak had been with Sarah. The thought of her and the twins brought up another wave of anger, the old and ever-present and awful anguish inside his heart. At the moment, anything anybody said or did made him angry.

"The killer's coming here," he told them abruptly, interrupting their teasing argument about Claire's new cabin.

Black and Claire went quiet. Stopped smiling, too.

"You're sure?" Claire asked.

"I'm positive."

"How do you know?" Black asked him, frowning and leaning toward him.

"Because that little girl in there? She's got a GPS chip embedded inside her body. That's the way he tracks people. I don't know if he put it in her or somebody else did, but it's there. I found it."

Claire jumped up and stared down at him. "Damn it, Novak. Why didn't you tell us?"

"Would it have made a difference?"

"Well, no, but Black could have taken it out before we left Belize."

Novak knew exactly what she was thinking. "You're right. He could have. I could have. And I know that you and Rico and Harve are all in danger if we stay here. So are all of those people out there enjoying themselves. But the only way for me to get him is to lure him onto our turf. He's too resourceful down there on his own playing field. He wants that little girl for some reason and he's not going to stop until he gets her. That's why we need to get him first."

Black frowned. "So you've got a plan to do that, I take it."

"That's right. First thing, we need to move the girl out to Claire's cabin on the cove. I'll go with her, and I'll protect her there. The rest of you stay here. I don't want to worry about anybody else getting hurt because of me. No telling what this guy would do if he got hold of any of us. He'd either murder you outright or use you as a pawn to get the child back." He paused, thinking of Jenn again—how she must have looked with her throat cut, how it must have gaped open as blood gushed out. Novak swallowed down that god-awful vision. "I will understand if you don't want me to do this here on the lake. This guy is dangerous. Just say the word and I'll take the girl down to my house at Bonne Terre. I probably should have taken her there in the first place. Almost did do that, in fact, but she's still not out of the woods and I wanted Black to take care of her until she gets well."

Claire was still standing in front of him. Now her fists were planted on her hips. She did not look pleased. "Get real, Novak. No way are you doing this alone. Not against this guy. I'm going out there with you. Black can stay here and guard Rico and take care of the little girl."

"Like hell I'm staying here," Black told her emphatically, but still as calm and reasonable as always. "I've got bodyguards on staff who protect Rico around the clock. He likes them. Doesn't know their job is to watch him. Nobody can get through my hotel security and get to either one of those kids."

"Looks like it's two against one, Novak." Claire again.

"Yeah, it does. Okay, I guess I'm glad to have your help. If you mean it."

Claire gave Novak a look. "Do I ever say things I don't mean, Novak?"

"No. Okay, thank you. I just don't want anything else to happen. He cannot get his hands on her again." He paused and looked at Black. "How good is that security you put in at Claire's cabin?"

"Best in the world. Bar none."

"Infrared?"

"That's right, and top-of-the-line. Live and recorded video feeds into the safe room."

"Just inside the cabin?"

"No. I had them put night vision cameras all around the woods Harve owns across the lake from Claire's cabin, plus behind the cabin and all down the road and up the shoreline to where the main channel of the lake starts. Anything bigger than a mouse moves on her property, or Harve's, we'll know it."

For the first time in days, Novak felt good about the state of affairs. "Okay, then. Let's get going. We have a very small slice of time to set up. This guy cannot best us this time. And we all know now what that bastard's capable of."

Encouraged, Novak sat down with them to plan it out. They had the element of surprise this time. But the Mayan thought he did. He thought they didn't know he was coming. He didn't know they knew about the child's chip and had removed it. So they would be waiting, and he was in for one hell of a nasty surprise.

Two nights later, Novak sat in Claire's brand-new living room in front of her brand-new gigantic A-framed window. The drapes were wide open, every light in the house switched on. On the wall to the left of Novak's big leather recliner, a giant flat-screen TV was tuned in to *Scooby-Doo*. Novak was not watching it, and the sound was turned off. Instead, he was staring down at the cell phone he held in his lap. It displayed live feeds from the impressive infrared security system that Black had set up for Claire's safety. Novak had never seen such a home protection system in his life, nothing even close. Fort Knox would probably envy this system. It must have cost Black a pretty penny. The guy definitely wanted to keep his wife safe. And good luck with that. Not with her track record with the bad guys she pursued, first as a homicide detective and now in private work. She seemed to attract murderous serial killers. The security system fully illuminated any movement on any property edging Claire's cove, and that meant from the beach to the outer perimeter roads. Anything moved out there, Novak saw it. A control center with large monitors had been set up in the safe room upstairs, right beside their master bedroom. It was, of course, the most secure place in the house, with steel-enforced doors and fortified locks—impenetrable, unless the intruder had a hunk of C-4 and a death wish. Black was protective, all right. But he had reason to be, considering Claire's past. Not to mention Black's own background.

Since they had formulated the plan on the day they'd arrived at the lake, they had been carrying out surveillance religiously, twenty-four hours a day. They took turns with Black's team of hotel security guards, but Novak pretty much stayed on duty and grabbed a few hours whenever he could. He was always in that chair when darkness descended on the lake, because that's when Novak expected the Mayan to strike. Claire was now upstairs in the safe room, heavily armed. Harve Lester was at his house with a couple of other guys, watching the entrance road and his end of the lake, all of them equipped with night vision goggles. More security guards were stationed around the perimeter, some up in tree stands, others concealed on the ground, all watching for the Mayan to show up. Because he was coming.

Novak estimated the time and figured he would strike soon, maybe even tonight, tomorrow night at the latest. He would not have wasted time getting to the lake; he wanted the little girl too much. Well, that was just fine and dandy, because the killer was walking into a trap this time. The child was conscious most of the time now, but not saying a single word, not telling them her name or anything else. She was safe in her bedroom at Cedar Bend tonight, with Claire's former police partner here at the lake, Bud Davis, and her friend Joe McKay on duty inside and outside her room. None of them were taking the Mayan's skills lightly. Novak had told them how deadly he was. Novak was pretty sure the killer would be approaching Claire's cabin sometime tonight. He'd come in the dark, and he'd come in over the water. The cove was an isolated place, private and quiet and dark, and all that lined up with the Mayan's past preferences. He'd infiltrate the cabin and kill its occupants, and then he'd either take the girl or kill her, Novak was sure of it.

To the right of Novak's chair, which faced the window, lying on the big dark-gray sectional was a police homicide dummy approximating a child's size and weight, the kind used to determine how a victim would land if thrown off a cliff or out of a building. Claire had gotten it from the Canton County sheriff's department, where she'd once worked as a homicide detective. The dummy's head was lying on a pillow facing the television, where it would be hard for anyone to see it. The rest of it was covered with blankets. It looked real. It would've fooled Novak if he had been outside watching with binoculars, the way the Mayan would have to do. It looked like a beaten and slashed-up little girl watching cartoons before going to bed. At first, Novak had not been sure the dummy would work, but after Claire had arranged it on the couch, he felt a lot more comfortable with the ruse.

Now, just like they'd done for the last two nights, Novak would sit and watch the phone and wait for something to happen. Claire would scan the security screens upstairs in the safe room. So far, all they'd seen were some squirrels, raccoons, and a deer or two. Black was outside the house, well hidden and well armed and ready to do whatever was necessary. Novak was on edge tonight, his instincts telling him this was it. This time, the Mayan would get the surprise of his life.

"There's a breach in the woods, across the cove from the cabin. See him?" Claire's voice said inside Novak's earwig. She sounded excited, ready to get this thing done. All of them were ready.

Novak stared down at the phone and watched the figure moving stealthily toward the lakeshore directly across from Claire's place. "Yeah. That's got to be him. You ready, Black?"

"I'm ready. I'm coming inside now. Up through the back porches."

The other men hidden around the property checked in one at a time.

"Remember, this guy is mine," Novak told them all softly. "I take him down myself."

Nobody objected.

Novak expanded the live pictures of the area in question to full-screen. He could see the outline of the small figure clearly now. He was creeping along on the ground, from tree to tree, thinking he was undetected, thinking Novak was alone in the cabin with the child he intended to kill. Looked like he wore night vision goggles. Novak could see no canoe, no sniper rifle, no equipment at all; the killer probably had just his ritualistic green obsidian dagger. Maybe a handgun, too, but more likely a garrote. Novak felt his pulse accelerate. This was the moment he had been waiting for. Showtime.

Novak stood up and made a show of stretching and yawning. He messed around in the kitchen a minute or two as if cleaning up, put a cup in the dishwasher, and then he went around turning off most of the downstairs lights. He walked over to the couch and carefully picked up the dummy. It felt just like the little girl had felt in his arms, so small and light. He made sure the head was hidden against his shoulder, and then walked to the staircase and moved up the steps. Up top, a banister fenced off a wide hallway, open on the side that faced the gigantic front window, that led to several bedroom suites. He opened the middle door, which led to Claire and Black's master bedroom. The lights were off, but, through an open door connecting the two rooms, he could see a dim light burning inside the adjoining safe room. He walked into the master bedroom, shut the door, and dumped the dummy on the king-size bed. Then he strode to the safe room.

Inside, Claire sat in front of the massive control center that took up an entire wall. Black was now standing behind her. Both of them were watching the intruder. No one else was moving on any of the screens, everybody still in place. The Mayan had come alone. Novak had known he would. He always worked alone.

"He's still over there, but he's stopped now and is watching the house," Claire told Novak. "He's got night vision goggles. I think he's waiting for you to come back downstairs so he'll know where you are. Just like you thought he would."

"Okay, let's do this." Novak stripped off his red-and-black plaid flannel shirt and baseball cap and handed them over to Black. Black slipped into the shirt quickly, and then snugged on the baseball cap. He had a .45 in his hand. He slid the gun down into a belt holster and arranged the shirt over it. "Okay, I'm going down. Claire, shut that door after we leave and don't open it for anybody."

Claire laughed at him. "Yes, dear. But do remember, I am a trained police officer. I know what to do. I saved you, remember?"

Black grinned down at her, but he waited outside in the master bedroom until she shut and bolted the door to the safe room. Then he looked at Novak. "Good luck. If you need reinforcements, say the word."

"I won't."

Black left the room, kept his face averted as he descended the stairs, and sat down in a chair in plain sight of the big window. He would wait there, pretending to watch television. No chance of him getting shot through the windows. They were bulletproof throughout the house. Black was nothing if not thorough. He and Claire had faced their share of danger since they'd met. Now that they were married, Black wasn't about to let anything happen to her, not in their own home, anyway.

Novak dipped his fingers in a jar of black greasepaint and smeared it over his face and hands. He watched the guy across the lake on the cell phone the whole time. The Mayan was huddled in the same spot, patiently watching the house. Novak knew what he was doing. He was waiting for the man he thought was Novak to turn off the lights and go up to bed. Maybe he planned to sneak in and kill them all in their beds. Cowardly, but efficient and effective. But he wouldn't get that far.

Novak had the Ruger strapped in a shoulder holster. He had a bowie knife in a sheath at his waist. He was ready. He stood alone in the bedroom and waited for the assassin to make his move. The guy was cautious, prepared, and maybe smart enough to fear a possible trap. He would come in across the cove, using the water as cover. Thirty minutes later, Novak was proved correct.

The Mayan must have decided not to wait longer, because the glowing green figure on Novak's screen got down on his belly and crawled down to the edge of the lake. Then he eased into the water and started an easy breaststroke approach toward the cabin on the opposite bank. Novak smiled, adrenaline racing like crazy, and moved quickly out through the French doors that opened onto an upstairs back porch. The wait was over; the time was at hand. There were no steps from the porch down to the ground, another example of Black's overprotective zeal. Novak swung a leg over the rail, got on the other side, and then dropped to the ground, into the deep shadows under the porch.

It was dark outside, and all the security lights were turned off. The night was quiet and the lake looked like a piece of black glass. Squatting down, Novak glanced at the woods behind him and listened for sounds. The Mayan could have brought backup, but Novak didn't think so. They would have been seen on the security cameras by now, and the Mayan liked to work alone. Aware of the killer's night vision goggles, Novak got down on his belly and crawled around the side of the house until he was down close to the big boat dock. He had on night vision goggles, too. Surprise, surprise. He detected the Mayan's head in the water, coming slowly, leaving a gentle chevron wake. He was about halfway across the cove now. Only his face was above the surface. He was like a giant anaconda writhing its way toward unsuspecting prey. Not this time, buddy.

Novak inched his way down toward the lake, keeping out of sight. He crawled across the rocky beach and entered the water behind Black's big Cobalt 360 cruiser. But he kept his eyes trained on the Mayan's progress and angled his way into a good position to intercept him. Slowly, he submerged himself into the cold water until only his eyes and nose were above the surface. Then he waited.

The moon had risen, slipping in and out of rain clouds that had been building up all night, and suddenly the night won that battle of dominance. The moon disappeared, and thunder growled somewhere far away. Light drizzle began to fall, cold and steady, gradually increasing to a steady downpour that clattered the surface of the water and tore down dead leaves in the big oak tree above the dock. Novak welcomed the extra noise and distraction, thinking it a stroke of good luck, a good omen that gave him the edge. Maybe it would conceal his movements and muffle his sounds.

The rain also impeded Novak's night vision, and he lost sight of the Mayan coming at him in the water. He yanked the blurry goggles off and searched the surface frantically, not moving at all, but ready to panic if he didn't spot the assassin soon. If the guy evaded him, he might make it into the house. Novak was not going to let that happen. He went rigid when the Mayan suddenly broke through the surface, not a yard in front of him. The killer came out of the water ready to fight, lunging at Novak with a blade already in his hand. Novak was quick enough to evade his attack, and he grabbed the Mayan's shirt and jerked him down under the water. He went with him, trying to hold him under, but the Mayan slashed at him frantically and too quickly for Novak to get out of the way. He felt the blade cut through his shirt and then felt pain as it sliced across the top of his shoulder. But that was the intruder's last free move, because Novak had both his hands locked around the Mayan's wrist, twisting it brutally until the knife dropped into the water. After he was disarmed, Novak used his superior strength and got the smaller man turned around and in a blood choke hold that Novak applied so hard against both sides of his throat that he never had a chance. One-on-one, the fabled serial killer was no match for Novak's size and strength. Once he lost his edge of stealth and surprise, he was just a little guy shit out of luck. Rain pelted their heads, and Novak flexed his forearm harder against the guy's neck. He went limp in a matter of seconds. Then Novak dragged him out of the water by the back of his shirt and dropped him facedown on the muddy bank. Rain poured down on them as Novak stood above him and waited, until he watched the dazed assassin revive and struggle weakly up onto his knees.

"Say your goodbyes, you sick son of a bitch," Novak ground out between clenched teeth, and then he hit him in the face with his doubled fist, about as hard as he'd ever hit anybody in his life. The Mayan went down on his back in the mud and didn't move.

Chapter Twenty-one

Almost an hour later, Novak sat in that same leather recliner in the living room of Claire Morgan's new cabin. He had on dry clothes now, and the bleeding stab wound on his shoulder had been cleaned and pulled together with a couple of butterfly bandages. One lamp burned in the corner. The drapes were closed, and the rest of the house was dark. He stared at the little man who had heretofore seemed so deadly and elusive. He didn't look so tough anymore. Novak was somewhat surprised at how easily he'd been taken down. The guy was good when he had the advantage but not so good when he didn't. He should have known that Novak would be waiting for him, long before he encountered him in the lake. The Mayan had made a big mistake this time, a mistake that would end his bloodstained career. First, however, Novak wanted some answers, and he was going to get them. So he waited, relaxed now and in no particular hurry.

Across from him, the Mayan hung by his arms from ropes tied to the upstairs banister. Novak had spread out a painter's tarp under his feet so he wouldn't mess up Claire's new floor. The killer's face was a mess, both his eyes already swollen and beginning to turn black, his nose smashed and broken and still trickling blood. The house was silent and deserted.

Right after Novak had dragged the Mayan into the house, Claire and Black had gone back to Cedar Bend by water, roaring out of the cove in the big Cobalt 360. The final inning of the assassin's deadly game had begun, and he was losing. Novak had counted on the killer to come alone, and he had. Now Novak had the bloody bastard, dead to rights, and the rest of the night was probably going to be the most unpleasant evening that the killer had ever experienced.

After some time had passed, Novak did get impatient. He stood up, walked into Claire's spacious new kitchen, got a glass out of the cabinet, and filled it with water. He drank it down, staring at the assassin where he sagged unconscious against the wall. Then he refilled the glass, took it out to the living room, and stood in front of the Mayan. He tossed it into the assassin's face, damn sick and tired of waiting for the bastard to come to. He wanted to end this thing, once and for all. The Mayan roused a bit, sputtered, coughed and gagged on blood, and then slowly came out of it. Novak sat back down in his chair and watched the Mayan remember that he was in a shitload of trouble.

It took a couple more minutes for the killer to lift his head and figure out where he was and what had happened. Novak sat and watched him. Said nothing. The Mayan spit out more blood. His nose was definitely broken and he was struggling to breathe. Novak liked to go for the nose first. A hard blow there caused his opponent lots of pain and took the fight out of him faster than anything else. Except for a hard kick in the groin, maybe. The Mayan's eyes were bleary and bloodshot when he was finally able to focus them on Novak.

"Bravo," he sputtered out, his words hoarse and strangled. "You got me. Be proud of it. Nobody else has ever come close."

Novak was surprised the Mayan's English was so good. He hadn't expected that. He had expected him to speak exclusively in Spanish again. "Yeah, I've got you. Good for me. Bad for you."

"Why not just kill me out in the lake when you had the chance? Hold me under and let me drown?"

Novak watched the guy pull at the ropes, testing them, still thinking he had a chance to escape. Wrong. He couldn't get out of those knots in a million years. Novak had made sure of it. "Because I want answers. I want to know why you targeted me and more important why you abused that poor little girl I found tied up on your boat. You cut up her arms and legs and terrified her. She's just an innocent little kid. That bugged me. Pissed me off, if you want to know the truth. So now you're going to answer for it."

"Is she still alive?"

Novak scowled, angered by his question. "She is. No thanks to you."

The Mayan let his head hang down again, his chin resting on his chest. Poor guy was too tired to hold his head up. He was all dressed up in his ninja outfit, but his clothes were sopping wet and muddy and covered with his own blood. When he lifted his face again, he said, "I didn't hurt her. I didn't do anything to her."

Novak grimaced. So now that the guy was caught like a mouse in a trap, he was going to deny his crimes and try to save his own skin. Damn coward. "So what's that mean? You saying she cut herself up like that? I don't think so."

"I'm saying I was helping her. Just like you are helping her now."

Novak felt his teeth grind together. "You murdered my friend Jenn. You killed her, and you killed that young woman with her, and now I'm going to kill you."

"I didn't kill either of them. And I didn't hurt the child."

Halfway surprised that the assassin was denying his crimes, Novak stared at him, absolutely disgusted. He figured the killer would be proud of his murderous prowess. Most assassins were. "So I guess you didn't kill all those guys on that beach, either? Or the Asian woman back in the jungle? Li Liu? Remember her? You sayin' you weren't back there in that house, slicing off her skin inch by inch? We heard her screams. Guess you didn't do any of that, either, did you?"

"I killed them all. I admit it. They deserved to die, every single last one of them. They were thieves and rapists and slavers. The woman was the worst of them all. I knew her well. After she received the ransoms, she executed many of her victims with bullets in their heads and left them to rot in the jungle. I do not regret my actions that night. It is better that they are dead."

"Oh, I get it. You're a good guy now. Just getting rid of all the other bad guys."

"That's right. I kill bad guys."

The Mayan turned out to be even smaller than Novak had first thought. He looked five feet three, maybe, if that. He was muscular and fit for his size, and probably very quick—not quick enough tonight, though. He had long black hair tied back at the nape and a small goatee. He had the handsome visage of a Central American Indian, might even be descended with a pure lineage.

Their gazes locked. Neither blinked. Neither looked away. The

Mayan did not seem afraid of Novak or of what was coming next. He should be. He should be terrified. But he wasn't. He was quite calm.

"I'm ready to make a deal now," the Mayan told him. "It will be in your best interests to come to terms."

Novak actually laughed at that one. "No deals. You are soon going to be too dead to make any deals. My friend Jenn? She was a good person. An innocent woman who spent her life helping other people. I cared about her, and you murdered her in cold blood. You took her body and dumped her out in the ocean like a bag of garbage."

"I did not hurt her. I helped her."

Novak sighed, weary of the whole damn mess. He didn't like to think of Jenn out there, alone, dead, and drifting around on the bottom of the ocean. "Quit lying. I know who you are and what you do. You murder for hire. You work for Arturo Ruiz. But you've killed your last victim. Now you are going to find out how they feel the moment before you slice open their jugular."

The Mayan remained silent. Then he took a deep breath and blew it out. A burst of blood droplets hit the tarp in front of him. "You are wrong, my friend. Your lady, the one you call Jenn? She is not dead."

All right, that stunned Novak. He sat up straighter, hope flaring alive and then dying almost as fast. He set his jaw, angry again. Probably just another cruel game the Mayan wanted to play.

"I saw how much blood you left inside her house. I saw where you clubbed her or knifed her out on that deck. I saw where you killed Marisol."

The Mayan's eyes held his, dark and intense but with a look of utter serenity. "They were attacked, *sí*, very brutally attacked. But I did not touch them. When I arrived at that house, your friend Jenn was lying outside, unconscious and bleeding. The other girl was inside. She had been butchered like a sacrificial lamb. Her name was not Marisol Ruiz as you believed. Her name was Luisa Mendez, and she has been Marisol's best friend since they were children. They plotted this whole thing together, and I guess Marisol decided to leave no witnesses when everything started going wrong. As you probably know, Luisa was not a strong person, not a monster like Marisol is. She would have been easy to dupe, and she would be easy to kill. She would have fallen to her knees and begged for her life. It was clear from the scene that Jenn fought to stay alive, and maybe that is why she was in better shape when I got there."

"Then how come we found the blue butterfly tat on Luisa?"

"Marisol and Luisa both have that tattoo. Identical butterflies, done at the same place at the same time. I can remember when they got them, years ago. Luisa adored Marisol, wanted to be like her in every way. That's how Marisol manipulated her the way she did. They played you."

Novak didn't like that, but it made more sense than the rest of it. "You're a damn liar. There was too much blood in that house for either of those women to have survived."

"I'm telling you the truth. I suspect Luisa contacted Marisol and told her where they were and about the trade, you in exchange for Marisol. I believe Luisa probably panicked when she thought she was being taken to the Ruiz compound. Arturo would have had her shot for tricking him. She knew that, and I know that. I don't know how she contacted Marisol, but she did."

"At the exchange, the blond girl said they were alive and waiting for me at the beach house."

"Surely you didn't believe her? She is a consummate liar, just as Luisa was. Marisol killed Luisa and then tried to kill Jenn. Your friend only survived because I followed Marisol and got there in time. Jenn is still alive and in a safe place."

"How the hell did you find them? We cut the chip out of the girl you're calling Luisa."

"I wasn't tracking Luisa anymore. Couldn't find her signal. So I went back and tracked Marisol. She has the same kind of GPS chip inside her body. I know, because I'm the one who implanted both girls. Her father ordered it done when I had brought them back home to him after they'd run away. I did it while they were sedated. Neither of them had any idea I could track them. I tried to find Marisol first, but she moved around too often for me to catch up with her. So I started tracking Luisa. I knew she could tell me where Marisol was. Marisol's the one I want."

Novak considered everything he'd said. "Say I believed you for one single second, which I don't. No way could anybody, especially some young girl like Marisol Ruiz, get the jump on Jenn. Jenn's a trained operative, as good as they come."

"You don't know Marisol Ruiz. She is a deadly woman. Believe me, I trained her myself."

"You're saying that the blonde that they exchanged for me was the real Marisol Ruiz."

"Yes, when things started going wrong and she had a chance to return to the safety of her father's compound, she apparently decided going there was her best bet. She knew I was coming to kill her. That girl you pulled out of the water and tried so hard to protect was her friend Luisa. As I just told you."

Novak said, "You were after Luisa. You came after us with everything you had."

"That's right. She was just as guilty as Marisol is. I am not innocent of crimes. I admit freely that I have been an evil man for most of my life. I have killed many people. I will answer to God for those souls on the day I die."

"Today, you mean." Novak wasn't buying what the Mayan was selling.

"I did not kill the woman named Jenn. I swear it. She is still alive. I treated her wounds right there on that beach to try to stop the bleeding. Luisa was already dead, but the American woman lived, and I figured her life meant something to you. I assumed she might come in handy as a bargaining chip if you should ever get the better of me. You are an adversary that I can respect. I do admire your dogged determination."

"You're lying. Jenn's dead." But Novak wanted to believe him. He wanted to believe she was still alive, about as much as he had ever wanted to believe anything in his entire life.

"Then let me prove it. Cut me down and I will show you."

"Prove it right now."

The Mayan bent his head back. His nose had started bleeding again. It ran into his mouth and made him choke and cough. Novak was unmoved.

"I can give you a mobile number. You can even use FaceTime, if you've got it. A nurse will pick up at the other end and hold the phone so that you can see the woman named Jenn. You will see her with your own two eyes. She is severely injured but still breathing. Then you will know that I did not kill her. I saved her life. She will tell you that, too. She will tell you that Marisol Ruiz attacked her and left both her and Luisa for dead."

Novak considered his story, considered what kind of ruse he might be trying to pull. This guy was clever, no doubt highly adept at getting himself out of tight situations. Novak suspected he'd never been captured until tonight. Still, if Jenn was alive, if there was any hope of it, Novak had to know and had to find her. He considered how the Mayan could be perpetrating a trick or a trap and why the killer would give him a way to verify his assertions. Novak couldn't figure how calling a phone number could put him at a disadvantage. He had to know. If Jenn was alive, he wanted her back. He wanted to go get her. The Mayan had a bargaining chip, all right, and he had just laid it on the table.

"What's the number?"

The Mayan told him, and Novak punched it into his phone. They stared at each other while it rang at the other end of the line. Two rings. Three. Then somebody picked up. A woman's face appeared very briefly. Then the screen turned around, and Novak could see Jenn. She was lying on a bed, her head propped atop white pillows. She had bandages on her face and wrapped around her forehead. She had on a hospital gown and was covered with a white blanket. Her eyes were swollen almost shut, but she was awake and aware and was trying to focus her eyes on the phone. She couldn't quite do it.

"Novak? Is that you? I thought he killed you."

Her voice sounded as if her lungs had been affected, maybe collapsed from the attack. But it was definitely Jenn. No question about it. And she was alive. Novak felt his throat constrict, close in on itself and almost strangle him with emotion. His muscles went tight. He was relieved, so damn relieved to see her alive and talking to him.

"Are you okay? Are they treating you all right?" Novak asked her quickly, glancing at the Mayan.

"I'm hurt pretty bad, I think. They're giving me something in an IV to help with the pain."

Across the room, the Mayan grinned at Novak. His teeth were bloody, both his lips raw and split open. Novak still could not believe Jenn was alive. But she was, and she was talking to him. "Where are you?" he asked her. "I'm getting you out of there."

"I don't know. A hospital, I guess. They give me sedatives and I sleep most of the time. There's a doctor here and some nurses who take care of me." She stopped and took some rasping breaths. It was hard for her to talk, hard for him to understand her. "I'm handcuffed to the bed. I don't remember how I got here. The Mayan came here once, I think, and told me you might call and talk to me if I didn't try to escape. I was afraid to believe him. He told me I was his safety net."

"I went to your house, Jenn. I saw blood everywhere. He said the girl was already dead when he got there and you were close to it. Tell me what happened, Jenn. Tell me who did this to you. Did the Mayan attack you?"

She shook her head. "That girl you pulled out of the ocean. She wasn't Marisol. I don't know who she was, but she's dead now. I think she got hold of my phone somehow, maybe when I was in the shower, and called the girl who attacked us. She must have let her in to the house. The girl had been so compliant after you left that I let down my guard." She stopped, licked dry lips, rested a moment. She was in a lot of pain, all right. Her eyes were dull with the drugs. "I heard them whispering, and then the girl screamed. I ran into the living room, and she was already down beside the couch, throat cut, and she was just, God, she was just down there gargling on her own blood. Then some other girl came out of nowhere with a big knife and started slashing at me. She was screaming and yelling, in some terrible, crazy frenzy. I got a shot off, but she stabbed my arm and I dropped my weapon. I got out to the deck, and then she was on me so quickly that I couldn't get away. She just kept stabbing me." Jenn's words trailed off and she shut her eyes. "I passed out, I guess. I don't remember much after that."

"Was the woman who attacked you tall with blond hair?"

Jenn nodded.

"What does the Mayan have to do with this? Was he with her when she showed up with the knife?"

"I didn't see him, but it all happened so fast. When I came to again, I was on a boat. Down in some dark place. I was bandaged up and he was feeding me pills. He had my arm chained to the wall. Water was sloshing around on the floor, I think. I was only half conscious then." She stopped, took more breaths that seemed to hurt her. "He asked me who had done this to me, and he said he was going to get her. He told me that if you kept interfering, he would use me to make you see reason."

"I'm seeing reason. He's tied up by his arms and bleeding all over the place and offering me deals. I haven't killed him yet. Doesn't mean I won't."

The Mayan showed his bloody teeth again. "You won't kill me. Because those doctors and nurses taking care of your friend? They have been instructed to leave her there without food and water or medical attention if I do not call in at scheduled intervals. She'll die slowly, chained to that bed, dehydrated and starved to death."

Novak knew then that he didn't have a choice. "Are you okay, Jenn? Are they hurting you?"

Jenn revived a bit, looked slightly more alert for a moment. "They're giving me what I need, but they'll leave me here alone if he tells them to. They answer to him."

"Okay, try to hold on a little longer. I'm coming to get you. It might take me a while but I'll get there, I swear."

The nurse hung up the phone before she could answer. Novak felt a hell of a lot better. He turned to the Mayan. "Okay, now you can tell me where she is."

The Mayan sighed audibly. "You must know that I will die before I tell you that. Not unless you give me what I want in return for her."

Novak grimaced. "I guess what you want is that poor little abused girl I found on your boat, right? The one you tortured and starved? The one who can identify you as the bastard who did it to her? I'll never turn her over to you, not in a million years."

The Mayan started desperately jerking on the cords. Then he just stopped, panting hard, and stared at Novak. "That poor little girl you took? She is my daughter, Carmelita. I would never hurt her. Never. I want to see her. I want to know that she is all right and being cared for."

Okay, now that sure as hell wasn't anything Novak had been expecting. But he'd be stupid to believe it. "Your daughter, huh? Yeah, right. If she's your kid, why'd I find her on your boat, bruised and beaten half to death and chained up in the bilge?"

"Is she all right? You haven't hurt her, have you? Was that her you carried upstairs a while ago. Is she up there now? Please let me see her."

"I don't hurt children. She's holding on. That guy on that island that you paid a visit to was the one who got an IV in her arm before it was too late, if you want to know the truth. If she makes it, he saved her life."

"I'm telling you the truth. Ask my baby, ask Carmelita who I am. Ask her who did those terrible things to her. She will tell you. It wasn't me. I have never hurt her in my life. I couldn't."

"She hasn't spoken a word since she came around. She just lies there and stares at us, or cries herself to sleep."

"Let me see her. Let me see that she's all right." The Mayan's voice was getting a tad shrill now, so he cut it off and controlled his anxiousness. Then he spoke more calmly. "Please, I beg you. Let me see my child."

Novak stared at him, not sure what to think. It seemed preposterous, but then again, maybe the guy was telling the truth. "You expect me to believe that if I bring that little girl in here, she's going to tell me that you're her father?"

"Yes, yes, she will. She must be frightened to death. She's been through so much. Marisol Ruiz took her from us. I swear that on the Holy Mother. She took her to blackmail me."

"Know what? I don't believe a damn word you say. I want to know where Jenn is. Tell me that and then we'll talk about the kid."

"No way. Not until I see my daughter is alive and well. Is she upstairs? Tell me. I saw you take her there." He was twisting around, trying to look up at the bedrooms.

Novak thought about it a moment, then decided it wouldn't hurt anything to let him see the girl. No way could he harm her, not tied up the way he was. But it would tell Novak a whole lot. He pulled out his phone and dialed up Claire. When she picked up, he said, "Can you bring the little girl over here? This guy says he's her father and she was kidnapped. I want to see her reaction to him. It's safe enough. No way in hell can he get loose."

"You sure it's not some kind of trick?" Claire asked, her tone telling Novak that she didn't like the idea one bit.

"He's hanging by his arms from your banister. He's not going to do anything I don't want him to."

They hung up. The Mayan watched him. "Where is she? Is she not upstairs? Who was that I saw you carry up there?"

"It wasn't her. We would never put a child in danger like that. Don't worry about it. She's been in a safe place. They're bringing her over, and then we'll see if your story pans out, or not."

It took about forty-five minutes before the Cobalt roared back into the cove. The instant the Mayan heard the boat's powerful motor, he strained to see out the window. Minutes later, the front door opened, and Black walked inside carrying the little girl in his arms. She had her head lying on his shoulder, her face turned away. Claire was right behind them. She had her Glock out, and she immediately pointed it at the bound man.

"Carmelita! Carmelita, come, come to me!" the Mayan cried out.

The child raised her head off Black's shoulder, and when she saw the Mayan, she struggled desperately to get down. Black placed her on her feet, and she ran and hugged the killer around his legs. She burst into tears.

"Papi, Papi!" she kept saying.

"It's okay, baby. I'm here now. Don't cry."

That's when Novak started believing the Mayan's story.

"Cut me down, please," the Mayan was begging them. "Let me hold my child and I'll tell you everything. I won't try to escape. She is why I am here, the only reason."

"What do you think?" Novak asked Claire.

"I think she knows him, all right. Cut him down. I'll keep my weapon on him. He's not going anywhere."

With some reluctance, Novak pulled out the bowie knife and slit through the ropes. The Mayan fell to his knees and gathered the child into his arms. She couldn't stop crying, and he held her tightly against him. But he stared across the room at his captors as he whispered reassurances into her hair.

Novak realized that there was a lot more to this story than the Mayan was telling them. At the moment, though, he was more interested in getting Jenn back. "Okay, you have the kid. Where's Jenn?"

"She's at my ranch in the mountains south of Merida. She'll be all right there for a few days. Right now, we have to finish this. We have to find Marisol Ruiz and kill her."

Novak picked up his cell phone. "Tell me where Jenn is, or I'm turning you over to the American authorities. You can guess what they'll do to you."

"Do not call in the police," the Mayan warned, "or my men will take Jenn away and you'll never find her. My ranch is quite secure. They will have time to escape with her. Do not play games with me, Novak. I will be true to my word and take you to her. I am an honorable man."

Claire did not like that. "You are not honorable," she said.

After that exchange, they sat in silence and watched the assassin sit on the floor, leaning against the wall and rocking his frightened daughter in his arms. Novak and his friends sat there, relaxed, but with weapons drawn and trained on the notorious assassin. He didn't seem to mind. He only seemed relieved to have his daughter back with him. When she went to sleep in his arms, the Mayan waxed conciliatory. "I owe you my thanks for taking care of my daughter. She was very sick when I found her on that boat. I gave her all the medicine I had on board and was bringing antibiotics back to the boat when you stole the *Calakmul*."

"When I stole your boat, you had her chained up in a dark and filthy bilge. How could you do that to your own child?"

"She had been in bed up in a cabin since I got her back that night off the *Orion's Trident*. I only put her down there when I had to leave the boat. She was breathing okay and sleeping comfortably. I was afraid she'd wake up and wander off or that somebody would find her, that Marisol would find her. I couldn't risk that. I knew Marisol was getting close to you and Luisa because I was keeping track of her GPS chip, and that meant she was close to me, too. I couldn't let her get my baby again, so I hid her while I went out that night and tried to find you. I wanted Marisol dead. That's all I could think about after I found Carmelita, all cut up and beaten." He stopped as if overcome with emotion. Probably anger. "I managed to sneak aboard and surprise Luisa and Diego that night. Then I chained them up the same way they'd chained up my baby, and took my child up to a stateroom so that I could tend to her wounds and stop the bleed-ing. Those devils had tortured my little girl, you have to understand that. And then when she was finally calm and sleeping, I went back down and methodically beat the truth out of both of them. I wanted to know where Marisol was. I intended to kill them as soon as I got Carmelita down into my inflatable boat. But they got loose somehow and tried to escape." He stopped, his face as hard as a stone carving on a Mayan temple. "I made them tell me everything down in that bilge. Then you showed up and interfered with my rescue of Carmelita." He looked at Novak and held his gaze. "I took pleasure in beating them. I wanted Luisa and Diego to suffer for what they'd done to my baby, and then I wanted them dead. They were as guilty as Marisol was. They sat back and watched Marisol torture her. I got him first, shot him down, but then you started shooting at me before I could finish off Luisa. I thought it was Marisol shooting at us. I thought she had returned to the yacht with her men, so I just took off."

"Tell us how the hell this all went down. Don't think you're going anywhere until I find Jenn and get her out of there."

"I will uphold the bargain. All I want is my daughter. That's all I wanted from the beginning. Now that I have her back, my only desire is to kill Marisol for the crimes she's committed."

"What crimes?"

"Let me take her upstairs while you talk," Claire said. "Put her to bed. It's the middle of the night. She's tired and still weak. Then you can tell us the rest of it."

"Please allow me to hold her," the Mayan whispered softly. "She can tell you the parts of her abduction that I cannot. You can keep your weapons on me. She needs to be in my arms when she wakes up. She has suffered terrible things."

Novak sat there, still unsure. A lot of questions still needed to be answered. The child knew the Mayan, no question there. She loved him. The Mayan rocked his child and said nothing for a few minutes. Novak wasn't sure what else the Mayan was going to tell them, but Novak was willing to listen. One thing he did know. The rest of the story damn well better be good.

Chapter Twenty-two

The cabin had grown quiet again. Novak was waiting to hear the real story of the Mayan and his little girl. The Mayan had been allowed to mop off some of the blood and move with the child to one of Claire's new leather recliners. He had the little girl on his lap and was rocking and patting her back. She had begun sobbing again when she was moved, but was now lying against her father, calm and almost asleep again.

Novak stared at them. Carmelita had finally gone to sleep. He wasn't sure what to believe. He did not want to trust a killer—an assassin, for God's sake—who suddenly decided to play loving father to a kid that Novak still considered to be one of the man's victims. Maybe he'd brainwashed the kid while she'd been in the bilge. Maybe she was exhibiting signs of Stockholm syndrome. Maybe the child had developed fondness for the captor holding her prisoner. It was obvious that she trusted him now. Worst-case scenario, maybe this guy was a pedophile and had made her think he loved her. The idea made Novak sick to his stomach. But it was a possibility.

"Where would you like me to start?" the Mayan asked softly.

"Just get on with it. I want to get Jenn somewhere safe. Maybe you should start by telling us your real name."

"My name is Sebastian Desoto. I was an assassin for many years. But for the last ten years, I've spent my time as a professor of Mayan history at the Museo Nacional de Arqueología in Guatemala City."

The Mayan gently shifted the child so that she lay against his shoulder. She didn't stir. "Few people know my name."

"So go ahead."

"I grew up an orphan, starving and stealing on the streets of Guatemala City until Arturo Ruiz found me and took me in. He trained me to become what I am. He convinced me that by killing his enemies, I was helping him to eradicate evil people who preyed upon the weak ones suffering such as I suffered as a boy. I believed him, because he raised me out of poverty and gave me a home. I lived at his estate in the mountains. He treated me as if I were his own son, and called me the Mayan. He educated me in the finest schools. He told me he loved me more than he did his own daughter, Marisol, because I was a male and she was not. She resented me from the beginning. So I learned to kill from him, and kill well, and kill without thought or remorse. I did the jobs he gave me without question. I became very good at it."

Novak frowned. "Yeah, we know all about you. You're going to pay for those crimes, by the way. You should've stayed a thousand miles away from me and mine."

The Mayan gave a slight shrug. "I suspect you're right, as I sit here with those weapons pointed at me. To shorten my saga, I met a woman, a woman that I love more than life itself. I married her and she gave me my only child, little Carmelita here. Then the two of them became my life. I no longer wished to kill, not even to please Arturo. So I quit killing and left the Ruiz compound for good. He allowed it because he loves me." He stopped, shook his head. "It was a violent business into which he indoctrinated me and then Marisol after me, when she showed an aptitude for murder. But I loved him as much as any son could love a father. I have always been loyal to him. To this day, I am loyal to him. I would die for him."

"That might happen."

Desoto stroked his daughter's soft hair.

"Luisa said you kidnapped her," Novak said. "Is that true?"

"I never took Luisa or Marisol. Nobody took them. She was lying to you from the beginning, about who she was and about why she was on that yacht. Luisa Mendez was a talented liar."

"Look, I saw you slug her in the head with the butt of your pistol. I saw you knock her into the water."

"I told you that I wanted her dead for kidnapping my child. You must believe me. Luisa lied to you about everything. I swear it."

"You're saying that Marisol abducted Carmelita and held her aboard the *Orion's Trident*. You tracked them down, killed Diego, failed to kill Luisa, and got your child back."

"Yes, that is the truth. They kidnapped my baby. Marisol called me on FaceTime and made me watch while she used her knife on Carmelita. She made me listen to her screams. She doesn't know it, but I recorded those screams. I recorded Marisol laughing as she tortured my child. You can hear the audio recordings if you like. I have them on my phone. After that, I just wanted Marisol and the other two dead for what they did to my baby. But Marisol left before I got to the boat that night, so I found only Luisa Mendez and her boyfriend aboard. They had been left to guard Carmelita."

"You are sure the others were in on the kidnapping?"

"I told you, they were all in on it. Luisa and her boyfriend kept her chained up on that boat. I found them because I knew about the chips. Marisol and Luisa never knew we could track them. Arturo was determined to know where they were and what they were doing because he knew what his daughter was capable of." He paused. "After Carmelita was born, I did the same thing after a few years, in case she was abducted. I implanted her with the chip. Many wealthy families in Mexico and Central America implant their children, because kidnappings are so rampant now. That's how I found them out on that boat the night you saw us. I went there to get my daughter and take them out. I told you all this. You need to listen and believe me. Now they're all dead, except for Marisol. I want her dead, too. I saw her hit my daughter and swipe her knife down through her skin with my own eyes. I heard Carmelita cry and scream and beg me to make them stop. It was sickening. I want her dead. I am going to see her dead."

Desoto paused there, and Novak could see the emotions churning inside him from the awful memory of his daughter's torture.

"I will get Marisol soon," Desoto continued. "Luisa led Marisol straight to Jenn's beach house. She was a stupid girl, influenced by Marisol's beauty and money. She was expendable, so Marisol killed her so that Luisa could never tell Arturo what she had done to my daughter. Marisol tried to kill Jenn for the same reason. She only returned to her father's house because she knew I was right behind her and wouldn't stop until I killed her."

Novak stared at him. "That's it? That's what you want us to believe?"

"That is the truth. You need to believe it. You have been duped by those evil girls. They were on that boy's boat, Diego's, and I surprised them. I do not regret killing him, and I wish I had ended Luisa, too. You, *mi amigo*, would be much better off if you had left her out there floundering in the ocean to drown. Can you deny that?"

Now that was something Novak could readily agree with. "Why were they holding your daughter? Were they blackmailing you? What did they want?"

"They didn't want money. Marisol wants her father dead. She wants me to kill him, because she knows I'm the only one who can do it. Arturo knows that she is evil. He has been trying to control her for years. She was born bad. That's why he sent her to the convent, where she and Luisa concocted this plot against him. Marisol Ruiz is crazy, filled with a kind of bloodlust that I've never witnessed in anyone else. After I retired to be with my wife, Marisol took my place as her father's assassin. She likes to kill and she does it well. She's the one who has taken the scalps of her victims. I was a pro. I never wasted time on theatrical stunts and stupid calling cards. I have never done that, never, except on that one night after I tracked you and Luisa to Li Liu's camp. I wanted to send Luisa a message that night if I didn't get to kill her. That I was coming. That I was right behind her with my knife. I wanted her to run. I wanted her to lead me back to Marisol."

"Where was Marisol?"

"She was hiding out but moving so often I couldn't catch her. I knew Luisa would lead me to her, sooner or later."

"Luisa was terrified of you."

"She knew what Marisol had done. She and Diego just sat back and watched her do it. She knew I would seek vengeance, if it took me the rest of my life."

"Why does Ruiz's daughter want him dead?"

"He controls her, and she doesn't like it. She didn't want to be in that convent, saying the rosary every day. What she wants is to head up the Ruiz cartel. With him dead, she could take it over. Some of his men are loyal to her. She was trying to coerce me into murdering him because he trusts me. She knew I could get into his inner sanctum. I refused, of course. So she abducted Carmelita and used her against me. So I tracked them out to sea, boarded, and took my child back. I was just sorry that Marisol wasn't there. If she had been, none of this would have happened. I would have killed them all and taken my baby home and stayed there. I have no wish to kill anymore. Except for Marisol. I will kill her."

The whole sordid story sounded complicated but legitimate. Novak glanced at Claire and then at Black. They sat together on the couch and listened, weapons ready but never saying a word. Claire nodded, and he knew that she believed Sebastian Desoto's story. Novak got up and knelt down in front of Carmelita. He had questions, and she was the only one who could answer them. He touched her shoulder, gently, so as not to frighten her. She woke and raised her head off her father's shoulder. Then she stared back at Novak, solemn and silent. He spoke to her in Spanish.

"Is this man your daddy, Carmelita?"

She nodded.

"Did he save you from Luisa and Diego out there in the ocean?"

"Yes." Very low, very scared, shivering all over.

"Was Marisol Ruiz the one who hurt you?"

She nodded again, and spoke so softly they could barely hear her. "She slapped me and pulled my hair and chained me up and left me in the dark." She closed her eyes and kept them shut. "She said she was going to kill me, even if Papi did what they wanted. She showed me her knife and then she kept coming in and cutting me. She told me she was going to cut off my head and send it to Papi in a box." Then the child started crying.

The Mayan stared hard at Novak. "You see? I tell the truth. They put my child through hell. That's why I boarded that boat, to get her and to kill them. You assumed all the wrong things, but that is understandable."

Novak gestured for his friends to follow him into the kitchen, and they stood there together, speaking in low tones. Claire kept her weapon trained on the Mayan. Just in case.

"What do you think?"

"I think he's telling the truth," Black said. "I was watching him the whole time, and all the indicators told me he wasn't being deceitful. But that's not infallible. Just my professional opinion."

"Carmelita loves him. No doubt about that. Their relationship feels real to me," Claire said. "Poor little kid."

Novak didn't want to believe it. He wanted the pleasure of killing the guy right now, tonight. Nope, he wasn't in for the hug-and-make-up scenario. Not until he got Jenn back. He walked back into the living room. The Mayan and his daughter both watched him with identical dark eyes.

"You said that Marisol came to the beach house, killed Luisa, and attacked Jenn, right? You had nothing to do with that."

"That's right. Absolutely nothing. I showed up not long after."

"How'd you find the beach house? We took out Luisa's chip."

"I told you. I was following Marisol's signal. She led me there. I was right behind her, as I have been so many times. She is crafty, moves often and erratically. By the time I got there, she had already left to trade herself for you. Luisa died a terrible death at her hands. I didn't wish to tell you this, but you should know: Marisol attempted to scalp Jenn, as she did to Luisa. She cut her badly but did not take her hair. Your friend lost a lot of blood. When I got her on my boat, I didn't expect her to live through the trip."

Novak envisioned the bloody crime scene inside that house. He visualized Jenn's beautiful hair, so soft and blond and silky, revolted at the thought of it being sliced to the scalp. But she was still alive, and that's all that mattered to Novak.

"Marisol was in a hurry, I guess," Desoto continued. "In any case, she took Luisa's place in the trade, and that's how we ended up here."

They stared at each other, Novak hostile, Sebastian Desoto serene.

"I'm going to kill Marisol for what she did to Jenn," Novak told him.

"I'm going to kill her for torturing my child."

"Sounds like a match made in hell," Claire said.

"I don't trust you," Novak said to the Mayan.

"I don't trust you, either."

"Great, maybe you two ought to think this through before you do something you'll regret." That was Black, still in psychiatrist mode and, as usual, the voice of reason.

The Mayan remained serious. "Marisol's father adores her. Arturo will protect her with all he's got. He will use his men and his money and his weapons to keep her safe. He will not easily believe she wants him dead, but he might believe me if I tell him—if I let him listen to my recording of her laughing as she tortured my child. He loves Carmelita. She is his goddaughter. If he hears what Marisol did to her, I think he will believe me."

Claire was not so sure. "If all this is true, why didn't you just go to him and tell him the first time she tried to blackmail you?"

The Mayan smiled, showing them all those sharp little white teeth. The light from the kitchen reflected in his jet eyes. "Because I wanted to kill her with my own two hands, 'up close and personal,' as you Americans like to say. He would never let me do that, because she is his only child. He dotes on her, but he is fair. He will listen to me, especially once he hears the recording, but I do not know if he will agree to let me kill her."

Novak knew that feeling, that craving for vengeance. He understood the reformed assassin's overwhelming obsession to get his hands around the throat of Marisol Ruiz. Novak had seen the woman only twice, but the desire to put her down ate like acid dripping onto the fabric of his soul. She had pulled all the strings but kept herself alive. He thought of how she'd smirked at him during the exchange at the Ruiz compound. That little knowing smile, when she was fresh off the butchering of Luisa and the attempted murder of Jenn. Then his mind went back to Jenn, and Jenn alone—her kindness, her smile, her hair, how it would look now after that devil had tried to slice it off. If the Mayan hadn't gotten to Jenn when he did, she would have bled to death. He did owe the assassin that one debt of gratitude, even if he didn't like it.

"Thank you for saving Jenn's life." His words sounded begrudging, because it hurt like hell to say them.

"Thank you for taking good care of my daughter."

Novak sighed and laid down his weapon. He didn't like this turn of events, not at all, but he wanted that woman dead. Right now, she was alive and under her drug lord daddy's protection. The Mayan could get Novak around that obstacle.

Novak looked at the Mayan. "Then let's do this together. As a team. Let's kill Marisol Ruiz for what she's done to us."

Claire still had her gun pointed at the Mayan, not one to forgive and forget so fast. Not one to disarm herself around an assassin, either. "Now c'mon, Novak, let's not get too hasty here. This guy's still an admitted assassin. He could put a knife in your back the

minute you turn around. Cut your throat, sever body parts. You need
to think this through some more."

"Look at the child cuddled up against him and tell me that he's
the one who cut her up and beat her."

Claire couldn't, of course. The love between them was obvious.
The little girl clung to Sebastian Desoto as if she'd never let go. He
was a bad guy, just as evil as Marisol Ruiz apparently was, a killer
for hire, nothing more. He probably didn't deserve to live another
minute. But he could get Novak into that compound on the hill outside Mexico City, and that's where Novak wanted to go. They would
make the Ruiz girl pay for the string of bodies she'd left behind.
First, though, Novak wanted to get Jenn out of the Mayan's control
and make sure she was in a safe place.

He turned to Desoto. "Will you agree to keep Carmelita here at
the lake? Over at the hotel, under guard, where she'll be safe?"

"Never. I am taking my daughter home to be with her mother.
Marta is grief-stricken. She thinks our only child is dead and never
coming home. I promised her that I'd get her back. I will not make
her wait any longer. Carmelita goes home with me before we do
anything else."

Claire wasn't having any of this unholy alliance. "Novak, you
need to think about this. At least, sleep on it. We're talking about a
powerful drug lord's assassin here, for heaven's sake. This guy is no
saint. You can't trust him."

"Like you thought things through last summer when those crazy
people had Black?"

Claire shook her head. She couldn't deny what she'd been willing
to do in order to save her husband. "Well, be careful, damn it. Just
because you both want that crazy psycho bitch dead doesn't mean
this guy won't stick a knife in you, too. Watch your back."

"Don't worry."

"Same here. I will watch my back," said the Mayan. Then he
rocked the frightened little girl until she fell asleep in his arms
again. The other three sat silently and watched him. Novak itched to
pull the trigger, as he'd hungered for days to do—get the bloody assassin right between the eyes, but he didn't. He needed Sebastian
Desoto at the moment, but after that, all bets were off.

Chapter Twenty-three

Novak, Sebastian Desoto, and his daughter flew back to Mexico, with Black's personal pilots at the controls of his sleek Gulfstream jet. Novak sat in a large tan leather seat and kept his gun on his lap, while the Mayan sat on a white couch across from him. He and his daughter were snuggling and looking at pictures in a magazine, acting as if he weren't one of the most ruthless assassins ever seen or heard of in Central America. Yeah, just a loving *papi* reading one of Rico's superhero comic books to his kid in Spanish. Not likely. Novak was on edge and ready for anything, and he had better keep it that way.

Black and Claire had stayed put at Cedar Bend Lodge, much to Claire's discontent. But they'd done enough to help, had come through for him big-time. Novak needed to finish this by himself. He wanted to see Jenn first, actually talk to her in person, hide her somewhere safe, before he made Marisol Ruiz pay for what she'd done. He wasn't sure he believed everything he'd been told by Desoto, but he believed most of it. Marisol had proven herself to be no angel, but Jenn could tell him in detail more about what had happened to her. Upon that revelation of truth hung Marisol's life. If she had done what the Mayan had accused her of, if she had tried to scalp Jenn, then Novak was going to make her pay. If not, he still might make her pay for what she did to Carmelita and the pathetic little trusting Luisa. But somehow, he figured the Mayan just might save him the trouble.

They put down in Merida, an ancient city and the capital of the Yucatan province. Signs in the airport said it was founded by the Spanish in 1542 and that its present-day population was just under one million people. It was purported to be a beautiful city, with big white cathedrals and ancient buildings, but Novak saw little of that. A car met them at the airport. Novak instructed Black's pilots to return home to Missouri and that Novak would find his own way back to the States. He just might be on the run after dealing with Marisol and her father, and he didn't want to drag Black and Claire into his troubles again.

Outside on the tarmac, the three of them got in to the backseat of a shiny new dark blue Lexus. A big, burly driver in a white shirt, black tie, and black pants whisked them away. The man wasn't as big as Novak, but he looked like he'd be a competent opponent. He looked like an Olympic weight lifter—strong, but slow as molasses. Novak would deal with him in time, if need be.

Novak was not in a chipper mood. He was ready for something to happen. He wanted payback for way too much suffering all around. He wanted to throttle somebody, and at the moment, he didn't much care who it was among the evil cast of characters he had dealt with since he had awoken from that nightmare aboard the *Sweet Sarah*, which was still sitting on the bottom of that bay. He wanted his boat back, too, salvaged and refurbished, damn it. That was the second thing he had to do before returning to Bonne Terre. If he ever made it back there alive.

Carmelita slept on her father's lap for the entire ride. Nobody said much—not much to say—not Novak, not the Mayan, and not the tough driver with all the muscles. The kid just slept. It was probably the first time in weeks that she hadn't been scared out of her wits. That gave Novak more time to think. He was worried about Jenn's health, as they drove on, and about blithely waltzing into the Ruiz compound with the Mayan. It could very well be a trap, and the Mayan's long involved story an imaginative pack of lies. Jenn had talked to Novak, but she had not looked so good. She had looked like she was going to die. Still, he wanted to believe she would be all right. Once he knew she was all right, then he could enjoy the revenge he was about to exact.

The ride took almost an hour, driving up through wooded hills on dusty dirt roads. It appeared the Mayan did not want his home to be easily found, and it wouldn't be. They passed periodic intersections with iron gates chained across isolated roads. Men stood guard and saluted the car as they drove past, as if Desoto were the president of

Mexico. Maybe the Mayan had set up his own personal little crime syndicate and/or kingdom on the hill. So Novak held the gun on his lap, ready to fire. After a while, the Mayan turned to him.

"You don't need that weapon."

"I'll be the judge of that."

"I was frantic when you took the *Calakmul*. I was afraid you'd kill my daughter."

"I don't kill children. Do you?"

"Of course not."

"You just kill whoever you're told to, that it?

He shook his head, scoffing at the idea. "I was a professional. Those to whom I was assigned were very bad men. I went in and did the job and got out. Marisol kills for the pleasure of it. She likes it. She is godless and amoral."

"And you're saying you aren't?"

"I am not godless and I am not cruel. I finished my jobs quickly and efficiently. I never hurt anyone for the sake of hurting them. After I found my wife and had this baby, I quit the business and have lived a quiet life for the last ten years, teaching at university or staying up here in the hills with my family and men who are loyal to me. Marisol is heartless, a killer who used her knife to terrify and scar my child who had done nothing to her or to anyone else. She is the monster, not I."

"You were right behind us all the time."

"Never close enough, apparently. I knew Luisa's GPS code because Ruiz told me to keep an eye on her and Marisol. This was his way of keeping them safe. I was tracking you and Luisa from a distance after you took her aboard your boat. When I saw the helicopter and four boats heading your way, I figured out who they were. Then you got in my way at the beach by stealing my canoe and escaping with Luisa. You are quite formidable, Mr. Novak."

Novak said nothing. This guy, this assassin for the drug lord, spoke softly, enunciated every word like a learned professor of the King's English. He was a family man when he wasn't whacking people, an in-and-out killer, like some kind of damn burger joint drive-through window. And he was good at what he did. So was Novak. Marisol Ruiz? Not so much. She was toast.

Finally, they drove out into a large lawn cleared out of the jungle. There was a big house, square, white, with the usual decorative arches and lots of potted plants and fountains. A very nice and peaceful place. Assassins must be paid on par with American brain surgeons. They had no more than come to a stop in the front courtyard when a small woman came racing out of the house. She was dressed in mourning black and wore a lacy black mantilla and was weeping and calling out the little girl's name. The child awoke and responded with the same kind of excitement, jumping out of the car on the opposite side and running hard into her mother's arms.

The Mayan got out, too, and then he looked down at Novak, who still sat in the backseat. "You see, it is as I said. My wife is distraught, as was I. Please, come inside. I owe you every consideration and every amenity. *Bienvenido, mi amigo.*"

Yeah, right. Sure, they were best buds now. That'll be the day. Novak got out, but he was wary as hell. Sometimes extra-nice former assassins were polite because they had a sharp green obsidian knife in their pocket with which to slice out your heart. Literally, in this case.

"All I want is to see Jenn, and then I want to get her out of here. Where is she?"

"She is upstairs in our guest wing. Please allow me to take you to her."

So Novak followed Desoto across a dusty patio and into a dim and cool foyer similar to the one at the Ruiz estate but maybe half as large. It was homey and inviting inside, while Ruiz's had been austere. There were several women who looked like lifelong servants huddling together in a doorway and watching them, maybe maids or cooks or the kid's nannies. They pulled little Carmelita into their circle of ample bosoms and nearly hugged the life out of her. All of them, including the mother, wept without stopping.

Novak remained where he was, the Ruger held down close behind his right thigh. He was beginning to feel like Alice in Wonderland, knocked down the rabbit hole with a rifle butt to the head and not sure who had the murder weapons. Everything going on around him seemed kosher. The place appeared to be a regular, peaceful rural Mexican home. Maybe it was. Maybe it wasn't. He kept up his guard. He didn't trust anybody anymore. He probably never would again.

The Mayan was speaking in rapid-fire Spanish now, a mountain dialect that Novak couldn't follow completely, but he was telling the women something to the effect that Novak had saved Carmelita's life. He'd taken the child to a doctor who'd given her the drugs she needed. He left out the part about Novak saving her from being chained up in her own father's dirty bilge. That's when Carmelita's mother turned and rushed over to Novak. She fell on her knees in front of him, grabbing his left hand and pressing kisses onto it. "*Gracias, gracias, señor.*"

"She doesn't speak much English, but as you see, she is very grateful. She is a fine woman. I am lucky to have found her."

"*De nada,*" Novak said to the woman, wanting her to cut out the excessive show of gratitude. All the other women started calling out thanks, too.

"All right, Señor Novak, let us go upstairs and find your friend. Just as I promised."

Novak walked the length of the foyer, his eyes darting from one person to the next, mostly female servants, still not sold on the Mayan's show of friendly goodwill. There were no armed men inside, but he'd seen plenty outside. Sebastian Desoto had his own personal army. At the rear of the hall, a wide stone stairway turned to the right and rose to the second floor. They climbed it together, Novak just behind the assassin, mapping a way out if escape should become necessary. They arrived at a long hallway, with arched windows facing the rear lawn lining one side. They strolled to the far end. The Mayan opened a door and stepped out of Novak's way.

"Please, your friend is inside this room. I will return to my family now and celebrate the return of our daughter."

As Desoto walked away, back down the hall in the same direction from which they'd come, Novak stepped inside and shut the door behind him. A nurse dressed in modern white scrubs and soft-soled white shoes sat beside the door, knitting something red. He motioned her out with a jerk of his head. She looked startled, but then she gathered her yarn and needles in a hurry and scurried out of the room. Novak set the lock behind her. He looked over at the bed. It was Jenn lying there, all right. She lay in a swath of snowy white sheets near an open casement window. A soft breeze was billowing white gauzy curtains in toward the bed. A large and beautifully wrought black iron cross hung on the wall above her head. Jenn was lying on her side facing him.

Novak crossed the room and stood looking down at her for a moment. His gut clenched. Her eyes were closed. Her forehead and the front of her skull were covered with bandages, professionally applied. No blood spotted the clean white gauze. She was being well cared for. Her eyes were still swollen. Novak looked around again, and then he shoved his weapon down in his back waistband. He pulled a plain wood chair close to the bed and sat down. She didn't move when he took her hand and held it between both of his. Two IV tubes snaked up from her arms. Antibiotics and sedatives, most likely.

"Jenn," he whispered, leaning down close to her.

That's when she opened her eyes, blinked, and brought him into focus. Her eyes were bloodshot from what must have been one hell of a fight for survival. Then she recognized his face and squeezed his hand. "Novak, thank God. I thought you were dead."

Novak spoke softly, stroking her hand. "I'm sorry, Jenn. I got you into this god-awful mess. I'm so damn sorry that you got hurt like this."

"I'm all right. Whoever these people are, they're very kind. They are taking good care of me." She took a deep breath, swallowed hard. She hadn't raised her head from the pillow. She was weak.

"Good, good. You're gonna be all right now. You look good and you're going to be fine." Novak was lying like a dog. She didn't look good. He wasn't at all sure she'd be all right, but he was going to make sure she got everything she needed. She was going to survive Marisol's attack, if it killed him.

Jenn didn't buy it. Too damn smart, as usual. "She surprised me, Will. I was not expecting anything to happen. I messed up."

"You didn't mess up anything. That girl we had with us? The one we called Marisol? Her real name was Luisa Mendez. She was working with Marisol, and I guess Marisol decided she didn't need her anymore."

"She cut her throat. It was awful."

"Marisol Ruiz did this to you? You're sure it was her and not the Mayan?"

"Yeah, she grabbed my hair and then she—" Jenn stopped, squeezed her eyes closed. "Then she started slicing—"

"Ssh, she didn't get it done. We'll get you all fixed up, I promise.

We'll find the best doctors in the world. But you are definitely sure it was her?"

Jenn was getting worked up, trembling. "Yes, I heard the other girl calling her name out when they were fighting over the knife. Claire had just called earlier and told us where the exchange would be in the morning. I guess Luisa told Marisol about it. I don't know, I don't know." Her voice trailed off. "If that little guy hadn't gotten to me, I'd be dead, too. I'd be dead, Novak."

Novak squeezed her fingers. "Hey, don't think about it anymore, Jenn. Just stay right here and let them take care of you until you're better. The Mayan said he's got a doctor watching over you. As soon as you can travel, I'm taking you back home with me so you can get well. I'll take care of you."

"Don't leave me here, Novak," she said, trying to raise up off the bed. "Don't leave me here alone."

"I'm going after Marisol Ruiz. I've got to. She's not getting away with what she did to you. This whole thing goes back on her. I'll come back for you, I swear. It'll just be a couple of days. You can trust these people. I'm trusting them until we get back."

She closed her eyes and was quiet. "Please stay with me, just a little while."

So Novak did stay with her for a little while. He sat in that chair drawn up close to her bed, holding her hand, giving her small sips of water when she roused up and wanted it. He could hear voices outside in the courtyard, some laughter, lots of happy chatter. Seemed deadly assassins could enjoy cheerful homes on their off hours, no matter how many people they'd put in the ground. Nobody bothered Novak and Jenn, nobody entered the room, except the wary nurse who came on an hourly schedule to check Jenn's vitals and bring food that Jenn did not touch. She brought him a tray, too. He ate his tamales and cheese and papaya and something else that he didn't know what the hell it was. Best of all, nobody attacked him with bloodstained machetes or green obsidian ritual daggers.

Chapter Twenty-four

The next day dawned bright and clear. Blue skies, cloudless, no wind, no breeze wafting Jenn's curtains. Hot as hell before the dew dried. Maybe that was an omen. Maybe they were preparing for a trip down into hell. Novak knew that what they contemplated posed a huge risk. Breaking into a powerful drug lord's heavily guarded compound and taking out his beloved, if evil as hell, daughter was not something done every day—or any day, actually. But it was possible, and the two men knew it. Both of them had done similar things in the past. Both of them wanted this woman dead, and in the worst way.

"So, what's your plan?" Novak asked the Mayan.

The two of them now sat downstairs alone inside a large, airy dining room with white walls and white curtains. Novak had gotten some sleep in the bedroom next to Jenn's sickroom. Then he'd been summoned downstairs, where several women had served a breakfast of orange juice, *chilaquiles* (which turned out to be enchiladas with eggs), nice warm flour tortillas, and mangoes and oranges and some kind of sweet bread. Novak wasn't hungry, but he ate what he was served and drank plenty of the strong black coffee and lots of water. He needed the nourishment, and he wouldn't get another opportunity, if things went as he figured they would. If it was there and available, eat it and be grateful. The Mayan sat across from him, ate less, and said nothing. Which was fine with Novak. They might be out to kill a mutual enemy, but they were never going to watch *Monday Night Football* and eat pizza together.

Desoto leaned back in his chair. "We enter the compound, find the girl, and then I will slice her flesh as she did to my Carmelita, and then I will kill her in the most painful way imaginable. Then we will leave her to rot in hell."

"Don't sugarcoat it or anything, Desoto."

"I don't understand what that means."

"You're just planning to kill her at her father's house, just like that? Slice her up, slit her jugular, and mosey on out? That's your plan?"

"Of course."

"That's a terrible plan."

"What other way is there?"

"Maybe a way where we both don't get shot dead in the first three minutes."

"We can get out alive. I know the house, the entire compound, very well. I grew up there. If Arturo catches us and knows we killed her, I will explain what happened to Carmelita and that Marisol wants him dead. I will play the audiotape I have on my phone of his daughter torturing Carmelita. He will listen to me. He is like a father to me. He trusts me."

"I'd say that takes a whole lot for granted, wouldn't you?"

The Mayan's dark eyes flashed with anger. "Let me explain this to you. Arturo is a loving father, to me, to her, but he is the most brutal, mean-spirited man I have ever known. He can be extremely cruel to those he loves as well as those he counts as enemies. I have seen him whip Marisol's back bloody when she defied him. She hates him for that and other cruelties. That is why she wants him dead, but she is afraid of him. She knows he will not hesitate to kill her if she betrays him. And she has betrayed him. She tried to coerce me to kill him for her. If I tell him that, he will not show mercy to her. Marisol has caused him much grief and worry throughout her life. He has become weary of dealing with it."

"If he believes you over her. That's a big *if*, Desoto."

"I think he will."

"She's his blood daughter. You are adopted."

"He loves me the same."

Novak observed him. Drained his coffee cup. "You've been in the army, I take it."

"I have been in several private armies. No more. This is my last mission. I wish to stay here in this house with my wife and daughter until I die peacefully in my own bed. But what Marisol did to me was a grievance that no father could leave unavenged. But that is the end of my killing. Are you a father, Señor Novak?"

Novak stiffened, as he always did when somebody brought up his children, his beautiful little twins, gone before they had a chance to grow up. He didn't answer.

"If someone abducted your child, beat her, and chained her? Used a knife to slice into her flesh? How would you react?"

Novak didn't need time to consider his answer. "I would find them and kill them. Just like you intend to do. But I would do it on my terms, not on her home turf with her father's goons there to protect her."

"They are loyal to him, not her. That is why she wanted him dead. They will never obey her while he still breathes."

"If he's likely to show no quarter to her, why not just call and tell him the truth about her plot to kill him? He trusts your word, right? Let him listen to that tape and then handle it his own way."

"Because I cannot be sure how he will react. If he forgives her, which I doubt, but if he should, I would lose the element of surprise. Now, at this moment? They will not be expecting me to attack them, not inside their stronghold. But Marisol will be on guard and wary of what I will do. She knows me. She knows now that she should never have crossed me. I doubt very much that Arturo knows half the truth of what she's capable of. She has probably told him lies about both of us."

"I say we surveil her movements for a couple of days. Wait for an opportune time. Get her outside the compound. Use our heads."

"No, señor. You are very good, but you are wrong this time. I can and will do this alone, if you do not want to be involved. Take that poor lady upstairs and go along on your way. I will avenge Marisol's crimes against you as I avenge my own."

"She tried to murder and scalp my friend. No way am I letting that go. I'm in. I just think there are better ways to proceed. Safer ways for us to pull this off."

"I know the place. I know that mansion. Every room and hallway and back stair. I can get us inside and find her without alerting a single soul. You must learn to trust me."

Sure, but that was the thing. Novak didn't trust him, not completely. Not at all, truth be told. He considered for a moment doing exactly what Desoto had suggested: taking Jenn and getting her out of Mexico, for good. His head was telling him that was the smart thing to do. But his gut was telling him to kill that crazy bitch who scalped women and cut up children, and make sure she died the kind of painful death she parceled out to others. Nobody got away with butchering his friends. Nobody. Not ever. It was just a thing with him.

"I'm going with you. But if I think you're making a bad move anywhere along the way, then I'm going to do it my way. Got that?"

The Mayan showed him all those little sharp white teeth. No blood this time, but lots of bruises and black eyes that neither of them mentioned. Novak didn't complain about his slashed shoulder, either. Nick Black had stitched it up and given him painkillers, but it still hurt. He just ignored the pain.

"Of course I do," the Mayan answered. "We both must seek our own personal vengeance. I hoped I had put killing behind me, and I did so for a long time. But my little Carmelita has suffered greatly. When I boarded their boat and found her below, lying on a mattress, soaked in her own waste, her little face bruised and arms striped with bleeding gashes, I knew I would kill Marisol. She does not deserve to live another day. Luisa and Diego were guilty for allowing my child to be hurt. None of them cared if Carmelita died. Marisol Ruiz is a woman with no conscience, no feeling, no compassion. She was born that way. Soon she will have no heart in this life because I am going to take it from her."

Novak said nothing to any of that. The Mayan was right on in his analysis. The Ruiz girl had a severe mental deficiency, all right. Why she did, he couldn't say. But he'd seen what it had spawned, seen what she'd left behind. But she had messed up when she had attacked Jenn. Novak liked Jenn. Maybe he even loved her, not like he'd loved Sarah, but in his own way. Marisol was not going to get away with hurting her. No way. She had messed with the wrong man. Two of the wrong men. She was going down.

"All right, let's get something down on paper. I want to get this done. Get in, get out, and get Jenn out of the country."

"I, as well, *mi amigo*. Let us talk."

As it turned out, their plan remained fairly simple. Too simple, in fact. The Mayan knew the Ruiz property like the back of his hand, or so he said. Novak wasn't stupid enough to believe everything the assassin was telling him. He had never been much of a kumbaya type, anyway. Being buddy-buddy with a murderous assassin with a hundred notches on his obsidian knife went against his grain. He called a spade a spade and entered every situation with his eyes wide open. He trusted no one, with the exception of Claire and Black and Jenn and a few army buddies. That habit had served him well and kept him alive. He had no need to deviate.

One thing Novak did know—they should be creating a diversion for their escape. All they needed were a few timed bundles of C-4 at the front gate and a couple more at strategic points along the adobe wall around the house. The sun-dried brick wall would crumble like soda crackers under the blast. But the Mayan didn't have any explosives lying around and nixed the idea because the guards checked the perimeter on the half hour. Novak didn't like that, but he listened as the Mayan told him how they could go in over the inner east wall, very close in to the kitchen and servants' quarters. The Mayan said it was a virtual dead zone late at night. Novak approved, but he had plenty of reservations about all of it.

They flew to Mexico City on a private aircraft. Sebastian Desoto didn't tell him who it belonged to but just took him back to the Merida airport, where they boarded without incident. Novak didn't demand details, didn't care, didn't even want to know any details or names involved. He just wanted to get the job done and get Jenn home. A jeep had been left for them in the long-term parking lot at the Mexico City Benito Juarez Airport, and they got in and drove off toward the fortified hilltop where Novak had been taken before with a black hood over his head. Neither of them said anything. Conversation was no longer required. Novak checked his gear and found everything to be in order. Made sure he had plenty of ammo clips, because he was going to need them. The compound was an armed camp. He'd seen that himself. And he could be walking into a big trap, a double cross by the Mayan and his murderous adoptive family. Novak couldn't come up with a good reason for them to want to do that, but he didn't know them all that well. He only knew that they were all brutal, godless killers.

Sebastian Desoto took the jeep up a ton of winding roads that seemed to go round and round to nowhere. They passed through wooded tracts skirting eroded volcanic peaks, the dirt road gradually climbing higher into the scrub. Twilight descended with a slow pink-and-amber sunset and then a black velvet night. A good thing, considering where they were headed. They finally pulled off the narrow path they had been following, and Desoto stopped the jeep in a thicket of trees and killed the lights and the motor. They both climbed out, footsteps muffled on thick layers of rotting dead leaves, and started their trek west. Novak followed Desoto, not thrilled, but he didn't know the area. He had to trust the Mayan to get them there. He kept his rifle ready and his eyes peeled.

Maybe half an hour later, they came out at the back edge of the Ruiz compound. The white wall rose in front of them, seven to eight feet tall. Novak could see the lights on inside the house where it stood high on the hill, maybe two football fields away. He boosted the little guy up first, and then he jumped, got a grip, and swung himself onto the top. His injured shoulder screamed with pain, but he ignored it. He lay there on his stomach and gauged the fields before them with his night vision goggles. Nothing stirred. Nobody. No guards. No alarms. Probably nobody in the whole of Mexico would be stupid enough to penetrate the inner sanctuary of the most deadly drug lord in Mexico. Except for them.

They dropped to the other side, hunched down, and ran across the fields, keeping about thirty yards between them. The second wall was lower and no problem to scale. Once they were on the other side, Desoto suddenly cut diagonally across the grass that led around the far end of the house, past the pool that shone brightly in the night and cast wavering reflections onto three stories of balconies rising high above. They saw nobody, except for the guards on duty at each corner of the house, standing around and smoking cigarettes. It was very serene and silent. A few lights had gone out since they started up the big grassy fields. Bedtime for the mafioso and his devil daughter.

On the other side of the mansion, it was extremely dark under the overhanging jacaranda trees, just as Desoto had described. Novak kept up, alert. Seemed too damn easy so far. That made him nervous and upped his cautiousness. They moved quietly through the darkness, keeping plenty of space between them, and Novak had to admire Desoto's stealth. He really did move like a shadow. Novak could hardly spot him. He was even better than Novak and his buddies in Special Forces. The Mayan was deadly, too. Novak had seen his work, up close and personal, something he wouldn't forget.

When they reached a space under a long line of kitchen windows,

Desoto pointed up to the balcony above their heads. It looked about sixteen feet up, but there were thick vines covering the side of the house and all kinds of water spouts and trellises. A burglar's welcome mat. Novak took hold of a tangled mass of the vines and jerked hard on it. It held, enough to support his weight. Desoto was already halfway to the wrought-iron balcony. They both still had on night vision goggles, and the scene around them was a glowing green landscape. If anybody else moved, the two men would see them first. Novak stood there a moment, incredulous that he was with the guy he had tied up and threatened only hours ago. Somehow that made him nervous all over again.

Shaking off his misgivings, Novak climbed up quickly, following the Mayan past the second-story balcony and on up to the third floor. He stepped over the rail and hunkered down beside the Mayan, keeping himself tight against the wall of the house. Their luck ended there.

The door beside them suddenly opened and a guard walked outside. He didn't see them. He stopped at the railing and lit a cigarette, looking down into the darkness below. His pant leg had almost touched Novak's shoulder. Novak didn't give him time to sense their presence. He came up fast and got him around the throat. It took under ten seconds and the guy went limp as a rag. Novak lowered him to the balcony floor, and Desoto immediately thrust his obsidian knife into his neck. The blood spurted out, and Novak stepped back to avoid it.

"You gonna kill everybody we see?"

"Only the bad ones. He is Marisol's man. I know him. I have seen what he does to people. She uses innocent looks and beauty to convince gullible men to support her. Her father's people are much more loyal to him."

Novak shrugged, no soft spot in his heart for drug lords' murdering minions. That included the Mayan. Probably the world would be better off if they crept about and methodically killed everybody residing in the place, like the Mayan had done to the pirates. The dead guy seemed incompetent to Novak. Wasn't observant, that was for damn sure. It had been very easy to infiltrate the heavily guarded stronghold. Too easy, maybe. Again, thoughts of a double cross entered his mind.

Desoto headed off down the porch to their right. Novak followed him, keeping his back to the wall, his gun pointed down toward the garden below. The Mayan was walking upright and unafraid, apparently quite sure of himself. Probably had done the same thing a hundred different times on a hundred different balconies. Probably thought nobody could see him anymore, that he really was the Invisible Man. Novak was too cautious to be overconfident, and he still had no idea where they were headed. Desoto could be leading him into a death trap, but somehow Novak doubted it. He had seen Carmelita's condition. He had seen the love of a father for his daughter, the way he'd held her, the way he'd whispered that he was there and she was safe.

They moved down alongside what Novak assumed to be a row of bedroom windows and French doors. At the back corner, they stopped, with the swimming pool directly behind them and far below. The Mayan's face swam with reflections off the water. Novak picked out two guards below them, one at the top of the steps that led down to the pool, the other one at the far end of the pool, out by the grassy fields. They were both leaning against iron gates, probably half asleep. None of them would expect anybody to storm the place. Not if the intruders wanted to keep their heads intact.

"Her room is halfway down the back balcony," Desoto whispered to him. "Stay low. We can surprise her while she's sleeping. She's quick with her knife, so take care."

Novak was beginning to get a bad feeling. His gut was telling him that something was amiss and things were going to go south—and fast. "Wait a second, something's not right," he whispered, grabbing the back of the Mayan's shirt.

"Stay here then," the Mayan whispered, jerking out of his grasp. "I will go inside and kill her. Then I will come back with her heart still beating inside my hand to prove to you that she is dead."

"Just kill her and stop with the Shakespearean dialogue."

Desoto was already moving toward Marisol's bedroom, keeping so low that he was practically on his belly. Novak stayed put, pretty sure Desoto was going to run into trouble before he stole Marisol's heart. He watched the man move, like a shadow on a wall, small and agile and deadly. Like an angel of death, floating in close to snatch someone's soul. Then the Mayan stopped, right outside the girl's door. He looked back at Novak and then pushed it open and eased inside. A few moments later, the lights flared on, and a shot rang out.

Well, shit, thought Novak. He pulled off his night vision goggles, dropped down, and headed forward in a low crouch. When he reached the door, he saw Desoto lying on the floor. Two guards were standing over him. Marisol had her back to Novak and was yelling curses down at the Mayan.

"You think I didn't know you would come after me?" she screamed, giving Desoto a kick in his side. He grunted and curled up into a fetal position. Novak could see blood seeping through his pants, wet and shiny, midpoint on his thigh. Marisol's arm was in a sling. Jenn must have gotten her before she went down.

Novak swiftly stepped up behind the girl, grabbed her by the throat, and put his rifle up under her chin. She struggled, so Novak clubbed her once across her nose with the barrel, and she stopped fighting. The two guards had swiveled around and beaded their weapons on him.

"You move a muscle and she's dead," Novak said, very low.

They didn't want her to die, it seemed. They looked at each other and then looked back at Novak.

"Go ahead. Put your weapons on the ground," he told them, listening for guards running up the iron steps. Not yet. The two men obeyed, and then he glanced down at Desoto. "Can you get up? Grab those guns and let's go."

The Mayan pushed up, groaning as he got to his feet, using the bedpost for support. Then he grabbed his gun and disabled the guards, one, two, down you go, with a rifle butt smash to the head. The two guys were out for the count. "Kill her, Novak. Do it now, while you can. Or I will."

"She's a hostage that can get us out of here. Just get the guns and come on."

Novak dragged the girl backward out of the bedroom, his biceps flexed hard against her throat. He hoped to God that Desoto got his act together. Below them, several guards had gathered and were yelling an alarm. He ducked down, took Marisol down with him, and then headed back toward the kitchen side of the house. She acted dazed now, but he wasn't going to loosen his grip. She stumbled along with him. They could hear men shouting and the thud of running feet as they clamored up to the balcony. Just as they made the corner, a couple of guys appeared at the other end of the balcony. Novak headed toward the vine-covered lattice, but it was way too late. Men were waiting below on the ground and others were at the far end and also on the balcony behind them now. They were trapped.

Thrusting open a door right behind him, Novak backed inside, holding the woozy girl in front as a shield. The Mayan followed and slammed it and set the lock. Before they could barricade it, a light flared on inside the room. Novak swung around with the girl. Arturo Ruiz sat up in a huge four-poster bed. He held a very big and nasty looking .357 Magnum in his hand. He pointed it at Novak's head, very calm and collected, as if people attacked his compound, shot up his house, gun-whipped his daughter, and invaded his bedchamber every night of the week.

"Release my daughter, or I will shoot you."

"I think not," Novak said, keeping the gun barrel pressed hard up under the woman's chin. She was his one and only bargaining chip, and they were in some serious trouble. "Call off your men, or she dies. I will shoot her, Ruiz. And she deserves it."

"Do so and I will kill you."

"Might just be worth it, after what she's done to us."

Ruiz frowned, taken aback, Novak hoped. The big man hesitated, and long enough for Novak to know they had a chance. Several armed men burst through the interior door and held them at gunpoint. Novak kept his back to the wall and held the girl tight. Everybody just stood there, in a frozen-armed standoff.

"Stand down," Ruiz said to his men. Then he looked at his daughter. "Are you all right, my dear?"

"They hurt me, Papi. I'm so scared."

Marisol's nose was bleeding a bit. She sounded scared and whined like a frightened child, like she'd probably heard Carmelita cry when she tortured her.

Ruiz swiveled his attention to the Mayan. "Sebastian, I am shocked to see you doing this to me. What have I done to make you hurt me like this?"

Novak took that as a good sign. Sebastian's take? Not so good. He looked angry as hell. His leg was bleeding profusely, darkening his pants and staining his boot and the white carpet under his foot.

"You must know the truth. Marisol, the daughter you love so much? She kidnapped my little Carmelita. She tortured her. Tortured Carmelita, your own sweet goddaughter. Marisol is evil, Arturo, but you know that, do you not? I will not let that vicious attack on the honor of my family go unavenged. I will gladly die in defense of my child."

Well, Novak wasn't gonna die in the defense of anybody, not tonight. "I'll kill your daughter if you make a move against either of us. I want safe passage out of here and then we'll let her go, alive and well. If you attack me or the Mayan, I will kill her where she stands and not think twice about it."

Ruiz paid no attention to Novak, so Novak took a step backward toward the balcony door, holding Marisol tightly around the neck. The girl tried to pull away and he cut off her breath. After that, she stood still. Ruiz was more interested, it seemed, in Desoto's motives.

"Why, Sebastian? You are my son. I chose you myself. I took you in. Raised you as my own. Why are you turning on Marisol? I don't understand."

"I think you do understand. I think you understand that your daughter is corrupt and evil. And I can prove it. You can call my home. Carmelita will tell you what happened to her. How your daughter starved her and beat her and slashed her with knives."

"Oh, come now, Sebastian. I believe your daughter was kidnapped, but that is hardly a novel thing around here. Why would Marisol want to hurt her? Carmelita is like a little sister to her. She could not harm her."

"I've got the sound of it, if you have the stomach to listen. Here on my phone. Listen to Marisol laugh as my daughter screams in agony. Listen to that and you will know I speak the truth."

Ruiz just seemed befuddled. He didn't look so intimidating in his blue-and-white-striped pajamas, either.

Novak took advantage of his confusion. "When my friend and I tried to help Marisol's friend Luisa, your daughter repaid us by killing Luisa and leaving my friend for dead. She scalped Luisa. Does that give you an idea what your daughter is capable of?"

Ruiz ignored him, still horrified that his adopted son had turned on him. "Why, Sebastian? Why would she do such a thing to your precious child? I provide her with everything. She has just come back to me, and she is happy here now. She wants to stay home. She swore she did."

Desoto hesitated, looked unsure now. "Because she was black-mailing me. She lured my daughter away from home, telling Marta that she wanted to take her into town for ice cream, and then she took her. Let me tell you why, Arturo. Because Marisol wanted me to kill you so she could take over your business. That's the truth. I swear it on the Holy Virgin. Ask Juan. He was in on it, too. Go ahead, ask him."

Arturo looked at his bodyguard, and Juan froze where he stood, and then he tried to run. He was taken down to the floor, dis-armed, and held there by the other guards. Ruiz got up out of bed, slipped on his blue house shoes, and then stared down at his former friend. "Is that true, Juan? Do you know of this plot against me? Tell me now, and perhaps I will spare you."

The man said nothing, but Marisol apparently saw the writing on the wall. She started crying. "Don't believe them, Papi. It's not true. None of it's true. I love you. I would never want to hurt you."

"Cut his throat," Ruiz told the guard holding Juan. All casual and nonchalant, like asking somebody to hand him the salt.

Juan didn't like the sound of that. He found his tongue real fast. "It's all true, *patrón*. She was blackmailing the Mayan to kill you. She said she would kill Carmelita if he didn't. I helped her kidnap the little girl, but I never laid a finger on that child. I'm sorry! Please, please, forgive me."

"Do it," Arturo instructed the other guards, still calm. He watched as they slit the man's throat. He gargled and choked, and Ruiz turned back to his daughter. He had a look in his eyes now that boded well for Novak and Sebastian. Not so much for Marisol.

"Release Marisol. I will deal with her myself."

"You think I'm just going to believe that?" Novak kept inching slowly toward the outside door. He had a firm grip on Marisol, and he wasn't going to let go anytime soon.

"I give you my word. Let my daughter go. I will deal with her treachery. I give you my word. My word is law here."

Novak had noticed that. The unfortunate man on the floor was still gurgling blood. Novak glanced at Desoto. The Mayan was star-ing at Ruiz, giving him a long and searching gaze. Then Sebastian

Desoto spoke up. "I beg your forgiveness, Arturo. But I refused to consider what she asked of me. I have always been loyal to you. Always, even after my retirement. I came here only to avenge my daughter's suffering. Marisol is evil. You understand the seriousness of her crimes, do you not?" Desoto tossed him his phone. Ruiz caught it and looked down at it. "There is the evidence. Listen to it. Listen to your daughter torturing your goddaughter. Listen to Carmelita screaming and begging her to stop."

"I will listen to this tape, but I believe you. You have never lied to me. I will handle my daughter's sins myself," Ruiz said again. "You both may leave the compound now and no one will molest you. You have my word, Sebastian, and you know my word is true. Go."

Novak didn't know his word was true, hell no, but Sebastian limped across the room to where Novak stood with the girl. She was shaking like a leaf, terrified of her father. "Let her go. He will not harm us."

"Sorry, but I'm just not that stupid."

"He is a man of his word."

"Honor among thieves, that it?"

"That's right."

Desoto walked past him and out onto the balcony. Ruiz shouted out for his men to back off and let them pass. Novak hesitated a long and anxious moment. The whole thing had been a disaster from beginning to end, and he didn't like letting Marisol off the hook. Not after what she had done. She deserved to die, right here, right now, and her father would never kill her. On the other hand, Novak had no choice. So he backed his way out the door and found the outside coast clear. The Mayan was halfway down the curving concrete steps that led to the second floor, leaning heavily on the wall. Nobody was touching him. He was leaving smears of blood on the stones behind him. Nobody was following him. Novak sucked in a breath, pushed the girl back inside the room, and took the steps slowly, inching down them backward, his rifle aimed at the men watching from the third-floor balcony. Their weapons were down. They followed orders, and Novak was damn glad they did.

Desoto seemed to accept the situation for what it was, more concerned now with getting the hell out of the place. Novak had too much innate caution to be so sure everything was going to work out in their favor. They made it to the second floor and then on down to the big concrete patio at ground level. They started down more steps to the pool. Novak still walked backward, weapon trained high above them, at the top of the steps where most of the guards were congregated. Nobody tried to stop them. It was as if they all had been frozen in time. But Novak was afraid it wasn't quite over yet. He was waiting for the bomb to drop, maybe in the guise of an M16 barrage the minute they reached the open field.

When they made it to poolside, Desoto sat down on a low wall and ripped off part of his shirt and fashioned a makeshift tourniquet on his thigh. The bullet had not hit the femoral artery or he'd be upstairs and dead on Ruiz's bedroom floor. Novak watched the back of the house. He jerked his attention to the third-floor balcony when he heard Marisol screaming. Arturo Ruiz stood up there, holding his daughter sitting on top of the balcony wall, her feet hanging off the precipice. Desoto stood up, his wound forgotten, and they both watched as the big drug lord waited a few seconds and then he shoved his daughter off the wall. Novak and Desoto stared in shock, watching her fall, her long and drawn-out shriek of horror stopping abruptly when she hit the patio below. The sound of her body hitting the concrete was horrendous. Nobody moved. Not Novak. Not Desoto. Not the guards. It was surreal.

"There is your vengeance, Sebastian!" Ruiz shouted angrily from high above them. His voice echoed down over the pool and out across the fields. "There is your family's honor. And mine."

Then Arturo Ruiz turned and walked back into his bedroom. His guards scattered in all directions, afraid of the same fate, no doubt. Nobody went near Marisol's body. Novak supported the Mayan with one arm and helped him move down past the pool into the grass. But Novak kept looking back, expecting gunshots to ring out at any moment.

"He will not attack us. We are free to go now."

"He's just letting us walk away?"

"He knew she was a psychopath, that she liked inflicting pain on helpless people. He had seen her do terrible things to animals and to his servants from the time she was a mere child. He had talked to me about it, worried himself about her. That's why he had kept her a virtual prisoner. He knew her defective character. He suffered greatly because of her mental instability. He didn't know what to do about it."

"Yeah, well, I guess he figured out what to do tonight."

"I will never see him again. He will never forgive me for coming here tonight. He will mourn her death until he dies."

"Well, he'll be the only one. Let's get out of here. We've done what we came to do."

Epilogue

As soon as Jenn was almost well enough to travel, Novak left the Mayan's mountain ranch and drove back to her house on the beach in Belize. Once there, he cleaned up the blood and gore on the floors and the walls and the deck, Jenn's blood and the blood of Luisa Mendez. He had scrubbed it clean with a bottle of bleach, and then he had aired the foul stench out of the house and straightened the furniture and cleared away the debris and placed a fresh bouquet of red roses in a vase beside her bed. After all that was done to his satisfaction, he had brought Jenn back home. He had carried her inside and put her in her bed, and once she was settled and comfortable, he hovered over her and nursed her back to health. When she was well enough and invited him into her bed, he made love to her, and that was as good as it ever had been. They stayed there together by the beautiful sea for nearly a month, while he had the best boat salvage company in Mexico City raise his boat and completely refurbish it at great cost. But it was a cost that was worth it to him a million times over.

Novak and Jenn were good together, just as they had been in the past. Doctors in Belize City had reattached the small part of her scalp that had been severed, and her hair was growing, just as fine and silky and blond as ever. After enough time had passed and when he knew it was time for him to go, he had the *Sweet Sarah* brought to Jenn's beach and anchored just outside the breakers. He hated to leave her there alone, but he had a life to live and so did she. When he told her goodbye this time around, it turned out to be a slow and gentle farewell that lasted almost two more weeks. And then he made her promise that she would come to Bonne Terre and stay with him for as long as she liked. She promised she would. So he boarded the clean and refurbished *Sweet Sarah* alone and took her out to sea, and then sailed north toward the Gulf of Mexico and home. It had been a terrible, bloody ordeal, but they had both gotten through it alive. Now he was ready to go back to his plantation in the bayou and see what awaited him there. Maybe Jenn would change her mind and come live in Louisiana with him for a time until she had healed enough, mentally and physically, to go back to work. She was welcome for as long as she wanted to stay. Maybe she would decide to take a flight and beat him back to Bonne Terre. Maybe she would be waiting on the veranda of his plantation house when he docked his boat on the bayou behind the old mansion. Maybe she would wave and laugh and beckon him to hurry. Oh yeah, that sounded good to Novak. He would like that, all right, but he wasn't counting on it. He wasn't counting on it at all.

If you enjoyed *Say Your Goodbyes*,
be sure not to miss Linda Ladd's

BAD ROAD TO NOWHERE

BAD MEMORIES
Not many people know their way through the bayous
well enough to find Will Novak's crumbling mansion outside
New Orleans. Not that Novak wants to talk to anyone.
He keeps his guns close and his guard always up.

BAD SISTER
Mariah Murray is one selfish, reckless, manipulative woman,
the kind Novak would never want to get tangled up with.
But he can't say no to his dead wife's sister.

BAD VIBES
When Mariah tells him she wants to rescue a childhood friend,
another Aussie girl gone conveniently missing in north Georgia,
Novak can't turn her down. She's hiding something.
But the pretty little town she's targeted screams trouble, too.
Novak knows there's a trap waiting. But until he springs it,
there's no telling who to trust . . .

A Lyrical Underground e-book on sale now.

Read on for a special excerpt!

Chapter One

Will Novak swung a leg over the starboard gunwale of his sailboat, got a good firm grip on the railing, and then stretched down far enough to reach the layer of salt and brine crusted at the waterline. Novak was a big guy with big fists and big shoulders and an intimidating look to him. People usually gave him a wide berth if they didn't know him well, and that's the way he liked it. It was a beautiful afternoon, late September in South Louisiana, and still hot as hell. Unseasonably so. He was shirtless, muscles straining with effort, sweat shining on his torso. His body was in peak physical condition, banded with thick, powerful muscles that he knew how to use and that he wasn't slow to put to good use if anybody messed with him. He followed the rigid daily workout he had mastered a long time ago while in the military, and still adhered to it almost every day. He wasn't quite as fit as when he ran special ops missions with the SEALs, but he wasn't too far off. He liked that kind of order and rigidity and purpose in his life, especially now when little else he had meant a damn thing to him.

The Jeanneau Sun Odyssey 379 on which he labored was a sleek and powerful craft, practically new and spotless after an entire day spent scrubbing her after over a week spent at sea. She was a forty-footer that he'd had for almost three months, new out of the factory and built to his own specifications. He'd made sure that the boat was perfectly suited to him. Everything was somewhat oversized, enough to comfortably accommodate his six-feet-six-inch frame. He'd sailed her from South Carolina on the Intracoastal Waterway to his home deep in the bayous of Lafourche and Terrebonne Parishes. He'd worked hard all day making her look like new again. Everything was spotless, inside and out, his gear clean and orderly and stowed in the proper places. That kind of thing was important to him.

On the eve of September 11, he had steered his gleaming boat down the wide Bayou Bonne that edged the back side of his property and eventually sailed her out into the deep royal blue waters of the vast Gulf of Mexico. He'd spent ten full days out there, completely alone, as was his habit every year on the anniversary of that day of infamy for all Americans. He had stayed out on the rolling waves, working through the most catastrophic event in his life, a trauma that he had fought to accept daily for so many years that he no longer kept count. It didn't matter how long it had been. Not if he lived to be a hundred. He wasn't going to get over it. He had accepted that now. He just forced himself to live with it. Endless day after endless day.

Out there, though, completely by himself in the dark, quiet, ever-swaying, ever-restless sea, under untold billions of glittering stars spangled across ink-black skies, he had suffered alone and wept fresh tears for his dead family while he fished for bonito and sea bass and flounder and mourned to the depths of his soul and studiously drank himself into oblivion every single night. But that's the way he liked it during his own personal, self-inflicted hell week, far away from every other living being on earth, alone and buffeted by ocean winds and rocking waves and the merciless sun, and most of all, the silent solitude where he could work through the grief that never left him, not for one hour, one minute, one second of conscious thought.

But now, on this sunny day, Novak was back at home, ready to live his miserable existence once more, an empty, futile objective that he never really accomplished. But that's the way it was. Swiping his sponge a few more times down the wide blue stripe painted along the length of the white hull, he took a few extra minutes to scrub the giant silver letters naming his boat. He had called her *Sweet Sarah,* in memory of his dead wife. Another way to keep Sarah close when she wasn't close and never would be again.

Once Novak was satisfied with his efforts, he hoisted himself back up and straddled the rail. He raised his face, shut his eyes, and felt the fire of the sun burn hot into his bare skin. He was already sunburned from his time out on the drink, his skin burnished a deep, warm bronze. After a few minutes, he shifted his gaze down onto the slow, rippling bayou current. It was good to be back home, good to be sober, good to be able to think clearly. He had wrestled his demons back under control, at least for the moment. He left his perch, stooped down, and pulled a cold bottle of Dixie beer from the cooler. He twisted off the cap and took a deep draft, thirsty and tired from a full day of hard physical labor. That's when he first heard the sound of a vehicle, coming closer, turning off the old bayou road and heading down through the swampy woods to his place.

Grimacing, annoyed as hell, not pleased about uninvited guests showing up, he lowered the beer bottle, shielded his eyes with his forearm, and peered up the long grassy field that stretched between the bayou and the ancient plantation house he'd inherited from his mother on the day he was born. He had not been expecting company today. Or any other day. He did not like company. He did not like people coming around his place, and that was putting it mildly. He was a serious loner. He liked to be invisible. Anonymous. He liked his privacy. And he was willing to protect it.

The sun broiled down, the temperature probably close to ninety, humidity hugging the bayou like a wool blanket, thick and wet and heavy. Drops of perspiration rolled down his forehead and burned into his eyes. Novak grabbed a towel and mopped the sweat off his face and chest. Then he took another long drink of the icy beer. But he kept his attention focused on the spot where his road emerged from the dense grove of giant live oaks and cypress trees and magnolias. The sugar plantation was ancient and now defunct, but it was a huge property, none of which had ever been sold out of his family. It took a lot of his effort to keep the place even in modest repair. The mansion on the knoll above him had stood in the same spot for over two hundred years. And it looked like it, too, with most of the white paint peeled off and weathered to gray years ago.

Once upon a time, his wealthy Creole ancestors, the St. Pierre family, had sold their sugar at top price and flourished for a century and a half on the bayou plantation they'd named Bonne Terre. They had been quite the elite in Napoleonic New Orleans, he had been told. They still were quite the elite, but mostly in France now. The magnificence with which they'd endowed the place was long gone and the house in need of serious renovation. Someday, maybe. Right now, he preferred to live on his boat where it was cooler and more to his liking.

Minutes passed, and then the car appeared and proceeded slowly around the circular driveway leading to his front gallery. It was a late model Taurus, apple-red and shiny clean and glinting like a fine ruby under the blinding sunlight. Probably a New Orleans rental. He'd never seen the car before. That meant a stranger, which in Novak's experience usually meant trouble. Few visitors found their way this far down into the bayou. Ever. That's why he lived there.

Claire Morgan was the exception and one of the few people who knew where he lived, but he trusted her. She was a former homicide detective who'd hired him on as a partner in her new private investigation agency. But it wasn't Claire who'd come to call today. She was still on her honeymoon with Nicholas Black, out in the Hawaiian Islands, living it up on some big estate on the island of Kauai. They'd been gone around eight weeks now, and that had given Novak plenty of time to do his own thing. Especially after what had happened on their wedding day. The three of them and a couple of other guys had gotten into a particularly hellish mess and had been lucky to make it out alive. Novak's shoulder wound had healed up well enough, but all of them deserved some R & R. Other than Claire, though, only a handful of people knew where to find him. He didn't give out his address, and that had served him well.

Novak wiped his sweaty palms on his faded khaki shorts and kept his gaze focused on the Taurus. Behind him, the bayou drifted along in its slow, swirling currents, rippling and splashing south toward the Gulf of Mexico. As soon as the car left his field of vision, he headed down the hatch steps into the dim, cool quarters belowdecks. At the bottom, he stretched up and reached back into the highest shelf. He pulled out his .45 caliber service weapon. A nice little Kimber 1911. Fully loaded and ready to go. The heft of it felt damn good. Back where it belonged. He checked the mag, racked a round into the chamber, and then wedged the gun down inside his back waistband. He grabbed a clean white T-shirt and pulled it over his head as he climbed back up to the stern deck. Picking up a pair of high-powered binoculars, he scanned the back gallery of his house and the wide grassy yard surrounding it.

Nothing moved. He walked down the gangplank and stepped off into the shade thrown by the covered dock. He moved past the boat-lift berths but he kept his attention riveted up on the house. The long fields he'd mowed the day before stretched about a hundred yards up from the bayou. The big mansion sat at the far edge, shaded by a dozen ancient live oaks, all draped almost to the ground with long and wispy tendrils of the gray Spanish moss so prevalent in the bayou.

The wide gallery encircled the first floor, on all four sides, twelve feet wide, with a twelve-feet-high ceiling. No wind now, all vestiges of the breeze gone, everything still, everything quiet. He could see the east side of the house. It was deserted. The guy in the car could be anywhere by now. He could be anybody. He could be good. He could be bad. He could be there to kill Novak. That was the most likely scenario. Novak sure as hell had plenty of enemies who wanted him dead, all over the world. Right up the highway in New Orleans, in fact. Whoever was in that Taurus, whatever they wanted, Novak wanted them inside his gun sights first before they spotted him.

Taking off toward the house, he jogged down the bank and up onto a narrow dirt path hidden by a long fencerow. Then he headed up the gradual rise, staying well behind the fence covered with climbing ivy and flowering azalea bushes. He kept his weapon out in front using both hands, finger alongside the trigger. Guys who were after him usually just wanted to put a bullet in Novak's skull. Some had even tried their luck, but nobody had tried it on his home turf. He didn't like that. Wasn't too savvy on their part, either.

When he reached the backyard, he pulled up under the branches of a huge mimosa tree. He crouched down there and waited, listening. No thud of running feet. No whispered orders to spread out and find him. No nothing, except some stupid bird chirping its head off somewhere high above him. He searched the trees and found a mockingbird sitting on the carved balustrade on the second-floor gallery.

Novak waited a couple more minutes. Then he ran lightly across the grass and took the wide back steps three at a time. He crossed the gallery quickly and pressed his back against the wall. He listened again and heard nothing, so he inched his way around the corner onto the west gallery and then up the side of the house to the front corner. That's when he heard the loud clang of his century-old iron door knocker. He froze in his tracks.

Directly in front of him, a long white wicker swing swayed in a sudden gust of wind. He darted a quick look around the corner of the house. Three yards down the gallery from him, a woman stood at his front door, her right side turned to him. She was alone. She was unarmed, considering how skin-tight her skimpy outfit molded to her slim body. While he watched, she lifted the heavy door knocker and let it clang down again. Hard. Impatient. Annoyed. She was tall, maybe five feet eight or nine inches. Long black hair curled down around her shoulders. She was slender and her body was fit, all shown to advantage in her tight white Daisy Dukes and a black-and-white chevron crop top. She turned slightly, and Novak glimpsed her impressively toned and suntanned midriff and the lower curve of her breasts. She was not wearing a bra, and her legs were naked, too, shapely and also darkly tanned. White sandals with silver buckles. She looked sexy as hell but harmless.

On the other hand, Novak had known a woman or two who'd also looked sexy and harmless, but who had assassinated more men than Novak had ever thought about gunning down. Keeping his weapon down alongside his right thigh but ready, he stepped out where she could see him but also where he'd have a good shot at her, if all was not as it seemed. The woman apparently had a highly cultivated sense of awareness because she immediately spun toward him. That's when Novak's knees almost buckled. He went weak all over, his muscles just going slack. His heart faltered mid-beat. He stared at her, so completely stunned he could not move or speak.

Then his dead wife, the only woman he had ever loved, his beautiful Sarah, smiled at him and said in her familiar Australian accent, "How ya goin', Will. Long time no see."

LINDA LADD is the bestselling author of over a dozen novels, including the Claire Morgan thrillers and the Will Novak thrillers. Linda makes her home in Missouri, where she lives with her husband and her beagle named Banjo. She has two adult children and two grandsons. In addition to writing, Linda is an expert markswoman and enjoys target shooting with her Glock 19. She also loves reading, traveling, swimming, and enjoying her family. She is currently at work on her next novel featuring Claire Morgan. Learn more at lindaladd.com.

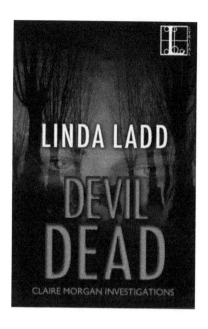

LINDA LADD

DEVIL DEAD

CLAIRE MORGAN INVESTIGATIONS

LOST GIRL

She was last seen in New Orleans. Her father, a rich, powerful
arms dealer, believes she was abducted. For ransom. For revenge.
For reasons too horrible to imagine.

LOST INNOCENCE

Claire Morgan, recent former cop turned private investigator,
and her new partner begin their search at the girl's school,
where a violent junkie attacks Claire with scissors, raves of
"demons and devils," and then takes her own life.

LAST RITES

Sinister clues lead Claire on a twisted trail through the bars and
bayous of New Orleans to a bloodstained altar in Paris.
Vast, secret, and powerful, it is a world that few enter or escape.
And Claire is going in—*the devil be damned* . . .

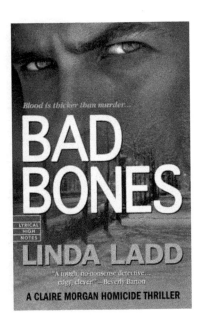

BAD OMEN
Homicide detective Claire Morgan has a bad feeling when a man's body is found in a Missouri state park. The crime scene is buried in snow. The corpse is frozen in ice. And nearly every bone has been broken, shattered, or crushed . . .

BAD BLOOD
Claire's suspicions only get worse when the body is thawed and identified. The victim was an ultimate fighter on the cage-match circuit. His wife blames her ex-husband, a Russian mafioso. But Claire knows this is no mob-style execution. This is something worse. Something evil . . .

BAD BONES
Raised from childhood to inflict pain, the killer uses rage as a weapon. Punishing without mercy. Killing without conscience. Upholding a dark family tradition that is so twisted, so powerful, it destroys everything in its path.
And Claire is about to meet the family . . .

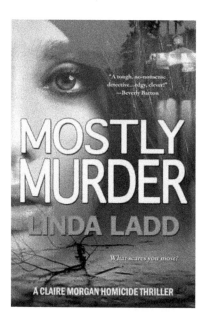

"A tough, no-nonsense detective...edgy, clever!"
—Beverly Barton

MOSTLY
MURDER

LINDA LADD

What scares you most?

A CLAIRE MORGAN HOMICIDE THRILLER

MOSTLY FEAR

She suffered a terrifying coma. She survived a serial killer's obsession. Now homicide detective Claire Morgan hopes to forget the nightmare of her Missouri past in the city of New Orleans. But when a body is discovered near her home, her darkest fears come rushing back . . .

MOSTLY SUPERSTITION

Surrounded by candles and skulls, the victim is bound to an altar like a human sacrifice. More disturbing to Claire is the voodoo doll in the woman's hands. A doll pierced with pins and wearing a picture on its face. A picture of Claire Morgan . . .

MOSTLY MURDER

Claire doesn't believe in voodoo. But she does believe in the power of superstition to warp a person's mind and feed a killer's madness. It is here, in the muddy bayous where it festers, that Claire must face her fear head-on— and meet the man who's marked her for death . . .